THE
LONELY
S • U • N

THE
LONELY
S • U • N

LEE E FULLER JR

iUniverse, Inc.
New York Bloomington

This is a work of fiction. All of the characters, names, incidents,
organizations, and dialogue in this novel are either the products
of the author's imagination or are used fictitiously.

iUniverse books may be ordered through booksellers or by contacting:

iUniverse
1663 Liberty Drive
Bloomington, IN 47403
www.iuniverse.com
1-800-Authors (1-800-288-4677)

Because of the dynamic nature of the Internet, any Web addresses or
links contained in this book may have changed since publication and may
no longer be valid. The views expressed in this work are solely those of
the author and do not necessarily reflect the views of the publisher, and
the publisher hereby disclaims any responsibility for them.

ISBN: 978-1-4401-5729-5 (sc)
ISBN: 978-1-4401-5728-8 (ebook)

Printed in the United States of America

iUniverse rev. date: 07/15/09

CHAPTER I

A SOFT CHIMING INTERRUPTED the sleep of Donald George Stuart. With a muttered curse he reached over to the panel next to his bunk and slapped at a switch. With the previous weeks of practice of doing so he hit the switch dead on. Unfortunately, the chiming continued. It was not his alarm.

Sitting up in his bunk he blinked the sleep back from his eyes and dreams until he realized that the chiming was the ship's onboard AI enhanced computer system requesting his attention. If he did not respond the chiming would continue with the volume increasing until he did respond.

"Alright, Athena I'm awake. Is this something that can wait for a few minutes?" he asked into the room knowing that Athena would hear him.

"This can wait for a few minutes, Commander. Please come to the bridge at your convenience." A soft feminine voice responded.

"Thank you, Athena, I'll be up shortly."

"Acknowledged Commander," The nebulous voice answered.

Stuart shook his head slightly as he crawled out of his

bunk. Here he was at the edge of the Sagittarius arm of the galaxy and the only companion that he had was the AI, Athena. The voice of the AI had been programmed to be that of a polite young woman.

It damn near drove him nuts to hear that voice and not have a face to put to it. So, like a century of deep space solo explorers before him he had created a vision in his mind of what his AI looked" like.

In his mind Athena was a petite woman, blond hair flowing down her back and pacific blue eyes, a small scattering of freckles across her nose and slight dimples in her cheeks. She had a gymnasts' frame with a small waist and long muscular legs.

Stuart briefly examined himself in the small mirror as he quickly dressed. He saw the face that always looked back him from the mirror, ice blue eyes with the faint beginnings of crow's feet forming at the edges above a strong aquiline nose. His mouth was well centered above his chin which was narrow and at the moment needed to have the growing stubble shaved. Atop his head was sandy brown hair that was still tousled from sleep to which he now ran a comb through to straighten it out and as he did so he realized that his hair was beginning to get a bit long and needed cutting when he next reached a facility where he could obtain the services of a good barber. He left his cabin and headed for the ships small informal mess room. Standing at 5 feet 10 inches tall he was average height for an officer of the fleet, his arms were a bit long for his frame which he didn't mind as he had always enjoyed the extra reach they provided him. Once at the mess hall he proceeded to order up a large breakfast of eggs, hash browns, toast and coffee. When the dispenser opened he saw a glass of orange juice had been added to his breakfast tray.

Athena was making sure he had a well-balanced meal. Just the part of her programming that ensured his health was maintained while journeying through the vastness of outer space.

———————————
———————————

Stuart stepped onto the bridge a few minutes later and proceeded to the command chair. His eyes briefly examined the readouts on the command console to see if anything was amiss and he determined that all was well.

"OK, Athena, I'm awake fed and here, what's the story?"

"I have located something unusual Commander. With your permission I will display it on the main screen." Athena answered him, her "voice" coming from a speaker behind him and to his right. Her voice came from exactly where the science station on the bridge was located. Athena would project her "voice" from whatever station on the bridge she deemed was the proper station for whatever type of response was necessary.

The bridge was a large rectangular affair with work stations set into the port and starboard sides and the command chair with its command console located in the center of the bridge. At the front of the bridge was a large view screen. To the rear of the bridge were the elevator, a small bathroom for on duty personnel and the Captain's Office.

"What exactly have you found?" Stuart asked.

"I have located a star system that is not listed in our star charts."

"Really, that doesn't seem strange. After all we're out here to map this sector of space. What makes this system so special that you felt it was necessary to wake me up early for it?"

"The location of the system, Commander; May I put it on the main view screen?"

"Sure, let's see it"

✦

The main view screen changed from a simple star field to an image of a single star surrounded by blackness.

"Athena, I see one star and a not very impressive star at that."

"As I said Commander, its location is unique."

"Fine, where is this star located that makes it unique?"

"The star is located 87 light years beyond the outer edge of the Sagittarius arm, 77 degrees above the galactic plane." Athena answered. She continued, "It has not been detected before in part due to its location above the galactic plane and also due to the cosmic dust that obscures objects outside of the galaxy.

"Had we not been traveling outside of the galactic edge mapping the outer systems, we would not have detected the star."

"OK, so this star is above and beyond so to speak. Do you have any other information about it?" Stuart replied to Athena. He was not particularly impressed.

"It is a G type star. I would like permission to send a hyper speed probe to the star to gather further information. I have detected the usual wobble in the star indicating planets are present."

"Planets huh? OK, Athena, go ahead and launch the probe. Let's see if that sun has any Earth type planets. Probably all gas giants, but you never know."

Stuart knew that due to its location above the galactic plane the star was in a unique position. The Federation could use such a hidden system in its ongoing war with the Vegan Empire. A system located outside of the galaxy above the galactic plane could be used to conduct research or hide a colony in case the war should suddenly go against the Federation.

The Vegan Empire and the Terran Federation had been at war for over a hundred years, neither side able to gain an advantage over the other. No one knew what name the

Vegan's had for themselves, they were the Vegan's simply because they were first encountered in the Vega system.

We only know what they look like from far off photos that have been heavily enhanced by computer programs. They are wormlike in form, with artificial arms, hands, and fingers. Even after a century of warfare, no one knew how or where they obtained those artificial appendages. Researchers theorize there may be another race that we have not seen that is either enslaved or symbiotic to the Vegan's that construct and attach the appendages.

We do know that they favor implosion weapons. Their implosion weapons do not go boom, they go Fwoomp! Whatever they target collapses inward on itself instead of exploding outward.

The first starship to encounter the Vegan's was the Sisu. She was a Federation heavy cruiser mapping the Vega system. She had been in the system for three days when the Vegan ship appeared. For 12 hours the Sisu attempted communication with the Vegan ship. The Vegan ship finally answered with an implosion cannon aimed at the Sisu's main engines.

With the loss of their engines, the Sisu could not run, but she could still fight. Captain Roth returned fire. The beam weapons of the Sisu were not powerful enough to penetrate the Vegan shields. The Vegans quickly imploded much of the Sisu. After the Sisu was effectively rendered inert the Vegans boarded her. They took a few prisoners and killed everyone else.

Then they left.

By losing that one battle, the Terran Federation was spared. Had the Sisu won that battle, an entire Vegan fleet would have scoured the entire sector until Earth was located and annihilated.

By losing the battle that day, the Vegans determined that there was nothing in this part of the galaxy that threatened them so they turned their fleets to their other enemy, the Hrosions.

Little is known of the Hrosions except for two facts, they are reptilian and they have been fighting the Vegans for at least two hundred years.

One last thing we do know about the Hrosions, and great lengths are taken to keep this piece of knowledge secret from the general population, human flesh is a delicacy to them.

"The probe is away, Commander." Athena announced from the speakers at the helm station in front and to the left of Stuart.

"What is the probe's ETA?" Stuart asked.

Athena answered from the helm station. "22 days, 13 hours and 45 minutes."

Stuart thought about it for a few seconds then gave his next order.

"Alright, that gives us time to finish scanning this corner of the sector. Set course for the next system"

"Course laid in for system H42."

"Set engines at cruising speed 4 and engage."

———————————
———————————

The sun rose over the city, its light reflecting off of the polished spires and domes of the local temples. People were stirring as they rose to greet the new day with their morning rituals. Some were opening up stalls in the central bazaar of the city; others were sitting down to breakfast. The city guard was changing as the sleepy night guard was being replaced by the alert morning guard.

The gates of the city were being opened for the day and travelers that had been caught outside the city the previous evening were now starting to enter to attend to whatever business they had within the centuries old walls.

One of these travelers was Erat. He was a large man,

very heavily muscled with bronzed skin from constantly being in the sun. His hair was long and the brown uneven bangs often fluttered into matching brown eyes. He stood head and shoulders above the average man and in a crowd he would be able to see across the heads of those around him. At his hip he wore a great sword.

It was obvious to the city guard that he was a barbarian.

Erat wore robes that matched the color of the sands that surrounded the city for leagues in every direction. If he were to lie down next to the road no one would see him until he rose up before them, like a ghostly specter rising from the hells below to steal a soul.

The city guard eyed him warily; barbarians were known to draw their swords if they thought they had been insulted. But the guard did have to question all travelers entering the city.

"What business do you have in Qualor?" the guard asked nervously.

"Business, I have no business. I am only staying here long enough to get a few supplies. I will be gone by midday." Erat answered gruffly. He did not like being asked such questions. He had grown up in the hills of Gran, many weeks to the north by horseback. In Gran no one asked questions when you wanted to enter a city.

Well, to be completely honest, Gran had no cities, only villages scattered throughout the valleys that the rocky hills surrounded. Those villages did not have walls made of stone that stood hundreds of feet high as did cities of Vanithiria such as Qualor. Some of them did have wooden palisades, but only a few of them.

"Very well barbarian. You may enter Qualor, but make sure you are gone by nightfall."

Erat glared at the guard but proceeded on into the city,

leading his horse. He hadn't taken more than a few steps when the guard called out to him again.

"You can't take your horse into the city; you will have to stable him. The stables are inside the wall and to your left."

Erat simply grunted and headed into the city. Once he had passed beneath the Great Outer Wall of Qualor, he turned left and looked for a suitable stable for his horse. He had not gone very far until a boy of no more than 9 years accosted him.

"Mighty Barbarian," The boy cried upon seeing Erat. "I am Losian! Follow me and I will take you to a stable that will see to your magnificent steed. They will see to it that your noble mount is well fed and watered. They will brush him down and make sure his hoofs are well shod!"

Erat stopped and eyed the boy. He was dressed in simple home spun garments, with dirty bare feet. His hair was long and unkempt. He stared into Erat's eyes without flinching or looking away. He may be dirty but he was not afraid.

"So, this stable that would do all of this would be expensive. I have not the willingness to pay such coin as would be asked for these services." Erat replied to the boy as he proceeded to push past him.

The boy darted around the side of Erat's horse to block Erat's progress down the avenue. "I tell you that they will not ask for high coin, simply follow me and you may see for yourself. Besides, how can you tell an expensive stable from a cheap stable?"

"Very well boy lead on, I will look at your stable!" answered Erat.

Erat followed the boy for a few minutes, passing various stables and livestock markets along the way to his destination. Erat stopped at one such livestock market to watch as horses were auctioned off. Losian waited patiently while the barbarian watched the bidding for a horse that stood no higher than his hips. Even though it was the size of a small pony, Erat knew that it was a full grown horse.

He had heard stories of these miniature horses from the plains of Ahgoaristan, far to the east. It was rumored that the peoples of Ahgoaristan were as small as their steeds, but he had met a man from the city of Movara during a campaign for King Tugast last summer. That man, Judquin was only slightly smaller than Erat himself.

Judquin explained to him that the small horses, known as Bree, were used exclusively for herding sheep.

Erat was not sure if he believed him or not, but obviously the little horse could not be ridden by anyone but a child.

He gestured to Losian to lead on after the auction for the little horse finished. He was surprised at the high price that the Bree had brought. It was higher than his horse would have brought.

Erat followed Losian for a few more minutes until the boy stopped in front of another one of the stables that the avenue seemed to teem with. The stable looked no different from any of the others they had passed.

It was a simple building comprised of stalls for the horses that were its chief occupants. In the rear a blacksmith was at work banging some piece of metal on an anvil.

Losian turned to Erat. "Here we are Master Barbarian, the Stables of Bron!"

Before Erat could say anything Losian darted into the stables interior only to emerge a moment later with a man in tow. The man looked so skinny that Erat was sure a strong wind would blow him away. But upon a second look Erat saw that the man had a sinewy strength about him.

"So, Losian, this is the barbarian, eh?" said the man.

"Yes Bron. Is his horse not magnificent?" Losian replied excitedly.

"The boy said your stable is good. I only need you to stable my horse for a few hours while I go into the city."

✦

"Hmmm, short term rental? Do you want the horse fed and watered or only stabled?"

"How much for stabling and feeding the horse?"

The barbarian and the stable master haggled for a few minutes until they both reached a mutually satisfied agreement. Bron would feed and water Erat's horse while he kept it stabled.

Erat turned the horse over to the stable master then turned to go into Qualor proper. He headed back the way he had come. The stables were within the great wall but there was a smaller secondary wall that separated them from the city itself. Erat was heading back to the gate where he had entered the great wall when Losian caught up with him.

"Master Barbarian, where are you going? I thought that you were going into Qualor?" he called after Erat.

"I am boy." He answered back over his shoulder.

"Then why are you going back to the gate? There is an entrance gate just a short way beyond Bron's stable. Here, follow me and I'll show you."

Erat turned and followed Losian back past Bron's and a few hundred yards past where there was a smaller gate set into the inner wall down another side avenue.

Erat parted ways with Losian at the gate as Losian returned back to the main gate to see if he could acquire more customers for Bron.

Once inside the inner wall, Erat saw the street that he was on was blocked in on both sides by buildings that all seemed to run together. He followed the street for a few minutes until it let out into a small square where two other streets came together.

Erat stopped and looked about the square. There were a few people milling about, a couple of city guards were loitering by a fountain that was in the center of the square, they were filling their drinking skins from it and wiping down their faces with the water.

Off to his left one street ran off into the distance while off to his right another street curved out of sight back towards the inner wall.

Erat set off to his left; he wanted to find a market where he could stock up on supplies before setting forth from Qualor.

As he moved down the avenue more people were appearing as the morning headed into midday. There were women moving along the avenue some with children in tow as they headed off to market, there were mercenaries seeking employment with the Qualor city guard or simply passing through to other places. Merchants moved along the avenue, some with personal guards to protect them from thieves that were sure to be roaming the avenue as well. Here and there a priest of this or that deity moved through the street, the only ones that Erat recognized wore the saffron robes of the sect of the god Gereator. Other priests that Erat saw had orange robes, black robes, and in one case no robes at all.

Erat did not bother with gods and their priests; he had learned long ago that it was best to leave priests and gods alone. He only knew of the sect of Gereator from a smuggling operation he was briefly involved with some years ago. He had come face to face with the living representation of Gereator and had barely escaped with his life.

Erat eventually arrived at a large square that was filled with temples. The crowds were not large but there was a certain sense of reverence underlying the feel of the square. People here were speaking in lowered voices bringing an unnatural hush to the square. Even the birds that were roosting in the temple eaves were quiet.

Erat was halfway through the temple square when a man bumped into him. The man was dressed as a nobleman, but went about without any sort of body guard.

Erat was immediately suspicious of him.

But the man did not act like a nobleman. "My apologies

barbarian, I was not paying attention where my feet were taking me."

Erat automatically felt for his pouch and upon finding it intact he simply glared at the man who hurried off through the square and off into a side avenue.

Discarding the matter Erat moved on, just as he was leaving the temple square a squad of soldiers burst into the square and began questioning people. They were looking for the nobleman that had bumped into Erat only moments before.

Erat simply moved on, leaving the temple square behind him. He wanted no part of any questioning by the city guard. Whatever trouble the man was in Erat wanted no part of it.

Soon he came to the main bazaar of the city and proceeded to find the supplies he was seeking. He spent the better part of an hour haggling for the items he needed then he proceeded to a tavern where he ordered flagon of ale and a leg of the pig that was roasting on the spit.

Sitting on the bench after acquiring the ale and pig's haunch he felt something digging into his side beneath is loincloth. Thinking that his belt was rubbing through his loincloth again he automatically reached for it to make an adjustment when his fingers encountered a small crystal cube lodged in between his belt and loincloth.

Pulling it out he examined it briefly before dropping it into his pouch to rest with what few coins he had left. He knew where it came from, the man in the temple square that bumped into him. Instead of stealing his pouch, he put this cube in his belt.

If the city guard caught the man they would not find the cube but would eventually find out through interrogation where the cube was.

Erat did not hurry his meal; he knew that the man was probably captured by now and probably being interrogated.

But he did not wish to draw attention to himself by acting abnormally.

When he finished his meal he left the tavern and quickly made his way back to Bron's stable. He was apprehensive as he passed through the temple square but he forced himself not to dash through it.

When he arrived at Bron's stable he quickly located Bron and collected his horse. He knew that he needed to leave the city as quickly as possible, but he also knew that he could not leave through the same gate that he entered through. A traveler could stay within the outer wall until they reached the gate on the opposite side of the city, passing behind stables, taverns, guard barracks, and the other establishments that lie against the outer wall of the city.

Erat mounted his horse and rode the avenue between the walls. Three hours later he was approaching the gate on the far side of the city. He dismounted his horse before he approached the gate and joined the line that was leaving the city.

He held onto his horses reins as he waited in line. He was beginning to get surely as the line was moving slowly. The guards were questioning people as they left the city.

Finally Erat was close enough to hear the guards questioning the people leaving Qualor.

"How long have you been in Qualor" one guard asked another barbarian that was also leaving the city.

"I have only been here a few hours. Now I am leaving." The barbarian replied. His answer was noticed by other guards who quietly moved closer to the barbarian as they loosed their swords in case they should need them.

"Only a few hours? What business did you have here?" the guard asked.

"Nothing that need concern you, now stand aside!" the barbarian growled at the guardsman.

By reply all the guardsmen drew their blades and surrounded the barbarian.

"What treachery is this?" the barbarian cried as he drew his sword. Before he could raise his arm to strike arrows suddenly blossomed from his arm holding the sword. He cried out in surprise as the blade fell from his hand. The guardsmen quickly subdued him and dragged him off.

Erat and the others in the line had fallen back at the confrontation, now they all queued up in line again so they could leave the city. New guards replaced those that had dragged off the barbarian.

Soon it was Erat's turn.

"How long have you been in Qualor, barbarian?" asked the guardsman that confronted him.

"I have been here for two days." Erat lied to the guard.

"What business did you have here?"

"None, I am passing through on my way to Kusar."

The guard looked Erat and his horse over for a moment. Then he motioned other guardsmen over.

"Then you will not mind if we search you and your horse before you leave?" he asked Erat as the guardsmen all moved their hands to their swords.

Erat glared at the guardsman, but he offered no resistance. "Search all you like, I have nothing to hide from you." He told the man.

The guardsman did not move he simply stared at Erat for a few moments. The he gestured at the gate. "Go on, get out of here." He ordered Erat.

Erat grunted and led his horse out of the city. He did not mount his horse until he was well out of sight of the city gate. When he did mount his horse he urged it into a trot. He wanted to put as much distance between himself and Qualor as he could.

He rode for a few hours along the road until darkness descended over the countryside. He then turned off of the main road and rode slowly into the rocky wastes that the rode cut through. He reasoned that if anyone came looking for him they would search along the road.

After riding for an hour through the rocky wasteland he decided to stop and make camp for the night. He dismounted and tended to his horse, watering it and attaching a crude feedbag to it. He then looked to his own dinner.

He did not want to make a fire as it might attract anyone looking for him or other things that lived in the wasteland where he was spending the night. He dug through his pack and pulled out some cured meat and a skin of water.

After he had eaten, he bedded down for the night, wrapping a blanket around himself and leaving his sword within reaching distance.

He was not worried about anyone sneaking up on him during the night; he was a very light sleeper and would come awake instantly if someone or something approached too closely to his camp.

As he was drifting off to sleep his thoughts turned back to the crystal cube that he had suddenly found to be in his possession. He had meant to look it over but had forgotten about it in his determination to leave Qualor far behind him as possible.

He would look it over more thoroughly tomorrow.

Captain Avril of the Qualor city guard drew his hand across his brow wiping away the trickle of sweat that was forming in the warming morning air. He was sitting on his horse watching as a member of his guard approached.

He had been ordered out of the city onto the trail of a barbarian that had been allowed to leave the city yesterday afternoon. The guardsman that had let the barbarian leave was now dead. It was rumored that the Grand Vizier had not been gentle with him.

Avril believed the rumor. The Grand Vizier was not known to tolerate failure or stupidity.

The rider had reached Avril and drew up in front of him and snapped off a salute. "Sir, the barbarian has not been seen by anyone at the outpost. They do not believe that he has passed by them."

Avril sighed; he now had to determine where the barbarian had left the road. Normally this would be an impossible task, but he had a Mujari tracker with him. The Grand Vizier had seen to it that one of his prized trackers accompanied his squad.

"Very well Corporal, fall in with the squad." Avril ordered the man as he turned in his saddle and looked for his sergeant.

"Sergeant, bring the tracker to the front of the column."

"Yes, sir!" the sergeant answered even as he turned to ride back and collect the requested Mujari.

Avril looked out into the wastelands that the road ran through. He did not relish the thought of riding into the rocky terrain. Every man in his squad would have to be paying close attention that their horses did not step wrong and break a leg. If the barbarian had ridden into the wastelands he had done so after darkness. That could turn into an advantage for his squad as the barbarian very likely had to abandon his horse and proceed on foot.

But barbarians were notorious for being able to do things that regular men could not accomplish; such things as riding into the wastelands at night without having their mount injured.

"You need Xipt to track the prey now?" a voice asked.

Looking down and to his left Avril saw the Mujari tracker, Xipt was his name, he could not pronounce the word. He was a small man, he also tended to run more as a dog or a wolf would run using all four limbs. But his senses were much keener that those of a normal man. It was said that a Mujari tracker could sense a man hundreds of yards away, downwind by just hearing the man breathe.

From the things that Avril had seen in the service of the Grand Vizier, he believed the abilities attributed to the Mujari.

"Yes, we believe that the barbarian left the road before he reached the outpost." He answered the tracker.

"I will find where the prey has gone. It cannot hide from Xipt. I know it has not left the road before here, its spirit moves forward of here."

And with that Xipt turned and moved down the road. He moved quickly, head lowered close to the ground. A slight shiver went down Avril's back as he watched the tracker lope down the road as a dog would have. No, not as a dog, but as a wolf low to the ground his passage being completely silent, not a single noise did he make as he flew forward.

Yes, a wolf fit the tracker better than a dog did.

Avril called out to his sergeant, "Get the squad moving out Sergeant. We follow the Mujari!"

"Yes, sir!" the sergeant replied to the Captain then he turned to the rest of the squad. "Alright you bums! You heard the Captain! Move out, I want everyone in side-by-side formation!"

The squad began moving forward following the Mujari tracker.

Erat scanned the horizon in the direction that he had come. He could not tell if anyone was following him or not, but he did not think that anyone would be able to follow him out here in the wasteland that he was traveling through.

He had to pick his way carefully as there were small holes everywhere that his horse could step in. The gods must have been looking down on him last night when he moved over this terrain in the darkness.

He had not wondered very long about where all the holes had come from when he saw small creatures poking their heads up from the holes from time to time. They looked to be some type of small rat. They tended to avoid him and his horse; he only caught glimpses of them from a distance.

Only after he had broken camp and rode farther into the wastelands did he bring the crystal cube out to examine. It was a perfect cube, only about a half inch to a side. It was perfectly smooth, and mirrored as if it had been polished. It was not clear but opaque.

The cube was cold to the touch, almost like holding a piece of ice in his hand. The sun shone off of it causing it to sparkle.

Erat had never seen anything like it in his life. He could see that it might be valuable as a rare item. He figured that it was probably also stolen and the man had stuck it in his belt as he feared capture by the city guard.

Shrugging his shoulders, Erat placed the cube back into his pouch and looked ahead to see where he was headed. Off in the far distance he could see the flat expanse of the wasteland becoming hilly terrain backed by mountains. From this distance the mountains were only a dark line on the horizon.

Erat knew that the mountains were over a month away at his present pace and that he could have reached them in only a few days had he stuck to the road. His current destination was the city of Kharam on the other side of the mountains. He had told the guardsman at the gate that he was headed to Kusar.

The city of Kusar was on this side of the mountains, but many leagues south of his present location. Kusar was a major trading port along the southern coast. It was the last port before the Rowad Ocean. Sailing from Kusar one would either follow the coast back to the west or sail directly out into the Rowad Ocean until one reached the southern lands.

The southern lands were hot and humid, with jungle thickening the farther into the interior one traveled. The men who lived there tended to keep to themselves, shunning strangers. There were a few trading posts along the coast, but few people traveled to those posts as the danger was great. But the traders that went there and returned were now men of great wealth.

The city of Kharam lay beyond the mountains. It was the western most city of Sumter, a great empire that covered much of the land east of the mountains. Kharam served as a trading center and military outpost for the Sumter Empire.

It was here that Erat was to meet Porar, a man who reportedly held a map that Erat was seeking. The map was to show a route traveled by Hurakos of Yannos over a thousand years ago. Along this route Hurakos had found a doorway into the earth itself which led to a vast underground chamber filled with unimaginable wealth. Erat had been searching for this map for the last two years.

He would miss his appointment if he was forced to continue through the wasteland. He turned his horse back towards the road. This was a dangerous thing to do if someone was looking for him, but he would make better time returning to the road. He had come a good distance through the wastelands; he should be past the outpost that he knew was located along the road.

He would just have to take the chance and stay alert for anyone looking for him.

――――――――
――――――――

The Mujari tracker suddenly stopped and stood up. He looked around then turned to Avril.

"The prey slept here." Xipt called out to Avril.

Avril looked around the area, but he didn't sec any

telltale signs of the barbarian. He did notice that the sky was darkening rapidly since the sun had dropped over the horizon.

"All right," Avril said to himself.

"Sergeant!" he called out. "Have the men dismount and set up camp."

"Yes, sir!" the sergeant answered back. He then began to call out orders to the squad. Avril didn't pay any attention to the sergeant as he was busy dismounting from his own horse. He handed the reins off to a guardsman that was standing ready to take them.

He then looked around and was amazed at how many little holes were scattered everywhere. He knew that the holes were made by wastrels, little rat like animals that lived mostly underground. He had never seen so many in one place before.

He wondered what they found to eat out here. Whatever it was, there must have been a great number of them also. Perhaps whatever they ate lived underground also.

With all the little holes everywhere, it was a wonder that his squad, let alone the barbarian, had managed to get so far without losing a horse.

Xipt was patiently crouching by one of the holes. As Avril watched he suddenly struck out with his left arm and pulled a wastrel from the hole. With a grin he proceeded to eat the creature, still alive and writhing as he tore into it with his teeth.

Avril looked away in disgust. He appreciated the Mujari's tracking ability; he did not appreciate its eating habits.

The Grand Vizier had a very considerable number of servants; the Mujari were not the most disgusting or disturbing of them.

Erat continued along the road as the sun set. He allowed

his horse to proceed at a steady walk. He let the animal follow the road as he dozed in the saddle. He did not worry about being pursued in the darkness as he would hear any riders and could simply slip off of the road to be swallowed up by the darkness until any riders should pass by him.

As Erat slipped into sleep his mind was filled with strange dreams.

The dreams contained images that he had never imagined, images that he could not conceive of in his waking mind.

They contained blazing suns and fantastic machines hurtling through the darkness between suns. Men and women dressed in suits that were blindingly white and covering their entire bodies, even with helmets that covered their entire heads. Some of the suits were black and not white and the wearers of those suits had blazing red eyes.

He also saw other things, things not human. Things out of his own worst nightmares. Things which looked like huge insects which stood upright and pursued human prey with grisly intensity.

He saw men in strange clothing fighting these insects with weapons that killed with light and fire. And he saw the insects also fighting with similar weapons.

He dreamt of a great battle between the two sides. Men and women in deadly ships fighting the insects who fought from their own deadly ships. Cities burning, consumed in huge mushroom clouds, entire worlds cracking apart and throwing debris into the blackness of space.

Suddenly the dream was interrupted by the sound of hooves striking stone in a fast gallop.

Erat came awake and quickly pulled off of the road. He moved his horse into the wasteland away from the road and held his mount still.

The riders that came down the road were in a full gallop. They quickly passed his position. He remained still until the sounds of the riders faded into the distance until he could hear them no more.

He returned to the road and kicked his horse into a quick trot. He was concerned that the riders were taking word of him to the final outpost at the base of the mountains. He decided that he would follow the road until dawn then he should be out of the wastelands and into the hills before the mountains.

When he reached the hills he could leave the road and travel into the mountains at any point that he wished. While following the main road one could pass over the mountains in a few days, there were other less traveled paths that would only take a few days longer.

He had enough time to locate and travel one of these other paths.

He wanted to avoid any member of the Qualorian Guard that might be looking for him. It did not seem like a good idea to let them catch him.

Curse that man for sticking him with the cube.

CHAPTER II

STUART WAS SITTING AT the command console on the bridge studying the image on the main view screen. It was an image of a nearby nebula.

Athena had sent a probe into the nebula a couple of hours ago and was currently receiving telemetry from the probe. The image on the view screen was being transmitted from the probe within the nebula.

They had been approaching the nebula for two days, only giving it cursory attention as they mapped a star system that was on their approach to the nebula.

The system they had just finished mapping only had 4 planets, three of them were gas giants and the fourth was an airless rocky world closer to the sun than Mercury was back in the Sol system.

The second gas giant was in an orbit within the "life zone" of the star but as it was a gas giant it could not support life. However, it had 14 moons and moon number 5 was capable of supporting life. In fact, it was slightly larger than Earth and was covered in jungle.

Stuart had submitted a report on it a few hours ago

recommending a full survey team be dispatched with an eye to colonization.

As the image was coming from the probe it tended to be interspersed with static every few seconds. The gasses and radiations in the nebula were interfering with the probe's signal.

"Commander, I am receiving a message from Admiral Higgins, Starbase 12."

Stuart sat up a bit straighter in his seat. "Put it on the main screen please, Athena."

The image of the nebula was replaced by that of Admiral Higgins sitting behind his desk on Starbase 12. The Admiral was a man of medium build with a balding head and piercing blue eyes. He sported a large handlebar mustache that he was very proud of. When he spoke a slight British accent could be heard that was remnant of his childhood on Excalibur IV where he had grown up.

Excalibur IV had been colonized by a contingent of colonists from Great Britain. They had colonized the planet and had remained isolated for over a century until a Federation cruiser had made contact with them on a routine patrol mission. Due to their being isolated, their accents had remained strong as there was no interaction with the rest of the federation for so long.

All the inhabitants of Excalibur IV were extremely proud of their accent.

"Admiral, Lieutenant Commander Stuart of the Pegasus here." Stuart stated to the Admiral.

"Lieutenant Commander, "the admiral responded. "I have just seen your report of the star you have discovered outside of the galaxy. I believe that your report states it is well above the plane of the elliptic?"

"Yes Admiral. It is 77 degrees above the plane."

"Commander Stuart, the Pegasus is a Class Two

Exploration and Scout vessel, I believe?" Higgins asked as he looked down at a display set into his desk.

"Yes Admiral. The Pegasus has a crew capacity of eleven, although her current mission only calls for myself as crew." Stuart replied, just in case the admiral was unaware of the Pegasus's current mission.

"Yes, of course. I realize that you are on a simple mapping mission, Commander. I was more interested in the range of the Pegasus than in her current personnel assignment." Higgins spoke without looking up from his desk's readouts. The he suddenly looked up at Stuart.

"According to the files I have here, the Pegasus is 3 months into the current mission, is that correct?"

"Yes, sir."

"I also see from your personnel record that you are on your 3rd solo survey mission on the Pegasus. It seems that you continue to volunteer for solo survey missions. Why is that, Lieutenant Commander? Do you have a problem being a part of a crew?"

"No sir. I just prefer mapping and studying spatial phenomena. I have no objections to being a part of a larger crew."

"Perhaps you prefer to be the captain of your ship rather than serving under another?"

"Not at all, sir. Truth to tell, I simply prefer the relative quiet that a solo mapping mission affords." Stuart answered neutrally.

"A lone eagle type eh? Well, there is nothing wrong with that considering that Fleet Admiral Carstair took seven solo mapping missions before he accepted a position in a more crewed capacity."

Higgins studied Stuart for another few moments then he looked back down at his in-desk display screens again. Abruptly he changed the subject.

"Lieutenant Commander Stuart, I am ordering you

to proceed to the coordinates that I am uploading to the Pegasus's A.I. and await the arrival of the Wellington. Upon rendezvous, the Pegasus will take on additional personnel to bring the ship's crew complement up to full staffing."

Higgins looked up at Stuart. "You have three days to arrive at the rendezvous point. You will receive new orders upon arrival. Do you have any questions Lieutenant Commander?"

"No, sir, your orders a perfectly clear as we are to proceed to the rendezvous point as ordered."

"Very well. Higgins, starbase twelve, out."

The screen changed back to the nebula display. Stuart stared at the display without seeing it. The admiral did not say that he would remain aboard the Pegasus, but he did not say that he would be reassigned either. He did say that he would receive new orders upon arrival. He was probably being reassigned to a larger ship, possibly the Wellington. He would end up in her astrogation department, probably on the third shift being the newest member of the team.

Well, it was no use putting it off any longer; he knew that this day would come eventually.

"Athena, set the probe for passive data collection and storage, and then set a course for our rendezvous with the Wellington. Adjust speed accordingly."

"Acknowledged, do you wish to know the rendezvous point?"

Stuart truly didn't want to know where he would have to give his ship up at but his curiosity pushed him to ask, "Where are we going, Athena?"

"Our destination is in orbit above Moldovan III."

"Never heard of it, what information do you have about it?"

"Moldovan III is an earth-type planet, although the gravity is 1.2 gees. It was discovered in 2278 by the solo survey vessel, Agrippa. Colonization was approved in 2311 but it has not yet been colonized. The main view screen changed from the nebula to a video of Moldovan III hanging in space. A large space station was in orbit above the planet. There was also a moon peeking out from behind the planet.

"Moldovan III has one moon. The moon has an ammonia atmosphere which is not conductive to human life."

"Athena, what information do you have about the space station in orbit?" Stuart asked. A space station in orbit above a planet was a rare occurance. Very few worlds outside of the core Federation systems harbored an orbital station. The expense to build, maintain and supply an orbital station in one of the core systems was huge, to build a station out here on the edges of the Federation had to be extremely expensive.

"That is the Argos research station, Commander. The research conducted there is for the most part classified. The only information about what type of research conducted there states that it has to do with trans-dimensional inference."

"Trans-dimensional inference, what exactly does that mean?"

"I am not really sure, Commander, but I can postulate from what records that are available across the galactic-net that it may have something to do with extra dimensional travel."

"Sorry I asked. What is our eta to Moldovan III, Athena?"

"Fifty-Seven hours and forty-two minutes. The probe has acknowledged passive data collection, course laid in for Moldovan III."

"Very well, activate engines and engage."

"Affirmative, we are now en route," Athena answered.

Erat left the road as the sun rose over the horizon. The wastelands were behind him now and rolling hills led off into the distance. He was able to ride at a gallop here as the holes scattered throughout the wastelands were not in evidence in the hills.

After a while Erat allowed his mount to slow to a walk, he could not afford to have his horse drop from fatigue. He kept an eye out behind him but could not spot any sign of pursuit, but he still believed he was being trailed. He just did not know how far behind him his pursuers were. They could be an hour behind him or a day, he just didn't know.

The hills were covered in a short scruffy looking grass. But the color had gone from the sandy gray of the wastelands to a dull uninspired greenish hue. The farther he rode into the hill the higher the grass was becoming. Soon the grass was up to his horse's knees forcing Erat to continue at a walking pace as he was not able to see any pitfalls that might cause his horse to stumble and fall or worse yet break a leg.

After a few hours of riding in this manner Erat came to a small stream running through the small depression between hills. He decided to stop and let his horse rest and graze through the grasses.

Erat decided to make camp for the night as the sun was getting low in the sky. He watched as the sun sank out of view and the sky darkened. He gazed up to the usual nightly view of an entire galaxy above his head, filling the night sky.

He could make out individual spiral arms, each filled with literally millions of pinpoints that were suns burning in space.

Erat did not know that the stars were suns; he only knew that they filled the sky with their brilliance. When he was a boy he had asked an elder of his village about the stars.

"Why do you care about the stars, Erat? They are beyond the reach of any of us, they do not affect us, they simply are there," the old man had replied. "It is better that you learn how to keep a blade sharp, how to care for a horse, how to fletch an arrow than to worry about the stars. The stars were there before any of us were born and they will be there long after we are gone. Pay them no mind."

The problem was that Erat could not help but to notice them. This was especially true when he was alone and out in the open at night as he now found himself to be. The starts filled the entire sky after dark. If it was a clear night as tonight was then he could see the entire galaxy of stars laid out as if they were on a platter ready to be served up as a feast for some unseen gigantic creature.

The biggest problem that Erat had was that the stars made him feel small and insignificant. He did not like this feeling, even though he suspected that it was true.

Erat finally tore his attention away from the stars and concentrated on his dinner. He still did not make a fire. If he was being pursued, he did not want to give his position away. If anybody was following him, he was sure they would have a hard time finding him.

———————————
———————————

Captain Avril was fuming. This Mujari was having a hard time tracking this barbarian. They had followed the spoor through the wastelands and back to the road. Then off the road to the south for a short distance, then back to the road, then along the road throughout the day, at some points leaving the road to ride alongside it as caravans passed.

Finally, just before nightfall they left the road, heading north into the hills. Now they had traveled for three hours heading deeper into the hills. Finally Avril had called a halt to their pursuit to camp for the night.

At least there were no wastrels around for the Mujari to sink its teeth into. The creature tended to make Avril's skin crawl. If it weren't the Grand Vizier's creature he would have killed it out of disgust. The cursed thing was just not natural somehow. It stank of sorcery.

There was a great deal about the Grand Vizier that Avril did not like either. However, in the Grand Viziers case, Avril chose to keep his council to himself. One never knew when one of the Grand Vizier's spies was loitering around, just waiting for a chance to report back with incriminating evidence on someone.

Avril had ordered guards at the corners of the camp. They were close to, if not in, the territory of the Tribes of Hern; which is a most dangerous place to be if one were associated in any way, shape or form with the city state of Qualor.

The Tribes of Hern and Qualor were constantly skirmishing with each other. Both had territorial claims to the hills, with the tribes having the stronger claim as Qualor was located at the other edge of the wastelands. If the tribes could be conquered, then Qualor would go from being a city state to becoming a small nation.

Qualor had three outposts between the city gates and the foot of the mountains. Each of them was heavily fortified and the road well patrolled. The tribes tended to stay away from the outposts and the road.

The most dangerous outpost in the Qualorian Guard was the far outpost. Every few years the tribes made an attempt to overrun it. If they should ever be successful, it would be a difficult task to rebuild it.

The three outposts and the road they guarded were the only northern land route between the Rowad Ocean and the lands to the west. There was also a southern land route, but that was mostly in the kingdom of Donaria and was well protected from any external threat.

Donaria was a strong kingdom that few dared to even dream of attacking. Caravan master's never worried about being set upon by brigands when they drove through the kingdom. Mounted patrols were plentiful and well trained. The men comprising the patrols would never threaten a caravan with extortion or violence, as it was a death sentence if they were ever caught.

However, if a caravan was traveling from the Northern provinces then it was quicker for it to travel through the mountains, across the wastelands and come out through Qualor. This would literally take weeks off the travel time.

It also made for a good situation for Qualor to collect a "passage tax" as it was called. But the ruler of the Qualorian city state, King Phiponoux knew to keep the tax low so caravans would not take the extra time to go south to Donaria.

This had all been going on for over 70 years since Qualor had finished building the road to connect Qualor with the mountains. There was a natural road leading through the mountains which the Qualorian road builders had connected to when they finished building their road. It was at that point that the far outpost had been located.

The far outpost was the most heavily fortified of the three outposts. It had stone walls that were 20 yards wide and rose 50 feet into the air. On top of the walls were guard barracks and armories. Set into the walls one three sides stood iron gates that could be dropped in seconds.

The rear of the outpost was the side of the mountain. Straight up for hundreds of yards it was improbable that an attack would come from that direction. Set into the face of the cliff were caves that had been converted into a final line of defense. The caves had all been dug out deeper and had thick walls built into their mouths with small iron doors to prevent any from attacking in anything but single file.

The caves had been inter-connected so defenders could rally to any cave as necessary. The caves had passages that led to a humongous underground cavern. From this cavern one could travel through the mountain for hundreds of leagues and exit through a series of caves in Donaria.

Those passages were a very well kept secret and had a very select guard upon the Qualorian end. Only guarsmen that could be completely trusted to keep the passages a secret were allowed to guard the Qualorian end.

No attack had penetrated the walls of the far outpost, so the caves had never been needed for a last stand or as an escape route.

Avril knew nothing of the passages. He was only vaguely aware of the defense strategies for the far outpost. His main concern was his squad which normally patrolled the road between Qualor and the first outpost with an occasional patrol to the second outpost.

His squad had the misfortune to have been in Qualor when the Grand Vizier needed a patrol to locate and return the barbarian. If it had been a day later it would have Captain Skara's squad that would have been recruited for the assignment.

✦

Chapter III

15 MINUTES LATER STUART stepped onto the bridge. He glanced at the main view screen as he made his way to the command console. The image was of Moldovan III turning below them, the sun was opposite the planet so the view that Stuart was seeing was of the night side with cities sprinkled out between the darkness on the land masses below.

"Athena, can you display Argos station on the screen?"

The image of the planet changed. Now Stuart saw the opposite side, sunlight streaming onto the surface. He could make out a large continent bordered to the east by a larger ocean. There was a storm out in the ocean that looked to be a hurricane in the making. Above it all, hanging suspended in space was Argos station.

Argos station was a large tri conical structure. There was a large conical central structure which had three smaller conical structures attached to it via a series of tubes and struts. It was totally white in color with yellow light shining from its ports. There were blue and red blinking lights interspersed about it.

Below Argos station was a spherical structure whose size dwarfed Argos station. There was a large tube that emerged from the top of the sphere that spanned the distance between the sphere and Argos station and disappeared into the bottom of Argos station.

The tube was translucent and Stuart could see a small shape traveling from the station to the sphere. It looked like a simple transport tube, except for the fact that it was four times larger than any transport tube Stuart had ever seen.

"Athena, what is that below the station? It wasn't there when you showed me Moldovan III a couple of days ago."

"I was just running a cross check, Commander. The image I showed you of Moldovan III previously was a file image recorded seventeen years previously. At the time I showed you the planet I did not have a more currant image available." Athena answered. Stuart could swear she sounded miffed.

"No big deal, Athena. But next time you show me a file image could you inform me that it is a file image?"

"Acknowledged, Commander, should I contact the station now?"

Stuart chuckled silently to himself, Athena was changing the subject. He would never believe that Athena was not alive. She may have been a ship's A.I., but she had personality. He did not believe that she had been programmed that way. She had evolved over the years he had been aboard the Pegasus.

All A.I.'s were programmed to interact with their crews and to adapt to each situation. Stuart firmly believed that Athena had reached a threshold and crossed over it to become alive in every sense except biologically. He had a couple of ideas about that as well, but he was currently keeping those ideas to himself. If what he thought was correct, then a whole new chapter in intelligent life was about to be released upon the galaxy.

But that was for a future date to look into. Right now he had more pressing matters to attend to, the first of which was to contact Captain Martinez on the Argos.

"Yes, Athena, please send my compliments to Captain Martinez and inform him that I am available to him at his convenience."

On the main view screen Stuart saw the image of a middle aged man in a tan short sleeve shirt. He had coal black hair with white strands running through it. His eyes were a deep cocoa brown and he had a nose that looked like it had been broken at least one time. The one thing that truly stood out in Stuarts' mind was Martinez's teeth. His teeth were so white they seemed to shine as if electricfied.

"Ah, Captain Stuart, welcome to the Moldovan system." Martinez greeted him warmly. Even though Stuart was a Lieutenant Commander he was still addressed as Captain as he was currently in command of the Pegasus.

"Thank you Captain Martinez." Stuart replied, but he was at a loss of words for any kind of a follow up beside 'Glad to be here' which sounded lame to him, especially as he was not glad to be here. Fortunately, Martinez did not seem to notice any lapse as he continued speaking as if Stuart had not spoken at all.

"Can you tell me how long until you will be ready to accept personnel and load equipment aboard your ship?"

"I am ready to begin both when the Wellington arrives."

"The Wellington will not be here for another day, Captain. I have personnel and equipment that are ready to transfer to the Pegasus now." Martinez responded, his smile beginning to droop a bit.

"Captain Martinez, I am sorry to disappoint you, but I have no orders about anyone or anything from Argos station coming aboard the Pegasus. I was simply told to await the Wellington." Stuart answered. He didn't have any orders to not accept any personnel or equipment either. The only orders he had was to rendezvous with the Wellington and have a full crew transfer from that ship, nothing concerning Argos station at all.

"Hmmm, I see. Very well then we will simply have to await the Wellington. In that case would you consent to dine with me this evening over here?"

"I would be delighted to, sir. I am most curious about Argos station and what type of research you are conducting."

"Excellent, Captain I will expect you at 1800 hours sharp."

"I'll be there. Pegasus out."

Stuart frowned as the screen went back to the orbital view of Moldovan III. He drummed his fingers on the arm of his seat and sat quietly for a moment.

"Athena, the orders that Admiral Higgins transmitted, am I incorrect that they did not mention any type of personnel or equipment form Argos station?"

"No commander."

"Was there any mention of Argos station at all in those orders?"

"No commander."

"Well, Captain Martinez seems to think that we are here to collect personnel and equipment from his station. I wonder what he knows that I don't."

"I do not have any answers for you, Commander Stuart." Athena stated flatly.

"I did not expect you to have any, Athena. I was just thinking out loud. Well, I have about three hours until dinner; I think I would like to see any data that you have concerning Argos station. If you would be as kind as to pipe it over to my console so I can review it I would appreciate it."

"Transferring data now, commander," Athena's voice replied as his console lit up and began to fill with data.

Stuart bent over his console screens and began reviewing the history and other pertinent information concerning Argos station.

Captain Avril scratched his cheek where his beard stubble was itching. He hadn't had a chance to shave in two days and his stubble itched. The top of the stubble ended just below his high cheek bones which ran up to his eyes. His eyes were a deep blue and many a tavern serving wench had lost herself in them. Avril's nose was narrow and pinched and rose up between his eyes where his forehead ran the rest of the way up his face to end in a hairline that was beginning to recede and matched the blond of his beard stubble. Avril's mouth offset the rest of his face with full think lips behind which were a full set of teeth that were starting to yellow slightly. Avril stood just under 6 feet tall and had a medium build, his uniform was loose fitting, almost as if someone had simply draped it over his frame.

Avril frowned as he watched the Mujari tracker literally sniff at the ground on the other side of the stream. It was obvious to Avril that they had come upon the barbarian's campsite of the previous night. It was also obvious that the barbarian had ridden off across the hills, he could see the hoof prints in the mud on the opposite bank leading up and over the small rise that currently blocked his view of the hills beyond.

The Mujari turned and called out to Avril from the opposite bank, its voice just loud enough to carry to Avril's ears.

"Captain, wait here, the prey may be playing tricks." And with that he turned and proceeded to move up and over the hill out of sight.

Avril sighed, but he did not doubt the Mujari, it had

been right every time so far. He decided to give his men a rest.

"Sergeant, have the men dismount and stretch their legs. I want a sentry on top of that rise. See that the horses are watered and are allowed to graze but keep them close."

"Yes, sir," the sergeant repiled enthusiastically.

Avril dismounted and handed his horse off to a guardsman. He walked around the area that he could tell was the barbarian's campsite. He looked around trying to determine if he could find anything that might tell him what the barbarian was up to or which way he was headed. With the exception of the hoof prints, he couldn't tell anything.

The more he studied the hoof prints the more he was convinced that the Mujari was right about them being a diversion to lead any pursuers astray. The prints looked wrong somehow, but he couldn't put his finger on how they looked wrong.

Avril stood on the bank looking at the prints his eyes following them up the rise where they disappeared. He lightly jumped across the stream and followed the prints up to the top of the rise.

He nodded at the sentry that was at the top of the rise and looked out over the hills that rolled away into the distance. He studied the tracks to where they faded out of sight about halfway down the other side of the rise. He noticed that the Mujari was completely out of sight.

After satisfying his curiosity about the hoof prints he looked outward to the other hills in sight and began to worry about running into the Tribes of Hern. These hills were home to them and if they were around he would never know it until it was too late.

The hills were covered with grasses that grew taller the farther he looked. In those grasses right now could be a single Hern horseman watching him to an entire army headed his way, out of sight in the grasses or even behind the hills themselves.

He agreed with General Triptonis about the need to burn off the grasses and keep roving scouts stationed out here. The general had proposed this to the king 12 years ago. The king had then consulted with the Grand Vizier and had finally informed the general that while his idea had merit, he did not wish to antagonize the Tribes of Hern by burning the grasses.

The general had replied that the tribes did not worry about antagonizing Qualor when they continued to attack the far outpost.

The general was now retired and living abroad. Avril did not wish to follow the general into exile. His family was comfortable living in Qualor and Avril did not want to put them in jeopardy, so he obeyed orders and was a good soldier. But there were times he wished the Grand Vizier had never stepped foot in Qualor.

The Grand Vizier had come to Qualor 45 years ago. No one knew where he had come from, except perhaps the king. Upon his arrival in Qualor he had spent a few weeks quietly exploring the city and cultivating powerful friends. Eventually he had manipulated events so that he had been introduced to the king.

The king had been completely taken with the man who was to become the Grand Vizier. He had invited the man to dine with him and had spent the evening locked in conversation concerning what no one had been able to discover. For the next few months the king had kept the man at his side constantly, never asking anything of him which anyone could tell, not even advice.

Finally months after this began the king proclaimed the man to be the Grand Vizier. He made the announcement to a full audience of the assembled nobles of the city-state. He also stated that the new position of Grand Vizier would have

THE LONELY SUN

no claim to the throne if the king should become deceased. He said that it was at the Grand Vizier's insistence that this provision was announced so that no one would accuse the man of trying to usurp the throne of Qualor.

Avril did admit that the Grand Vizier had never shown any interest in ruling Qualor as the king ruled. But he believed that the Grand Vizier preferred to be the power behind the throne. He also believed that the man was interested in taking Qualor from a city-state to an empire.

For the past decade all three of the outposts had been strengthened, patrols increased and sent out better armed than ever before. New ring mail armor had been slowly replacing the leather corselets that had been the standard form of protection for the Qualorian Guard.

To the west, a new colony had been established. The primary purpose of this colony was farming, to make Qualor more self-sufficient and less dependent on food stuffs being brought in from Donaria.

Donaria produced much of the food that was consumed in Qualor. They had huge swathes of fertile farmland and were rich due to their food exports. Qualor had the farmland available but never farmed it due to roving bands of nomads that traveled the lands to the west of the city.

When the colony was established it had a barracks with a full time complement of two hundred guardsmen stationed there at all times. The colony had grown rapidly with farms springing up all around the main town itself. The guardsmen had fought two major engagements in the first year of the colony and had emerged victorious in each of the battles. The nomads had stayed away from the colony for the next few years, then started returning in small numbers to trade with the colonists.

Today a fair sized trading post had arisen in the colony along with an inn, a couple of stables, a flour mill, a few dozen houses and a small government building where townspeople and outlying farmers would meet to discuss the issues they had in establishing the colony.

Today it was no longer known as the colony but had been given the name of Farmington. An unoriginal and uninspired name, but it was accurately descriptive.

But it did not solve the issue of Donarian food stuffs being the main supply of edibles in Qualor. If anything, their imported foods increased as the population grew. The southern route to Donaria was well patrolled; it always had been in order to keep Qualor well supplied. But last year a new barracks had begun construction near the border with Donaria.

It was the larger than the barracks at Farmington. When completed, possibly late this year, it would house close to five hundred guardsmen with provisions for 10 times that number. It looked like the king was concerned that Donaria might attempt an invasion, or if he was perhaps planning an invasion of his own.

In response to this Donaria had increased the size of its military patrols in the border areas with Qualor. So far though there had been no incidents and all remained quiet.

Avril knew that his name was on the short list to be stationed at the new barracks. He might be offered the position of adjutant to the barracks commander. He would like to get the position, it would mean a promotion to major, and increase in pay and his status would rise a bit.

But first he had to capture and return the barbarian. He knew if he did that his name would move to the top of the short list, possibly even knock the other names off of the list and assure him of the position.

He looked out over the hills again before returning back down to where his men were. He saw no sign that the Mujari was returning. He might as well have the cook prepare lunch. They might be here for a couple of hours.

Erat continued riding his mount as hard as he thought the horse could take it throughout the day. As dusk was falling he decided to stop and make camp for the night. Tonight he would have a fire.

He was not convinced that no one was following him, but if he kept his fire small the surrounding hills should mask it from anyone who was not closer that a couple of hills away.

The hills were steadily becoming larger and beginning to look as if they belonged at the foot of a mountain range. Erat believed that he would reach the base of the mountains by midday tomorrow.

He tended to his horse first, feeding and watering it. He then brought out a brush that he carried with him to brush down his horse. He also checked each hoof before it truly became dark outside; he wanted to make sure his horse did not need any attention to its hoofs. He did not want the beast to suddenly become unable to carry him.

Only when he had satisfied himself that his horse was fine and tended to did he turn his attention to his surroundings before attempting to build a fire. He stared into the near darkness looking in each direction before he was satisfied that there was no one near enough that a fire might be noticed.

He could not be absolutely that no one was about anywhere except the small depression between the hills he had stopped at for the night. He could go on foot and check the surrounding nearby hills, but that would take a few hours. Sometimes you just had to take a chance.

Turning to his saddlebag he reached in and drew out a small kit for building fires that he carried with him. He gathered the materials that he needed and set to work with his kindling and flint.

Minutes later he had a small fire going that would do to prepare a small hot meal.

Sturya noticed the slight glow coming from the nearby hills. He quietly and quickly made his way closer to the nearby hill where the fire was emanating from. He dropped to his belly and crawled silently to the crest of the hill and looked down. His eyes managed to see a man and a horse in the small glow of the man's fire.

The man was sitting by his small fire, his attention focused on whatever it was that he was eating. The horse stood nearby, its head moving up and down as it ate of the grasses it stood amongst.

Sturya lay still and simply observed the man for a few minutes. He was a large man, but his manner of dress told him he was not one of the denizens of the cursed city to the west. He was not of that race which had built the road through the lands of his people.

No, this man was larger than those people, and his manner of dress was not of those men. He did not wear the armor nor carry the weapons they had. He did carry a large blade, wore simple leather boots and a shortened animal skin wrapped about his loins. A simple homespun tunic covered bulging muscles.

Sturya did not wish to arouse this man. The man looked like one of the barbarians that he had heard tales of in his youth. It was best not to disturb him. The man could probably break Sturya in half without even breaking a sweat. Sturya was only 5 and a half feet tall with a thin build. His people were all smaller in size than most others. Sturya had weatherbeaten skin which was stretched tightly across his bones. Although he was only in his late 20's he looked much older. His dark hair was pulled tightly back into a stern braid that hung at his back which in turn was covered by a leather jerkin. Sturya's most noticable feature was his nose, it had been broken long ago and had healed as a crooked thing that had flattened to the left side of his face. When he was being stealthy he would breath through his mouth as breathing through his nose produced a quiet rasping noise.

Sturya quietly backed down off of the hilltop and quickly put distance between himself and the stranger. He headed back to inform the tribes of this stranger. Sturya knew that there was a nearby camp.

An hour later Sturya entered one of the tribe's campsites. The site consisted of a large central tent with a scattering of smaller tents surrounding it. There was a horse corral at the edge of the camp and two men were sitting in front of a small fire by the corral. They nodded at Sturya as he rode up to them. They knew that had he not belonged here he would never have made it past the outlying sentries that guarded all approaches to the camp.

One of them stood and accepted Sturya's horse and proceeded to escort the animal to the corral. His horse would be cared for until he returned for the animal.

Sturya headed to the large central tent where the tribe's chieftain would be situated. Two guards stood in front of the tents entrance, both of them were armed with scimitars and the small throwing stars that every tribesman was proficient with. The throwing stars were taught to children starting at a very young age. By the time children became young adults they could hit a small moving target from the back of a galloping horse. All the children were taught, girls as well as boys.

The Tribes of Hern taught their children the arts of fighting. When the tribes went to war, only the extremely elderly and very young did not fight. All others would fight, men and women alike. The tribes always took care of their own people.

Sturya was admitted into the chieftain's tent. He was always allowed access to the chieftain as he was a Rover. He would report to whichever chieftain was closest. The Rovers had their allegiance to the entire Tribes of Hern, not a particular chieftain. This time Sturya just happened to be closest to his own family tribe.

The history of the Rovers was a long one going back centuries. To be selected for Rover training one had to show tremendous patience, endurance and tracking skills. Sturya had shown abundant aptitudes in all three plus he had proved that he could avoid the best trackers that the tribes had to offer.

The Rovers had watched Qualor build the road connecting the city to the mountains through the wastelands and through the southern reaches of their territory. At the time they did not see a need to interfere and it was only a road. Even the outposts did not concern the Rovers, as it was obvious to them that they were simply there to provide security for travelers.

It was not until some decades ago that one particular chieftain, Tragara decided that the outposts and the road was a threat to the tribes that military action was taken against the Qualorians. By this time it was too late, the far outpost was too strong to destroy and since they first tried the Qualorians had strengthened it and added more troops to its defense. It would take the combined might of all the tribes to hope to destroy it.

The Rovers had counseled against this course of action. The Qualorians were not trying to conqueror the surrounding countryside; they were only looking to protect the road they had built. So far, the tribes had not continued with their attacks, the debate continued and had for a few years now. A chieftains council would be held late next year where the issue would be debated further, until then all attacks were suspended.

Inside the chieftain's tent Sturya stepped to the side of the tent and sat. He was brought food and drink and would sit there until the chieftain called for him. If Sturya had urgent news he would have told one of the sentries outside and the sentry would have escorted him into the tent. As he did not have urgent news he simply sat and waited. It could be hours until the chieftain called for him, but usually a Rover was called upon quickly as they generally had news of events outside of the local campsite.

For now, Sturya would sit and wait.

The Mujari returned after an hour. Avril had to admit that he was impressed by what it had to tell him.

It seems that the barbarian had ridden over a mile then had managed to get his horse to backup, stepping exactly in his own tracks.

The Mujari had not been fooled; the deepness of the tracks had given away the ruse. If the barbarian had done it on harder ground, the Mujari may have been fooled; Avril definitely would have fallen for the deceit.

The Mujari was able to travel quickly to the end of the fake trail and back. It was much quicker then Avril's squad would have been.

The Mujari then spent the next several minutes hopping from one side of the stream to the other as it searched out the barbarians spoor. Finally it looked upstream and the turned to Avril. "The prey rides up the river. Its beast carries it in the water."

Avril considered this turn of events. He would have to follow upstream deeper into the territory of the tribes. He did not relish going further into their territory, but he did not have a choice. The Grand Vizier did not take well to

LEE E FULLER JR

failure. Going into back to Qualor because he did not wish to go deeper into territory controlled by the Tribes of Hern, would be failure. There could be only one excuse that the Grand Vizier would accept and that would be the death of Avril and his squad.

Avril looked to the sky, it was early afternoon, and they could travel a good distance further until nightfall. He did not want to stop for darkness at this point. He needed to find out if the Mujari could track in darkness.

"Xipt!" he barked to the creature. "Are you capable of following this barbarian's track after the sun goes down?"

"Difficult to follow in darkness, have to go slower," was the answer he received. But it was the answer he wanted, they would be able to travel throughout the night. With the barbarian stopping at night to camp they would be able to cut down the distance if they continued forward during the night.

"Good enough. Follow the trail we are right behind you." Avril ordered the creature.

"Sergeant, mount up, we are moving out." He informed the sergeant who was standing nearby in anticipation of the order.

Minutes later the squad was riding along the bank while the Mujari moved against the flowing water in the stream, following what tracks he could still make out that the moving water had not yet erased.

CHAPTER IV

STUART STOOD IN FRONT of his uniform closet and tried to decide whether or not to wear his dress uniform for dinner with Captain Martinez on Argos station. He was not averse to wearing it, he was just trying to decide if he should or not. Captain Martinez outranked him and had invited him to dinner, not the other way around.

He'd be damned if he was going to ask Athena for advice on this, her answer would be based on regulations and protocols and nothing else.

Captain Martinez did not state that dinner was formal, but he did not say it wasn't either.

These were the kinds of decisions that he dreaded. He could quickly decide what type of action to take in any military situation. But put him in any type of social situation and he was totally adrift in a sea of confusion.

He finally decided to wear his dress uniform. He had been invited to dine with a superior officer aboard that officer's command, so it would be the dress uniform to show proper respect for that officer.

A few minutes later he was admiring how he looked in the dress uniform of the Federation Spatial Naval Forces.

The uniform was a brilliant white with his rank insignia in a deep blue along his cuffs. His few ribbons and the one medal he had earned were attached to the left breast of his dress tunic. As he was visiting another facility located in space he was wearing his dress uniform type two. This consisted of a tunic, pants, boots and a small earpiece to keep him in constant contact with his own ship.

A dress uniform type one was similar except that it was for planetary functions and had the addition of a jacket and a hat. The last time he'd had to wear a dress uniform was when he formally took command of the Pegasus almost three years ago. He would have to wear it again tomorrow when he turned command over to whoever was to be the new commander.

"Commander, we are being hailed by a shuttle from Argos station. They are ready to dock." Athena informed him as he pulled on his left boot. He stood and looked in the mirror and found himself acceptably attired for the upcoming social occasion.

"Bring them in, Athena. I'm on my way to the docking port."

"Yes, commander."

Stuart then left his cabin and proceeded to the ship's lift. Once in the lift he headed down to deck five where the ship's docking ports were located. The Pegasus had two docking ports, one starboard and one port side. Deck five was a corridor that followed the inner hull around the entire level.

Leaving the ship's lift one would be facing the door into main engineering. Or one could turn to the left or right and follow the corridor all the way around and end up back at the ship's lift. Inward of the corridor were separate compartments, mostly storage and a couple for engineering such as life support controls and the like.

There were two ports on the outward corridor walls

and these were the two docking ports. Stuart knew that the shuttle from Argos station was docking with the starboard docking port as Athena had piped the communication with the shuttle through the ship's intercom system. Stuart was hearing such communications chatter as "thirty degree axis initiate, aligning docking ring, firing port thrusters" from the shuttles pilot and such things as "pitch alignment confirmed, docking sensors initiated and aligning" from Athena as she worked with the shuttle pilot to bring the two ships together.

Stuart reached the starboard docking hatch just as the light changed from red to green to indicate that the dock was active and that pressure was equalized between the Pegasus and the shuttle. He reached out and slapped the switch and waited while the hatch slid into the hull leaving him to stare at the hatch of the shuttle.

A few moments later the shuttle hatch slid back and Stuart found himself face to face with the shuttle's pilot.

The pilot snapped to attention and saluted.

"Lieutenant Watkins, shuttle one at your service, sir." He formally reported to Stuart.

Stuart returned the salute. "As you were, Lieutenant, are we ready to proceed to Argos station?"

"Yes, sir, if you will come aboard and strap in, we can boost for the station."

"Good enough. Athena, standard security protocols please."

"Aye, commander," Came the response in his left ear through the com unit he was wearing.

Stuart entered the shuttle and looked around. There were four seats available to him. He chose one and strapped himself into it while the pilot returned to the shuttle cockpit and prepared to leave the Pegasus.

Stuart watched as Athena sealed the hatch on the Pegasus then he saw the shuttle hatch slide into place and felt a slight pressure change within the shuttle. A few moments later he felt a slight lurch as the shuttle disengaged from the Pegasus and boosted toward Argos station.

Stuart didn't have anything to do for the few minutes that it took to reach Argos station so he simply sat in his seat and continued the battle within himself over his feelings about turning the Pegasus over to another captain. He couldn't believe how attached he had become to the little exploration / scout ship.

If this is how he felt about turning over command after only three years, then how would he feel about turning over command to a ship if he had been its captain for 10 years? 10 years was average for a person to be in command of a light to heavy cruiser.

But this was different; he wouldn't be turning command over but getting another command in return. He would be just another Lieutenant Commander in the astrography section of a heavy cruiser. At least the Wellington was a heavy cruiser. Officers tended to be promoted into command positions quicker after having served in a heavy cruiser.

With all these thoughts running around in his head, Stuart didn't notice the slight lurch of the shuttle as it landed in the hanger bay of the station. His subconscious mind did notice though as he automatically unbuckled and stood up from his seat. He didn't become aware that he was aboard Argos station until he noticed that he was standing in front of the hatch waiting for the atmosphere to finish filling the landing bay.

He nodded to the pilot as the hatch slid open, "A nice smooth ride, Lieutenant."

"Thank you, sir." Watkins acknowledged the compliment. "If you simply cross the bay to the hatch over there" he gestured to a hatch set across from the shuttle hatch some 30 feet away "Ensign Clark will be waiting there to escort you to the Captain."

"Thank you, Lieutenant."

Stuart then stepped out of the shuttle and crossed the distance to the hatch. As he approached it the hatch slid open to reveal a young woman wearing the uniform and rank of an ensign of the Federation Naval Forces.

The ensign came to attention and saluted Stuart. "Commander Stuart, I am Ensign Clark and I will escort you to Captain Martinez."

"A pleasure, Ensign," He answered as he returned the salute. "Please lead on; I am looking forward to meeting Captain Martinez in person."

"Certainly, sir, right this way please." Clarke responded as she turned and headed into the station.

Stuart followed her down the corridor. The corridor ran straight for quite a ways making him realize that Argos station was much larger than he had realized. They finally came to a lift. They waited for a few moments after Clark had pressed the call button. The lift carried them up and deeper into the station.

The lift deposited them in another corridor. This corridor split off into other corridors and was lined with doors every few yards. This corridor also had a good number of people moving through it.

There was also a constant murmur running throughout the corridor as conversations carried along its length blended into the underfoot thrum of its power reactors and air circulation systems.

Stuart had been alone on the Pegasus for so long with only Athena for company that he had forgotten that the sounds of a fully manned station could be so noisy. But the station would be quieter than any planet side city would be. So it was all relative anyway.

And with that thought a silly little smile appeared on his face as he followed Ensign Clark through the corridors of Argos station.

Erat was having trouble leading his horse through the rocky steepness of the mountains he was finally climbing. For the last several miles he had been leading his horse as it was becoming too difficult to remain mounted as the horse kept slipping due to the steepness of the mountainside.

He had reached the base of the mountains a few hours ago as the day was turning from morning to afternoon. He had found a game trail and had followed it for a few miles up into the mountains but it had petered out leaving him with the decision to continue upward or to turn back and try to locate another trail.

He had continued upward with the hopes that the way would not be too much for his horse. For a couple of hours he had been able to ride making good time in ascending the mountains then he had come upon this particular steep slope. He was finally nearing the top of the slope.

He struggled with his horse for the last few yards until they both stood at the top of the slope, which turned out to be a ridge. Looking back Erat finally spotted his pursuers. They were a couple of miles away from the base of the mountains, and a bit south of his position, but they were definitely following his trail.

He studied them for a few moments. They were obviously a squad of the Qualorian Guard. Out in front of them there was a smaller figure. At first he thought that it was a large dog as it was running on all fours but as he watched he saw it rise upright and look in his direction.

Suddenly he knew that they were using a Mujari tracker to stay on his trail. The entire squad stopped as he watched. The tracker was staring in his direction. Erat suddenly realized that he was standing in plain view on the top of a ridge. They were all looking at him. They all knew exactly where he was.

Erat suddenly saw two small bands of men coming up on either side of the squad using the hillsides for cover. The Tribes of Hern were about to ambush the Qualorian squad. He threw his head back and laughed. The hunters had suddenly become the hunted giving him the chance to cross the mountains unmolested.

He watched for a few more moments as the ambush unfolded, the Qualorians suddenly on the defensive. The little Mujari fell to the ground and lay still. Many of the guardsmen fell from their mounts before they were even aware that they were under attack.

Erat turned away and began to look for way through the mountains. He was quite happy that he had not had the misfortune to run into the tribes himself. He enjoyed being alive.

Avril led his squad behind the Mujari. He was still confounded at the stamina that the creature was showing. It scurried forward on all fours like an animal yet managed to stay ahead of the squad riding their horses at a steady trot.

Avril was keeping an eye out for a likely place to make camp for the night. He was in no hurry though as nightfall was still a couple of hours off. Behind him he could hear the muted conversations being carried on by his men. He knew they would keep their voices low as the sergeant was bringing up the rear and would not tolerate any loudness that would give away their position.

Suddenly the Mujari stood upright at stared at the mountains ahead of them, completely stopping in its tracks. Avril brought up his arm to halt the squad and rode up behind the Mujari. Before he could ask the creature pointed to the mountains.

"The prey, it is there!" It exclaimed.

Avril followed its pointing arm with his eyes and was

surprised to see a man standing on a ridge off in the distance. From this distance it could be anybody. But he believed the Mujari. Standing next to the man on the ridge was a horse. It had to be the barbarian.

Avril had just turned back to order the sergeant to have one of the men carry the Mujari so they could proceed at a gallop when he heard the Mujari scream. He turned back and saw a handful of arrows protruding from the Mujari as it fell to the ground even as its life fled from its body.

The tribes were here and they were attacking.

He turned back to his squad and saw his men falling from their saddles as they too were filled with arrows. The sergeant sprang from his mount yelling at the squad to do the same even as an arrow suddenly emerged through his throat, drowning the man in his own blood.

Avril watched helplessly as his squad was cut down. He quickly turned his horse and fled in the direction of the mountains. Arrows fell all around him causing him to prod his horse with his heels to get it to gallop faster.

He rode hard for minutes before turning to see how many were chasing him.

He pulled up his horse to give it a moments rest. No one was behind him.

They did not seem to even be interested in him at all. They were probably busy stripping his men of their possessions and rounding up their horses. He was sure they would be after him in short order.

He turned and rode towards the mountains. He needed to put some distance between him and the tribes. He knew that they had let him go. The tribes did not miss with their arrows unless they intended to miss. He knew that he was safe only as long as they let him be safe.

He was sure he knew the reason he had been left alive, as a warning to others not to ride into the territory of the tribes.

He kicked his horse into a gallop again; he desperately wanted to reach the mountains before nightfall. The tribes did not generally go into the mountains. They had a superstitious awe of them for reasons he did not understand, but he felt reasonably sure he would be safe from the tribes there.

Sturya waited for the ambush upon the Qualorians to begin. He had ridden slightly ahead of the doomed squad and awaited whatever rider that was allowed to survive to pass by so that he could follow him.

He had awaited the chieftain's attention in the tent until the small hours of the morning. He had been kept waiting as another Rover was speaking with the chieftain in hushed voices. They continued to confer as occasionally the chieftain would motion to one of the sitting warrior heads who would then move up and join the conference until he was motioned back by the chieftain whereupon he would return to his seating cushions on the tent floor.

This went on for a few hours until the chieftain dismissed the other rover then motioned for Sturya. When the chieftain had learned of the barbarian he informed Sturya that a squad of Qualorian guardsmen had ridden deep into their territory. He then concluded that the barbarian was the reason they were here.

Finally he decided that they would ambush the Qualorian guardsmen and leave one alive. Sturya was ordered to follow the survivor and see if he would turn back or continue to follow the barbarian. If he turned back to Qualor then Sturya was free to kill him and claim his horse and possessions. But, should he continue to follow the barbarian, then Sturya was to continue following and try to find out why the barbarian was of such interest to him.

Finally the sounds of combat brought Sturya back to the

LEE E FULLER JR

present. The ambush had been sprung on the guardsmen. Shortly he heard a rider pass by on the other side of the hill he was hidden behind. The rider was in a full gallop.

Sturya quickly kicked his horse into motion and rode in the same direction as the rider that had passed. Sturya kept the hillsides between himself and the rider he was shadowing. The hills in this area had a tendency to run parallel so the route that the rider was taking would be the same route with only a hill between.

Sturya pulled in his horse after a few minutes as he heard the other rider stop. He held his horse's reins tight. His horse had been trained to be silent when he held the reins tightly. He sat and waited, listening. Finally after a few moments the other rider rode off again, in the direction of the mountains.

Sturya loosened the reins and prodded his horse after the rider, keeping the hillside between himself and the Qualorian guardsman. He was not yet sure if the guardsman was still following the barbarian or if he was simply putting distance between himself and the ambush site. He could still turn south and head for the distant outpost they had established at the base of the mountains.

Only time would tell. For now Sturya would be patient and follow the rider.

Erat had found another trail leading deeper into the mountains. It did not go any higher but went east along the mountainside. He followed it allowing his horse to set the pace at a slow walk. He was content to let his horse walk as dusk was settling over the day. He would stop soon and sleep on the trail if he could not find any type of clearing as he would not risk riding the narrow trail in darkness. A single misstep by his horse would send them both tumbling down the mountainside to end up lying broken and lifeless on the plain below becoming food for the vultures and other scavengers.

As the trail bent around the curve of the mountain Erat spotted a cave opening up ahead. He pulled up before his horse had crossed in front of the cave mouth and dismounted. He drew his sword and cautiously approached the entrance. He could only see a little ways into the cave, darkness shrouded its interior.

He moved back over to his horse and pulled his tinderbox out of a saddlebag along with the materials he needed to make a small torch. Soon he again approached the cave, torch in his left hand and sword in his right hand. He held the torch out in front of him, knowing that most animals would back away from fire.

He did not think that any animal was in the cave as his horse seemed completely unconcerned by the cave. His horse would be skittish if there was any scent of a dangerous animal emanating from within. But it was better to be sure if he was to spend the night here.

Erat entered the cave and slowly moved his torch around his eyes following the light it emitted. The cave was not shallow as he had at first suspected. He could not see the back of the cave at all. He moved further into the cave, alert for any sign of danger.

The floor was smooth, a few rocks scattered about, the walls were dry and the ceiling moved up into darkness the further into the cave he moved. There were no signs that any animal had ever lived in this cave. That worried him more than finding bones from a carnivore's kills.

He slowly moved deeper into the cave. Still nothing to indicate that any creature ever called this cave its home. It was as if he was the first to ever come across this cave.

Considering that the trail he had been following ran past the mouth of the cave was not reassuring.

He decided that he would be safe enough if he stayed near the cave entrance for the night. Turning he returned to where his horse awaited. Sheathing his sword he tossed the torch to the cave floor then saw to his horse's needs.

After the animal was fed and watered he made his own camp for the night. He had enough wood and dried horse dung with him to build a small fire. After he had his fire going he prepared a small meal for himself and ate.

He returned to the trail and carefully made his way back the way he had come until he reached a part of the trail that looked out over the hills he had ridden through during the past couple of days.

His eyes looked out in the darkness. Here and there he could make out signs of life by the small winking dots spread throughout the hills indicating fires. He did not see anything in the darkness to indicate that the Qualorian guardsmen that followed him still survived. He decided that he would check again in the morning when there would be daylight to see the hills by.

As he headed back to the cave he stopped to pick up some wood lying next to the trail. Looking up he could make out the outline of tree tops against the night sky. They looked to be up beyond the ridge he was currently halfway up. The wood must have fallen from those trees and come to rest here.

When he returned to the cave his fire was getting low. He added about half of the wood to the fire and dropped the rest of it against the cave wall behind him. With the fire built up he still could not see the rear of the cave, but he did notice that the little bit of smoke that the fire was giving off was blowing back out of the cave entrance.

He positioned himself by the fire so that he could keep an eye on the rear of the cave as well as the entrance of the cave. His horse was standing outside the cave, its head down. He slid his sword out of its scabbard and set it beside him on the ground so he could grab it quickly if needed then lay back and closed his eyes and slipped into a light sleep.

His dreams were nightmares. Huge insects chased him through cities beyond wonder. He tried to escape them by boarding a lengthy sailing ship. The ship suddenly engulfed him, surrounding him within white walls that rose up from the deck and met above his head sealing him in. He ran through the ship until he came to a high window that looked out the front of the ship.

The view out the great window was not of the ocean but of the night sky, stars everywhere, but he was not looking up at the stars, he was among them, moving about them. He came close to one star and as he neared it the star grew into a sun. Then he was past it and suddenly he was bearing down upon a world the oceans and land masses speeding up to meet him.

Suddenly the ship was on the ground and he fled from the great window and dove through an open doorway onto hard ground. He rolled to his feet and looked about only to find himself standing in the ruins of mighty towers of shattered glass and twisted metal. He heard the chitinous sounds of the giant insects nearby and ran.

He ran right into a swarm of the bugs. They turned upon him and attacked. Their large multifaceted eyes seemed to bore into his very soul, their large over sized mandibles reached out for him.

Erat suddenly sprang to his feet, covered in sweat and fully awake. His sword was in his hand and he swung about looking in all directions trying to locate the menace that he had dreamt about. Finding nothing to attack or defend against he suddenly sagged and let out a huge breath that he had been holding without even realizing it.

Then he noticed that there was light coming from his

pouch, leaking out through the leather straps that held it closed. It was so bright that it was practically bursting through the leather skin of his pouch. Yet the pouch was not hot as it should be if a fire was burning inside it.

Erat quickly tore the pouch from his belt and threw it across the dimly fire lit confines of the cave. It hit the opposite wall of the cave and spilled forth its contents when it hit the floor. What few coins he had rang against the stone floor of the cave and were brilliantly lit by the cube that also flew from the pouch.

The cube illuminated the whole cave as far back as Erat could see. It was as if a small sun was suddenly shining in the cave. He heard his horse whinny in fright as the light spilled forth from the cave and into the night.

The rear of the cave was now illuminated and there was no rear to the cave, it became a passage that ran down into the mountain. And coming up that passage was a man with no face. The man was not wearing any clothing. His skin was gray and flat looking, he moved up the passage quickly.

Erat backed away from the thing; it was clear now that it was not a man. It had three legs and three arms, the arms were long and slender and waving about as if they were tentacles. The legs were acting exactly as the arms, waving about except that they propelled the thing forward.

It reached the center of the cave and simply stopped. Erat could feel his heart beating, superstitious fears rising up within him, making his legs weak and his breath come in shallow gasps. The thing suddenly moved, lightening fast and the cube was now being held aloft by one of the tentacles that the thing used as arms.

Then the light from the cube exploded into brightness so bright that Erat had to turn his head and shield his eyes with his arm.

When the light faded Erat, the thing with no face and the cube were all vanished from the cave. Erat's horse whinnied then settled down. Slowly the night sounds of the mountains returned and all was quiet again.

———————————
———————————

Sturya inadvertently let out a howl of superstitious fright as a bright light lit up the mountainside. He fell from his horse and buried his face into the earth as he babbled prayers to his gods. He pounded his head into the earth and his fists beat at the ground as he allowed his fear to rule him.

So involved with his protestations to his gods he did not hear the horse ride up. He did not notice the sounds of a rider dismounting. The soft footfalls of someone approaching him from behind went unnoticed as he wailed his prayers into the ground beneath him, his tears moistening the hard packed soil.

He did hear the sword slide from its scabbard. But before he could make any move to defend himself he saw another bright light. This time the light came from within his own head as the pommel of the sword smashed against the back of his skull, dropping him into unconsciousness.

Avril sheathed his sword and looked towards the mountains. The bright light was only now fading away, returning darkness to the night. He did not know what the light represented, but he was convinced that the barbarian had something to do with whatever events had caused it to spring forth from the darkness.

Sighing, Avril looked back down at the unconscious tribesman. He reached down and felt for a pulse and found one. Now he had to decide to bring the tribesman with him or simply to kill him and be done with it.

Avril was a soldier, not a murderer. He tied up the tribesman then tied him to his horse. Avril then mounted his own horse and took the reins of the tribesman's horse

LEE E FULLER JR

in his left hand. He then began to carefully pick his way forward to the waiting mountains.

He was to going to find the barbarian and capture him. He may have lost his men but he would complete his mission. He still had his pride.

Chapter V

Stuart pushed away the empty plate and sat back in his chair. He was full after eating such a large dinner. Captain Martinez put on a very grand table in his opinion.

The dinner began with a salad and an excellent vegetable barley soup, with the vegetables being grown here in the station hydroponics section. Then after those were finished and the waiter had taken away the plates and bowls the main course arrived. It was a crustacean like creature prepared in a sort of Alfredo type of sauce. Delicious did not begin to describe the dish.

There were also the usual accompaniment of breads, appetizers and wines to go with the meal. Then after that he was faced with dessert. That consisted of a chocolate confection of ice cream, graham crackers and a sauce over the whole thing.

There were also different entrée samples for tasting. All in all he was stuffed.

As the waiter put a cup of coffee in front of him Captain Martinez let out a sigh of contentment and patted his stomach as he reclined back in his chair.

"Did you get enough to eat, Commander Stuart?" Martinez asked.

"More than enough, sir, that was an excellent dinner. Thank you very much for inviting me over."

"Not at all, simple courtesy demanded that I invite you. But I will admit that I am also quite proud of my kitchen staff especially Chef Hoover. He was trained by the Cordon Blue Academy in Paris, back on Earth."

"I hate to admit this, but I have never heard of that school." Stuart replied as he sipped his coffee.

"No problem, commander, not many people have heard of it way out here. But I will tell you this it is a centuries old cooking academy that is very well known throughout the inner systems. Chef Hoover is probably the only student of the academy that is practicing his craft outside of the inner systems."

"Captain, I must say that I am not disappointed to have dined on one of his meals. It was delicious."

"I am willing to bet that it was better than anything you have had aboard the Pegasus." Martinez stated matter-of-factly.

"Indeed it was, Captain, indeed it was."

Stuart finished his coffee and set the cup back on its saucer. He was hoping to get a second cup but Martinez chose that moment to rise to his feet. He dabbed at the corner of his mouth with his napkin and dropped the napkin onto the table in front of him. Stuart also rose, following his host's example he also left his napkin on the table.

"Commander, what do you know of our work here?"

"Pretty much nothing, Captain. I ran a brief check of the station before I arrived but all I could discover on the galactic-net was some vague reference to trans-dimensional inference. But, I confess, I have no idea what that means and there was no explanation on the net either."

Martinez grinned. "Nor should there be any information.

I am surprised that the galactic-net even has that much information to offer. I will have to look into that and try to find out who uploaded that much info."

"Well, I can save you the trouble there, Captain. The info I got was around seventeen years old."

"Ah, that explains it then. That was when the station was first approved as the location for the research. My predecessor spent fifteen years getting the research equipment installed, calibrated and running before I took over."

"So you have only been here for two or three years, then?"

"No, I have been here for twelve years. I was second in command until five years ago when the admiral retired. I was then placed in command."

"Which admiral was that, sir?"

"Admiral Cartwright. He was in charge of this station and the security for this entire sector."

"I'm afraid that I haven't heard of him."

"I'm not surprised, commander. He was not a glory seeker, he was interested in two things and two things only, the research being conducted here and keeping that research secure."

By this point Stuart had accompanied Captain Martinez from the dining hall through several corridors and a small lift located near the center of the station. At the lift Martinez placed his eye up to an optical sensor and spoke his name.

When the doors of the lift opened he indicated Stuart was to proceed ahead of him. Inside the lift Martinez again went through the optical sensor security routine. When he was finished the door to the lift closed and a small panel inside the lift opened revealing a standard 10 digit number pad complete with the standard pound and asterisk keys. Martinez punched in a code on the keypad and the lift proceeded to move in a downward direction.

Martinez kept up his end of the conversation throughout

the entire security routine. "Commander, I took the liberty of checking your security clearance. Your security clearance is high enough for me to show you some of the equipment that we use here and to also give you a slight overview of what we do here."

Stuart was intrigued, but he had never given any thought to his security clearance. He was just beginning to realize how important this facility must be if its commanding officer had to check his security clearance just to show him some of the facility.

"You said you saw trans-dimensional inference listed as the research we are conducting here at Argos station, but do you have any idea what that phrase actually means?"

"No, sir."

"I am not surprised, taken simply as a phrase it means pretty much anything. Let me see if I can explain this to you without having to go through a bunch of complex mathematical formulas."

The lift slowed and stopped. Martinez again had to enter a code onto the keypad before the doors would open. Stuart followed him out of the lift and down a corridor. They ended up in a small briefing room and he was waved into a seat.

"Let me ask you a question, commander. How did you feel when you washed out of basic training?"

Stuart looked up at Martinez with a slightly bemused expression on his face. "I'm sorry, captain, but I didn't wash out of basic training. Commanding a survey ship should prove that in itself."

"Oh, it does, it does. But look at the screen here, commander and you tell me."

Martinez hit a button and one wall of the room became a large view screen. Displayed upon it was Stuart's service record. It had his photo and showed the date that he had entered basic officer training at the academy; it showed everything correctly including his performance evaluations and test scores. But then it suddenly diverted from the norm three months after he had entered the academy showing him to have been discharged after having been caught dealing hypercaine, a genetically enhanced form of cocaine, an extremely addictive drug.

"That's not true!" exclaimed Stuart. "I've never dealt drugs; I didn't get busted out of the academy, either!"

"Of course not I am just using this as an example of inter-dimensional inference. Everything on the screen is completely false. But it could have happened that way, who knows what strange twists and turns our lives can take?"

"I don't know what twists and turns my life may take, but dealing drugs is not one of them."

"No doubt, commander but this record on the screen could be true, actually probability indicates that it is true, somewhere else."

"How can that be? It is not what happened at all," insisted Stuart.

"I know it's not what happened to you, commander. But probability shows that it is what happened to another version of you. An alternate you that went on to end up in prison, or dead."

"I'm not following any of this at all, Captain. In fact I am more confused now than when I first sat down."

"Alright, commander let me try this a different way. You know what happened to the Sisu when they had first contact with the Vegans?"

"Of course, the Vegans opened fire on them, disabling the Sisu. They boarded the ship, took a group of people prisoner and then destroyed the ship."

"Exactly and today we are at war with the Vegans. Currently we are basically at a stalemate as neither side can seem to get the upper hand, so both side continue to search for a way to break that stalemate and win the war."

"Now, suppose instead of disabling the Sisu, the Vegan ship had been disabled. We would probably still be at war, but perhaps we would have learned more about the Vegans earlier giving us an advantage. Or imagine that both ships had opened communications instead of shooting, we could be at peace today."

"This is what inter-dimensional inference is all about."

"What, changing the past? I don't see how we could go back in time, let alone get the Vegans to open communications with the Sisu instead of shooting."

"We cannot travel in time, commander. That has been proven over and over again. What we are trying to do is travel to alternate dimensions, where events have happened differently. That is what trans-dimensional inference is all about."

"You are telling me that there are alternate universes?"

"No, not alternate universes, simply different aspects of this universe some have called it a multi-verse, but here we refer to them as alternate dimensions."

"OK, I can grasp that. But how would being able to travel to these alternate dimensions help us win the war against the Vegans?"

"Think about it, commander from a military viewpoint. You assemble a fleet here. Dozens of heavy cruisers, fighters and landing craft and thousands of assault marines. Get everything assembled here and ready to launch an invasion."

"Then you translate everything, the entire invasion fleet to an alternate dimension where there is no Vegan Empire, no Vegans at all. The fleet then proceeds to the Vegan home system and translates back to this dimension. A complete surprise attack with the final result being that the Vegan home world becomes completely under our control."

"Can you see how that would be of advantage to us?"

"I'll say we could probably end the war in a matter of weeks."

"Exactly! But there is more, commander that is only the tip of the iceberg so to speak. We can colonize alternate dimensions where no intelligent life has arisen at all, we can exploit resources for our dimension, there are so many opportunities available to us with this technology, and it is simply mind boggling!"

"I do have one question, Captain." Stuart said in a hushed voice.

Martinez looked expectantly at him.

"You say anything that can happen that paths not taken here are taken somewhere else. Entire alternate dimensions exist where no intelligent life has arisen, an entire galaxy of resources just for the taking by anyone that can get there and start mining, or harvesting or whatever."

"My question is this, what happens when we run into beings that have already perfected this technology and are spreading out into all of the alternate dimensions and are technologically advanced over ourselves?"

"A very good questions commander at this point the only answer I have is to hope that they are peaceful."

"That's not very reassuring, Captain."

"No, it's not commander, but it's the only answer that I have."

Stuart turned his attention to the view screen and pondered his possible other existence that was still displayed. He didn't like what that existence implied about himself and he felt uncomfortable about this entire alternate dimensional thing happening here.

"Commander Stuart, would you like to see some of the results that we have attained?"

"Results? What kind of results?"

"Well, to be quite frank I doubt that you would

appreciate them. It is mostly wave form analysis, probability returns, causation inference, and things of that nature."

"Captain, has anyone actually seen an alternate dimension?"

"No. We have mathematical proof of the existence of these other dimensions, but no actual physical proof as yet."

"Have you tried sending a probe into another dimension?"

"Well, yes actually and it disintegrated. We concluded that the gravitational resonance was too great for it to translate." Martinez answered. He had a sheepish look on his face, as if he did not want to admit failure but was forced to tell the truth.

"The gravitational resonance was too great? Could you be a little clearer on that, please?"

"We believe that is myself and the senior research staff believes that the reason the probe did not translate into an alternate dimension was due to the high gravity within the galactic hyper mass. We believe that we can achieve a successful translation outside of the galactic hyper mass."

"Outside of the galactic hyper mass? What exactly is the galactic hyper mass?" Stuart asked, his mind beginning to understand where this was heading.

"What we refer to as the galactic hyper mass, simply put is the effects of gravity within the galaxy. We believe that the lowered effect of gravity outside of the galaxy will allow a successful translation."

Stuart looked at Martinez in complete astonishment for a few seconds then he burst out laughing. Martinez looked completely shocked that Stuart appeared to be laughing at him.

"I'm sorry, Captain Martinez." Stuart said after taking a moment to compose himself. "I really do apologize for my outburst. But all of your great ideas for ending the war in a few weeks by dropping a fleet at the Vegan's home world just fell apart. If you can't make this whole thing work inside the galaxy then that is not going to happen. It just struck me as absurd."

Martinez glared at Stuart for a moment then he suddenly broke out into large grin.

"It does sound absurd, doesn't it, commander? I have been here for so long that I often forget how it looks to an outsider. And you're right; we wouldn't be able to drop a fleet into the Vegan home world's system if we can only do this outside of the galaxy. But that is simply another obstacle to overcome."

Martinez pulled out a chair and dropped into it as he continued.

"What we could do though is build a fleet in another dimension and then translate it here. No spy would be able to report on it as we could completely seal off the alternate dimension so no one could get there while the work is being done. We could also have access to the Viridian system where the largest duotronium mines exist. The Vegans control that system here but they would not be present in an alternate dimension. Things like this would be possible if we can stabilize the translation technology."

"I suppose so, captain. But all of this looks to be decades away at best, not something that is going to happen tomorrow."

"Commander Stuart, I have given you more information than I should have considering your security clearance."

"I don't see how you could not have given me this much info about your research and expect me to even understand what you are talking about. But, rest assured, I don't know anything about the technical side of your research, only what you are trying to achieve and that a probe has been destroyed during deployment. Nothing of any real import."

"Looking at everything in that light I would have to

agree. I think that it is time for you to return to your ship, commander. The Wellington will be here tomorrow and you will have your new orders at that time. Come, I'll escort you back to the shuttle bay."

And with that Captain Martinez switched off the view screen and escorted Stuart out of the station.

———————————
———————————

Erat awoke in darkness.

He lay still, slowly taking in all the surroundings that his sense could perceive.

He lay in darkness, total and complete silence.

In his entire life he had never been in such completely silent darkness.

Erat suddenly remembered the horror that had grabbed him. His body tensed at the sudden remembrance. His senses became acutely heightened. Adrenalin coursed through his body. He was ready for anything. His muscles were tensed, ready for fight or flight.

Nothing happened. Minutes passed and still nothing happened. The adrenalin rush faded leaving him feeling tired and slightly disgruntled that he had been ready for an attack that had not happened.

Erat slowly rose to his feet. He stood in place for a few seconds before moving forward, his arms out in front of his body. He hadn't taken more than a few steps before he came to a wall. He moved along the wall, using his left hand as his guide sliding along the wall.

After a few steps he came to another wall. He turned to his right and followed that wall until he came to yet another wall. He followed this wall to yet a fourth wall which he followed until he came to another wall.

He had gone in a full circle in the darkness. He was in a cell of some sort. He had gone along four bare walls. He did not come across a door.

He must have been dropped into a pit. But yet, he could sense a ceiling above his head. He held his right arm straight up and jumped. His hand hit a ceiling. He repeated this throughout the cell he was in and hit a ceiling every time he jumped.

The ceiling was solid with no give.

Erat became concerned. The only explanation was that he had been permanently sealed into a cell to die of starvation.

But how had he been sealed into this small cell of darkness? He had run his hand along the walls and they were as smooth as any glass he had felt. There were no protrusions in the walls and they did not feel like stone, wood or metal. The walls felt smooth like glass, yet they felt different from the way glass feels.

He felt at his waist for his pouch but it was not there, nor was his scabbard for his sword. He then remembered that he had thrown his pouch in the cave and that it was probably still lying on the cave floor. His scabbard had to have been removed.

He had nothing to do at the moment so he simply sat his back against one of the walls. After a while his head dropped to his chest and he slept.

* * *

Avril reined his horse to a stop. The horse carrying the tribesman also came to a stop. The tribesman was securely tied to the horse and was probably uncomfortable as he was strapped lying over the horse's back, his head hanging down with his wrists bound to his ankles underneath the horse.

Avril dismounted and went to check on the man. He did not want him injured, just secured so he would not have to watch his back every moment that the tribesman was with him. He kneeled down and assured himself that the tribesman was still securely bound and could not escape his bonds.

Standing, Avril turned and gave his attention to what prompted him to halt.

The barbarian's horse was grazing on the trail next to an opening that appeared to be a cave. Of the barbarian there was no sign. He was probably within the cave, waiting to spring upon Avril if he strayed too close to the entrance.

Still, he was here to capture and return the barbarian to Qualor. Removing his sword from its sheath and moving forward he halted only when the tribesman called out to him.

"Guardsman! Beware! To enter these caves means instant death!"

Spinning around, Avril sprang back to the tribesman, grasped his hair and pulled his head up so that he could look into his face.

"Silence, fool!" he commanded. "If the barbarian did not know we are here he surely knows it now from your bellowing!" he hissed at the hapless tribesman.

"It is you who are the fool. That barbarian is long dead! What do you think that light was last night? It was the barbarian being carried into the afterlife."

"Preposterous! There are no monsters in these mountains other than stray mountain cats and bears!"

"Then it was a stray cat that made the light." The tribesman said sarcastically.

"What do you say made the bright light?" Avril asked with a condescending tone in his voice.

"It was the light of the hells burning through as the door to the hells was opened." The tribesman whispered through clenched teeth. "And if we do not leave we will also be dragged screaming through the door."

Avril let go of the tribesman's head and stepped back. He looked toward the cave entrance but did not see anything other than what was there before. The barbarian's horse still grazed peacefully, completely unconcerned by Avril, the tribesman, the caves entrance, the reins hanging down from its head.

"Tribesman, I am Captain Avril of the Qualorian Guard. What are you called?"

"Sturya," Was the answer.

"Sturya, I intend to enter that cave and search out the barbarian. You have two choices; remain as you are, tied to your horse until I return, or not as the case may be. If I do not return then you will probably become freed after the horses wander back down the mountain and into the hills until your people come across you."

"Not something I would like to happen, Captain Avril. If my people were to find me tied to my horse they would kill me and take the horses. What is my other option?"

"That you accompany me into the cave."

"I like that option even less than the first option. Either way I will die."

"We all die, Sturya. You can wait here, I'll return shortly." Avril said. He then turned away from his prisoner and the horses and proceeded toward the barbarian's horse. Sturya remained quiet behind him.

Avril calmly went up to the barbarian's horse and took hold of its reins. He then led it back to where Sturya and his own horse waited. He tied the reins of the barbarian's horse to his horse in the same manner that Sturya's horse's reins were tied to his horse.

"Untie me, Avril. I will go with you into the cave."

"Very well I am curious to see if you run away or if you actually have the courage to accompany me into the cave." Avril said, knowing that he would anger the tribesman. They valued their courage thus making it legendary.

Sturya was not angered though. "Do not doubt my courage against anything that breathes and bleeds, Avril."

Avril grunted as he leaned down and cut Sturya's bonds. He then stood up and pushed Sturya off his horse. Sturya slid off the beast and landed with a thump on the hard ground. Avril knew that he would be stiffened from being bound as he was for so long and did not worry about Sturya attacking him.

Avril went around his horse and retrieved Sturya's water skin and tossed it to him.

Sturya grasped the skin and drank deeply before looking up at Avril who stood above him with drawn sword.

"Do you mean to kill me then?" Sturya asked looking Avril in the eye. Avril responded by sheathing his sword and taking a step back so Sturya could stand.

"I have no desire to kill you. Even though your people ambushed my squad and killed them."

"You were invaders in our territory."

"We weren't invading, we were pursuing a thief."

"You did not have any right to pursue anyone into our territory."

"What does it matter now? My men are dead, we're here and the man I'm pursuing is in that cave. Either you go into that cave with me or you get on your horse and leave."

"You would let me go just like that?"

"Why not? I don't need you as a prisoner; you would just be a liability. I don't even know if I want you to go into the cave with me, I would have to keep one eye on you and the other eye looking for the barbarian to lunge out of the dark." Avril looked at Sturya and came to a decision.

He walked over to his own horse and untied Sturya's horse from his own. He then pulled Sturya's sword out from where he had stashed it on his horse and tossed it over to Sturya.

"You have your horse and your sword. You don't like being here in the mountains, so go, return to your hills."

Sturya slowly crouched down and retrieved his sword

from the ground where it had landed and strapped it back on to his waist. He then took hold of the reins to his horse and slowly stepped back, away from Avril.

"How do you know I won't wait for you to return from the cave and then jump you?" Sturya asked, eying Avril warily.

"Because you don't want to go near that cave it terrifies you more than the mountains do. You may wait for me to return at the foot of the mountains, but I am not worried about that either. Now go, I have a barbarian to retrieve." And with that Avril turned away from Sturya and started towards the cave entrance.

Sturya called out before Avril could take more than a dozen steps.

"Wait!" He called out as he let the reins to his horse drop. He stepped forward as he drew his sword.

"I will go with you Avril. You may be a guardsman of Qualor, but you have shown great courage and I cannot allow you to enter that cave alone. To do so would be to show cowardice, and that I will not do. Better to die at the claws of a monster within that cave then to run away!"

Avril eyed him warily.

"Have no fear, captain. I give you my word that I will stand by your side as long as we are in that cave."

"Very well but remember, one sign of treachery and I will run you through without a second thought."

Sturya answered by moving up alongside Avril and nodding at him to proceed.

The two men cautiously moved toward the cave entrance. Avril indicated to Sturya that he should move to the left while he himself moved to the right. They came up to the cave from either side.

Avril looked into the caves dark interior and waited a moment for his eyes to adjust enough for him to make out certain features within the cave. He could make out the ashes of a fire and the barbarians saddlebags. He did not see the barbarian.

He quickly ducked into the cave, moving to the saddlebags and dropped into a crouch as he looked about.

Sturya followed him and took up a position a few feet to his left. Avril noticed an unlit torch lying beside the barbarians blanket on the other side of the ashes where he had made his fire.

Avril moved over and retrieved the torch.

"He isn't here, Sturya. We need to check the back of the cave and then search outside. Here," Avril said thrusting the torch at Sturya. "Light this torch while I check his saddle bags."

Sturya took the torch as Avril began going through the saddlebags. He went through the barbarians bags but did not find the cube that the Grand Vizier's aide, Scoros, had described to him. He had just finished searching the bags when the torch flared to life illuminating the cave.

Avril spied the pouch lying on the cave floor with its contents of coins scattered about it. He also noticed that the cave had a passage in the rear leading into darkness. He moved over to the fallen pouch and retrieved it from the cave floor. He tipped it into his hand, but only a few coins spilled out.

He motioned Sturya over and instructed him to move the torch around the cave floor where the pouch was. He scooped up the fallen coins but did not find the cube he was searching for. He dropped the coins into the pouch and tossed it over to where the saddle bags lay.

"Well, Sturya, it seems the barbarian may have gone deeper into the cave. I think he has taken that passage and has not yet returned."

"What do you mean to do, Avril?" Sturya asked anxiety in his voice as he dreaded the answer he knew Avril would give.

"I intend to follow him. What would you have me do? Wait here for him to return?"

"No, leave this place. Return to the hills."

"There is nothing here to be afraid of, no monsters hiding in the corners. Look, this is only an empty cave!" Avril barked out at Sturya in frustrated anger. He waved the torch about to illustrate his point, bringing the dark shadowy corners of the cave into brief illumination.

"The only living things in this cave are us! We need to follow the barbarian down that passage."

"I do not need to follow the barbarian anywhere. I am going to return to the hills. I will give you safe passage back to the road, Avril. But I will not go down that passage. Only death lies that way."

"Nonsense there are no creatures lurking down there waiting for us. The barbarian is down there, possibly he has fallen and is hurt or he has followed the passage to a secret chamber that he has learned of, I don't know but I intend to find out and you are going with me."

Sturya was slowly backing towards the cave entrance, hoping to escape what he considered to be a man on the edge of madness. Only a man hovering at the chasm of insanity would enter these cursed mountains. And only a man who had gone over the edge into the chasm would go down that passage into the bowels of the mountains where the gods themselves would not willingly go.

Avril saw that Sturya was slowly moving toward the cave mouth and was about to leap back and intercept him when he suddenly decided upon a different course of action.

"On second thought," he began causing Sturya to stop in his attempt to reach the cave entrance. "I think that it is best if you just leave. I don't have the time or patience to baby sit you."

"Baby sit me? Are you calling me a child that needs its

mother to cling to?" Sturya demanded, taking offense to the allegation.

"You jump at every shadow, start at every noise!" Avril pointed at the passage with his sword as he held the torch up higher. "Just the thought that you may have to enter that passage turns your bowels to water and causes your legs to shake!"

Avril lowered his sword and looked at the passage. "No, it would be best if you just leave, I'll need to focus my attention on the passage and be prepared for any surprises it might hold. I won't have time to hold your hand."

Sturya bristled at Avril's words. He had basically called him a coward, a child to be left with his mother rather than a man standing tall and facing his fears even though those fears would bring death to him. He was about to refute Avril's words with his sword when he suddenly realized that from Avril's point of view he had been acting like a child and worse still that by acting that way in front of Avril he had brought shame and dishonor upon himself and his people.

The only way to restore his honor was to accompany Avril into the passage and face whatever demons and hells lay beyond. He did not like it, he was completely afraid of that passage, but he had no choice. If suicide could restore honor he might have chosen that path, but his people believed that suicide was one of the most dishonorable things a man could do; it prevented a man from taking responsibility for his actions and correcting any mistakes that he may have made.

Sturya stood up straighter and faced Avril, looking him directly in the eye he answered the charges set forth against him.

"You are correct, captain. I have been acting like a frightened child. My people have always believed that these mountains are filled with demons from the hells. We believe that the door into those hells are within these mountains, simply waiting for a fool to come and throw that door open allowing the demons to escape into the world and lay waste to all in it. If I had not let my fears rule me I would have gone into the mountain with you, my sword held at the ready.

"Instead, I have had to have the shame of you calling me a coward and your words bringing forth the truth, opening my eyes to the dishonor I have brought to myself and my people. To regain that honor I will travel with you into the depths of the hells themselves. You will have no need to worry that I might betray you; I will watch your back as if you were a clan mate."

Avril was not sure if he believed the tribesman. Sensing Avril's skepticism Sturya stepped forward, took the torch from Avril's hand and proceeded to the passage entrance at the rear of the cave. He turned his head and said "Ready when you are, Captain Avril."

Avril mentally shrugged his shoulders, scooped up the few pieces of wood that the barbarian had gathered into the cave to use as torches when this one gave out and proceeded to follow Sturya.

CHAPTER VI

THE WIND WAS BLOWING his hair across his face. His hair had grown down past his shoulders this past year. He hadn't bothered to keep it cut since he had left the service after turning command of the Pegasus over to Captain Martinez. He remembered Admiral Higgins laughing at him during the ceremony.

"To think we would let a Lieutenant Commander retain command of the Pegasus for a real mission!" Higgins roared with contemptuous laughter at the command exchange ceremony.

Stuart had felt his cheeks redden as everyone laughed along with Higgins. Martinez had stood there, grinning as he formally accepted command of the Pegasus. Stuart had then voiced the command codes and Athena had logged the transfer.

"Command shifted from Lieutenant Commander Stuart to Captain Martinez." Then Athena had turned the knife that Higgins had already stuck into him. "As the ship's AI I look forward to serving under a real captain."

The audience had broken out into roaring laughter at that. Stuart could not take anymore and had stormed out of the enormous hall. He had torn his tunic off and resigned from the service.

Now he stood, a year later, on a high promontory, looking out over a valley filled with the remains of an ancient city. The city was crumbling into dust, even as he watched. Strong winds blew over rusting steel towers; glass turned to sand and blew away in the winds. Within hours the city would be gone, nothing left to indicate that it had ever been here.

Only the soft chiming of the wind would be left to mark the passage of the city. He turned away from the passing city and strode down the station corridor. He passed sealed doors on both sides until he came to the central lift. Its doors opened and he stepped into the lift.

He mindlessly stabbed at the controls that would send the lift to the main bridge. Looking down he saw through the clear floor of the lift and saw Argos station circling the planet below him. Argos station was changing from white to blue as he watched. By the time the doors of the lift opened Argos was a brilliant orange color.

He stepped out onto the bridge and walked up to the main view screen and peered into it. A Vegan cruiser was slowly going past; it guns shooting fireworks out into the blackness of space. As he watched the fireworks exploded into huge patterns then imploded back onto themselves becoming black holes that turned and consumed the Vegan cruiser.

The only sound was the soft chiming of the environmental control panel he was now standing before, its lights flashing blue then red then blue again.

"Don't be alarmed, Lieutenant Commander Stuart." He heard Captain Martinez say from behind him. "There is a full oxygen / nitrogen atmosphere throughout space in an alternate dimension. No need to worry."

He turned to ask Martinez a question and saw the

✦

sandstorm heading toward him. He was stuck to the spot he stood in by the sand he was sinking into. It was up to his knees and he couldn't free himself. The sandstorm moved closer to him. The chiming of the wind was getting louder as the storm neared.

Suddenly his legs were free and he fell backwards, arms out stretched and his whole body suddenly cart wheeling. Everything was spinning; the chiming of the winds was getting louder and louder.

"Can't you stop that damned noise?" Higgins bellowed at him. He was yelling at him, but the chiming was drowning him out. The more Higgins yelled, the louder the chiming became. It wasn't the wind it was Higgins. The chiming was coming from Higgins. Higgins looked down and tore his uniform open revealing a Vegan tearing its way though his chest.

Stuart suddenly came awake and sprang upright in his bunk. Upon sitting up the chiming stopped. His alarm had awakened him from a nightmare.

"Alarm off!" he barked at the automated system. The chiming stopped. He sat in his bed for a minute regaining his composure and allowed his breathing to slow back down to normal. Finally he swung his legs off the bed and stood up.

He made his way into the bathroom and looked at himself in the mirror. His hair was sticking up everywhere; he idly noted that he needed a haircut. There were lines in his face that weren't there a few short years ago, and not only were those lines there, they seemed to be deepening. He frowned at the thought. There was dark stubble on his face but then he suddenly noticed that one of the facial hairs that comprised the stubble was not the proper brown color, it was white. Not gray, but white!

He reached for the shaver; his mood was quickly going from bad to worse.

A half-hour later he stormed out of his cabin and headed to the dining compartment. No matter what else he noticed his appetite was still healthy. The exercising program that he maintained had kept the weight off of him and his body physically fit and toned. He was not yet to the point in his life that he needed extra exercise to keep his weight down or the dreaded 'spare tire' off his waist.

When he entered the dining compartment he headed over to the food dispenser and dialed up ham, eggs, hash browns, toast, orange juice and coffee. He waited for the minute or so it took for the dispenser to prepare and deliver his food then took the tray and sat down at the closest table.

He was halfway through his breakfast when Athena greeted him.

"Good morning, Commander."

"Morning, Thena" he mumbled back through a mouthful of eggs.

"The Wellington is scheduled to arrive at eleven hundred hours. Do you have any orders for me in regards to the arrival of the Wellington?"

"No status quo, Athena," He answered as he glanced at the clock above the food dispensers. It currently read 08:47. Just over two hours until the Wellington arrived. Stuart sighed as he finished is breakfast.

He decided to indulge himself this morning. He retrieved a second cup of coffee from the dispenser and headed to the bridge, cup in hand. When he stepped out of the lift onto the bridge he headed straight to the command console. He set his coffee cup into the cup holder of his chair and leaned back into the seat.

"Athena, can we have some music please."

"Yes, commander, what would you prefer?"

"Classical, Mozart perhaps. No, scratch that! I would like to hear something a little softer, more natural. What would you suggest?"

"Perhaps you would like something from Bragg?" Athena suggested.

"No, his music is too, I don't know, wistful? Anyway, not Bragg. Who else?"

"Trundle? His sonatas are quite timeless."

"No, I want something from Earth. Can we get something pre-star travel?"

"Kitaro? His Silk Road passages?"

"Perfect, Athena! Pipe it in."

For the next few minutes Stuart studied displays and reviewed reports. He wanted everything in perfect shape for the command handover that he was expecting. He didn't want anyone to question his abilities.

"Athena, I see you had to reroute power through a secondary relay earlier this morning, um, at 03:23 hours, on hydroponics bay one. Please elaborate."

"The primary power relay indicated a possible overload. I rerouted power through the secondary relay and ran a level one diagnostic on the primary relay. The diagnostic indicated that the micro-connectors were in a failing state. I had maintenance droid 2A replace the micro-connectors and then routed power back to the primary power relay." Athena answered.

Stuart could swear that Athena sounded, well, insulted. He paused and looked up from his reports.

"Athena, no need to be upset I just want to make sure that everything is in order for the command change."

"I am not upset or offended, commander. I have no feelings to hurt, as you are aware. Also, if I may, why do you think that there is going to be a command change?"

"Athena, I am in command of the Pegasus for survey missions. They are placing a full complement aboard her. I will probably be re-assigned to the Wellington and a more able officer placed in command of the Pegasus."

"Commander, you do not know that they will replace you. It is just as likely that they will leave you in command as you are familiar with the Pegasus as you have been the Captain for three years."

Stuart sighed. How could you explain politics to an AI? You could try but you might as well bang your head against a wall. The result would be the same, no progress and a big headache.

So far his only consolation was that he would have three years of command experience under his belt, which would go a long ways to his getting another command in a few years. He knew how it was on a larger ship such as the Wellington. He would be just another member of the astrogation section waiting for the opportunity to advance.

His uncle had been a Lieutenant Commander in the astrogation section of a heavy cruiser for five years. He had finally volunteered for a solo mapping mission into the Scorpious sector. That was 11 years ago, he was officially listed as overdue. He would not be listed as deceased for another nine years. Due to the vast distances involved in space travel, one had to be missing for 20 years before listed as deceased. Even then, people who had been missing far longer had turned up on follow up surveys, stranded on planets when their ships had developed problems and they had to abandon their ships to the stars.

With human life spans running to a hundred and 50 years, opportunities for promotion were far fewer than in the early years of manned space travel. The only place where one could advance was in solo survey missions. Small survey ships such as the Pegasus were cheap to build compared to the large cruisers and capital ships that patrolled the human sectors of the galaxy. If not for the Vegan War there would be no solo mapping missions.

The solo survey missions started 20 years after the Sisu incident that launched the Vegan War. Resources and habitable worlds were needed. The fastest way to locate those worlds and resources was to send out small scout ships that had faster engines and better sensors than the larger ships of the day. Over time, the larger ships were equipped with better sensors and engines, but the smaller ships had become cheap to build and maintain.

Today, ships such as the Pegasus were the standard of the survey scout class ships. They could be run by a single person with the AI interface handling all the day to day operations and a small complement of tech droids to handle routine maintenance and light repair jobs.

"Athena, push our sensors out to maximum range, we should be able to pick up the Wellington's wave front any time now." Stuart ordered. He wanted to have as much lead time as possible to finish up any loose ends.

"Aye, sir extending sensors to maximum range and changing subject of conversation." Athena replied, highly amusing Stuart. And she claimed that she didn't have any emotions!

"Commander, I am picking up a wave front, however it is in the opposite direction of approach vector to that of the Wellington."

"Can you identify?"

"Negative, it is still too far out for identification. I am also picking up another wave front vectoring in where the Wellington should be. Ninety percent chance that it is the Wellington."

"I want that unknown tracked. Is it on course for this system?"

"At current speed and trajectory it will reach the Moldovan system minutes before the Wellington."

"You mean provided that the second wave front is the Wellington. I don't like the idea of that second wave front appearing just now. Athena, contact Argos station, see if they are expecting another ship to arrive today."

"One moment, commander," Athena replied. Stuart sat and waited while she communicated with the station. While he waited, he brought up a real time animated display that he could watch showing both wave fronts approaching the system.

"Commander, Argos station reports that the second wave front is most likely the Antares, a supply freighter and passenger ship that is scheduled for arrival anytime within the next three days."

"Yet it just happens to appear at the same time that the Wellington is on approach?"

"Coincidence, commander."

"I don't know, maybe. Wait! What was that? Athena, move the display on monitor 3 to the main screen and playback the last thirty seconds."

The view on the main view screen changed from the orbiting Argos station to the real time animated wave fronts that Stuart had set up on his consoles monitor. As the display tracked back through the last 30 seconds there was a brief flash in the wave front of the supposed Antares freighter. Then the wave front simply continued as if nothing had happened.

"What was that flash, Athena?"

"Unknown, commander possibly a sensor glitch, a radiation flash or perhaps a mirroring of the wave front."

"Mirroring of the wave front?"

"Yes. It is a known phenomenon that occurs when sensor bounce contacts the previous sensor reflection on a tangent angle of …"

"I know what it is Athena. Check for it, see if that caused the flash we witnessed."

"Reviewing. Review complete. Mirroring was not the cause."

"Athena, what is the ETA of that ship?"

"One hour and thirty-five minutes at present speed."

"They will arrive fifteen minutes before the Wellington. Athena, I have a bad feeling about that ship. I don't think it is the Antares, but I have no proof. However, I want the Pegasus on yellow alert."

"Going to yellow alert, commander shall I notify Argos station?"

Stuart hovered in indecision for a moment. If he went to yellow alert then he should notify Argos station and request that they go to yellow alert also. He may look foolish, but that would be better than not being prepared in case it was a hostile ship incoming.

"No, I'll do it. Get Martinez on the screen."

"Aye, commander."

A few moments later Captain Martinez appeared on the main view screen, pushing the animated real time display up into the top right quad of the screen.

"Commander, what can I do for you?" he asked. He looked a bit annoyed that he had been pulled away from whatever it was he was doing.

"Captain, I have a ship coming in on a vector that I'm told could be a resupply ship, the Antares. However, the timing of this ship concerns me. Also there was a brief flash that we observed."

"It probably is the Antares, commander. As to the flash, it is probably mirroring of the wave front. It is a common phenomenon with our current sensor technology."

"I am aware of that, Captain. However, Athena has ruled out that as a cause. As it is, the ship will arrive fifteen minutes prior to the arrival of the Wellington. I personally feel that there is something amiss here and have put the Pegasus on yellow alert."

"What? Commander Stuart, I can assure you that the

ship you are concerned about is the Antares. Have you tried hailing them?"

Stuart kicked himself mentally. He hadn't thought of trying to contact the ship. But before he could answer Athena stepped in.

"There is no reply from the incoming vessel, commander"

Martinez frowned at hearing her reply. "Try using the lower band frequency, her captain has a tendency to keep his comm. gear on low power during star flight."

"Try it, Athena." Stuart commanded.

Moments passed while Stuart and Martinez waited, neither saying a word.

"No reply, commander."

"Commander, you said it will arrive fifteen minutes before the Wellington?"

"That's right, Captain."

"You sensors are better than those here on the station, commander. I am going to put Argos station on orange status, that way if it turns out to be the Antares we can go back to condition green, no one is inconvenienced, but if it turns out to be a threat, we can go to yellow alert quicker."

"Orange status? I haven't heard of that before."

"It is a fairly new designation for large orbital facilities. Due to their size it takes considerably longer to go on full alert. I am sure your AI can fill you in on the details if you are interested. In the meantime, as soon as you can make a more positive ID on that ship, the better."

"Understood, Captain, Pegasus out."

The image of Martinez faded out and the other image grew to fill the screen again. Stuart stared at the wave front. Was it the Antares? Or something more sinister? Only time would tell.

✦

Avril and Sturya were cautious as they made their way deeper into the mountain. Cautious of the path they were on, cautious of each other. Avril held a flickering torch in his left hand and his sword in his right hand. Sturya carried his sword in his left hand and nothing in his right hand. Both men kept a wary eye on the other. Their truce was fragile, but for the time being it held.

The path they followed was a tunnel through solid rock. The floor and walls were smooth. The ceiling was only a few feet above their heads giving both men the feeling of claustrophobic tightness. The cave was far behind and above them; the passage they were traveling led deeper and deeper into the mountain.

"We travel away from the mountains," Sturya whispered to Avril through clenched teeth.

"How can you be sure which direction we're going through these passages?" Avril asked as he slowly moved forward.

"My sense of direction has always served me well, something a city bred dog like you could never have developed always trapped inside your walls."

"Careful who you call dog you superstitious lout. Just because I was raised inside the walls of Qualor does not mean I am ignorant of tracking and stealth."

"Hold!" hissed Sturya urgently enough that Avril abruptly froze in place and waited. Sturya crouched down and quietly slid forward, his head tilted as he listened for any noise coming from the darkness in front of them.

Sturya motioned for Avril to wait and moved stealthily into the darkness beyond the range of the flickering torch that Avril had lowered to limit its effectiveness against the inky blackness of the underground passages they traveled through.

Avril waited, his breathing loud in his own ears. He

nervously flicked his sword in the air in front of him, stabbing at imaginary foes.

Minutes passed, the only noise coming from the torch as it burned, small hissing and popping sounds that disturbed the quiet.

Sturya returned and motioned Avril to backup. The two men quietly moved back a few dozen yards before Sturya spoke.

"There is a deep chasm in front of us and it glows with enough light that the torch is not needed. There is a stone bridge that crosses the chasm, it is very narrow but has knee high walls on each side. Across the bridge the passage continues, I followed it far enough to determine that it no longer moves down but is level."

"So we do not travel any deeper into the earth then?" Avril asked.

"Not here anyway," Sturya replied. "But I do not know how much farther this passage continues."

"Then the only way to find out is to keep going." Avril declared.

"Wait, Avril. Why do we need to continue? We have come far enough, we don't need to keep going. We can return to the cave and our horses and leave this cursed place to the spirits." Sturya argued. He did not relish going deeper in to the passage they traveled through, his instincts told him danger lay ahead and the part of him which was steeped in superstitious fear of these mountains was causing his courage to wane.

"You can go back if you want to, I have to find that damned barbarian or my life is worthless. Here, take the torch and go." Avril said as he thrust the torch at Sturya.

Sturya searched Avril's face and approved of what he saw there, courage and determination, no fear showed at all. Sturya felt shame to know that this city born man was showing more bravery and courage than he was and he cursed himself for being a weak cowardly fool.

Sturya reached out and took the proffered torch from Avril's hand and he said, "We will not need this torch for as I said the passage has a glow to it from the bridge and beyond."

And with that having been said the two men turned and moved into the darkness as Sturya casually tossed the torch to the ground.

A few moments after the two men had moved off into the darkness, a supple metal tentacle reached out and picked up the torch and extinguished the flame.

Erat awoke to find himself lying on a stone slab that was supported by chains to a stone wall in a small cell. He sat up and looked around. The small square room he had been in was gone. He now found himself sitting in a prison cell. Standing he moved over to the iron bars that kept him from leaving and looked about.

From what he could see he was in the middle cell in a row of three cells. Across the stone floor were three more cells. The stones were clean as were the cells. To Erat's left the cells ended in a stone wall and to his right was a stout wooden door. Sitting on a small wooden stool next to the door was a man wearing the uniform of a Qualorian guardsman.

"So, barbarian you are finally awake. You were snoring loud enough to wake the dead when they brought you in last night," the guardsman rumbled.

The man stood up and walked over to stand in front of Erat, only the iron bars separated the two men. The guardsman was at least a hands width taller than Erat and had a muscular build to him. He also had long blonde drooping mustaches that matched his eyebrows and hair in color. The man had his hair pulled back into a long pony tail with an iron ring at the end.

"Who brought me here?" Erat demanded.

"Who indeed!" laughed the guardsman. "The Grand Vizier's own personal guards. I have been tasked in watching over you to ensure that you do not escape though I doubt that you could break out of that cell."

Erat took a step back from the bars and briefly inspected them for any sign of weakness but knew they were strong and solid; the guardsman was right, he would not be breaking out of this cell. At least he would not break out without any help from outside, help he did not have.

"So, barbarian, do you have a name?" the guardsman asked him. Erat eyed this man, he was not hostile, only matter of fact.

"I am Erat." He replied.

"Erat, hmm, I've not heard such a name before. Where do you hail from Erat?"

"You talk too much," Erat answered. He did not want to speak any further with the guardsman, he may have been caged, but he did not have to listen to the prattering of this lackey.

"Talk too much do I? Maybe it is so. But I am not the one locked in a cell." The guardsman grinned at Erat.

Erat suddenly became amused as rarely happened.

"No, you are not locked in a cell, but you have to stay here anyway to watch me. So we are both prisoners, I am a prisoner of your Grand Vizier and you are a prisoner of mine." Then he threw his head back and laughed.

The guardsman's features changed from amusement to consideration. Then he suddenly laughed also. "We are both prisoners. You are funny for a barbarian." Then he returned to his wooden stool and sat there, quietly chuckling to himself as Erat dropped back down to the stone slab that was to be his bed for the near future.

The Grand Vizier of the city-state of Qualor stood to the left of the king and waited patiently for the royal personage to finish his current audience with General Aubu. The king had just placed the general in charge of the eastern garrisons and was going over everything that he expected of the man. The king was quite specific of what he wanted the general to accomplish.

Finally the king waved dismissal to the general who bowed low to the king, retreated the prescribed five steps upon which he snapped a salute to the king. The king nodded at the general who then did a smart about face and marched out of the Royal Hall of Reception and away to attend to his new duties.

"So, my Grand Vizier, what news do you have for me today?" the king quietly asked, he did not want those standing nearby to eavesdrop on their conversation. The reception hall had been designed and built with materials that naturally dampened sound. Even though the hall was cathedral in size, it was unnaturally quiet which caused everyone entering the hall to speak softly. The one thing you did not want to do in the hall was to whisper, whispers were carried around the hall. If a man were to whisper into his companion's ear his words would be plainly heard by another across the hall as if the man were standing next to that other. Softly spoken voices carried not at all.

"The usual reports my lord," the Grand Vizier replied. His voice was soft spoken and warm. Whenever he spoke people would be put at ease and everyone always listened attentively when the man spoke.

"The usual meaningless census figures, crop productions, treasury assets and the like I suppose?" the king asked as he drummed his fingers on the arm of his throne.

"Yes, and also last night's guard logs of course." The

Grand Vizier replied, amusement in his voice at the king's nonchalant show of boredom.

"And do the guard logs have anything interesting in them? Perhaps a tavern smashing brawl or some such exciting occurrence?"

"No your Excellency, nothing exciting I'm afraid." The Grand Vizier replied. "Only the usual all's well reports. Qualor is a quiet and peaceful city, as always."

The king looked at his Grand Vizier and wondered about the man. His looks were intimidating, yet the man himself always seemed gentle and kind. He always wore the mask and robes of his office; in fact, the king could not remember ever seeing him without his mask and robes.

The mask was extremely detailed, the work of a talented artisan. The mask was a face, bearded and not smiling so much as smirking, the nose was aquiline but the eyes were the part of the mask that disturbed everyone, even the king. The eyes were blank, simple pools of opaque whiteness. No one understood how the Grand Vizier could see anything, yet the man saw extremely well.

The king had never seen his Grand Vizier without his robes or mask. As the king knew a different person could have been under the robe every time he was summoned to the royal presence. If not for the same soothing comforting voice the king would wonder who it was under the robes. The king suspected that the man had to be ancient. When the king was a small boy the Grand Vizier had first appeared.

The king remembered the day although some of the details had grown fuzzy over the years. His father had been king then and was holding court in the Royal Hall of Reception. Duke Grakfor had just bowed and backed away when the Grand Vizier was announced. He was not the Grand Vizier then, he was simply called Tomas. He had worn the mask and robes even then.

His father had looked the man over without speaking; he simply waited and watched the man. The entire hall had grown quieter than usual as king and supplicant looked at each other. Finally his father had spoken.

"Well, Tomas what is it you wish of me?" he had asked.

When the man answered all were taken aback by the warmth and compassion that his voice conveyed. "I wish nothing, your highness. I simply wanted to look upon you with my own eyes."

"And what do your eyes see?" his father had asked.

Everyone in the room seemed to lean forward in anticipation of the answer.

"I see a man who is just and rules with love for his people. I see a father that loves his son and I see a boy that adores his father, too. It is a very rare thing indeed to find a man that is perfectly suited to his position and that is happy in his position.

"This is what my eyes see and my heart tells me that my eyes are correct."

A palpable silence filled the hall as the anticipation built for his father's response, but before his father could respond he himself had stepped forward and answered this stranger.

"How does your heart talk to your eyes?" he had asked.

The future Grand Vizier turned his face toward him then stepped forward and knelt before him. His opaque white eyes were level with his own piercing blue eyes.

"Young prince, how can my heart not speak to my eyes? Your own heart speaks to your eyes and guides your actions does it not? When your eyes gaze upon your father does not your heart tell you that here is the man whom you love and worship?"

Then the man who called himself Tomas stood and stepped back.

"My lord, I would ask a favor of you. I would ask that I be allowed to serve you in whatever capacity that you should find useful."

The audience continued on for some time after that but he had been ushered out of the hall then by his nanny to be taken back to his mother in her apartments.

After a rather long interview that covered everything from agriculture to military protocol, his father had appointed Tomas to oversee the rebuilding of the western outpost of Kalor.

Kalor had been devastated by a flood then overrun by the nomadic Trantha tribe and virtually wiped out. It would be Tomas's job to rebuild the outpost and to defend it against the ravages of nature and the raids of the Trantha.

Today Kalor was no longer an outpost but a respectable sized town. A full troop garrison was stationed there which protected the town and the surrounding area against any attacks form the Trantha.

Tomas had risen through the years until he had reached the position of Grand Vizier to his father. After his father had died and he had succeeded to the throne of Qualor the king had retained the man as his council had always been beneficial to Qualor and he had never shown any inclination to try to usurp the throne for himself.

"Well if, as usual all is well then I may as well hear the next petitioner unless you have something more for me?" he asked.

"I do not have anything else that requires your attention, Excellency." The Grand Vizier replied.

"Very well then, I give you leave to go. No need for both of us to remain here and listen to the various complaints of the people," Sighed the king.

"Sire they come here to seek your judgment. They know that you will fairly judge whatever matters they bring before you," gently chided the Grand Vizier.

"I know, but it does get monotonous sitting here day in and day out listening to people who always want something."

"Your highness, it has been a long time since you have visited the outer provinces, perhaps you should do so again and make a vacation of it," suggested the Grand Vizier.

"Perhaps, but it would necessarily be a working vacation I'm afraid," muttered the king. Then he brightened and straightened up on his throne.

"See to the arraignments, Vizier Tomas. I shall tour the western towns and settlements all the way out to Markam Outpost. I would like to leave in five days. Will that be enough time to make all of the arraignments?"

"Yes, sire. I shall see to the arraignments. Shall I inform Minister Stervos that he will hold court here in your absence?"

"Not unless you are planning on locking yourself in your chambers while I am away." The king replied with a mischievous grin on his face.

"What? Sire, I had planned on going with you," replied the Grand Vizier, plainly taken aback at the suggestion.

"Nonsense!" exclaimed the king. "I am perfectly capable of touring my kingdom without your assistance. Besides, I would feel more comfortable with you here guarding the capital in my absence."

The Grand Vizier knew that any argument against him staying and watching over Qualor while the king was gone would be moot. Once the king made up his mind it was near impossible to get him to reconsider.

"Very well, as you wish sire," replied the Grand Vizier with resignation in his voice. "I shall see to the arraignments and report back to you this evening."

"Thank you, Tomas."

The Grand Vizier, backed up the customary five paces, bowed and left the Royal Hall of Reception through an archway to the right of the throne. He traveled swiftly through the corridors of the royal palace until he reached a thick wooden door of which only he retained the key.

After passing through and securing the door behind him he descended the stone steps to their bottom where another corridor lay. The Grand Vizier traveled down this corridor, stone walls to either side of him. He passed numerous wood doors, all securely locked again with keys that only he had access to on his key ring.

He came at last to the end of the corridor where he was greeted by a stone wall. The stone wall was bare of any accoutrement. The Grand Vizier placed his hand on a particular spot of the wall and he very softly spoke a single word.

"Graza," the word was immediately followed by a soft clicking sound as a stone to his left suddenly recessed into the wall and the dropped down into the wall itself to reveal a lighted panel and a keypad.

The Grand Vizier reached out and tapped out a sequence on the keypad after which the stone slid up and pushed out to resume its position in the wall, hiding the panel. The Grand Vizier waited as a section of the wall swung away from him to reveal an ascending spiral stairway.

After he had stepped through the opening and began climbing the stairs the wall silently swung shut behind him.

The Grand Vizier reached the top of the stairs and passed through and archway where a smooth stone wall confronted him. He stood before the wall and waited while a small section of the wall disappeared in front of where he stood. From eye level a light shot out and moved across the opaque eye pieces of his mask.

After the light scan was complete the small section of the wall reappeared then the wall itself slid away to reveal a modest sized room holding a desk with a computer terminal mounted upon its otherwise stark surface.

The Grand Vizier moved around the desk and sat in the chair facing the computer terminal. He reached down and began typing on the recessed keyboard. The terminal sprang to life as he entered commands through the keyboard.

Presently an image of a cell block appeared. A guardsman with long drooping blonde mustaches was sitting on a small stool and there was only one prisoner in the six cells of the cell block.

The prisoner was a muscular barbarian from the northern reaches that had been captured by a drone in the caves at the foot of the eastern mountains. The barbarian had carried the holocube that the Grand Vizier had been seeking for over 50 years, since before he had ever come to Qualor.

"So my barbarian friend," he spoke aloud to the image of the man in the cell. "Do you have any idea of what it was you carried?"

The Grand Vizier brought the holocube forth from within his robes.

"Hopefully the data I need is here. I have waited a very long time to retrieve this information. It is imperative to the survival of this world and all human life in the galaxy."

And with that softly spoken statement the Grand Vizier placed the holocube into a data retrieval slot and began downloading the information.

Chapter VII

Stuart watched the monitor in anticipation. A few minutes time would tell him if that was the supply ship Antares or something else entirely. Watching the screen he came to a decision.

"Athena, get me the Wellington please." he asked the ship's AI as he smoothed his tunic down.

"Acknowledged, Commander," the AI responded.

Stuart watched the approaching wave front. He suddenly knew that it was not the Antares. He suspected that it might be an enemy vessel and that the flash they recorded earlier was the Antares being destroyed by the vessel. The only thing was he could not provide any facts to backup his certainty.

"Commander I have the Wellington standing by for you. Captain Carson."

"On the main screen Athena," he replied as he sat up straighter in his seat.

"Commander Stuart, what can I do for you," Captain Carson asked. He was sitting in his own command chair on the bridge of the Wellington. The bridge was substantially larger than the bridge of the Pegasus. Behind Carson Stuart could make out three other officers at their stations.

"Sir, our sensors have picked up another vessel on course to the Moldovian system. We have been tracking it for one hour and at the beginning of our tracking we noticed this flash. Athena, will you forward the sensor logs to the Wellington?"

"Forwarding now, Commander," Athena replied.

"At first we believed that the approaching ship was the supply ship Antares and that perhaps the flash was a mirroring of the wave front but my ship's AI has eliminated that theory."

"One moment commander while we review the data you have sent us," Carson said before turning in his seat and motioned to another officer that was not within Stuart's view. A moment later the officer appeared in view and held a quiet discussion with Carson.

After a few moments the officer moved off screen again and Carson turned back to Stuart.

"Commander, I see from your logs that the ship has not responded to hails either. Have you contacted Argos station?"

"Yes, sir they have gone on orange alert." Stuart replied.

"Good, please stand by," said Carson.

Stuart sat and waited, watching the activity on the bridge of the Wellington increase as Captain Carson spoke to people off screen. Stuart let his eyes wander up to the upper right of his view screen where the tracking telemetry of the incoming ships was displayed. The ETA of the unknown ship was 44 minutes; the ETA of the Wellington was 56 minutes.

"Commander, we have analyzed the data you sent and we simply cannot tell if the incoming wave front is bring generated by the Antares or not. Due to the nature of the research being conducted on Argos station and to the uncertainty of the identity of the incoming ship I am increasing our speed to maximum. We will still arrive after the other ship, but it will only be by a few minutes."

"Understood, Captain," replied Stuart. He understood the Captain's concern. If the other ship was the Antares then everything would be fine and the Wellington would simply arrive a few minutes earlier, no harm done. But if the incoming ship turned out to be an enemy vessel then the Pegasus and Argos station should be able to hold out until the Wellington arrived which would give them much better odds of survival.

"I will contact you again in 25 minutes, Commander. I want to be in contact with you when that ship enters the system. Wellington out," stated Carson.

"Athena, get me Captain Martinez," ordered Stuart. He watched as the telemetry display remained in the upper corner as Carson's image winked out on the screen and after a few moments Martinez took his place on the view screen.

"Commander Stuart," greeted Martinez grumpily. "We are now also tracking the incoming ship. I also notice that the Wellington has increased their speed. Did you have anything to do with that?"

"I contacted the Wellington and apprised Captain Carson of our situation," Stuart answered somewhat defensively. He wasn't sure if Martinez was put out that he had contacted the Wellington or if something else was bothering the man.

"Probably not a bad idea," Martinez conceded after a moment. "I have made final preparations and everything is ready to be transferred aboard the Pegasus. We are ready when you are, Commander."

"How long will it take to transfer everything aboard?"

"No more than an hour, possibly less if we work quickly."

Stuart nodded. "Athena is the landing bay prepared?"

"Yes Commander, everything is ready to begin receiving

the equipment and technicians from Argos Station," the AI answered.

"Let's begin the transfer then, Captain," Stuart replied back to Martinez.

"Commander the fastest way would be for you to dock the Pegasus with Argos Station. We can transfer the materials quicker this way and we can also use shuttles from the station to transfer to the Pegasus as well." Martinez cautiously requested of Stuart. He knew that should an enemy appear while the Pegasus was docked to the station it would be a prime target, unable to maneuver.

Stuart considered the request for a moment before he consulted with Athena. "How much time would we save Athena?"

"Fourteen minutes, commander," came the immediate reply.

"Athena, dock us with Argos station and prepare to receive visitors."

"Aye, aye commander," Athena replied even as Stuart felt the faint vibration of the maneuvering jets firing.

"Thank you, Commander Stuart," Martinez said relief evident in his voice. He knew that Stuart was risking his ship.

Athena had added ETA displays to each of the incoming ships. 42 minutes until the unknown ship arrived, 47 minutes until the Wellington arrived. Athena had also added a time that was counting down on the equipment and personnel transfer from Argos and that timer was not yet active as docking had not yet completed.

Stuart drummed his fingers on the arm of his chair. After what seemed forever but was only a couple of minutes the Pegasus was docked with the Argos and the transfers were beginning. The first shuttle landed in the Pegasus's landing bay shortly after the ship was docked.

"Commander," began Athena. "I have data coming in from the probe we launched 27 days ago."

"Athena, can you please refresh my memory a bit, oh wait was that to the star outside the galaxy above the galactic plane?" Stuart asked his concentration being taken from the main screen and its readouts of distances and ETA's.

"Affirmative commander," replied Athena. "The star if you will recall is located 36 light years outside of the galaxy and 77 degrees above the galactic plane. The probe data is indicating a system of twelve planets."

"Twelve planets, any of them habitable?" Stuart asked, his curiosity for new worlds being peaked.

"There is one planet that can support life, commander. It has 1.1 Earth gravity and a rotation of 26 1/3 hours. There is one unusual datum regarding this world," Athena stated.

Stuart knew that Athena was using her preprogrammed psychological programs to occupy his mind as there was nothing he could do while the equipment was being transferred to the Pegasus. Still, the suspense of this unusual datum was beginning to intrigue him.

"Ok, Athena, you have my complete and total attention. What is this unusual datum?"

"The planet is 428,952 kilometers in diameter." Athena replied.

Stuart was stunned. No habitable planet had ever been discovered that was so large. The largest habitable ever discovered was Meridian III and it was only 1 ½ times the size of Earth.

"Athena if the probe data is correct that planet would be at least 3 times larger than Jupiter!" Stuart exclaimed.

"Affirmative commander, I have verified the probe data and ordered a full diagnostic of all probe systems and everything checks out."

"Jesus," Stuart whispered to himself. Three times the size of Jupiter and habitable. How was that even possible?

The gravity alone should have been crushing. "Athena you said that the gravity is 1.1 Earth standard normal?"

"Yes commander that is what the probe data indicates."

"How is that even possible? The gravity should be crushing for a planet that size."

"Not necessarily commander, the mass of the planet may be much less than its size would indicate."

"What mass does the probe data indicate?"

"Zero mass commander."

Stuart stammered for a moment then managed a slight gasp of incomprehension.

"1.1 Earth standard gravity, zero mass, a habitable ecosphere, Athena this planet is just begging us to come and have a look. Out of simple curiosity, how far away is this monster planet at top speed?"

"The Pegasus can reach the system in 16 days at top speed."

Stuart murmured the time under his breath, 16 days. He looked up at the view screen. The unknown ship was 31 minutes out with the Wellington only 5 minutes behind that. The Pegasus would be ready to disengage from Argos Station in 37 minutes, 1 minutes after the Wellington was due to arrive in system.

"Athena, please pipe the probe data to the science console," Stuart ordered the AI as he moved out of his command chair and strode over to the science station. He sat in the science station seat and began going over the probe data that was rapidly filling the science console screens.

He was so intent that he did not hear Captain Martinez enter the bridge. He visibly started when Martinez spoke after viewing the data over his shoulder.

"That is incredible!" he exclaimed. "How can this be? Zero mass, 1.1 Earth standard gravity, a diameter three times the size of Jupiter? Astounding! My god, its location is perfect for our experiments! 77 degrees above the plane of the ecliptic and 36 light years away from the outer most edge of the galaxy!" Martinez was filled with uncontrollable excitement.

"Commander Stuart you have found the ideal location for the final phase of our experiments. You are to be commended." Martinez happily told Stuart as he slapped him on the back in pure joy of the find.

"Well, the Pegasus always aims to please, Captain." Stuart lamely replied, totally taken aback by Martinez's outburst after his startlement had passed.

"I'm sorry, commander, I am just so excited by this system you have discovered. We have been searching for a suitable location for final testing and the best we could come up with is the Tipotex system. Then you come along and have a perfect system in your hand, so to speak." Martinez proclaimed, his eyes shining with near religious fervor.

"Captain, how is the transfer going?" Stuart asked wanting to change the subject.

"We are making slightly better time that we originally anticipated. We should finish loading in another 25 minutes."

Stuart looked at the main view screen and saw that the unknown ship was 23 minutes away. Two minutes after its arrival the Pegasus would be ready to go. Not bad, thought Stuart to himself. There was six minutes between the arrival of the unknown ship and the completion of the transfers. The transfer teams had managed to shave four minutes off of that.

"Captain, how many shuttles are being used" Stuart asked, an idea forming in his mind.

"We are using two shuttles, commander. While one is here offloading the other is on Argos loading."

"Can the Pegasus's shuttle be used? I know it isn't a cargo shuttle but it does have a good sized cabin, you could conceivably cram quite a bit of things into it and we could simply land it in the bay and not have to unload it until after we are underway."

"Hmm, not a bad idea unfortunately I only have two qualified pilots. We did have three but one of them was injured and is not able to fly right now," Martinez stated. He was still giving most of his attention to the probe data.

"That shouldn't be a problem, Captain. Athena can pilot the shuttle remotely from here."

"Then by all means, let's do it commander. That should save us a little more time. Contact Commander Harland and inform him. Do you mind if I sit there and go through that data?"

Stuart rose from the science console and offered the seat to Martinez. Martinez nodded at him as he took the proffered chair and dove into the probe data, quickly absorbing himself with the aspects of the giant planet.

Stuart gave him a wry smile and quickly ordered Athena to prep the shuttle for a run to Argos Station and to inform Commander Harland to be contacted and informed of the shuttles arrival.

He then went back to his command chair and settled into it and watched the incoming ships. Time was getting short with only 20 minutes until the unknown ship arrived. Shortly Athena chimed in.

"Shuttle launched and Commander Harland will have a team ready to load it upon arrival."

"Good. When the shuttle is loaded, bring it alongside the Pegasus and hold it there until the other shuttles are finished." Stuart ordered. He wanted the Pegasus's shuttle kept out of the way until everything was finished.

"Sir, the Wellington is hailing us," Athena stated in way of reply.

"Main screen please," Stuart ordered.

The tracking display moved up into the corner and

Captain Carson appeared on screen. Carson nodded at him and held a hand up indicating Stuart to wait.

Stuart watched as Carson said something to someone out of his view on the screen. A moment later the screen split and Admiral Higgens at Starbase 12 appeared on the right side of Stuart's main screen.

"Captain Carson, Commander Stuart." The admiral acknowledged each of them. Both of them replied with "Admiral" at virtually the same instant. Carson simply raised an eyebrow briefly at Stuart.

"Gentlemen we have a situation on our hands. The 3rd fleet has engaged a Vegan contingent at the Shoal system. The battle was inconclusive as each side was virtually annihilated."

Both men remained silent, shocked at the news of the loss of the 3rd fleet. The 3rd fleet was the largest and most decorated fleet in the federation. 37 ships with over 95,000 officers and crew. The 3rd fleet had engaged the Vegans twice before in the last 2 decades of the war and had defeated the Vegans each time.

"Admiral," asked Carson, "Are there any survivors?"

"One ship managed to limp away, captain. That was the Andoria; otherwise the rest of the fleet is gone. What is more, as both of you are aware I am sure is that the Shoal system is our first line of defense for the federation itself. We currently hold the system, but if the Vegans should follow up with troop transports we stand a good chance of losing the Shoal system. This would be a major blow to the federation and would push us to fighting a defensive war for the immediate future."

Both men knew that this was grim news. After the Shoal system would be the Altair system, where major ship building yards were constantly producing federation naval ships. Should that system fall then the federation would have its ship building capacity cut by a third.

"Commander Stuart, your orders are as follows as the Wellington is now needed for the defense of the Altair system. You are to transport Captain Martinez and his staff along with all of the equipment they require to a location of the captain's choice. Once there you will give all assistance that is requested of the Pegasus and yourself to the captain and his staff."

"Stuart nodded and acknowledged the admiral with a crisp, "Aye, aye, sir."

"Captain Carson, you will immediately change course and proceed to the Altair system."

"Sir," answered Captain Carson. "We may have an incursion happening at Argos Station." Carson then quickly briefed the admiral on what was happening. The admiral looked down for a moment as if considering something then he looked up at Carson, "Captain, continue on to Argos Station, keep me linked in."

"Aye sir," Carson acknowledged.

The display showed that the unknown vessel was 11 minutes out and the Wellington was 16 minutes until arrival at the station.

Stuart quietly conferred with Martinez for a few moments then quietly checked the progress of the transfers to the Pegasus. The minutes ticked by slowly. Stuart had practically forgotten that the admiral and Captain Carson were still linked on his main screen so intently was he concentrating on the incoming ship display.

Finally time was up and the unknown ship dropped out of hyperspace and into the Moldovan system.

"Commander the unknown vessel has entered the system and is on course for Argos Station," announced Athena.

Everyone was now watching Stuart, Martinez from his seat at the science console, Carson and Higgins from the view screen.

"Athena can you give me a visual please." Stuart ordered.

The view screen split again and the unknown ship came into view, although it was at the outer range of the ship's sensors Athena still managed to get a visual lock on the ship.

The ship, although very faint, looked to be the Antares supply ship. It was slowly growing larger on the screen.

Martinez visibly relaxed. He had been sitting very rigid in his seat until the image of the Antares appeared.

Stuart still had a tickling feeling telling him something was not right.

"Athena, hail the Antares," Stuart ordered the AI.

Athena hailed the Antares so all could hear. "USS Pegasus calling the Antares, do you read, over."

Silence was the reply. Athena tried a second time and still only silence answered the hail.

"Athena aim the main antenna at the Antares and scan it," Stuart ordered. No one questioned him why he was doing this. He was in command of the Pegasus and even though he was only a Lieutenant Commander he was still responsible for what happened aboard the Pegasus. While Martinez outranked him Stuart was the ship's captain which meant that even Martinez was required to obey any orders that Stuart might give.

Captain Carson and Admiral Higgins could over rule him but would have to explain themselves to a board of inquiry if they did so.

Finally Athena acknowledged that the main antenna was focused on the Antares and scanning was commencing.

"Commander the ship's mass is wrong for it to be the Antares. According to the sensors the mass of the incoming ship is 1,345,454 tons. The Antares is an Avaya Class Freighter which has a mass of 116,459 tons. Therefore this ship cannot be the Antares."

✦

Stuart immediately went into action. "Athena, bring the ship to red alert. How long until the transfers are completed?"

"Commander Harland has just informed me that they finished the transfers. Bringing the ship's shuttle aboard now, commander," Athena replied.

"Athena, inform Argos station of the situation and request that they also go to red alert."

"Acknowledged commander," replied Athena.

"Athena, have you made a positive ID on that ship yet?" quietly asked Martinez.

"Negative, Captain. The mass of the approaching ship is greater than any other ship I have on file," replied the AI with could almost have been a trace of frustration in its voice.

Captain Carson spoke up, "We have very limited information on any ship of that mass but what we do have is very disturbing. If I am correct that ship is a new class of ship the Vegans have begun deploying. We have designated it a Leviathan Class Carrier."

"Commander Stuart," cut in Admiral Higgins. "I want you to remain on station at Argos station until the Wellington arrives. As soon as the Wellington arrives and engages that ship you are to leave the Moldovan system at top speed."

"Captain Carson," continued the admiral. "You are to engage that ship and keep it occupied as long as you are able. We need to give Commander Stuart time to escape. Fight as long as you are able but do your damnedest to bring the Wellington out of there and to safety."

"Admiral," inquired Stuart. "What about Argos Station? Can't we do anything for them?"

"They are expendable I'm afraid. I don't like it a bit, but we have no choice in the matter." Higgins answered with bitterness in his voice.

Don't worry about Argos, Commander." Martinez

quietly said. "They will be ready for that ship. Contingencies exist for just such an occurrence. Can I please be patched through to Commander Harland?"

"See to it, Athena." Stuart said as he looked at Martinez. The man's face held no sorrow at the approaching destruction of the space station, only a strange look of determination.

Stuart had his attention pulled back to Admiral Higgins as Martinez turned toward the science console and began speaking to Commander Harland on a small screen inset into the console.

"Commander Stuart, Captain Carson, you both have your orders. Carson see to it that Stuart receives the orders for the Pegasus that I transmitted to you."

"Higgins out," The admiral signed off and the main screen display dropped his image and widened out to show Carson only.

Carson spoke to someone off screen then turned back to Stuart. "Commander that ship will be in firing range of Argos in three minutes. We will be in system in two minutes. I have just had your orders transmitted."

"Commander I have received new orders for the Pegasus from the Wellington," Athena confirmed.

"Relay them to my console Athena. Status on battle systems," Stuart asked as he looked at the small screen on his console where his new orders were now appearing.

"All systems are activated and ready, Captain Stuart," replied Athena. This caused Martinez to turn in his seat and grin at Stuart. AI's only referred to personnel by their official rank.

"Huh?" Stuart grunted as he came to the section of his orders that bestowed a field promotion to the rank of Captain upon him for the duration of his current mission. A two grade rank increase. He suddenly grinned also. If he was successful in completing this mission he might just be promoted to full Commander at its conclusion.

Martinez spoke up, "Congratulations on your promotion, Captain Stuart."

"Thank you Captain Martinez," replied Stuart. He believed he had been promoted to captain as he was the captain of the Pegasus and his highest ranking passenger was also a captain. This way he did not have to worry about Martinez trying to usurp his command.

The doors to the bridge opened and two more people walked onto the bridge. A Lieutenant Commander accompanied by an Ensign.

"Captain Martinez," began the Lieutenant Commander. "We have everything aboard and stowed away. Orders sir?" she asked.

"Commander Ivanova, Ensign Clarke, may I introduce you to Captain Stuart, the ship's commanding officer?" Martinez replied as he rose and nodded in Stuart's direction.

Stuart stood up as both officers turned their attention towards him. Ivanova was bringing herself to attention when she noticed his rank was equal to hers and mistakenly relaxed. Ensign Clarke did come to attention.

"Commander," Ivanova acknowledged him as Clarke snapped out a very crisp "Sir!"

"Welcome aboard, we are a bit pressed for time. Commander please take navigation. Ensign take the science station. Captain Martinez, if you please, would you take tactical?"

Martinez replied first, "Tactical it is Captain," and moved to the appropriate bridge console. Ensign Clarke replied with the enthusiasm of a first year cadet's "Aye, aye sir!" as he quickly moved to the science console and took the seat there, his hands already flying over the controls.

Commander Ivanova raised her eyebrow at him as if to question his judgment but then simply nodded and moved to the navigation console.

Stuart muttered quietly under his breath and took the command chair.

"Captain," Athena's voice chimed, startling Clarke who was not accustomed to AI's at all. "The enemy vessel is within firing range of Argos Station.

All heads snapped to the main screen. Captain Carson was still there also and his attention moved from someone off screen back to Stuart.

"The Wellington will be in system in 45 seconds, Captain, thinking you can hold out?" Carson asked Stuart.

"For a few seconds anyway, Captain," replied Stuart. "Commander Ivanova, move us to a position behind Argos Station." He ordered.

"What!?! You want to hide behind the station?" she exclaimed.

"I have my orders Commander as do you, move the Pegasus now." He responded tersely.

Instead of complying she turned to Martinez. "Sir, I believe that this ship is small enough that we can out maneuver that ship and hit it in a few critical spots and knock it out of commission."

Martinez snapped at her, "The captain of this ship gave you a direct order, commander, follow it at once!"

Ivanova's face turned beet red as she quickly swiveled back to her navigation console and moved the ship to a position behind Argos Station.

"Status of the enemy ship, Athena?" asked Stuart.

"Still approaching the station, it has slowed to one half sub-light. Unable to determine if it has weapons lock."

"Why not," Stuart asked.

"The shields of that ship are near impenetrable to our sensors, sir," answered Ensign Clarke. "I am trying to recalibrate them now."

"Very good, Ensign," Stuart answered the young man. He liked his gung ho attitude.

"Captain, the Wellington has just entered the system," Advised Ivanova in an icy tone.

On the bridge of the Wellington Stuart could see activity increasing as the battleship entered the system and headed for the enemy ship. Carson looked at Stuart, "Captain we are here and are preparing to engage the enemy. I highly suggest that the Pegasus now evacuates the system."

Stuart did not like the idea of turning tail and running, but if he did not leave then the Wellington's probable sacrifice would be for nothing. Plus he had his orders and they directed him to do exactly as Carson had suggested.

"Agreed, Captain," he replied. "Good luck, Pegasus out." Carson nodded at him and disappeared from the main screen to be replaced by a larger view of the enemy ship.

"Navigator, I am sending coordinates to your console, implement them and take us out of here at full sub-light speed."

Ivanova grunted an acknowledgement as she hunched over the navigation console and began programming the Pegasus's navigation system with the information provided by Stuart.

"Captain," calmly stated Martinez, "the enemy ship has slowed to minimal forward motion and is launching what appear to be fighter craft."

Stuart looked up from his command console and saw dozens of lights breaking away from the huge leviathan class ship. Most of them were heading toward the Wellington but a small group was headed toward Argos Station.

"How many headed our way, Mr. Martinez?"

"Sensors indicate 23, sir."

"How long until we depart, Commander?"

"Departing now, heading away from Argos Station. The station will shield us from sensor view for 30 more seconds and then we will be shielded by the planet for three minutes 22 seconds. After that we will be visible to their sensors.

However by the same token, we are now no longer able to see what is happening beyond the station"

The main view screen view changed to a rear view angle and they could see Argos Station growing smaller until the station itself was eclipsed by the planet.

"Hopefully that will give us enough of a head start that they will not be able to catch up to us," Stuart said aloud. Silently he added 'or else we are most certainly dead'.

"Ensign, see if you can get us a feed from Argos. I would like to see what is happening."

Ensign Clarke acknowledged and began to make adjustments to his science console. After a few moments the view on the main screen changed to the opposite side of Argos Station. The small fighter ships were now coming into view. They resembled infinity symbols with two circles making a figure 8 in the center. When they maneuvered the infinity symbol would change places with the figure 8 symbol and the infinity symbol would then become the figure 8 symbol and vice versa. It was very disorienting to the human eye.

"Why do they not fire on Argos Station? They are in range," Murmured Commander Ivanova loud enough for Stuart to hear.

"They are firing at Argos Station, commander. They don't use explosive weapons but implosive weapons. So the shields don't have the usual color glare when an energy or missile weapon impacts against it. The only way to know that the shields are taking hits is by the shield power readings.' Stuart explained as he turned toward Ensign Clarke.

"Ensign, what are the shield power readings for Argos Station?"

Clarke quickly returned an answer. "Shields are at 76% power, Captain. If the shields continue to take this pounding they will collapse in 1 minute 45 seconds."

A grim silence descended on the bridge.

"Sir," Ivanova uncharacteristically whispered. "The Wellington."

All eyes turned to the main screen and watched helplessly as the Wellington was being ripped to shreds by the quickly maneuvering fighter ships. The fighter ships were dying at a high rate as the more powerful guns of the Wellington was destroying them, but their number was too large for the Wellington to hold them off for very long. For every fighter that the Wellington took out there were two more fighters to take its place. The leviathan class mother ship was also firing on the Wellington, but the implosion weapons could not be seen on the screen.

Suddenly the entire front of the Wellington disintegrated. Following the disintegration explosions began moving down the length of the Wellington, completely rupturing the battleship until the main reactor was engulfed by the explosions which caused the main reactor to detonate and a temporary sun to blast outward. The explosion destroyed the fighters in the area and even caused the leviathan ship itself to sustain, at least superficially, damage to her hull.

The only things not affected by the dying Wellington were the fighters attacking Argos Station as they were all far from the blast.

"Captain," interrupted Ivanova from her console. "We are ready to go to go to hyperspace and depart the system."

"Activate hyperspace engines and gets us out of here." He replied. Ivanova responded by doing just that. Within minutes the Moldovan system was far behind them and soon dropped off of their sensors completely. The Pegasus was headed beyond the edge of the galaxy itself, to a super giant planet orbiting a star that was beyond the edge of the galaxy.

"We have been in these caverns for days, will they never

end?" Sturya moaned to Avril. For the past five days they had moved progressively through caverns filled with twisting passages. They would move down a path only to have it end in a solid stone wall with no egress. They would then backtrack and select another passage only to have a similar ending.

Their supplies had run out yesterday and only the fact that they had once come across a stagnant pool of water had they been able to fill their water skins. The water was clear but tasted slightly foul from the minerals that imbued it. Still, they had needed water to continue.

Reversing course and returning the way they had come was impossible as they were hopelessly lost and could not retrace their steps even if their lives depended upon it. So, having no other options they continued forward hoping to find an exit from these caverns they were trapped within.

"They must come out somewhere, they must, else we are truly doomed," replied Avril in a harsh whisper. Both men had fallen into the habit of speaking in lowered voices and whispers, neither feeling bold enough to speak in a fully normal voice. It was as if the gloominess of the caverns had seeped into their very souls.

The stone bridge the two men crossed was not the only manmade object they discovered. They had come across a cache of wood and wrappings which had allowed them to make a store of torches which they had been using to light their way. The torches were running low and they were down to each having three left. Sturya was currently leading with a torch in his hand. When his torch was about to go out Avril would light one of his torches from it then assume the lead.

Sturya was more cautious when leading than Avril was. Avril set a quicker pace and at times Sturya muttered under his breath that Avril was a fool. And sometimes he did not bother to mutter.

"Slow down fool," he hissed through clenched teeth. "You will lead us down a shaft!"

"The torch gives enough light; I'll see a shaft before I fall into it. Besides, if these passages don't have an outlet then it won't matter if we fall down a shaft and are killed. Better that then a slow death by starvation." Avril replied even as he increased his pace unconsciously trying to outrun his own fears of starvation.

Sturya did not reply but concentrated on moving faster to keep up with the Qualorian captain. He had put his head down and allowed his feet simply to move him forward while keeping his sense alert to any danger from behind. Even though it had been five days, he still felt as if they were being shadowed by some lurking creature of these cursed caverns. Avril did not share his concerns; he believed that they were completely alone down here.

Hours passed until Avril's torch was finally burning down. Both men were exhausted and becoming weaker from lack of food. Avril decided to call for a rest break. He set the torch down and let it burn out.

After a few seconds their eyes adjusted to the darkness, except it was not dark, the walls suddenly came alive with glittering images. The images were faintly glowing and both men started when their eyes adjusted.

Sturya suddenly dropped to the ground and began wailing in superstitious fear. Avril jumped when Sturya began his moaning as it was louder than they had been since entering the caverns. But he quickly forgot about Sturya as he began to study the images.

The images showed what looked like giant insects fighting men wearing strange garments. Both the insects and the humans looked to be hurling light at each other resulting in opponents blowing apart and the remains burning. Some of the images showed massive cities with giant mushrooms above them, while others showed great javelins dropping from the skies and insects emerging from them after they hit the ground.

Avril started walking along the passage while he studied the images. There were things here that greatly disturbed him. He did not understand what was being displayed most of the time, but he knew in his bones that these things had happened and that someone had gone to great lengths to put these images into this wall. He reached out and ran his hand over one of the images and it was smooth as the wall of the cavern itself. It was if someone had used dyes that cloth was colored with.

He suddenly had an idea and took out his tinderbox and worked for a few moments to produce a small flame. When he had his small flame going he raised it high in his hand. The images were gone. He stood staring at a blank wall for a few moments then doused the flame. After a few seconds his eyes adjusted and the images were once again on the wall.

"Astounding!" he exclaimed in a voice just above a whisper. "Images that only appear in darkness."

Suddenly he realized that is was totally silent. Sturya had stopped moaning and wailing. He retraced his steps to where he had left Sturya thrashing about on the floor of the passage. Only Sturya was not there. The torch that he had dropped was still lying on the floor but there was no sign of Sturya.

"Sturya, where are you hiding you mis-begotten son of a mongrel cur!" he yelled out into the passage, knowing that he could get past the other man's superstitions by angering him.

He searched for several minutes but could find no trace of the man. After back tracking their passage for an hour or so he came across Sturya's torches. They were lying on the floor of the passage as if they had been carelessly dropped. He gathered them up and bundled them to the other two torches he still carried.

LEE E FULLER JR

He stood and considered what he should do next. Should he continue to work his way back along their trail and see if he could find Sturya or was it time to let the man go. He was not responsible for him; it was obvious that the man had abandoned him due to his own superstitious fears. After pondering what he should do he finally decided on a course of action.

Turning he strode back to return where the walls held the images that he wanted to study further. To hell with Sturya, he was on his own and he would find his way out of these passages. After all, no one would travel five days, build stone bridges crossing chasms just to find a place to put images on a stone wall. No, there would be another exit nearer to these wall paintings, of that he was sure.

After he had gone a mass of metallic tentacles with a silvery orb atop of them silently moved out of the darkness, the still form of Sturya wrapped in their cold embrace. The tentacled creature moved silently through the passage until it came to a particular section of the cavern wall. Unnoticed by Avril, Sturya or anybody who was not paying strict attention to the wall were three small holes. The holes, even if noticed by anyone would not have been thought to be anything other than three small holes. The creature inserted the tips of three of its tentacles into the holes simultaneously. After a brief wait it withdrew the tips and waited while a small section of the wall silently moved inward and rose out of sight.

The creature passed through, still carrying the unconscious form of Sturya and disappeared into the darkness beyond. The wall closed behind it silently, leaving no trace of the creature's passage.

A moment passed and Avril stepped into sight and approached the wall. He examined the wall and pondered the three holes for a moment before he turned away. He removed his pack and began searching through the contents of it until he found what he was searching for and withdrew a small ink and quill set.

He laid aside his pack and pulled the stopper from the ink bottle. He then dipped the quill into the bottle then made a small mark on the floor of the cavern wall to the left of the section where the three small holes were located.

After doing this sealed the ink bottle and returned it along with the quill to his pack. He then shouldered his pack and again moved off down the passage. He moved quickly and did not bother to look over his shoulder. He knew that for now he was alone and able to return to the wall paintings to try to decipher them. He had an avid fascination for the cavern wall drawings. He had never encountered anything like them before. Drawings that only appeared in darkness and were as completely smooth as the stone they were inscribed upon.

He had seen the tentacled thing that had bourn Sturya off into the wall passage. He did not fear it, but he did not wish to tackle it just yet. He believed it meant no harm to Sturya; else it would have killed him. He knew that Sturya lived by the rise and fall of his chest as he breathed.

Finally he came upon the first of the cavern wall drawings. He stopped to study it. The image showed nothing but a great many dots on the wall with what looked like a tear in the image with a few lines emerging from the tear. The image did not make any sense. He finally moved to the next image.

The next image also had the dots but the tear was gone, then lines were gone and a circle was now where the tear had been. The circle was empty. He scratched his head and tried to figure out what the images were telling him. He finally moved on to the third image.

The third image was much like the first two. The dots were everywhere and the circle was there, but now the circle sat beside another circle. The second circle was in pieces

LEE E. FULLER JR

and there were little squares strewn throughout the second circle. Again, an image that made no sense to him.

Avril finally stopped looking at the image and went back to the first image then to the second image and stopped again at the third image. He knew that the images were related but that did not mean he could understand what was being portrayed. He was in the position that a caveman would have been in trying to comprehend what a telephone, something that he had no reference as to what it might be and could not place in context within his known world.

Avril finally gave up on the images and moved along until he again came to the images of the insects and the men fighting. This was something he could grasp a war or at least a battle between two foes. But the weapons were inconceivable to him. Beams of light that destroyed whatever they touched. Javelins that fell from the sky and disgorged huge insects with weapons of light. Great cities with mushrooms above them and moving along he discovered more of the javelins with men entering them and the javelins leaping into the sky.

Avril suddenly realized that the javelins were ships that could move through the sky! When he was a boy just entering his teen years he had accompanied his father to the Rowad Ocean. They had traveled through Donaria; else his father would have left him at home as the Qualorian road was even more dangerous 20 years ago than it was today. On the shores of the Rowad Ocean were the ships that plied the waters for trade and warfare. Huge war galleys sat moored beside swift merchant ships and even a few pleasure ships of the nobility. The one ship that he would never forget if he lived to be 100 was the huge galley of King Necolin. That ship had carried the king to a watery doom only a few short years after he had seen it tied up dockside in fair Khalimnor.

These javelins were not javelins but ships that carried the warriors and the giant insects through the sky. From whence they came there was no image on the wall. He could only wonder, but the images of battles and fighting were all about him. He moved slowly down the passage until he came to the final image that of an exploding orb. The orb was surrounded by many of the javelins and it was exploding outward, tossing debris is all directions, many of the javelin ships themselves were depicted as exploding balls of fire, caught up in the great orb's explosion.

Avril simply stood and pondered the final image, he was beginning to get an inkling of the image truly meant, but could not accept the idea of his thoughts; they were too unbelievable to comprehend.

With an audible sigh, Avril, captain of the Qualorian Guard sank down and sat with his back against the wall of the cavern. Presently his head dropped and he slept beneath the murals of the cavern.

———————————

Sturya woke with a start from a nightmare. He had dreamt that he was in prayer to his gods, prostrate on the ground and chanting the Prayer of the Great Incursion when suddenly all light dimmed and darkness completely took hold of the world. As he raised his head in growing terror huge tentacles had reached of the darkness and wrapped themselves around his body holding him tightly.

He could only cry out then even that was denied him as another tentacle wrapped itself around his head, covering his mouth and stifling his cries for help. He had felt himself pulled up off the ground and he could only look down and see his people dwindling as the light returned to the world. His people carried on about their affairs as if nothing out of the ordinary had taken place. Sturya was carried higher and higher until even the mountains dwindled into nothingness. Then the tentacles turned him away from the quickly world he had been snatched from and he came face to face with

LEE E. FULLER JR

what the tentacles were attached to, a huge insectoid like creature, huge mandibles clacking together in anticipation of the snack that Sturya was about to become, the tentacles drew him ever closer to those vile snapping things, the many faceted eyes all seemed to be staring directly at him. He was about to be devoured when suddenly the creature was shot through with a great blinding light that caused Sturya to shut his eyes as tightly as he could, then he was thrown away from this abomination and into the void itself.

He was completely free of the creature and falling back to his world. He was beginning to feel warm as he fell toward the ground. He was sweating then he was burning as great heat was beginning to consume him. Then suddenly a great blast of ice cold water drowned the heat and brought him out of the nightmare.

Sturya quickly jerked upright and sat sputtering for a moment as he shook the water from his head and hurriedly wiped his eyes so that he could see. What he saw surprised him greatly. He was sitting in a cell where a huge guard was standing outside the bars holding a now empty wooden bucket. Sturya suddenly knew how he had gotten a face full of water. This lout had doused him!

He leapt to his feet and stood before the guardsman.

"Where am I?" he demanded.

"You are a guest of the city of Qualor. By what name are you known Tribesman of Hern?" the giant guardsman asked him in a rumbling voice.

"How did I get here?" Sturya asked, ignoring the man's question.

"You arrived the same way that he did," answered the guardsman indicating the man in the next cell. Sturya looked over at him and his eyes widened with another new surprise. The man sitting there was the same barbarian that Avril and his squad were pursuing when Sturya's people ambushed them.

"Interesting," mumbled the guard.

"What is interesting?" Sturya asked as he looked over the barbarian who was sitting on his bench, eyes narrowing as he looked over Sturya.

"You recognize him from the look on your face," answered the guardsman. "Ho, Erat," he spoke to the other man. "Is this Tribesman familiar to you?"

Erat looked Sturya over and he did seem familiar. Then he suddenly remembered the ambush of the squad that pursued him. This may have been one of the tribesmen from that ambush, but at the time he was too far away to make out individual details.

"I know him not," he answered simply. Then he rose from the bench and strode over to the bars separating his cell from Sturya's.

Sturya took a step back, here he was with two huge men standing before him, yet he knew that he was safe in his cell, unless the guardsman decided to open his cell and enter.

"Strange, he knows you," the guardsman stated. "How is it that you know him but that he does not know you?"

Sturya considered the question for a moment; both men were now drilling into him with their eyes. He was becoming nervous. He knew if he answered that he had seen the barbarian riding through the territory of the tribes then the barbarian might very well pin the ambush of the soldiers on him. Even though it was true, he did not think it a wise idea to even have it mentioned here in Qualor.

"I don't know him. I thought he was someone else for a moment," he lied to the guard. Then he quickly changed the subject. "You never answered my question of how I came to be locked in this cell."

The guardsman simply studied Sturya for a moment and shrugged his shoulders. "You were brought in last night by the Grand Vizier's personal guards," he simply answered then turned away to return to his wooden stool by the door.

Sturya shuddered. He knew the rumors and legends concerning the Grand Vizier. If he had truly been brought in by his personal guards then he was in effect a prisoner not of Qualor but of the Grand Vizier himself.

Turning he saw that the barbarian was still standing there watching him. The man had a neutral expression on his face and then he said in a low voice that Sturya could barely hear, "I would not want it known here that I were responsible for an ambush of Qualorian Guardsmen either." Having said that the barbarian turned and walked back to his bench where he dropped down and went back to sleep.

Sturya shuddered and followed the barbarian's example, sitting himself down on the stone bench. He wondered what had become of Captain Avril. Now that the man was not around he found himself missing his company. He had been a loner all his life, never staying in one place for more than a few days at the most. He had never traveled with another unless he was part of a large raiding or ambush party. Now that he had a taste of companionship, he found that he liked it and he began to re-evaluate his life.

The Grand Vizier looked up from the computer terminal and nodded to himself. The information on the holocube was important. He was satisfied that he had finally obtained it after decades of searching.

The holocube was a complete record of a probe that he had sent out 70 years ago. The probe had traveled a preset course deep into the void between galaxies and through time in a way. It had traveled back through three previous universes. The data it had gathered was extremely valuable.

The Grand Vizier removed the holocube from the terminal and stood up. The cube needed to be secured in the Vault of Ages where it would be safe from further loss. He moved to a different section of wall and pressed his naked palm against a certain spot. A doorway sized section of the wall slid aside to reveal a small square room. The Grand Vizier entered and the wall slid back into place.

He then reached out and pressed the lowest most button on a 7 button panel and the room dropped quickly. Within seconds the drop ceased and the same section of wall opened to reveal a small subway platform with a small two-seater car sitting at the platform.

Exiting the elevator the Grand Vizier took a seat in the car and typed a series of commands into the car's controls. A clear covering rose up from the open edges of the car and enclosed its seating area then the car moved away from the platform quickly gaining speed as it moved along its rails through the subway system.

After many minutes of travel the car emerged into another subway station and slowed to a stop coming to rest precisely even with the platform. The passenger waited until the clear canopy opened then he exited the car and strode toward the open archway that led out of the station.

Beyond the archway was a corridor that curved away out of sight. The Grand Vizier walked down this corridor passing row upon row of other corridors branching off of this corridor. After some few minutes of walking he turned right into one of the intersecting corridors and walked to its end where a large door was situated. The Grand Vizier withdrew a small device from beneath his robes and pointed it at the door. He pressed a control on the device and the door swung inward to reveal a room of gargantuan proportions.

The room contained a large raised section made of an unknown alloy. It glistened and sparkled as if it was filled with diamonds. There were four separate ramps leading upward, each ramp had a door at its foot. Striding forward the Grand Vizier moved up the ramp until he reached the center of the raised section where a leather chair with controls in the arms sat empty, awaiting an occupant. The chair could swivel 360 degrees and currently it faced a large view screen.

The Grand Vizier sat in the chair and punched out a series of commands in the right arm of the chair. A small opening appeared into which the Grand Vizier placed the holocube. After a moment the holocube sank out of sight and the opening closed behind it. For a few moments nothing happened then the view screen came to life with swirls of color drifting across the screen.

The Grand Vizier placed a device upon his right ear. A voice began speaking into his ear.

"Welcome Tomas. I am analyzing the holocube and will be with you shortly," the voice said.

The Grand Vizier knew that the voice could converse with him while it analyzed the holocube but that it did this to put him more at ease. He knew much about the voice as he had lived with it most of his life.

He had been born 136 years ago in Donaria. His parents lived at the edge of Donaria at the trading outpost of Liuawe. A month after he had been born the outpost had been savagely attacked by an assembled collection of desert raiders. The outpost was virtually destroyed. It was only by a simple twist of fate that he had survived.

He had been plucked from the arms of his mother's body by a sentinel a day after the raiders had departed. The sentinel had brought him underground to this very chamber in which he now sat and presented him for approval to the Great Planetary A.I. He was approved by that vast consciousness and the sentinel took him and a bag of gold coins and returned to the surface of the world.

The sentinel was a silver orb atop a mass of metal tentacles. But in order to place him with the proper family to raise him it disguised itself with a hologram that concealed its true nature then proceeded to the Foisee farm stead in Southern Donaria. There he was placed along with the bag of coins. The Foisee's were to raise him as their own until he reached the age of 15 when the sentinel would return for him.

The years he spent with the Foisee's passed quickly and happily for him. The night that the sentinel returned was one of bitter sweetness for him. He was excited at the prospect of traveling afar, but saddened at leaving the only family he had ever known.

He was taken underground by the sentinel which maintained its holographic appearance so as not to frighten him. He thought that it was a mute man until he learned later what its true appearance truly was and discovered that the sentinels had no mechanism by which they could speak.

He spent the next 20 years studying and learning; Mathematics, biology, chemistry, astronomy, and all the history of Origin. Origin was the name of the world he lived on. The more he learned of Origin the more in awe he became of the ancestors of the human race.

Origin was a completely artificial world. It was constructed by the Planetary A.I. over six billion years ago. The Planetary A.I. had traveled from another universe, not a galaxy but a universe! It was tasked with maintaining the human race. It was a huge self aware computer system built by men over 18 billion years ago. It had protected and nurtured the human race throughout all that time as it would continue to do until it existed no more.

His task was to take the place of the current "ambassador" to the people in the surface. The current ambassador was nearing 900 years of age. The planetary A.I. could sustain a human life indefinitely. The current ambassador was asking to be allowed to retire and live out the rest of his life off world. At the time he was physically 70 years old and held the position of High Priest of Baltas. When he was ready the priest would be replaced with a cloned body that would be "pre-programmed" to expire in its sleep while the priest himself would return underground, undergo complete rejuvenation then take a ship and move out into the galaxy to join the humans that lived out there who knew nothing about Origin.

When Tomas had completed his training the Planetary A.I. bade him to travel around Origin and to find himself a place to establish himself. It did not matter where he maintained his existence as there were numerous passages underground all over Origin.

He had learned that the human population was confined to one large super-continent and that the other ¾ of the planet was kept free of human life so other more advanced things could happen, such as space ports, anti-matter power plants, and other highly technological sites free from human intervention. He had also learned that the human population on Origin was tightly controlled and kept at a lower technological level on purpose. The builders of Origin had determined that a low-tech level population was desirable to keep the human race going. So every few thousand years a great cataclysm would occur, decimating humanity. The Planetary A.I. would always stop short of total extinction and pull genes from the stored gene pool and add more people back into the mix then would guide civilization again until the time for the next cataclysm.

The first thing that Tomas did was to return to the Foisee farmstead to visit his foster parents. After 25 years they were still alive but had become older. They still remembered him and were glad to visit with him but they made it clear that he did not belong there and so after a brief stay he moved on, never returning there again. He had learned years later that they had both died peacefully in their sleep, his foster father died first followed three years later by his foster mother. They had two sons of their own, Marl and Geon. Marl had taken over the farmstead and married and had four sons and three daughters of his own while Geon had joined the Donarian Army and had risen up through the ranks to retire as a captain in the capital of Donaria. He had never married and had eventually died with his estate going to his nephew Luika, his brother's youngest son whom had also joined the Donarian Army.

After that Tomas had stopped following what happened with his foster family as he was two generations past the people he had known and loved. The Planetary A.I. had offered him rejuvenation when he was 60 years old and he had accepted. He could not believe how much his body had changed over the decades until he had undergone rejuvenation for the first time. He stiffening arthritis was gone, his slowly failing eyesight was restored, his hearing was sharp again and he suddenly had a renewed sexual appetite. He had gone from 60 to 20 in the span of a week.

When he hit 120 years of age he again went through rejuvenation and had a few enhancements added per the suggestion of the planetary A.I. His body was infused with microscopic robots the Planetary A.I. had told him were called nanites. These nanites would help him to heal from wounds and boost his immune system greatly. He would be practically immune from all forms of sickness, including the common cold and flu. The nanites would also increase his strength, speed and agility threefold.

He had become proficient with a sword when he was in his thirties. He had learned from the sword master Corvin of Daria. He had petitioned the man to train him and was soundly refused as he did not have a sponsor to recommend him to the sword master. The Planetary A.I. had provided the sponsorship. It had sent a sentinel to the sword master carrying a sealed letter for the sword master's eyes only. Tomas never did know what the contents of the letter were, but the next day when was preparing to leave Daria a messenger from the sword master suddenly appeared before him and stated that the sword master had requested to speak with him again.

Returning to the presence of the man Tomas saw a change in his demeanor and attitude toward himself. Where before he had been coldly arrogant and disdainful of him he now acted as if Tomas was a Great Lord of the Land. Tomas asked him why he had changed his mind so suddenly and the sword master drew him aside and told him of the sentinel and the letter he had received and would say no more about the matter. The next day he began his sword training.

For three years Tomas had studied along with a small group of students learning techniques of sword fighting. The students all trained together and were never allowed to use anything but wooden swords against each other. Corvin had insisted on this rule as his own teachers years before had also wisely insisted on this rule. By using only a wooden sword the worst injury that could befall anyone were scratches, bruises and splinters.

Another thing that Corvin did was to have the students use progressively heaver blades and chop away at wooden posts that had been set up in the courtyard of his estate. By chopping away for hours at a time the students all built up their upper body strength. When they finally were allowed to use their actual swords the blades were feather light in their hands and their endurance was dramatically increased. The increased endurance could mean the difference between life and death if battling an opponent that was well versed in the use of a sword.

The only thing that Corvin could not train against were the attacks of the great barbarian hills men of the far north. These warriors were berserkers and could not be contained by even the greatest swordsman. They would get into a killing frenzy and would only stop after their appetite for killing had been sated. Once into a berserker rage the northern barbarians could only be brought down by archers well out of sword range.

After three years Tomas was called into the sword master's office and told that his training was at an end. Tomas asked why he was being dismissed as he had only trained for three years when others had been here for far longer. He was told that Corvin had been tasked to train him for three years and no more. The sword master then handed him a sealed letter addressed to Tomas then asked to leave.

Corvin did say to him though that he had learned his lessons well and at his current level of knowledge that only those with more advance training would be able to stand against him. This put him above most of the world's populace and gave him a sense of confidence that few others maintained.

After leaving the sword master's office he stopped only long enough to gather his things, say goodbye to the other students who he had made friends with, saddled his horse and rode away from the estates of Corvin the Sword Master of Daria. After he had put some distance between himself and the estates of Corvin he reined in his horse and pulled the letter out of his tunic. He studied the seal for a few moments and recognized it as that of the High Priest of Baltas. He knew that the ambassador had already "died" and moved off world. So either the new high priest had business with him which he did not expect or the Planetary A.I. was using this to communicate with him.

He broke the seal and opened the letter. "Your training with the sword master is at an end. It is time for you to return to me." That was the complete letter. Two sentences. He knew it was not the high priest but the Planetary A.I.

He rode into the nearby hills and quickly located the entrance to the underground world he was returning to after his years of absence. He led his horse into the darkness and came upon a sentinel in short order. The sentinel accepted

LEE F. FULLER JR

the horse from him and took the animal off to be cared for until he should have need of the animal again.

Within a few short hours he was once again in what he referred to as the Great Audience Chamber of the Planetary A.I. Whenever he thought this he chuckled a bit as it was a very grandiose name and to him very tongue in cheek. But it was a name he had made up when he was only 15 years old and everything was new to him.

He conversed for a few minutes with the Planetary A.I. and was surprised to learn that he was going to continue his sword training with a mechanical teacher. A sentinel that was programmed to teach him advanced fighting techniques. Techniques that even Corvin did not know.

For two more years he trained with his sword and learned more in those two years than he had under Corvin. He also went through more education in something else that he had not even suspected existed, Psychology and Sociology. He was amazed that these sciences existed and could accurately predict what people would do alone and in whole societies.

He spent the next 20 years building a reputation as a powerful wizard in the western most kingdom of Skarlos. The kingdom of Skarlos was two years travel by caravan from Donaria. He arrived there overnight after riding the underground subway system. He had learned the language while training underground. When he emerged from the mountains that secured the country's eastern border he carried two things with him, a pouch filled with priceless gems and a pack with his sword and some assorted clothing kept inside.

He came upon the ruins of an abandoned keep by following the directions given him by the Planetary A.I. He unslung his pack from his shoulders and dropped it to the ground. Dropping to one knee he opened his pack and pulled a small hand held scanner from it. He did a quick scan to make sure no other people were nearby then stood and conducted a longer and more detailed scan. There was not another human within five miles of him.

He then returned the scanner to the pack and retrieved a signaling device. He activated the device and sat down and pulled a small lunch from the pack. He studied the ruins while he ate the lunch. The keep was crumbling; an entire wall had collapsed revealing interior chambers filled with nameless rubble. Some calamity had befallen this place in the not too distant past. From what he had learned from the library records this place had been the home of a cruel baron whom was destroyed by a traveling wizard at the behest of the local villagers.

The traveling wizard had called down the wrath of gods on the keep, killing the baron and heavily damaging the keep. In reality the traveling wizard was the High Priest of Baltas on assignment and the wrath of the gods was an orbiting defense satellite. That was 50 years ago. The area had been shunned by the local inhabitants since then. The traveling wizard had told them of another wizard which would return here one day and take up residence in the keep and that he would protect the people if he judged them as worthy of his protection.

Finishing his lunch he stood up as a small group of sentinels arrived. He simply nodded at them and they set off to work. He watched as they quickly began moving through the ruins of the keep. Following them were other construction droids, types he had never seen before. This did not surprise him as there were hundreds of specialized droids that he vaguely knew existed but had never seen.

As night fell the droids continued working, no lights were necessary as they all could in the dark as easily as in the light. Tomas gave up watching them and periodically checked the scanners he had set up and was satisfied that no other humans were approaching the area.

For a week he stood by the scanners watching for any approaching people and admired the work of the droids. The keep was finished at the end of the week and now stood completely restored. There were subtle additions, outer statuary that disguised laser cannons, hidden chambers that only he knew how to access and a new underground subway platform that was now accessible for his use.

Surveying the work he smiled and the construction droids and sentinels all departed. He pulled a small tube from his backpack and held it in front of him with the ends of the tube pointing to either side of him. He gave it s slight squeeze and applied pressure with his fingers in a certain order and the tube suddenly extended into a six foot long steel tube. Tomas gave a quick sharp twist of his wrist and the steel appearance of the tube blurred and took on the appearance of a great wooden staff with a huge opalescent stone at one end.

Smiling to himself he directed the staff at the newly restored keep and applied pressure at a certain point where he gripped the staff. A light spread out from the jewel at the end of the staff and the keep suddenly shimmered then it looked as it did a week ago, ruins and crumbled masonry.

Shouldering his backpack he turned and headed off in the direction of the nearest town in the area. He arrived at the town near midday and quietly made his way through the town until he came at last to the only local inn that the town boasted.

He stood for a moment and gathered his thoughts before he entered the inn. Stepping over the threshold he entered the inn proper and made his way to a table where he could sit with his back to the wall and prop his staff against that self same wall. All eyes were upon him as he leaned back against the wall and simply waited for the innkeeper to attend him.

The silence of the inn remained unbroken as the

innkeeper strode out from behind his stout wooden bar and made the short journey over to the table where Tomas awaited him. The inn keeper was a lean man with clean shaven face and dark brown hair; he would have looked more at home in a field behind a plow than behind the counter of an inn. He looked Tomas over warily, few strangers came to this town and even fewer that looked the part of a wizard.

"What can I bring you stranger?" the innkeeper asked Tomas, not getting too close to the table, yet close enough so as not to offend.

"A piece of whatever is roasting on that spit and a mug of hot tea if you have any," Tomas replied. He was one the one hand bemused by the inn keepers wariness but also on guard as he knew the unpredictability of nervous people.

The innkeeper did not move away to fill his request and Tomas shrugged. He slowly untied the pouch from his belt and opened it. He withdrew the smallest gem, a polished sapphire and laid it upon the table for the innkeeper to decide if this would do as payment.

The look on the man's face told Tomas that it would be more than enough. The man looked surprised to see such a well polished gem and seemed eager to take it, still he hesitated.

"Why do you pause?" Tomas asked the innkeeper. "Is it not enough for what I have asked of you?"

"It is more than enough, sir," he replied nervously. "But I fear it may be enchanted as you have the look of a wizard about you." Having said that fear swelled up in the man's eyes as if he had said too much.

Tomas smiled and nodded at the man. "I am a wizard. But fear not, the stone is not enchanted nor does anyone here have anything to fear from me. Unless I am not fed soon, I tend to get cranky when I'm hungry."

The innkeeper started at that, quickly gave a short bow, scooped up the stone and hurried off to retrieve Tomas's lunch. Tomas looked about the inn as he sat waiting and noticed that conversation had begun again after the innkeeper had left his table. One man sitting at the counter quickly finished his drink and hurriedly left the inn.

Tomas had just been served his lunch by the innkeeper when three local guardsmen entered the inn. The man who had left earlier accompanied them and pointed out Tomas to them. They nodded and two of them moved to stand by the door of the inn while the third one moved over to stand above Tomas. The man who brought them here turned and left quickly when he noticed Tomas eyeing him carefully.

"Greetings traveler," the guardsman said to Tomas. "What business do you have in Neidheim?" Tomas noticed that the guardsman had loosened his sword in its sheath and that his hand was resting lightly on his belt buckle. The man obviously was sure that he could draw and decapitate Tomas if he felt it necessary.

Smiling at the guardsman Tomas stated the obvious. "Lunch and then I don't really have any plans after that. Care to join me?" he asked the man as he picked up his mug and took a drink of the steaming tea.

The guardsman looked a bit less comfortable after his answer. He was used to people being deferential to him. So far Tomas had not done anything but stride into town, walk into the inn and sit down to a lunch which he had paid in advance for. Plus he had admitted that he was indeed a wizard. What was a guardsman supposed to do?

Tomas saved him the embarrassment of having to either become blustery or the danger of becoming threatening. "Who is in charge here?"

"Baron Rofen rules here and he answers to King Jaiper in the capital," the guardsman answered, his hand resting a bit more firmly on his belt buckle as he allowed himself to relax a bit. Then a sudden decision was made and he gestured at the innkeeper who nodded and drew a draft of ale for him. He waved his men off and they turned and left the inn.

Sitting down across from Tomas the guardsman waited until the innkeeper had set the mug of ale before him and moved back behind the counter. The guardsman hefted the mug and took a gulp of its contents before continuing.

"Will you be staying or are you simply passing through, um what is your name by the way?"

"My name is Tomas, and you would be?"

"I am called Bren, I am sergeant of the local garrison here at Neidheim."

"I see, Sergeant Bren. Are you a local or were you stationed here?" Tomas asked as he broke off a piece of bread that had accompanied his roasted slab of meat and the bowl of broth.

"I am stationed here; I go where my captain sends me. You still have not answered my question, are you passing through or are you planning on staying here?"

"Why? Is immigration to this area forbidden? You should try the roast, it is actually pretty good," Tomas replied stuffing a piece of meat in his mouth.

"Yes, I know. This inn has a very good reputation, and you still have not answered my question," Bren stated, his eyes narrowing in suspicion. He was used to having his questions answered quickly and he did not like the answers being questions directed back at him.

"I will probably be staying in the area. I came across some ruins on my way here. What do you know of them," Tomas asked as he finished up his dinner.

Bren carefully studied the man sitting across from him. A self professed wizard asking about the ruins of Keep Fris was the last thing he would have expected to happen to him today.

"The ruins you speak of are Keep Fris. From what I know another wizard cast the keep down on the head of Baron

Godu some fifty years ago. The wizard said that another wizard would follow him and take up residence there. Are you the one he foretold of?"

"Foretold of?" asked Tomas, raising his eyebrows. "I doubt that anyone foretold of my coming," he lied. "I was simply wandering and saw the ruins and thought they would make a fine place to take up residence."

"The keep is in ruins. It would take years to repair if you could find any that would leave their farms to clear away the rubble and begin rebuilding the place."

"Oh, that wouldn't be necessary, sergeant. I could take care of that with no problem. What I really need to know is who currently owns the place."

"No one owns it, wizard. It has been left abandoned and is cursed. None will go near it."

"Well then, I guess I can go ahead and move in then without having to worry about someone coming along and claiming it as theirs after I repair it," Tomas replied as he stretched after finishing his meal. He then stood and gathered up his pack and staff. Nodding at Bren he slung the pack over his shoulder, "I thank you for the information Sergeant Bren. Please express my regards to the local leaders and let them know if they need anything all they need to do is ask and I shall do what I can."

"Where are you going, to Keep Fris then?" Bren asked as he also stood.

Nodding Tomas replied, "Yes. I liked the look of the place. It would make an ideal home and the location is also excellent. It is far enough away from town that people will not be made nervous of me. I know that most people are a bit uncomfortable by having a wizard nearby."

"You know, for a wizard you have a way of sounding strangely, I don't know, normal." Bren stated matter-of-factly.

Tomas laughed. "I have never before been accused of

being normal, sergeant. You seem to me to be a good man. Feel free to come visit me sometime."

Bren had simply watched as Tomas left the inn. He was not going to try to interfere with a wizard, but he would keep an eye on him. He reported to his captain whom in turn reported to the town leaders. It was decided to send a party out to the ruins of Keep Fris and question this self-professed wizard. He only claimed to be a wizard and had not given one ounce of proof that he was indeed a wizard. The town had seen others come this way, mostly con men trying to convince the town that they were the wizard whose coming was foretold 50 years earlier.

Bren was chosen to command a small group of soldiers that would accompany the town representative to Keep Fris. Once there the representative, Jarl Kors would question the man and try to determine if he was indeed the wizard they were waiting for or if he was merely another con man. If he was a con man he would be either arrested or driven off.

Tomas waited hidden in the area near the keep for the inevitable party of townsmen that would come to question him and either accept him or drive him off. He was prepared, he had everything in readiness. The satellite was in position and primed if needed and he had changed into his white wizard robes, packing away his grey traveling robes.

Hours passed and he realized that the townsmen would not be coming until morning. He went into the 'ruins' and awaited the arrival of his guests. He set up a couple of long range scanners and went to sleep. He was awakened early the next morning by the scanners. Checking he saw that a party of six people were approaching from the direction of the town and that they would be arriving within the hour. He quickly shut down and packed away the scanners and made his way to his hiding place outside of the keep.

The sun was beginning to burn away the morning mists and evaporate the dew from the vegetation when the townsmen arrived at the 'ruins' of the keep. They stopped and looked around, none daring to approach very close to the actual 'ruins'.

"I think he has not stayed after all," one of the guardsmen stated nervously as he looked around the small meadow that surrounded the keep. Before anyone could answer him Tomas stepped out from behind the hologram appearing to look as if he had simply stepped around a fallen parapet.

"Good morning and how is everyone on this fine morning?" he asked cheerfully.

The entire party started with his unexpected appearance. Jarl Kors stepped forward and introduced himself.

"I am Jarl Kors and we are here on behalf of the town of Neidheim," he said, sounding very self-assured standing before the others.

Tomas nodded and gave him a slight smile. "I have been expecting you, but I thought that you would not be here for another day at least. I apologize for not having the keep ready to receive visitors. You arrived just as I was finishing my inspection."

"I see, and what does your inspection tell you?" Jarl Kors asked.

"That the keep was not so seriously damaged and that it should only take a short time to repair. Please, stand back, I do not wish anyone to come to harm while I conduct repairs."

Before anyone could say or do anything Tomas turned and raised his arms. He waved his staff and spoke an incantation with the hidden sound system within the staff amplifying his voice so it thundered across the meadow and over his visitors.

"Angorth, Karvas Soto goeth, Arvada karama grath!" he spoke and squeezed his staff in a certain manner. The preprogrammed holographic program began to play. The group from town stood back in fright and awe as they watched what appeared to be a keep repairing itself. The entire ground rumbled, not from magic but from the overhead satellite sending down a preprogrammed sonic signal that set everyone's teeth on edge and caused the ground to rumble.

Stone and mortar rose into the air and dust spread out from hidden sources buried by the construction droids further adding to the illusion of the keep rebuilding itself as Tomas stood waving his wand, directing the entire show.

Minutes passed until finally the rumbling ceased, the dust settled and the keep stood rebuilt, though in a different configuration from its original design.

Tomas lowered his arms and turned to the party form Neidheim and gave a slight bow.

"Gentlemen, my house is now prepared for guests, will you please enter and breakfast with me on this most wondrous day? Then afterwards perhaps you can tell me how I may be of service to Neidheim?"

That was how Tomas came to Neidheim and spent the next 20 years building a reputation as a powerful and good wizard to the surrounding countryside. His service there brought peace and prosperity to the area as none of Neidheims neighbors wanted to incur the wrath of a powerful wizard.

Then one day he was ordered to leave by the planetary A.I. He went to the town's people and told them he had a journey to take and that he would be gone for years. He also told them he was leaving hidden protectors so they would be safe. Before he left he preprogrammed a couple of sentinels, their true appearance covered by sophisticated holograms and left the area.

He returned to the underground chambers of his youth and spent three years there learning more about the eastern kingdoms until he was given a wardrobe consisting of new black robes and an intricately designed mask that he was to wear at all times. When he did have occasion to remove the mask a holographic image would cover his head. The image was that of a badly burned face, charred and deformed from the heat of flames.

"I have finished analyzing the data and have found that we have not been followed through the universes by the Screhaz as we were concerned. The one scout they had sent to track us was destroyed when we passed through universe 9537. The probe located the wreckage of their ship, their shielding was not sufficient to protect them from the proto-gravity waves of that universe when it was hours into creation."

"Then I assume mankind is safe in this universe from extra-universal threats?" Tomas asked.

"Yes, the facts do seem to support this theory. However, I will continue to monitor for any signs of an incursion. The seeds that we sowed here in this universe are growing rapidly. We have lost four of the worlds due to natural geologic conditions. Two others have been lost due to pre space flight atomic and biological warfare. One has survived pre spaceflight atomic warfare but is not currently technologically advanced. One is still within a pre industrial stage."

Tomas thought for a second then spoke up. "Wait, that is only eight worlds. Did you not seed nine worlds?"

"Indeed I did, Tomas. The ninth world currently has second generation hyper drive star flight. They are centuries away from localized trans-dimensional gate technology. They are actually the third world that I seeded, 53,168 years ago. I very nearly did not seed that world as it had an indigenous humanoid life form that at first seemed to have the potential for advancement into a technological civilization. Further studies indicated that the race was an evolutionary dead end. Their race was identical to that of Theta VII in Universe 456. The current inhabitants probably believe that this dead race was an evolutionary off shoot of themselves."

"Fascinating to be sure," Tomas wryly chuckled. He believed that the Planetary A.I. was a lonely intelligence. It would always give more information than was necessary, as if it were trying to make conversation. Sometime Tomas felt sad for the intelligence. If it was truly lonely it would always be lonely. Human life spans might be indefinite with the rejuvenation technology available to the Planetary A.I. but even those humans would eventually die, even if after thousands of years. The Planetary A.I. simply continued, ensuring that the human race never expired.

"So the people that have star travel, how are they faring?" Tomas asked out of actual curiosity.

"They are currently embroiled in a war with a race of which I have very limited knowledge. They have spread outward from their seed world and colonized nearly 500 worlds in the last two centuries. They have a democratic style of government which I predict will crumble within the next 120 years to be replaced by a Galactic Empire. All of the signs are there to indicate the change to empire has already begun."

"So they are on the way to galactic sustainability then?" Tomas asked remembering his history lessons on how only a true galactic empire could effectively unite a galaxy under a single government.

"Yes, Tomas eventually one of them will find their way to Origin and then we will have the opportunity to interview them and then determine in what manner we can assist them on their road to galactic supremacy."

Tomas sat and pondered that statement for a few moments. He knew that men like himself had designed and built Origin and the Planetary A.I. billions of years ago. The planet itself was completely renewable through the use of technology that he did not even pretend to comprehend and there were other technologies being used by the planetary A.I. that he was only vaguely aware of through casually dropped hints by the Planetary A.I. Only names such as Diurnal Existential Transfiguration Pod Architecture, whatever that was he had no idea. He also knew that there were other technologies that he was not aware of which he could not even conceive of without knowing more of everything.

He knew that Jonar Grend, the previous ambassador had gone off world and not been heard of since, at least that he was aware of. The Planetary A.I. did not always give him full information. He was only given information that he would need to know to complete whatever task he was assigned. He also did not know how much information that Jonar had been given, what knowledge he possessed or what training he had gone through during his tenure as ambassador.

"Tomas," boomed the voice of the Planetary A.I. "What of the barbarian that had the holocube?"

"I have him secured in a holding cell in Qualor. My personal guards are watching over him. I have also recently been informed that a Tribesman of Hern has been captured in the catacombs near the ancient historiography. He is also interred in the holding cells."

"A Tribesman of Hern? Interesting. They have been carefully conditioned through the use of religious indoctrination to avoid the mountains and the most especially the caves therein. It is meant to keep them from wandering into the cavern system and discovering the true nature of Origin. For millennia this arraignment has been successful. I shall have to cause an earthquake in the area to seal the cavern entrance the Tribesman used. This will preclude any other Tribesmen from following his example."

Tomas thought for a moment, "Ah, I understand. The earthquake shall serve a dual purpose, first seal the cavern so no others can travel into the catacombs and second let the Tribesmen believe that their gods are angry with them which will reinforce their fear of the mountains and keep them away."

"Excellent, Tomas your deduction is accurate. I believe that you are nearly ready for the next level of training. You will need to begin making arraignments for the Grand Vizier of Qualor to perish so that you may return for further training and your next assignment."

"How long will I remain in Qualor?" Tomas asked. He knew that eventually his position in Qualor would end; still he was bittersweet about it. He had lived in Qualor for close to 50 years and had enjoyed his position and life there. Still he was also excited at the prospect of further training and a new assignment.

"You shall be there for a few months to a year. The Eastern outpost situation needs to be resolved before the death of the Grand Vizier. Once Qualor has fully secured the eastern outpost then the country will be in a position to move into a position of equality with Donaria."

Tomas's original assignment was to bring Qualor up to a state of equality with Donaria. This had taken him decades to accomplish, strengthening the Qualorian Guard, subtly manipulating the opinion of the prince until his father passed away and he became king then being named an advisor of the king at that time. Then there were the public works projects, the completion of the new aqueduct and sewer systems, the animal husbandry programs, the agricultural programs, building up the treasury and establishing a regulated banking system, and a thousand other details that he had seen to over the years. He knew that if he would have been allowed to stay longer he could have raised Qualor to a position of major dominance over the entire eastern half of the Great Continent.

"Return now to Qualor and continue your duties, Tomas. Hold the barbarian for another fortnight then release him. His only crime was to be in the wrong place at the wrong time. Do see if you can find out how he came to possess the holocube. I would like to know if the barbarians of the north are a part of the tech underground. As for the Tribesman, hold him until I am ready with the earthquake. He will need to be seen by other members of the Tribesman in the area of the mountains so the earthquake will be effective."

"As you command," Tomas replied as he rose from the seat and retreated down the ramp to return to his quarters in Qualor. He had much to do over the next few days in order to prepare for the Grand Vizier's impending "death."

Chapter VIII

The Pegasus moved through hyperspace, the stars thinning and falling behind the ship as it moved further into the blackness of extragalactic space, the galaxy slowly receding away into the distance. With every moment the galaxy itself became the rear view of any on the ship that chose to look behind them. The crew and passengers were farther out from the galaxy than anybody in the Federation had ever been before. Athena was making a continuous recording of the galaxy spreading out below them and scanning in every direction. A complete scientific scan as was being made would be extremely valuable for the astrophysicists back at the Federation sciences academy on Earth.

Their destination was at the extreme edge of their scanners but not yet within visual range. They had been on a heading for the super-planet for 23 days. They could have reached the planet is 16 days at top speed but Stuart did not want to push the Pegasus that hard for such a prolonged period. Even traveling at close to 2/3 speed Stuart was aware that the maintenance droids were busier than usual. He had seen reports from Athena showing systems having minor issues where none had shown up before, circuits overloading, chips needing replacement, and other issues cropping up that needed immediate attention.

He had gotten to know his crew a little better since their arrival. Ensign Clarke had assumed the duties of science officer and had been working closely with Athena in interpreting the data from their continuous scans. Lieutenant Commander Ivanova still maintained her position as helmsman but remained cold and formal when dealing with him. She no longer questioned any orders he gave but the atmosphere between them was tense.

Captain Martinez he only saw occasionally in the dining area. He had barely spoken to him, but when he did Martinez was always friendly. He spent his time in the company of a fourth person who had come aboard at Argos Station, a civilian scientist by the name of Joe Granson. Granson appeared to be in his mid-nineties. He had developed the theory behind the project that the Pegasus was now transporting for field testing. He didn't know much about the man, had only been briefly introduced to him two weeks before after their hurried departure from the Moldovan system.

A small cadre of technicians had also come aboard the Pegasus at Argos Station. There were 7 of them and their primary duty was to assemble and operate the trans-dimensional inference equipment they had brought aboard. Stuart had seen them going over their EVA suits earlier in the week, all the equipment needed to be assembled in the vacuum of interstellar space.

Stuart stepped onto the bridge. It was the middle of what would normally be the 3rd shift, the middle of the night. The bridge lighting was dimmed and Stuart silently moved to his accustomed command only to come up short when he suddenly noticed that it was already occupied. The occupant gave a start when Stuart suddenly appeared and looked up guiltily as if they had just been caught performing an act of espionage.

Stuart was surprised to see Commander Ivanova in his seat as much as Ivanova was surprised to see him. She suddenly realized that she was sitting in the captain's chair and quickly vacated the seat and moved back a few steps to give Stuart room to assume the command chair.

Stuart nodded at her and waved her back toward the chair. "Please, Commander Ivanova as you were, I was just out for a stroll and automatically came to the bridge."

She warily watched Stuart and finding that he was not annoyed or upset she relaxed a bit. "It would not be proper for me to sit in the command chair when the ship's captain is on the bridge," she responded as she took another step backwards then reached behind her and turned the helm chair around and sat there.

Stuart shrugged then stepped up to the command chair and sat down. He sat and studied the commander for a few moments then he began his attempt to make peace with her.

"Commander, we got off on the wrong foot. When we first met conditions aboard ship were hectic and confused," he said.

"To say the least," she replied sardonically.

He chuckled a bit at that. "I have heard nothing but praise for you from Captain Martinez. Your performance since coming aboard the Pegasus has been exemplary leaving me no room for complaint or any doubts in your abilities," then standing Stuart faced Ivanova who quickly jumped to her feet.

"Commander Ivanova, welcome aboard the USS Pegasus," Stuart intoned as he saluted her formally.

Ivanova automatically returned the salute and could only give the time honored response, "I am honored to be here, sir."

Stuart nodded and became less formal. "Commander, would you care to join me for late night snack?"

Ivanova considered for a moment, "Perhaps another time, Captain. I am truly very tired and simply could not sleep. I am going to turn in if you do not mind."

"As you wish, we should arrive at our destination in two more days. I expect that things will get very interesting at that time. Sleep well, commander."

"Thank you, sir. Goodnight."

Stuart waited until she had left the bridge. Then he again sat in his command chair. He wondered if he had made any progress towards Ivanova thawing towards him at all. He knew that she would follow orders, her dedication to the fleet and duty was too strong for her to abandon only out of a personal dislike for a superior officer. "Or at least an officer of superior rank" he muttered aloud.

Curiosity about the commander suddenly grabbed him by the throat and shook him. He looked over his command console and activated his personal monitor. He called up the commander's service record.

Lieutenant Commander Lyudmila Ivanova. Born 2245 in Minsk Russia. Went to the Federation Fleet Academy in 2263, graduated 11th in her class, class of 2266. Served as Senior Cadet aboard the USS MacArthur which shaved a year off of her academy schooling. Was promoted to Ensign in 2266 upon graduation then assigned to Fleet Headquarters under Captain Laughton. 2268 transferred to USS Halsey as a newly minted Lieutenant working in the astrogation section, was third shift navigator during her second year aboard. 2271 assigned to Argos Station under Captain Martinez, promoted to Lieutenant Commander in 2272, just last year. Three commendations and one medal, the Order of the Sisu.

"The Order of the Sisu?" he said aloud. "That is only given for the highest act of valor." He looked through her record but there was nothing about why she received the medal. It was awarded during her Senior Cadet year aboard the MacArthur but the details were not there and the reason for her receiving the medal were listed as classified.

"Commander Ivanova you have an interesting record," Stuart muttered aloud as he cleared his monitor. He was just locking down his console when Athena suddenly shattered the silence.

"Captain, we have a contact on an intercept course."

"Do we have visual?" he demanded, coming fully alert.

"Affirmative," Athena replied as the main view screen switched from the forward view to an image of the incoming ship. The ship was a Vegan Heavy Scout, an even match for the Pegasus.

"Red alert, Athena call all hands to their stations," he ordered as he brought shields online and activated the weapons systems.

"Evasive maneuvers, pattern delta gamma omega," he spewed out as he brought the weapons to bear on the enemy ship. Ivanova and Clarke spilled onto the bridge and quickly assumed their stations. Moments later Martinez appeared and took the weapons station.

"Shields are down to 89 percent," Martinez informed him. Stuart swore under his breath. The Vegan scout was firing on them, only the draining shield power revealed this information. Had he not raised shields when he did the Pegasus would have a hole in the hull at best, destroyed at worst.

"Return fire, full power to particle beams and launch 2 number three missiles, sending coordinates for missiles to your board now," Stuart quickly replied. He had to move fast. By getting the first shot in the Vegan had the advantage.

"Firing Particle Beams, coordinates input for missiles and firing them now," Martinez acknowledged. Stuart could feel a slight vibration as the missiles shot out of the Pegasus.

LEE E FULLER JR

He had programmed them to launch from the opposite of the Pegasus so the implosion weapons of the Vegan would not destroy them as they left the launch tubes. The missiles shot away from the Pegasus and split up, one going over the Pegasus and the second missile traveling to the rear of the Pegasus and continuing away until it suddenly turned in the direction of the Vegan scout.

The Vegan continued firing the implosion weapons that were so deadly to Federation ships while the particle beams from the Pegasus tore at the enemy ship's shielding. Their shields were a kaleidoscope of colors, the energies of the particle beams cascading across their shields, weakening them.

The first missile was close to the Vegan when it suddenly collapsed upon itself, the victim of the implosion weapons being fired at the Pegasus. The second missile was approaching the enemy scout from the opposite angle and hopefully, the crew would not see it until it was too late.

"Shields at 34 percent, enemy shields at 74 percent. Continuing to fire particle beams should I ready more missiles?" Martinez asked his voice calm and his bearing just as seemingly calm.

"No time, either the other missile already out there gets him or he gets us. Channel all power to shields," Stuart ordered hoping it would buy them enough time so that the other missile could do its job.

The lights dimmed as power was rerouted, red emergency lighting spread to life on the bridge. Suddenly on the view screen a large explosion hit the rear of the Vegan scout. The missile, nuclear tipped, had detonated upon impact with the Vegan scout's shields. The explosion was enough to overload their shields and hurtle the ship directly towards the Pegasus. The continually firing particle beams sliced into the now unprotected ship shredding the hull and spilling its occupants into space.

"Evasive, full sub-light speed forward!" Stuart quickly snapped as he saw the Vegan headed directly toward the Pegasus. Ivanova's hands flew across her navigation board and the Pegasus shot forward. The Vegan scout only barely missed the aft of the Pegasus as it moved out of the way.

"Full stop," ordered Stuart. "Ensign Clarke, full scans of that ship. Athena, rear view on screen."

The wreckage of what was a few minutes before a Vegan scout ship now appeared on the main view screen. The ship was tumbling end over end as it moved away from the Pegasus debris trailing after it including the bodies of its recently deceased crew.

"Scans indicate that the ship is out of commission. Engines are totally gone, power readings are minimal, even those readings are fading, nope, all power is gone now. The ship is dead and drifting," Clarke reported.

"Any survivors, Ensign?" Stuart asked quietly.

"No sir," Clarke replied, his eyes glues to the sensor readout.

"Very well, stand down from red alert, I want yellow alert just in case that ship was not alone out here. Commander Ivanova, bring us as close to that ship as you can without endangering the Pegasus, match courses and spin with it."

"Aye, aye captain," she replied with a nervously raised eyebrow wondering why he would want to get so close to the wreckage of the scout.

"Captain," Martinez said quietly. "Do you think it might be a better idea to put some distance between us and that ship?"

"I know what you're thinking; they always self-destruct when they are near to losing a battle. My first instinct is to move us away, but this is an opportunity for us to gather information on one of their vessels. We haven't gotten any decent intel on their ships since first contact."

"I know Captain Stuart, but suppose they are playing

possum? Just waiting for us to get close enough to be destroyed when they initiate their self-destruct?"

"You heard Ensign Clarke, no power reading from the vessel at all." Turning to Clarke he continued, "Deep micro scans, ensign. If there are any systems with power onboard that ship I want to know about it immediately."

"Full micro scans, aye," Clarke replied as he bent further over his instruments. His fingers moved seemingly of their own accord across the control surfaces of the control panels as his eyes remained glued to the screens that provided full readouts of the ship being scanned.

"Sir, sensors indicate a low level of power onboard the ship. Not enough to run anything with the possible exception of emergency lighting."

Stuart stood up from his seat and paced the bridge, going from command seat to main view screen and back again. He then stood by his chair until Ivanova informed him that they were 2500 meters from the wreckage of the scout and had matched course and spin with the remains of the scout. He stood, rooted to the spot as he considered the situation. A boarding party could make interior scans of the ship, gather information on how the Vegans designed their instruments, perhaps retrieve some type of ship's logs, even a manual on how to remove a baffle plate would be useful, and it would give them a sample of their written language.

Stuart decided the opportunity was far too valuable to waste.

"Ensign Clarke, I want you to head a boarding party to the scout. Take one of the crewmen and search that ship, I want it's logs, we need to find out why they were out here."

Ensign Clarke practically jumped out of his chair in his excitement; this was to be the first boarding party he had ever had the chance to lead. Aboard the Argos Station he had never had a chance to do much of anything that was exciting.

Stuart stopped him before he moved three steps from the science station. "Ensign, use extreme caution, we don't know for sure that all of the Vegan's are dead, there may be survivors, shielded from our sensors by debris, shielding, radiation, or what not. Do not assume that the ship is safe. You are responsible for the safety and well being of those in your party, use common sense. Understood?"

"Yes, sir," an obviously abashed ensign answered.

After Clarke left the bridge Ivanova gave him a withering look. Stuart did not want to lose any progress in the truce they had achieved only within the last hour. So he explained his reasons to her.

"I know, commander that my words seemed harsh. I understand his assignment at leading the boarding party, but I just want to bring him back down to earth a bit. His life and the life of whoever he chooses to accompany him are in danger the moment they leave the airlock. He will still have the thrill of excitement but it should now be tempered with caution also."

Ivanova suddenly nodded in understanding and turned back to her board, her fingers moving swiftly so she could monitor the Ensign's party for herself. Stuart allowed her this privilege as Martinez had told him she had taken young Clarke under her wing since he had been assigned the post on Argos Station.

"Athena, full sensor sweeps in all directions and inform me immediately if anything at all appears out of the ordinary."

"Acknowledged, Captain," Athena replied.

"Captain Martinez, would you please monitor the energy reading of that ship? If you detect any change at all, no matter how insignificant it may seem, inform me immediately."

Martinez nodded acknowledgement as he assumed the science station and began monitoring the enemy ship.

Minutes passed the only sounds those of the normal instrument noises on the bridge, an occasional click or beep, a constant steady humming and a quiet chirping every few seconds. All three sat at their stations, Martinez at weapons, Ivanova at navigation and Stuart in the command chair. None of them spoke.

Ivanova was hawkishly watching the sensors she had trained on the wreckage where Clarke was preparing to go. Martinez was making sure the weapons remained powered up and that the missile tubes were again ready for full launch capability. Stuart simply sat and studied the wreckage displayed on the main view screen.

Finally Ensign Clarke reported in to the bridge. "Bridge, this is Clarke, I am in airlock two with crewman Edwards. We are ready to depart."

"Stuart here, Ensign. Please activate your helmet cameras gentlemen," he ordered. He wanted to see what they saw.

The camera images appeared on the left side of the main view screen, Clarke's camera image in the upper left and Edward's on the lower left.

"You are authorized to leave the ship, Ensign. Good luck." Stuart announced.

Clarke acknowledged Stuarts order and activated the airlock. The inner door closed, sealing the two men into the lock. Less than a minute later the lights changed from green to yellow as the air left the lock then to red as the air was gone and only vacuum remained. Clarke pressed the control and the outer door opened, exposing both men to the vast openness of space.

Edwards raised his right arm to reveal a grappling gun in his hand. He sighted on a section of the wreckage and fired the device. A cable shot out of the gun and quickly spanned the distance between the Pegasus and the wreckage of the scout. With no atmosphere to offer resistance the cable did not lose any of its firing speed and hit the wreckage with enough velocity to punch through the metal of the hull that it impacted with.

Edwards then gave a sharp tug on the line to stop its forward motion and the grapple caught firmly and held. He then secured his end of the line to a ring set into the wall of the airlock. Then getting the hand signal from Clarke to move ahead, he pulled a line from his suit's belt and attached it to the grappling line and pulled himself out of the airlock and let his momentum carry him across the gulf between the two ships.

Clarke followed suit and went trailing after Edwards. Clarke looked down as he crossed the span and saw nothing but blackness. He then looked up and again saw nothing but more blackness. The blackness was the void between galaxies where no stars shone. Clarke then looked to his right and saw more blackness. Finally he looked to his left and he let out a small gasp. Laid out to his left was the Milky Way galaxy spread out in all its vast grandeur. Millions of stars burned hot in the clouds of the galaxy. Somewhere in that vastness was the Federation, not even visible from where he was so small in comparison to the hugeness of the galaxy.

Those on the bridge also saw what he was seeing but their view was only a quarter of the main view screen, the significance of what Clarke was seeing being lost on them. They were more intent on seeing what Edwards was looking at as he had just reached the hull of the wrecked Vegan scout.

Edwards stepped through a tear in the hull of the scout and after he had secured his footing he reached out and unclipped his tether line from the cable connecting the Pegasus to the scout. To do this he simply reached down and unhooked the tether from his belt and let it hang off of the cable for the return trip.

Edwards then switched on a light that was strapped to his suits right wrist. He shone the light around and the observers back on the Pegasus were able to make out a damaged corridor of the enemy scout. The hole in the side of the hull carried across to the opposite wall of the corridor and into the room beyond. Edwards swung the light to his right and there was only an impassable wall of wreckage from the explosions that had destroyed the ship. Looking to his left the light picked out the details of the corridor which ran straight for a dozen or so meters and abruptly turned right and out of sight.

Clarke moved up beside Edwards and similarly unhooked his own tether and activated his own wrist light. He scanned the area with his light just as Edwards did and his voice carried over the suit's comm system to Edwards and the bridge crew also.

"We need to see if we can locate the bridge. That hole is too jagged for us to try and pass through; we could tear our suits trying. We'll only do that as a last resort. For now let's follow this corridor and see where it leads."

He then moved off, following the corridor with Edmonds taking up the rear and following him. When he reached the turn in the corridor he stopped and shone his light down the corridor and was surprised to see an intact corridor with no signs of damage. It ended in a set of doors that could only be access to a ship's elevator. He shone his light against each side of the corridor before moving ahead. On the left there was only one sealed door and on the right there was simply a blank wall.

Setting off he moved quickly down the corridor until he reached the elevator doors. He made a few motions at Edwards who then proceeded to examine the doors and the surrounding wall areas to either side of them. He found an access panel whose cover he removed and carefully set on the deck so it would not float away and possibly damage their suits. He studied the wiring for a moment then he discovered a lever recessed into the upper part of the panel.

Reaching up he pulled the lever and the doors opened about halfway before stopping.

Looking into the empty elevator car Clarke saw it was empty and motioned to Edwards. Together they managed to pull the doors the rest of the way open. Looking up they saw an access panel at the top of the car, but they had no way to open it. If they did not have to wear the pressure suits they could have pushed the panel open but with the suits on they were restricted in what they could and could not do.

Reluctantly Clarke led Edwards out of the elevator and to the one sealed door in the corridor. Edwards, now knowing what to look for, had the access panel off and the doors opened in no time. This time the doors opened all the way when he turned the lever.

They doors opened onto a small room whose purpose was obscured by the fact that the two men did not know for what purpose the equipment strewn about was used for. The room had no other access so Clarke said, "Ok, nothing here either. Let's try to see if we can maybe get through the hole in the wall where we came in and see if there might be a way forward from there."

They moved back down the corridor and returned to their entry point. Edwards and Clarke investigated the jagged tear in the inner wall of the corridor and after a few moments of examination Clarke made his decision. "We should be able to pass through safely; I'll go first and check out the other side. If there is no way forward from there then there is no point in both of us risking a suit breach."

Clarke carefully maneuvered himself through the tear in the wall and entered the room that it led into. He looked about and apart from the tear in the wall he had just passed through the room was relatively undamaged. The door to the room was to his right and he moved over to the door and located the access panel. Reaching up he grasped the lever and gave it a quick tug and the doors to the room opened about an inch then froze.

Clarke let go the handle and reached out and grasped the right hand door, set his feet and pulled. The door slowly gave way then suddenly snapped into the wall recess it was designed to fit into when open. Clarke tried the same procedure with the opposite door but it was frozen and would not budge.

Clarke studied the doorway for a few moments it was smaller than the doorways on a Federation ship. The Vegan's themselves were only 5 feet tall at most, although they could rise up to 7 feet when threatened or when they were getting aggressive.

He carefully pushed his head through the half open doorway and looked to his right. He could see the wreckage that blocked access in the corridor and he could also see flashes of light form Edwards's wrist light as he moved his arm about.

To his left the corridor continued to another set of doors, these looked like they might lead to the engine room as they were larger than normal and were thicker than the rest of the doors on this corridor. The doors stood open and there was a slight red glow coming from a distance beyond them.

"Edwards," he said into his comm system. "Come on through, I think I found the engine room. We should be able to find a hatchway that leads to the bridge from there."

"On my way sir," Edwards replied as he began to slowly and carefully make his way through the tear in the wall.

A few moments later he was standing next to Clarke and the two men began to struggle with the stuck left hand door. Clarke pushed while Edwards pulled and finally the door gave enough so that the two men could squeeze past and gain the corridor beyond.

Standing side by side they both lifted their arms and

shone their individual wrist lights ahead of them into the darkness. The lights picked out details here and there as they swept across the open doorway into the engine room of the smashed Vegan scout.

The two men advanced forward into the engine room and stopped just beyond the doorway. Vegan bodies floated through the vacuum, their bodies partially exploded from the vacuum. They were almost like giant worms with artificial arms. The bodies themselves were priceless as none had ever been retrieved, whenever the Vegans were close to losing a battle they would self-destruct their ship completely annihilating the vessel and crew.

"Ensign Clarke," Stuart called over the comm System. "Immediately retrieve one of those bodies and transport it back to the Pegasus. You can explore the engine room while Edwards brings the corpse to the Pegasus."

"Aye, sir," Clarke answered as he gestured to Edwards to retrieve one of the three corpses floating through the engine room. Edwards pulled a cord off of his suit and wrapped it around one of the bodies and secured it to his belt. Then, his left hand clutching the line he moved out of the engine room and began his return to the Pegasus.

Clarke slowly moved through the engine room, shining his wrist light into all the nooks and crannies that the darkness covered. He arrived at a central console. The console was on a raised dais in the exact center of the engine room. It was covered with dark banks of monitors and had numerous switches and controls moving around in a complete 360 degrees.

Clarke studied the controls trying to grasp their functions. He tried overlaying in his mind the engine room controls that would be on a similar ship of the Federation, a ship such as the Pegasus. Those controls could be environmental controls, those over there could be shield and gravity controls. He stopped suddenly when he noticed the red light that was shining steadily suddenly started to blink.

He shone his light over the controls in that section of controls as he tried to determine what they were for. The red light was blinking a little more rapidly than it was a few seconds ago.

"Ensign!" Stuart's voice suddenly exploded in his ears through the comm System. "Get out of there now, move it!"

Stuart had realized what it was that Clarke was seeing and with his warning understanding suddenly flooded through Carter. The self-destruct device had been activated but it did not have enough power to fully initiate. Now the scout ship power reserves were increasing enough so that the self-destruct sequence had begun; in minutes the ship would become an expanding ball of super hot plasma that would completely dissipate in a few days time.

Clarke moved as fast as he could and left the console and the engine room behind him. He took one last glance behind him as he pushed through the doors into the small room where the tear in the wall was at and saw that the light was blinking very rapidly now.

He threw caution to the wind as he plowed through the tear in the wall, catching his suit and tearing it slightly, creating a small air leak. Then he was at the tether line and quickly snapped it to his belt then he pushed off against the scout ship's hull and was heading toward the Pegasus, moving at a rapid speed.

He suddenly realized that he would not be able to safely halt his momentum in the airlock which had just cycled open to reveal Edwards standing there waiting for him. He grabbed the tether line with both hands and felt himself jerked suddenly as his forward momentum was slowed. He then let go of the tether line and let himself fall the rest of the way into the airlock. As soon as he was in the airlock

Edwards hit the control button and the outer door slid shut.

Clarke turned in time to see the wreckage of the Vegan scout slide away as the Pegasus moved away, quickly picking up speed as it went. Suddenly a blindingly white light filled the portal of the airlock and both he and Edwards were thrown to the floor of the airlock as a shockwave hit the retreating Pegasus.

The shockwave hit the Pegasus and caused it tumble through the depths of space. The engines that were only seconds ago moving the Pegasus away from the wrecked scout were now silent as safety overrides kicked in and shut them down. Emergency lighting activated all over the ship as the main power couplings disengaged automatically to prevent an overload that would force other safety systems to eject the main reactor core to prevent it exploding inside the ship.

The voice of Athena carried throughout the ship. "The Vegan scout ship has self destructed. Due to our near proximity to the explosion we have sustained minor damage. There have been no casualties."

Then all was quiet as the crew and passengers all lay unconscious while Athena guided the Pegasus through the darkness of space and sent repair droids throughout the ship.

―――――――――
―――――――――

Avril sat on the cold stone floor of the corridor and simply stared at the wall drawings. He was trying to grasp what they showed. The walls portrayed images of men and women fighting insects as large as a man, and in some cases even larger than a man. He shuddered to think that such things existed and couldn't even ponder what he might do should he come across one of the bugs.

Finally after sitting on the cold stone floor for so long

he could feel the chill seeping into his body he stood up and stamped his feet to get the circulation going again in legs that had gone to sleep. He rubbed his arms and stretched, yawning. He took one last look at the final drawing then turned and made his way back down the corridor.

After a few minutes he reached the spot where he had made the ink mark on the floor. But there was no ink mark where he thought he had drawn it. He slowly moved along the corridor, his torch held low as he searched the cavern floor. Finally he stopped and retraced his steps back the way he had come until he was where he thought he had made the ink mark.

Convinced that this is where he made the mark he began to examine the wall for the three holes that he knew were there. He searched for minutes before he located the holes. Once he had the holes located he looked again for his ink mark but it was gone. This could only mean that someone had erased it somehow.

Avril suddenly stiffened with the realization that if someone knew the ink mark was there and had erased it then there was the possibility that he was being watched, even now. He suddenly thrust the torch into the air and drew his sword as he whirled to look in every direction.

He froze when his eyes lit on a mass of tentacles with a silvery mirrored orb set atop them. The creature suddenly lunged at him and Avril leaped aside, his sword swinging wildly as he tried to avoid those tentacles. He felt the sword's blade slice into the creature as he felt a tentacle wrap around his other arm in which he held the torch.

The grip of the tentacle was strong and he involuntarily opened his hand letting the torch drop to the floor of the corridor. He again swung his sword at the creature and again he felt more than saw the blade slice into the creature. The blow was strong and he had hit a weak spot in the creature.

He watched as the silvery head flew off the top of the

mass of tentacles. Small explosions of light flew up out of the creatures severed head and miniature snakes writhed in the opening where the head had sat. The tentacle that gripped his arm suddenly relaxed and he yanked his arm free as he jumped away from the quickly collapsing creature.

He watched as the creature's tentacled body twitched, writhed and finally lay still on the cold floor of the corridor. He stood gasping and panting as his sudden rush of adrenalin wore off then he carefully moved forward and prodded the seemingly dead creature with the toe of his right boot. His sword was at the ready in case the creature should prove to be not dead but only pretending so it could draw him in again.

The creature did not respond so Avril kicked it this time and still it did not respond. Avril decided that it truly was dead. He looked the body over and a dawning realization washed over him as realized that this was no living creature. The tentacles were metal and not flesh.

Avril put aside his sword and began to examine the creature in detail, his fear gone replaced by curiosity of the unknown that had always driven him to find answers to mysteries which in turn had quickly propelled him to his current rank of captain in the Qualorian guard.

He gingerly lifted up one of the tentacles in his left hand and examined it more closely. It was flexible and smooth just as if it were made of flesh rather than metal. He then dropped the tentacle and examined more closely the miniature snakes that protruded from the creature's neck. Each of the miniature snakes were different colors, green, red, blue, orange and black. The ends of these snakes revealed what looked to be very fine copper strands. Avril was fascinated by what he was seeing.

He stood and went to where the head lay on the floor and knelt beside it. The base where his sword had passed through it also had the miniature snakes protruding and they were all the same colors as the ones from the now inert body. His sword must have severed these things which in turn killed the creature. He rolled the head over and saw scratches on its surface where it had skidded across the floor, marring its silvery smoothness.

He went back to the wall and located the three holes. Setting down the torch he used both hands and inserted his fingers into the holes. Nothing happened. He tried again and again nothing happened.

He knew that these holes would open this section of the wall as if it were a huge door. An idea suddenly occurred to him and he went back to the body of the dead creature and drew his sword. He carefully aimed his sword and cut off a tentacle then cut off two more of the tentacles. Gathering them up he moved back over to the wall and inserted the tips into the holes.

He pulled the tentacles out and suddenly the wall moved then opened. He jumped back and waited for the wall to complete opening. Finally it was open and he stood there and waited. Then when no danger presented itself he tied the three tentacles to his belt, gathered up the torch and moved through the opening.

He held the torch aloft and peered ahead and saw only another corridor of stone leading off into the darkness. Giving a mental shrug he proceeded forward into the darkness. As an experiment he set his torch down and moved ahead into the darkness. He slowly moved forward until the light from his torch was completely extinguished by distance and he stood in the darkness until his eyes adjusted.

Only darkness met his gaze. He waited but no drawings appeared on the wall and the inky blackness that was a complete absence of light filled his vision, momentarily giving him the impression of what it must be like to be blind and deaf as the corridor was completely silent.

He slowly backed up, retracing his steps until the glow

from his torch in the distance appeared, and at that point he turned around and quickly walked back to where the torch sat burning on the floor of the corridor. He retrieved the torch then turned again and moved back down the corridor. This time he could view the floor and walls and when he looked up he could see the ceiling was sloping downwards to completely entomb him in the corridor. He was beginning to get a feeling of claustrophobia as the ceiling progressively lowered as he moved forward. Finally the ceiling leveled out only a few feet above his head. He could see the smoke from his torch rise up and hit the ceiling only to spread outwards if he stopped.

He quickened his pace to keep ahead of the smoke from the torch so it would not sting his eyes. Then as he looked ahead he saw a faint light far ahead as if the light of day was at the end of a tunnel.

Hoping for an egress from these caverns to the outside world he broke into a sprint. As he moved toward the light he could begin to make out the opening he was fast approaching then he suddenly broke through the opening and quickly stopped, the torch flying from his hand as he waved his arms and backpedaled trying to maintain his balance.

The torch flew backwards to land beyond the entrance to the corridor he had just vacated and landed on the stone floor amidst a shower of sparks. Avril stood blinking in the sudden light of the morning sun that he had not seen in over six days. Looking down through watering eyes, with his right hand over his eyebrows to cut the glare of the sun's light he saw off in the distance the city walls of Qualor. He was standing in a cave opening along the Khoranain hills that overlooked the city from the west.

Avril could not believe his eyes. He had traveled the entire journey back to Qualor underground all the way from the mountains at the eastern border of Qualor's territory. Not only that he had to have passed underneath the city itself, deep in the bowels of the earth itself. Then he wondered, for he had traveled straight through this last passage from another passage that he had turned off of. The caverns he and Sturya had traveled had twisted and turned but the last few miles were straight.

Avril looked about and found a small path leading down from the cave entrance to the floor of the valley. Upon reaching the valley floor he headed directly toward Qualor knowing that when he reached the city he would be able to clean up, eat and rest. Then he shuddered as he marched across the valley floor, he still had to report to his company commander and explain how he had lived when his squad had died in an ambush from the Tribesmen.

Still he knew that his first duty had been to locate, capture and return to Qualor the barbarian he and his squad had been dispatched for originally. They never did find that barbarian. He figured that the man had gotten lost in the caverns among all the twists and turns and side passages that he and Sturya had avoided in an attempt to stay on the main passage.

Still, he believed the barbarian yet lived and if not underground lost among the labyrinth that was the caverns that he had traversed then perhaps the man had exited the cave before he had arrived there and had escaped into the mountains, perhaps even now he was leaving the eastern edge of the mountains behind as he journeyed east.

Avril had marched for hours through the countryside leading to Qualor and was becoming exhausted by the journey and burning from the noon day sun when riders approached him from the direction of Qualor. They rode up and surrounded him, so exhausted from his travels and weak from lack of food and water that he practically walked into one of the horses before he realized that the riders were there.

As he stumbled to a halt and looked up a hand reached down and clutched at his arm, steadying him so that he wouldn't fall. He looked into the face that the arm led up to and saw a captain of the Qualorian Guard.

"Captain Avril, what are you doing wandering around out here?" the other captain asked sardonically. "Don't you know that the sun at midday is bad for your health?"

"What?" replied an obviously dazed Avril. He was having trouble understanding what this other captain was saying to him.

Suddenly there was a commotion among the squad as to a man they all turned and drew their swords. They all faced the direction that Avril had come from and they were staring at a creature which was fast approaching.

Avril instinctively drew his sword and turned to face whatever this new threat might be even though he was near exhaustion and half dead from the effects of marching through the valley in the full heat of a summer day and from lack of recent food and water.

Looking up between the riders he saw another tentacled creature tearing across the valley floor in pursuit of himself. He had no doubt that the creature was after him. He had expected pursuit of some kind; he just did not think it would be another of these tentacled monsters.

He physically shoved aside a horse and rider and charged at the creature. He ducked beneath a swiping tentacle and slashed his sword across its torso; the wound splattered him with the black blood of the creature. Spinning he again slashed his sword and lobbed off a reaching tentacle. The severed tentacle continued along its arc and landed behind him with a sickening splattering sound even as he moved back away from the still advancing creature.

The Qualorian squad simply sat astride their mounts and watched as the battle unfolded. Avril backpedaling and swinging his sword wildly, the creature advancing, dripping

LEE E FULLER JR

gore from its open wounds where Avril's sword continued to slice and tear at its flesh. Avril's foot landed on the creatures severed tentacle and slid out from under him taking him down to the ground where he hit his head, leaving him on the ground, dazed and bleeding.

Right before he slipped into unconsciousness he saw the creature transform into Captain Garrig of the Qualorian Guard.

"He is mad!" exclaimed Garrig. "Attacking us like that, he fought as if we were devils chasing him!" he spoke to the soldiers surrounding him and the fallen Avril. The next words he directed at the unconscious man, "Well, Captain Avril never fear, we won't harm you, but we will get you back to Qualor where you will have some explaining to do concerning the whereabouts of your squad and why you are not with them."

"Hurkos, Swinda," he called out to his squad. "Secure the captain to a horse, and then we head back to Qualor. Make sure he is tied down tight, too. I don't want him waking up and attacking us again."

The two men dismounted from their horses and gathered up the fallen Avril. They dragged his unconscious form over to one of the extra horses that they had with them and lifted him onto the animal. They then took ropes and tied him into the saddle and secured his hands to the pommel. One of the two guards retrieved Avril's sword and placed it into a pack on the horse and the he gathered up the horse's reins and guided the animal back to his own horse.

"Wait," cried out Garrig after spotting the tentacles tied to Avril's belt. "What are those things he has tied to his belt?" he asked rhetorically as he dismounted and quickly walked over to where Avril was tied to the horse. He reached up and pulled on the leather cord that secured them to Avril's belt. They slid off of his belt and landed on the ground at Garrig's feet.

Garrig looked at the tentacles in puzzlement trying to decide what these things were. Finally after a few seconds of indecision he bent down and retrieved the tentacles and studied them. He saw how pliant and flexible they were and that they were constructed of metal and not leather as a whip would have been. Frowning he handed the tentacles to a soldier with instructions to guard these carefully then he remounted his horse and the squad rode away toward Qualor. They were observed by a multi-tentacled metallic creature just inside the cavern entrance where Avril had exited hours earlier. After the sentinel had determined that they were heading back to Qualor it silently sent a message to its master and upon receiving a reply it turned and retreated back in to the caverns.

Night was falling as Garrig and his squad rode up to the Eastern gates of Qualor. The soldiers at the gate were standing at attention as they rode up, which informed Garrig that a senior officer or even an aristocrat was present. He used hand signals to line his squad up and slow them down from a fast trot to a slow time march as they approached the gate.

As he neared the gate, General Ophister strode into view and raised his hand to halt Garrig and his squad. Garrig swiftly stiffened to attention and saluted the general.

Returning his salute the general spoke, "Captain Garrig, it is good to see you have returned safely to Qualor. I understand that you have rescued Captain Avril from the outer valley. Where is he?"

Garrig automatically answered, "We have him near the rear of the squad, sir."

In reply the general strode past Garrig and quickly stepped past Garrig's men until he came to the horse where the now conscience Avril sat, his hands still tied to the pommel. Before he could say another word the Grand Vizier suddenly appeared from within the gates and strode up to Captain Garrig.

"Captain," he began. "You and your men are to accompany me on a most urgent mission. General Ophister, please see to it that Captain Avril is taken care of, see to his injuries and keep him guarded. It is important that I speak with him upon my return."

"When will you be returning, sir?" the general inquired as he took the reins of the horse where Avril sat, his nose twitching from a sneeze that was not yet fully ready to explode out of him.

"Within three days, general. Captain Garrig, we leave now!" the Grand Vizier of Qualor commanded in a loud and reverberating voice that quickly brought each man of the squad to full alertness and readiness.

Garrig turned his horse around and rode the rear of his squad and each man turned his own mount to follow. The Grand Vizier rode directly behind Garrig; he seemed a menacing shadow so close did he follow the captain.

After the entire squad were all galloping behind Garrig, the Grand Vizier took the lead and led Garrig and his squad down the road for miles, slowing to a trot after a while.

Garrig was puzzled, the Grand Vizier had his own cadre of soldiers to guard and escort him anywhere he needed to travel. Why did he suddenly and without any explanation grab Garrig's squad just as they were returning from a three day patrol?

Garrig was trying to ascertain what was going on when a sudden realization of what had occurred at the city gates struck him like a thunderbolt. He suddenly pulled up on his mount and raised his hand halting his entire squad. The Grand Vizier rode on for a few more yards before he realized that the squad was no longer following.

The Grand Vizier reined his horse in to a halt and turned back toward the squad. Captain Garrig was sitting astride his horse and simply watching the Grand Vizier, his squad were all sitting on their horses watching their captain with looks of confusion on their faces. Knowing what he must do the Grand Vizier guided his horse forward a few steps and halted facing Captain Garrig.

"Why do you and your men stop, captain? I have not called for a halt." The Grand Vizier's voice was quiet but all heard it. His words were soft spoken, but all could hear the danger that they bespoke.

Garrig suddenly became nervous, still he was not about to back down. "How did General Ophister know we had Captain Avril with us when we arrived at Qualor?"

"A new device that was brought to us from a merchant hailing from Donaria. This device is called a telescope; looking through the device whatever is far away can be made to appear much closer."

"I have heard of telescopes, I had an opportunity to look through one a few weeks ago. Even looking through one and seeing Avril clear enough to make out who he was we would only been a few hundred yards away from the city walls. Yet the general and you were both at the gates by the time we arrived. There would not have been enough time for the two of you to arrive at the gates before we did."

"You are essentially correct, Captain Garrig. But you could not have known that the general and I were already at the gate. I had a message for the general from King Phiponoux and the general was in the vicinity of the gate. When word was brought of Captain Avril we both rushed to the gate."

"A very nice coincidence I am sure," answered Garrig, his nervousness suddenly vanishing from him. He suddenly knew that he and his men were forfeit. He began to wonder if he could strike down the Grand Vizier in the coming fight.

"Captain Garrig, if you and your squad do not wish

to accompany me further then I give you leave to return to Qualor. I have no more time to spend explaining my actions to you. I have a vital matter to attend to and I need to hurry. You and your men can either follow me or return to Qualor."

Garrig could not believe what was happening. The Grand Vizier had spun his horse around and galloped off into the distance and quickly disappeared from sight. He did not attack them as Garrig was sure he was going to do as soon as he confronted the man.

Garrig suddenly became very worried; if anything happened to the Grand Vizier when he and his men were to be guarding him then the king would have all their heads. Yet, the Grand Vizier had given them leave to return to Qualor, absolving them of any possible blame if he should come to harm.

Garrig was just about to chase after the Grand Vizier when suddenly one of his men shouted, fear prevalent in his breaking voice.

"Look out! They are all around us! Run, they're demons!"

Garrig twisted around in his saddle and saw creatures composed of multiple tentacles with silvery orbs on top of the writhing tentacles. The creatures were attacking the squad and men were dying and horses were neighing in terror and throwing riders from their backs in their panic to escape these things that swooped in from the darkness of the valley.

Garrig suddenly became aware that the tentacles of these creatures were identical to the two whip like things that Avril had tied to his belt. Avril had fought one of these things and survived!

He quickly took a count and realized that his men were almost all dead and that there were at least six of these creatures attacking. Quickly reaching a decision he twisted back in his saddle to face front and jabbed his heels into his mount's sides. The horse flew forward, the animal's fear spurring it into greater speed than it normally would have galloped.

Garrig turned his head, trusting the horse to follow the road and saw the last of his men get pulled from his mount and be quickly dispatched by two of the creatures. Then the slaughter faded from sight as the darkness of the night swallowed them from his sight. He continued riding hard, trying to catch up to the Grand Vizier.

Minutes passed and he reined in his horse to a halt. He listened and all he could hear was the heavy breathing of his horse. After a few moments the breathing of the animal quieted and Garrig strained to make out any noise but his ears could detect nothing. Not even the normal night noises of insects were to be heard.

Knowing that danger lurked Garrig drew his sword and sat waiting, ready to defend himself or attack. Then in the distance he heard the clip clopping of shod hoofs approaching from the darkness ahead of him. He tensed, ready for whatever foe that was drawing nearer.

Out of the darkness appeared the Grand Vizier. He rode up to within a few yards of Garrig and halted his horse. He spoke not a word but simply sat astride his mount, completely still his mask with its white eyes staring in his direction unnerving Garrig with its lifeless stare.

Finally unable to stand the silence any longer Garrig spoke. "What were those things, Vizier?" he demanded, turning slightly in his saddle so as to present a smaller target should he be attacked.

"What things, captain? Where are your men?"

"My men are dead! What were those creatures that attacked us!"

"Creatures? I have no idea. I heard you riding up behind me and thought you had come to your senses and were again providing my escort as you were commanded to do back at the gate."

"We have been set up. Why? What has my squad done to deserve this fate at the hands of your minions?"

"My minions? I have no minions, captain. Your words are bordering on treason."

"Treason? It is you who are the traitor! I hear that the king leaves tomorrow on an inspection tour, leaving you in charge. He will never return alive will he? You will have him killed and usurp his throne!"

"Nonsense I have been a loyal advisor for the king and for his father. I have had ample opportunities to take the throne and rule Qualor had I wished to do so. I have no desire to rule Qualor. I also begged the king to allow me to accompany him but he refused and ordered me to stay here and keep his throne safe. Should you fail to believe me then we shall go directly to King Phiponoux and you may present your charges of treason to him."

Garrig paused, suddenly uncertain. He had never known the grand Vizier to act against the throne in any manner. Still the rumors that swirled about the man, rumors of dark magicks performed, people disappearing into the night, the creatures that he controlled such as the Mujari Trackers and the Gnoscitain Bowmen. He was hovering between sureness and doubt, between action and inaction.

Still his squad had been attacked immediately after the Grand Vizier had galloped off into the darkness. His men had been pulled from their horses by tentacled creatures that had flowed out of the darkness along the road.

"Garrig, I command you to sheath your sword and follow me. We will go find your men and try to determine what exactly has happened," and having said that the Grand Vizier rode past Garrig and headed to where the scene of slaughter had taken place.

Garrig cast aside all doubt and indecision and lunged

at the Grand Vizier as he rode past him, sword raised and ready to plunge into the man's heart. But the blow never landed as a thick silvery tentacle curled about his arm and another slid around his torso. He felt a stinging sensation in the back of his neck then all went black.

CHAPTER IX

STUART STIFFLY RAISED HIMSELF up from the deck as he slowly regained consciousness. His body ached all over after being flung to the deck when the shockwave generated by the exploding Vegan scout vessel slammed into the Pegasus. He regained his command chair and sank into it as he shook his head to clear out the last of the cobwebs that encased his thoughts.

Looking about the bridge he saw Ivanova sprawled across her navigation console as was Martinez. He realized that the impact had thrown the ship forward, flinging him from his seat and the others into their consoles.

"Athena," he tried to croak out through a dry mouth. He rose from his command chair and unsteadily walked over to the water dispenser at the rear of the bridge. He drew a small cup of water and sipped at it for a moment before swallowing the contents at a gulp. With his mouth and throat now feeling better he now made a successful attempted at coherent speech.

"Athena, ship's status?" he asked the AI as he leaned against the bulkhead with his head hanging down.

"Minimal damage with exception of the shields, they

absorbed the majority of the shockwave's impact but this also overloaded the primary shield generator. Repair bots are completing repairs. Shields will not be operational for another 45 minutes when the replacement shield generator will be installed and brought online."

"Any causalities?" Stuart remembered to ask. He was not used to having anyone else on board having been alone for so long.

"None, Captain. The entire ship's complement was rendered unconscious from the impact, but sensors indicate all are alive and unharmed."

Stuart was thankful for that. He didn't want anyone getting seriously injured on his watch. He knew that the odds were against him though so he was content that the crises had passed without injury.

Ivanova was beginning to stir at her console so Stuart returned to his command chair and started checking ship's status on his console. When Ivanova had sat up in her seat and began to look her navigation console over Stuart spoke.

"Ms. Ivanova, the Pegasus is holding position. Athena took control while we were all unconscious and brought the ship to a full stop. We will be remaining here until repairs to the shield generator are completed. Will you please see to Captain Martinez?"

"Ivanova gave a groggy "Aye, sir" as she went to check on Martinez. Then it occurred to Stuart that he had two people down in an airlock.

"Commander, after you have verified that Captain Martinez is alright, would you go to airlock two and see to Ensign Clark and crewman Edwards?"

Ivanova was helping Martinez to sit up in his seat and nodded her acknowledgement to Stuart's request. Stuart sat looking over the readouts on his command console when he suddenly remembered that a Vegan body had been brought aboard.

"Athena, are sensors online?"

"All sensors are functional and online."

"I want a full scan, full sphere out to maximum range. Verify that there are no other ships within range."

"Proceeding with scan, time to completion 25 seconds," Athena replied.

Martinez and Ivanova had both stood up, Ivanova left the bridge as Martinez made his way over to Stuart's command chair.

"Captain," Martinez said. "Is the ship badly damaged?"

"No, minimal damage to the ship, but the shield generator overloaded," Stuart answered, then directed his attention to the ship's AI. "Athena, what other damage was there?"

"No other damages, the main power couplings went offline to prevent an overload. The power couplings were brought back online three minutes after shockwave impact and are functioning normally. Scan complete, no other vessels are within scanner range."

"Good. Keep a continuous scan going and alert me immediately if another ship is detected."

"Captain Martinez, shall we go and see the Vegan corpse that crewman Edwards brought aboard?"

"After you, sir," Martinez replied, his eyes aglow with excitement. He was to be one of the first men to ever be in the presence of a Vegan, dead or alive. This was an historical moment.

Both men left the bridge, leaving the ship in the hands of Athena. They quickly made their way down to the ship's sickbay where Edwards had deposited the corpse.

Upon entering the sickbay they saw Ivanova tending to Ensign Clarke. Edwards was standing over by another table, looking down at the alien body lying upon its cold surface.

Stuart went first to Ensign Clarke.

"Good work out there, Ensign. Are you alright?"

"Yes, sir, just a sprained wrist from my plunge into the airlock," he said as he held up his wrist that Ivanova had just finished bandaging.

"Small price to pay for your dramatic escape from the jaws of certain death," Stuart responded with a mock seriousness.

Clarke suddenly looked very nervous and Ivanova was beginning to look defensive, Stuart laughed and slapped the Ensign on his back. "I am only teasing you a bit, Ensign. You performed admirably out there and I am putting you in for a commendation."

Ivanova relaxed as Clarke suddenly brightened with the praise from Stuart. Stuart nodded at Ivanova and joined Martinez and Edwards at the table where the corpse of the Vegan lay. He spoke to Edwards before turning his attention to the corpse.

"I am also putting you in for a commendation, crewman. Retrieving this body is worth a medal or two considering that this is the first time that we have ever been able to capture a Vegan." Stuart reached out and shook Edward's hand. Edwards was suddenly self-conscience as he realized the implications of what it was that he had done. His name would adorn history books alongside the names of Clarke and Stuart.

Stuart turned and looked down at the corpse of the Vegan that Edwards had retrieved. The corpse was lying on its left side and the body was twisted and bent. The head was simply an extension of the body just as a snake's head was an extension of the snake's body. The mouth was slightly open and small sharp teeth could be seen through the open orifice. A slit above the mouth could be seen and Stuart assumed that there was another slit on the hidden side of the creature's face. The eyes were open and staring, they were

✦

milky white with no discernable pupils, but that could be an effect of the body being exposed to the vacuum of space.

The most interesting aspect of the body was the mechanical arms that had been surgically attached about a foot below the head of the creature. The arms were approximately two feet long and ended in tendrils rather than hands with fingers. There were seven tendrils at the end of each arm and the tendrils were made of the same metallic substance as the arms.

Stuart noticed something at the end of a tendril and leaned closer to be sure. "Look at the end of the center tendril on each arm; doesn't that look like a camera lens?"

Martinez answered in astonishment, "Yes it does! Why that must mean that the arms are wired directly into the brain for the camera to be useful."

Ensign Clarke who had also moved over to stare down at the corpse spoke up, "It must be able to do tasks with a high level of precision buy using the camera to get a much better view of what the tendrils are working on."

Stuart continued the train of thought aloud, "I would also think that, but the very design of the creature itself looks to preclude it from bending close to what the tendrils are doing whereas we can bend down to our hands and see close up without any extra cameras or lenses."

"But if that is the case, what built the arms and attached them to the Vegans?" Martinez asked.

"Just another mystery for us to solve. The best images that we have of the Vegans are blurry shots of them through opening in their ships. Now we have an entire corpse to examine. I want this body placed in stasis until we can get it in the hands of the proper scientific personnel back on Earth."

Edwards started pulling on gloves while Ivanova prepared the stasis chamber for the corpse. Stuart watched for a few moments then left the sickbay and headed to his own quarters. He needed a few moments alone and wanted to consult with Athena in private.

Upon reaching his quarters he dropped down onto his bunk. "Athena, ship's status, please."

Athena's voice wafted from the speaker set in the bulkhead above his bunk. Stuart closed his eyes and again pictured in his mind the image he carried of Athena in human form. Listening to her voice he could almost believe that she was in the room with him, perched above him on his bunk.

"All systems are nominal, captain. The shield generator repairs are nearly complete. Estimate that the Pegasus can get underway in 7 minutes."

"Excellent. What is our ETA to our destination?"

"At standard speed we will reach our destination in approximately 23 hours."

"ETA at maximum safe speed?"

"11 Hours and 43 minutes."

"I need a secure link to Admiral Higgins at starbase 12."

"Affirmative, captain, establishing secure link."

Stuart stood and stretched while Athena was making the connection to starbase 12. He moved over to sit at his personal desk and await the communication link to be established. He was surprised when Athena announced that Admiral Higgins was online and ready to speak to him. Usually it took quite a few minutes to get through to the admiral.

He hit the screen activator button and Admiral Higgins appeared in his screen.

"Captain Stuart, report," Higgins ordered.

"Sir, we have just encountered and destroyed a Vegan scout ship."

"What? A Vegan scout in your area? This is not good captain. The Vegans must know something is happening that could turn the tide of the war against them and are making an all out effort to discover what it is that we are up to. They knew enough to hit Argos Station and now they show up on your route out of the galaxy."

"Admiral, I do have some good news."

"That would be a refreshing change, captain."

"We managed to take out the Vegan scout before they could self-destruct."

"Are you telling me that you are in possession of an intact enemy scout vessel?" Higgins voice rose in excitement.

"No sir. The scout did self-destruct, but only after I was able to send a two man team to board the craft. My team made it out alive and unharmed before the self-destruct mechanism destroyed the ship. We have full video footage of the engine room and a couple of corridors and we were able to retrieve a Vegan corpse which is currently being placed in stasis."

Higgins simply stared at Stuart. The look of total and complete astonishment on his face gave Stuart a warm feeling inside. He had always wondered if Higgins ever showed any emotion other than stern gruffness.

Higgins now astonished Stuart more that he had astonished the admiral. He spoke very softly. "Captain, what you have accomplished is completely amazing. No one has ever managed to get more than a zoomed in photo of a Vegan. Now you have an actual corpse."

Higgins looked troubled for a moment then he continued.

"You have given me a conundrum to deal with, however your present mission is designated as Alpha Priority, yet what you have in stasis is also designated Alpha Priority.

"What is your current position?"

"Transmitting our coordinates now, Admiral," Stuart replied as he tapped out the numbers for the admiral.

"One moment, captain," Higgins responded as he

studied the current coordinates of the Pegasus with his own current star charts.

"Captain Stuart, I can have the Pandora's Box rendezvous with you at these coordinates in 17 hours. You will transfer the item you have in stasis to the Pandora's Box and then proceed on your current mission.

"And one other thing, captain I can ensure you that your new rank of captain will be permanent and you will also probably receive a medal and your crew commendations. Good work and god speed. Higgins out."

The screen went dark and Stuart sat in his seat and just stared at the now dark screen. Then he grinned and shook his head, fate was being kind to him right now.

"Athena, are we ready to get underway?"

"Affirmative, captain."

"Please have Captain Martinez, Commander Ivanova and Ensign Clarke meet me on the bridge," Stuart requested as he left his quarters.

When he arrived on the bridge he had no sooner sat down in his command chair when the other officers emerged onto the bridge and took their stations.

"Commander Ivanova," Stuart ordered as he taped out the rendezvous coordinates on his command console and transferred them to Ivanova's console. "Set course to the coordinates I just sent you, standard cruising speed 4.

"Captain Martinez, will you see to placing an armed guard by the stasis chamber round the clock. I do not want anything happening to our guest while he is in our care.

"Ensign Clarke, I want all the recordings made while you and Edwards were aboard the Vegan scout analyzed thoroughly. Also, I would like a complete scan made of the corpse if it has not already been done."

He was met with multiple voices replying "Aye, Sir." He sat back and settled comfortably into his command chair and began going over his console and studying the readouts. This mission was getting more interesting all the time.

———————————
———————————

Erat sat on the hard bench in his cell and watched the guard through half closed eyes. He took in all the details, the iron ring at the end of the man's ponytail, the prodigious broadsword at his waist, his chain mail shirt that covered his torso, the helmet with the spike on top and all the other myriad details about the man.

Erat had his arms crossed above his chest and his legs were stretched out in front of him with his left foot crossed over his right. He carried a sullen look upon his face and was patiently waiting to either be released or for his chance at escape.

The man in the cell next to him was lying on his bench and staring at the ceiling. Occasionally he would mumble something unintelligible just loud enough for Erat to hear the man's voice.

The outer door of the cell block suddenly opened and in strode two more guards. One was an officer and the guardsman that was guarding the cellblock quickly jumped to his feet. Erat was interested to note that the man could move so quickly for one of his size.

"Sergeant Garlgnor, Captain Rasnov wants to see you immediately. Corporal Blune will guard the prisoners until your return." the officer said.

Garlgnor did not budge, but a look of consternation appeared upon his face then he spoke up, "Sub-Captain, the Grand Vizier ordered me to guard the prisoners until he brought my relief personally. Also, you are outside of my chain of command as is Captain Rasnov."

"Both statements are true, but the situation has changed. The Grand Vizier rode out of Qualor just after nightfall and has not yet returned. Grand General Yousef is reorganizing the entire Qualorian guard and you have been reassigned from the Grand Vizier's personal guard to the main gate garrison."

Garlgnor stood indecisively, gently swaying from foot to foot. He had been a loyal man to the Grand Vizier since his enlistment and now he was being told that he was being transferred out of the man's personal guard and being sent to the main gate garrison. He suddenly noticed that Corporal Blune has unobtrusively moved his hand to his sword hilt and his sword was loose in the scabbard.

Garlgnor was decided and nodded at the sub-captain. "Very well then, sir I will report to Captain Rasnov immediately." He turned toward the cells and raised his voice to Erat.

"Ho, barbarian, you will no longer have my good natured self to keep you company," he bellowed at Erat as, with his back turned to the sub-captain and the corporal he swiftly drew his sword and spun back taking the two men by surprise. His sword sliced clean through Blune's right wrist cleanly severing the hand, he quickly followed with a follow up and sliced into the sub-captain's right leg, his sword cutting deeply into the thigh.

The sub-captain staggered back and into the door of the cell block. Blune had dropped to his knees and was holding his right wrist in his left hand and could only watch as his life's blood spurted out of the stump of his right wrist.

The sub-captain was trying to get the door opened to make good his escape when Garlgnor drove the point of his sword into the base of the man's neck, effectively severing his spinal cord and killing him. He then spun to his left and swung his sword through Blune's neck, removing the man's head. Blune's body remained kneeling for a few more moments, the left hand still holding the right wrist then the body collapsed into a pile of no longer living flesh.

Garlgnor wasted no time but threw open the cell block

✦

door and heaved the bodies of the sub-captain and the corporal out into the corridor that Erat could spy through the open door. The last thing to be thrown into the corridor was the severed hand of Blune.

Returning into the cell block, Garlgnor slammed the door closed and dropped a bar into place to prevent others from opening it from the outside. He then turned and looked at the two prisoners that were now both standing and staring at him with questioning looks upon their faces.

"We are now under siege. I fear that some evil is afoot in Qualor and I can do naught but remain here and guard the two of you from whatever tries to assault us. I hope that the rest of the Grand Vizier's personal guards fare as well as we have to this point my friends."

Erat said nothing; he just stood in his cell and scowled at Garlgnor. Sturya however, had no compulsion to remain silent.

"So what now? We are trapped in here with no food or water and the entire Qualorian Guard soon to come and beat down the door."

"They will not break down the door, the corridor is designed in such a way that no battering ram can be used effectively and the door is reinforced, it is iron with wooden panels on the outside. The Grand Vizier designed this entire cellblock.

"Do not worry about food or water either, there is a sufficient store of each cached in this cell block, although cleverly hidden. We shall not starve, although we may wish we had after eating the same food for a few weeks."

"Weeks!" Exclaimed Sturya. "I don't want to sit in this cell for weeks! I have done nothing to be imprisoned for and I demand that you free me!"

"Nothing?" Garlgnor said quietly, a dangerous tone entering his voice. "Then you had nothing to do with the ambush of Captain Avril's squad some days ago? You have a twin perhaps that led the ambush?"

Sturya paled at the accusations as he knew they were true, and the way that Garlgnor was now holding his sword, pointed directly at him caused him to keep his silence.

"As I thought. You were discovered in the forbidden caverns beneath Qualor. Do you know why they are forbidden Tribesman?" At Sturya's slight shake of his head Garlgnor continued. "They are forbidden for two reasons, the first is that the city foundations reach down into them and those foundations need to be protected else the city collapse. The second reason is that the Grand Vizier himself has hidden and secret chambers down there, chambers that hold terrible secrets. All think that the Grand Vizier is a noble and good man, and truly he is all of that. But he is also a terrible wizard and he has powers at his disposal and some of those powers hold things imprisoned in those secret chambers. Things so horrible if even one of them should get loose then not only would Qualor be in mortal peril but the entire world could suffer so greatly that mankind itself could be eradicated from the face of the world."

Erat watched as Sturya stepped backwards away from the now terrible countenance of Garlgnor. He felt superstitious fears of his own chilling his spine but he refused to step back as had the Tribesman. No, he would stand his ground.

"Garlgnor speaks the truth little Tribesman," Erat rumbled. "I was captured by one of the demons that the Grand Vizier controls. It gave me a blow to the head and when I awoke I was in a small stone cave with no way in or out, only a wizard could have imprisoned me thusly. After a time I fell asleep and then I woke here, something that only a powerful wizard could have done."

"No wizard brought you in, barbarian; two men of my own squad dragged your unconscious carcass in here and placed you in that cell."

Suddenly there was a pounding upon the door, it was muffled and after a moment stopped to be followed by a muffled voice shouting for the door to be opened in the name of the Qualorian Imperial Guard.

"Ho now," said Garlgnor "the Imperial Guard now comes banging at the door. I'll not open that door for anyone until the Grand Vizier himself appears."

"How do you know that when he comes knocking it will actually be him?" Sturya asked.

"He will have no need to knock; he can open the door from without through his own means."

Erat said nothing as Garlgnor returned to his stool and sat down as if nothing had happened. He sat with his back to the wall as before, simply looking at the prisoners for a few moments. When nothing else was said by either of the two imprisoned men he then brought out a cleaning cloth and began to wipe down his sword.

"Have to keep my steel clean and ready for next time," he muttered under his breath. Then he quietly began to hum to himself as he worked on his sword.

―――――――――――
―――――――――――

The Grand Vizier stood by his horse and fed it small candies from his right palm while his left hand gently stroked the animal's mane. "What do you think Grapthar? Will we be able to ride gently today or shall we be forced to gallop down the road, eh?"

The Grand Vizier turned as footsteps approached from behind. Captain Garrig stopped and saluted smartly. "Sir, camp is broken and the squad is ready to move out," he reported.

"Very good, captain. Have your men mount up and we shall head back to Qualor."

"Yes, sir" Garrig answered then turned back toward the squad. He moved a few feet away from the Grand Vizier before he bellowed out to his sergeant. "Sergeant, have the men mount up, we're moving out."

The Grand Vizier turned his attention back to Grapthar. "Well my friend we are going home. I am sure you will be glad to return to the comforts of your stable." The horse nudged his arm. "Sorry, I am all out of sweets for you. When we get back to Qualor I will see to it that you have another sweet. Now, let's head home, shall we?"

The Grand Vizier mounted his horse and rode up beside Captain Garrig. He nodded once at Garrig and Garrig motioned the squad forward. The sound of the horses' hooves falling upon the stone road soon turned into background noise as the squad traveled down the road. The Grand Vizier was left to his own thoughts as Captain Garrig dropped back into position three riders behind him.

The Grand Vizier smiled to himself beneath his mask, remembering the look of shock upon Garrig's face two nights ago when the sentinels rose out of the darkness and pulled him from his horse. Garrig and his men all had different memories of the last few days, all believing that they had accompanied him out to meet with a chieftain of the Tribesmen of Hern for secret negotiations.

None of them questioned that they escorted him instead of his own personal guards as he was representing the king in this matter and not himself. This subterfuge was necessary to erase and rewrite their memories concerning Captain Avril and the sentinel tentacles that he had tied to his belt. They would remember rescuing Avril, but the tentacles were completely removed from their memories.

They would also remember escorting him last night to the secret negotiations with the chieftain and the fact that the chieftain never showed up. They would remember camping out for two nights and waiting for the man, the night sounds of the hills and even the stars twinkling in the clear air of the hills. They would not remember the sentinels reaching out to them in the darkness and tearing them from their horses.

Captain Garrig rode up beside him. "Sir, with your permission I would like to send scouts out to cover our flanks."

"Unnecessary, Captain there will be no tribesmen out there to guard against."

"I don't understand, sir."

"The chieftain that we were to meet would be here only if he could arrive without arousing suspicion of the other chieftains. Since he did not show up, there is no need to worry about tribesmen in the area. They have no reason to venture this far west."

"You are probably correct, sir, but I would feel a bit more assured if I could post a scouting picket. Perhaps the reason the chieftain did not show up was that he was discovered and now an ambush is being prepared," argued Garrig.

"No Captain, there will be no ambush. Were we to be attacked it would have happened yesterday at the latest. More likely it would have happened when we first showed up the night before last," the Grand Vizier responded.

"Very well, as you say, sir."

"Captain, I wish to be back in Qualor before nightfall, please speed up the column to a quicker pace."

"Yes, sir," Garrig replied, happy to move faster to leave the hills behind and return to Qualor.

For the next several hours the riders alternated between a quick trot and a steady walking of their horses. At one point the Grand Vizier ordered them along at a fast gallop for 10 minutes, burning up a few miles travel in the process. The sun was getting low in the sky when the valley that surrounded Qualor finally came into view. The Grand Vizier immediately halted the column. He ordered everyone to dismount as he dropped off of his horse and withdrew a small telescope from his saddlebags.

He extended the telescope and peered through the device at the city walls away in the distance. Garrig watched as the Grand Vizier moved the telescope from side to side peering at the walls of Qualor and the surrounding countryside.

"Captain, have your men move back over the ridge and set up a perimeter. I want everyone on full alert."

"Is there something wrong, sir?" asked Garrig as he motioned to the sergeant to do what the Grand Vizier had just ordered.

"I am not sure, but why would the city garrison be so heavily stationed on the walls and at the gates?" came the reply to which Garrig did not have an answer.

The Grand Vizier motioned to Garrig that the captain should take Grapther's reins and remove the horse back over the ridge. The grand Vizier then moved over to an outcropping of rock in the ridge and sat down. He brought the telescope back to his eye and began looking over the valley floor. Minutes passed as he studied the valley floor, moving the telescope back and forth, peering at the activity going on down below. Finally he rose to his feet and strode back over the ridge to where Garrig and the squad were awaiting his return.

"Captain, I need your best scout," the Grand Vizier said as he approached. "Quickly, time is of the essence."

Garrig called out to his squad, "Odelas! Up here, now!"

A soldier sprang to his feet from where he was sitting on the ground chewing a piece of jerky. He dropped the jerky into a pocket of his tunic as he trotted over to where the Grand Vizier and Garrig stood waiting.

"Odelas?" asked the Grand Vizier to which the soldier simply nodded his head. "Come with me."

Odelas followed the Grand Vizier back over the ridge. The Grand Vizier stopped and peered through the telescope, focusing on a certain area down in the valley where several groups of soldiers were gathered.

Handing the telescope to Odelas he said, "Observe those soldiers down there and examine the area. It is where you are going."

Odelas took the proffered telescope and gingerly peered through the device. He had never seen a telescope before, it was akin to magic. He gasped and nearly dropped the device when he looked through it and was suddenly brought closer to the soldiers moving about down in the valley. He soon became used to the telescope then he began to concentrate on his destination. He picked out his route down and his return route. He studied the layout of the area then quickly figured out how to slip in and out again. Finally he reluctantly handed the telescope back to the Grand Vizier.

Knowing that Odelas coveted the telescope the Grand Vizier made him a promise. "Find out what is happening and return here safely and I will give you this telescope."

Odelas's eyes lit up and he snapped out a crisp "Yes, sir!" before he moved off to infiltrate the soldiers down below.

The Grand Vizier watched Odelas's progress with the naked eye through the lens of the telescope. He would occasionally turn his gaze upon the groups of soldiers and to the city walls farther behind the milling warriors. Finally as darkness was descending upon the valley he rose up and retreated back to the other side of the ridge where Garrig and his squad were waiting.

Walking into the small encampment that Garrig's men had established he was pleased to note that no camp fires had been established and that the men were eating cold rations. He nodded his approval at Garrig and moved over to Grapthar and patted the horse's neck. He returned the telescope to the saddlebags and withdrew a cold ration for himself. He took the cold ration and moved up into the trees that rose up to the ridge. He quietly walked through the trees and carried his ration in his hand. Finally when he was well away from the small encampment of Garrig and his squad he took the ration and twisted the bottom of the container. There was a slight hissing noise he removed the lid. He carefully sipped the now hot soup and reflected on the activities he had observed down in the valley.

He stumbled upon a downed tree and sat down upon the broken and cracked trunk. He quietly finished his soup and peered into the darkness, listening to the noises of insects and small nocturnal animals going about their business. He sat and wondered what could be happening in the valley and with Qualor. The walls and gates were heavily guarded. The last time that many guards had been assembled upon the walls and manning the gates was when the Tribesmen of Hern moved west en mass several years ago. They never made it to the valley thanks to the combined hosts of Qualor and Donaria.

After a couple of hours had passed he stood and stretched. He returned to the camp and returned the empty soup container to his saddle bags. He brought out a feedbag and strapped it to Grapthar's face and moved over the where Captain Garrig stood quietly conversing with his sergeant.

"What news, captain?" the Grand Vizier asked with lowered voice.

"All is quiet, sir. Odelas has not yet returned. Are we staying here for the night?"

"I don't know yet. Have the men rest but ready to ride at a moment's notice."

"Yes, sir," Garrig answered then he and the sergeant moved away and began to go around the camp quietly relaying the information to the men who were sitting about and quietly talking, eating or sleeping.

The Grand Vizier moved up the ridge and again crossed over it to where he had earlier been standing. Now he could make out the lights of Qualor glowing in the distance, the thousands of lamps of the city throwing a welcoming glow into the valley. He could make out the multiple towers and spinnerets of the city rising into the night sky, light spilling out of the windows of each of them. Closer to where he sat he could make out multiple campfires where the groups of soldiers had encamped for the night. He wished that he had thought to bring the telescope with him; he might be able to locate Odelas.

He had been standing there gazing into the valley for a few minutes when a shadow detached itself from the shadows of the road and the silhouette of a man appeared. The silhouette shortly took on definition and the features of Odelas hove into view. He looked tired and was covered in dirt and bits of plant matter from the valley floor. He saw the Grand Vizier and approached him quickly.

"Sir, it is the king. He has been usurped by Baron Mugior. The soldiers are there to arrest you when you return. They know you will need to pass them to return to Qualor and they are waiting." Odelas was panting from his efforts to jog up the steep hillside and to the ridge.

"The Baron has the support of the military then?" the Grand Vizier asked.

"Not all, but enough. Those loyal to the king have been imprisoned or killed. Your personal guard the same," answered Odelas.

"Hmm, it seems we have to rescue the king and dethrone the baron. Come Odelas, you have done well, let us return to the camp and inform Captain Garrig of our predicament."

The two men returned over the ridge and walked back into the encampment where Garrig and his squad waited. "Everyone," the Grand Vizier called out. "Assemble into a line here," he gestured with his right arm. His left arm had slipped into his robes, his left hand completely out of sight.

After squad fell into line, the Grand Vizier motioned Odelas to join them. When everyone was lined up, Garrig turned to the Grand Vizier and saluted him. "Sir, the squad is assembled and ready for your commands."

Nodding at Garrig the Grand Vizier motioned him to also go and join the line. Puzzled at the request, Garrig nevertheless, acquiesced and moved into the line. When the Grand Vizier was satisfied that all were there and assembled he began. "Soldiers of Qualor, we have a problem. It would seem that Baron Mugior has usurped the throne of the king. He has imprisoned the king and even now sits upon the throne. What I propose is that we go into Qualor, rescue the king and remove the baron."

There was a sudden outburst of whispering among the squad. The Grand Vizier let it continue for a moment then he once again raised his voice to the men. "Before we can do this, however I need to determine which of you are aware of what has happened and are loyal to the baron."

This time there was shocked silence. Suddenly each man looked to the man standing on either side of his place in the line. Who might not be loyal? Who here would betray their oath to the king? No, it was inconceivable, yet there were those who had done exactly that and now stood up to protect the usurper Mugior.

The Grand Vizier suddenly withdrew his left hand from beneath his robes and held aloft a strange looking orb. He slowly looked from left to right going down the line of men then he spoke. "This sphere," he said holding the orb high into the air so that all may see it "contains the trapped soul of a demon. This demon is very special. This demon can sense truth from falsehood. I will now go among you and, one at a time, I shall ask where your loyalty lies."

Every man suddenly became nervous. They were to be judged by a demon held by their Grand Vizier. They all knew that the Grand Vizier was a powerful sorcerer, but none had realized just how powerful until now. Only the most powerful and greatest of sorcerers could trap and control a demon. They all watched as the Grand Vizier approached the man at the end of the line. The Grand Vizier held the orb up, inches away from the soldier's face. He gazed intently at the soldier for a few moments then he spoke.

"Are you loyal to King Phiponoux?" the grand Vizier asked, his voice barely above a whisper. The soldier blanched at the question and moved back slightly, giving way to the orb held up to his face.

"I am loyal to King Phiponoux, I swear it!" The words gushed out of the man's mouth as a waterfall would explode over the edge of a precipice.

The orb did nothing, until a golden glow emanated out from the sphere to envelop the man before fading away. The Grand Vizier looked up at the soldier then smiled grimly. "You are indeed loyal to the king. Draw your sword and follow me down the line." The soldier heaved a sigh of relief and did as the Grand Vizier bade him. The grand Vizier moved to the next soldier in line and repeated the process.

Within minutes only Captain Garrig remained. All the men of the squad had proven to be loyal to King Phiponoux. The Grand Vizier then raised the orb to the face of Captain Garrig and repeated the question again, "Are you loyal to King Phiponoux?"

"I am loyal to the king," replied Garrig without a trace of fear or apprehension in his voice.

The Grand Vizier did not move. He stood there and continued to stare into the eyes of Garrig. Then he spoke again. "Are you loyal to King Phiponoux?" his voice was quieter than the first time he asked. The men of the squad remained grimly quiet as they surrounded their captain.

Garrig looked nervous for the first time. He cleared his throat and took a moment to phrase his answer carefully. "I am loyal to the king," he again replied.

The Grand Vizier took a half step back then asked again, "Are you loyal to King Phiponoux, yes or no?"

Garrig began to perspire, even though the night air was cold at this altitude. The squad tightened up their circle around him. "I am loyal," he began but was cut off by the Grand Vizier.

"Are you loyal to King Phiponoux, yes or no!" he shouted at Garrig

"I am loyal to," Garrig was again cut off.

"Yes or no!"

"Yes!" yelled Garrig back at the Grand Vizier.

All eyes turned and rested upon the orb in the hand of the Grand Vizier. They all waited for the golden glow. The orb began to glow, not gold but red, a deep blood hued red. Captain Garrig was suddenly surrounded by a ring of swords all pointing at him. He didn't move, he didn't dare for to do so would have meant instant death.

The Grand Vizier still held the orb up to his face.

"Who are you loyal to, Captain? Baron Mugior?"

"No, not the baron," Garrig answered. The orb turned golden.

"If not Mugior, then who?" demanded the Grand Vizier.

Garrig looked around at the faces of the men he had once commanded. There was no sign of forgiveness or mercy in any man's eyes. He suddenly realized that the Grand Vizier could not protect him from the swords that were only inches away from his body. He had betrayed these men and they were ready to forgive his betrayal by plunging their swords into his body and killing him. The only thing that was keeping him alive was his refusal to answer the question of where his loyalty lay. He knew that as soon as he answered that question that he would die.

"Again, who are you loyal to, Garrig?" the Grand Vizier asked. "You will tell me now, willingly, or I shall pull the information from your mind in a manner most unpleasant."

Garrig suddenly made up his mind. He straightened up and looked directly at the Grand Vizier's milky white eye pieces f the man's mask and said, "My loyalty is not to Qualor or King Phiponoux. My loyalties are my own and you shall never know them!" Garrig then leaped backwards and was impaled by three of the swords that were pointed at his back. He stiffened briefly, his body convulsed then went limp as the life fled his body.

"Who do you suppose he was loyal to, sir?" asked the sergeant of the Grand Vizier.

Looking down at Garrig's body the Grand Vizier sighed as he answered. "I don't know sergeant, but I do have my suspicions. Have the body searched, although I doubt that you will find anything."

The Grand Vizier put away the orb and moved away from the soldiers. He needed to come up with a plan to rescue the king and deal with the baron. It was fortuitous that he had ridden out of Qualor two nights ago; else he would have been captured or killed. Since he was not present when the coup happened he now had a chance to put things right.

He had discovered a spy in Garrig that he would not have discovered had not the coup taken place, so that was a bonus. He did not know who Garrig was spying for or if the man had done more than gather information. He could only speculate who he might have been spying for and how long he had been spying.

Baron Mugior would have to be removed. He had always known that the baron was an ambitious man; unfortunately, he had not realized how ambitious the baron was until now. Yes, the baron would have to be removed and questioned. The Grand Vizier would personally do the interrogation of the baron; in fact, he looked forward to it with unmitigated anticipation.

✦

CHAPTER X

"Captain, the Pandora's Box is hailing us," Ensign Clarke informed him. Stuart sat up a bit straighter in his seat and nodded at Clarke.

"On screen, ensign," he replied.

"Pandora's box, this is Captain Stuart of the Pegasus."

"Captain, this is Captain Marshall of the Pandora's Box. I understand that you have cargo to transfer over to us for transport back to Starbase 12?"

"Yes, captain. Have you been informed to the nature of the cargo?" Stuart asked, wondering if Higgins had told them of the Vegan body.

"No we haven't, captain. I was told that you would have it ready for transport and that it was to have a full security team on it at all times."

"The cargo is ready for transport, captain. I will have it delivered to the Pandora's Box at your convenience," Stuart replied. He wanted to see the look on Marshall's face when the other captain saw the nature of the "cargo," but he would be remaining on board the Pegasus.

"Captain, I have been ordered to come aboard the Pegasus to retrieve the cargo so you can be on your way immediately. These orders come straight from Admiral Higgins."

"Understood, Captain I'll meet you in the hanger bay. Pegasus out," Stuart acknowledged. "Ivanova, you have the bridge. Captain Martinez, would you please accompany me to the hanger bay?"

"I'd be delighted to, Captain. I want to see the body again."

"Good enough, Captain. Mister Clarke, will you please have the crewmen bring the body to the hanger bay," Stuart ordered as he and Martinez left the bridge.

The two captains arrived at the hanger bay at the same moment as the stasis box with the body of the Vegan. Stuart and Martinez stood aside so the box could pass into the bay. Two anti-grav units were attached to the box, one at the front and the other at the rear of the box. Two crewmen were guiding the box, Edwards was at the front anti-grav unit and crewman Simons was at the rear anti-grav unit. The stasis box was similar in shape to a coffin as it was designed to contain the body of a person who had been badly wounded until that person could be transported to a full medical facility. The stasis box was commonly referred to as a 50-50 box by federation military personnel. This was in the early days of the stasis boxes, half a century ago, when military forces wounded in battle would be placed into the boxes and transported back to rear areas where surgeons waited for the casualties. The early stasis boxes would disrupt the neural pathways in the human brain 56% of the time, resulting in massive cerebral hemorrhaging when the boxes were deactivated. Being placed into a stasis box meant the chance of survival was 50-50. The stasis boxes no longer caused cerebral hemorrhaging, but the name stuck.

Stuart and Martinez walked up to the stasis box and peered into the clear foot square window inset into the lid. All that could be seen was a small portion of the Vegan's upper head. Not enough detail to even determine what was in the box. Were a human lying in the box anyone looking into the window would be seeing the face of whoever was inside.

Stuart and Martinez continued looking into the window and neither man was satisfied with the view. They finally gave up trying to view the body of the Vegan and turned away from the stasis box. Athena's voice suddenly filled the hanger bay.

"Activating atmosphere shield and opening main hanger doors," the AI's voice boomed from the speakers throughout the bay. Stuart watched as a faint bluish glow sprang into existence in front of the main hanger door. Seconds later the main hanger door retracted into the deck of the hanger bay. The incoming shuttle floated to a halt outside of the hanger bay and was pulled forward by invisible tractor beams that brought the shuttle into the bay and landed it 10 feet away from where everyone was waiting.

The hatch of the shuttle withdrew into the side of the shuttle as a short ramp emerged. Moments later Captain Marshall emerged followed by three other men, another officer and two crewmen from the Pandora's Box.

"Permission to come aboard," Marshall requested from the top of the shuttle ramp. He and his men proceeded down the ramp only after Stuart replied with the standard, "Permission granted" answer of navel tradition.

Marshall stopped in front of Stuart and reached out his hand. "Captain Stuart, pleasure to meet you, sir."

Stuart took the proffered hand, shook it and said, "The pleasure is mine Captain Marshall. You are somewhat of a legend in the fleet."

"Not so much really, a couple of minor successes that could not have been accomplished had I not had a competent crew and a fine ship." Marshall replied contritely. Stuart made a point of Marshall's praise of his ship and crew. The man was giving credit to his crew for his successes. Stuart was sure that should the Pandora's Box ever have an unsuccessful mission that her captain would take full responsibility and protect his crew form any blame or backlash that might result.

"Captain, we have a very special cargo for you," Stuart said. He was using all his control to contain his excitement and appear cool and nonchalant.

"Of that I have no doubt whatsoever. Admiral Higgins was very particular concerning your cargo. Can you tell me what cargo I am to take aboard my ship? Is it dangerous?"

"Captain, it is dangerous in the sense that if any member of the Vegan race were to find out you carried this cargo then the Pandora's Box would become the primary target for the entire Vegan fleet." Stuart replied, perhaps over dramatically. Marshall raised his eyebrows skeptically. He knew that Stuart was a recently promoted Captain and thought that perhaps he was trying to impress a senior captain. He looked over to Captain Martinez whose face was neutral in expression. He had met Martinez years ago when he was a Lieutenant serving aboard the Lillehammer and the ship had patrolled the sector that had included Argos Station. He had found the man to be competent and professional. He wondered at his presence here aboard the Pegasus.

"Captain Stuart, I take it that the cargo is inside that fifty-fifty box behind you," Marshall stated.

"That's right. Come have a look at it before you take it aboard." Stuart said as he gestured Marshall towards the stasis box. Marshall moved over to the stasis box as Edwards and Simons moved aside for the captain. Marshall looked into the viewing window and tried to make out what the stasis box contained. He stared and stared but it was impossible for him to determine what was inside the stasis box. Finally he gave up trying to figure out what was inside the stasis box and straightened up. He turned around and gave questioning look to Stuart.

Stuart could no longer contain his excitement and a huge grin broke out on his face. "Captain Marshall you are not going to believe me if I tell you what is in there. Athena, can you please show us the recording from sickbay?"

A holographic projection sprang up on the deck to their left. The projection was full scale and showed the Vegan body on the examination table in sickbay. Captain Marshall looked at the recording for a few moments until the realization of what he was seeing hit him. He suddenly spun and stared open mouthed at the stasis box.

"Captain Stuart does that fifty-fifty box contain a live Vegan?" he asked incredulously.

"No, sir the Vegan is dead. We retrieved it after we disabled the scout ship it was on. Crewman Edwards here, "he nodded at Edwards, "went aboard with Ensign Clarke and they retrieved this body and made some recordings."

Marshall looked at Stuart and Edwards with astonishment. "Captain Stuart you called me a legend, I think that you are going to become a larger legend than I could ever hope to be." Then Marshall was suddenly all business. "Lieutenant Marks, get this stasis box loaded and let's get out of here."

While the lieutenant and crewmen attended to the loading of the stasis box Marshall stepped aside with Stuart. Martinez joined the two captains.

"How did you manage to disable a Vegan ship?" Marshall asked Stuart.

"We managed to get a missile through their defenses. My report has all of the pertinent details. But the condensed version is that we managed to fire a missile away which then arced around on an oblique trajectory and we held their attention with missiles fired directly at them and our particle beams on full barrage. The one missile came at them from behind and detonated on impact with their shields. Once their shields overloaded we continued the full barrage of the particle beams. Our beams shredded their hull and then they lost all power as their hull integrity collapsed."

"You scored a hit on their main reactor that took it out without destroying their ship?" asked Marshall.

"Correct. And our beams shredded enough of their hull that the crew died when vacuum replaced their atmosphere. There was no one left to activate their self-destruct. At least that is what we originally thought. It turns out that they did get the self-destruct activated, but when they lost their main reactor the self-destruct shut down. They did have battery backup, but it took 30 minutes for their batteries to charge enough for the self-destruct to resume the sequence."

"Amazing. You have found a weakness in their defenses that no one else has found."

"No," Stuart firmly stated. "We did not discover a weakness; we got lucky all the way around. If they would have detected that missile we would not be here now. Maybe they had a sensor that was out, maybe they were inexperienced, but whatever the reason, we got lucky."

"Yes, you did. But your luck has gathered a wealth of information that will provide us with opportunities for decades to come. With one of their bodies, we can determine their biological makeup and construct bio-weapons that will be effective against them. With the data you gathered on their ship, we can find clues to their implosion weapons, what type of star drive they utilize, how they power their ships. We can also analyze your attack data and use it to better aim our weapons during confrontations with their fleets.

"Captain Stuart, what you have accomplished is incredible and it will pay dividends for our ships for years to come. Your decision to board a disabled Vegan ship rather than to move away in anticipation of it destructing shows courage and determination in the face of the enemy. Sir, I commend and congratulate you and your crew." Marshall finished then came to attention and smartly saluted Stuart.

Stuart was completely taken aback but his training took over and he snapped to attention and returned the salute in his best parade ground manner. Martinez took a step back, away from the other two captains. He did not wish to intrude upon this small tribute from one captain to another.

"Sir, "Lieutenant Marks called out to Marshall. "We have the cargo aboard and secured for transport.

"Very good lieutenant, prepare for departure," Marshall replied. He then turned to Stuart and held his hand out again. Stuart took and shook Marshall's hand. "Good luck in whatever mission you are on Captain Stuart."

"Thank you, sir. Godspeed on your journey back to Starbase 12," Stuart offered.

Stuart and Martinez watched as Marshall boarded the shuttle. The ramp retracted into the hull and the hatch closed. A few moments later the shuttle lifted a few feet off of the deck of the hanger bay and rotated to face the open hatch. Athena used the tractor beams gently to push the shuttle from the bay. After the shuttle had cleared the hanger bay the main hatch closed and the atmosphere shield deactivated.

"Captain to bridge," Stuart said into a comm unit located next to the door into the landing bay. "Resume course, top speed."

"Resuming course at top speed, captain," came the reply from Ivanova.

"Let's head back to the bridge, we have a ways to go before we can test your equipment," Stuart said to Martinez.

Minutes later Stuart was again on the bridge, seated at his command console. He watched the main view screen as the Pandora's Box faded into the depths of space. He scanned his console then sat back in his seat and relaxed for a moment. So far everything was proceeding favorably and they were finally on their way to the isolated star outside of the galactic plane. There was one giant star with one giant planet just waiting for them to come and explore everything and find out all the system's hidden secrets.

"Captain Martinez," Stuart said. "What do we need to do to get your equipment set up?"

"Very little, Captain. Everything is ready to be assembled by my technicians and crewmen. We need access to the main reactor."

"That shouldn't be a problem. Athena, please coordinate with Captain Martinez and provide any assistance or access that he requests."

"Acknowledged, Captain," Athena's voice replied from the overhead speakers.

"Athena, will you please share the information that we received from the last probe that the Pegasus launched with Ensign Clarke?" Stuart addressed the AI. He then turned his attention to Clarke. "Ensign I would like you to go over the probe data and present your conclusions to me. As we don't have a lot of time until we reach our destination, I would like to hear your conclusions in three hours."

"Yes sir," Clarke replied before he turned his attention to the task that Stuart had assigned to him.

"Commander Ivanova, what is our ETA at our current speed?"

"4 hours and 16 minutes, sir." She replied looking down at the readouts in her helm controls.

"Ensign Clarke, have that report ready in 2 hours, not three."

"Aye, aye, sir," Clarke replied.

"Commander, you have the bridge," Stuart said to Ivanova as he stood up from his command console. He then left the bridge and went to his cabin where he seated himself at his desk and started bringing his ship's logs up to date and taking care of the requisite paperwork that his position as ship's captain demanded. Were he the captain of a cruiser or larger vessel a yeoman would have been assigned to him and the basic paperwork forms would have been all filled out for his review and signature. Unfortunately, the Pegasus was a small ship and he had to fill out all the forms himself. Athena could have done everything for him, but as Athena was an AI there were restrictions in place that prevented her from completing any paper work associated with the running of the Pegasus. Technically, Athena was the mind of the Pegasus. If the crew were to become incapacitated Athena could assume control of the Pegasus and guide it back to a starbase for assistance.

Stuart was just finishing up the inventory usage report when his comm whistled for his attention. "Stuart here." He said after slapping at the comm respond button.

"Ensign Clarke here, sir. I have my completed analysis of the probe data ready for you."

Stuart started; he didn't realize that 2 hours had already passed. Plus his stomach was growling for attention. "Pipe it down here, ensign, Stuart out."

Stuart looked at his desk's built in monitor as he hit a series of switches until Ensign Clarke's report appeared. He began to read what the ensign had put together. The star was five times more massive than Sol. There was a single planet in orbit about the star. The planet was five times larger than Jupiter, yet its gravity was .05 below Earth normal gravity. The planet had 17 moons in orbit. The moons ranged in size from 4530 kilometers in diameter to 21,117 kilometers in diameter. The probe did not give atmosphere readings on the planet or the moons. Ensign Clarke had added other data to his report that he garnered from the probe. The planet was 2 AU in distance from the star. Since the star itself was much larger and hotter than Sol this made for the possibility that the planet, or one of the moons, could support life provided a suitable atmosphere was involved.

Stuart finished the report then sat back and looked at the amount of paper work he had finished and the stack he had yet to process. "Athena, are we in sensor range of our destination?"

"Not yet, Captain. Sensor range in 23 minutes."

"Stuart to Clarke."

"Clarke here, sir," answered the ensign.

"We will be in sensor range in 23 minutes, ensign. I want a full scan undertaken as soon as we are in range."

"Aye, sir."

———————
———————

The Grand Vizier held his hand up bringing the squad to a halt. He had taken the squad and ridden a trail that led alongside the ridge, hidden from view to those in the valley below. The trail had wound in and out of the forest that surrounded the valley where Qualor lie sleeping in the early morning darkness.

Turning in his saddle he spoke to the squad behind him. "We dismount here and proceed on foot from this point. Odelas, you will remain here and see to the horses."

The Grand Vizier dismounted from his horse and quickly went through his saddle bags where he pulled several items forth and secured them beneath his robes. Then, indicating that they should follow him, he moved up the ridge until he reached the top where he dropped down to his belly and peered into the valley below.

The rest of the squad followed suit and all waited for the Grand Vizier to indicate what they should do next. He scanned the valley for a few moments before he scrambled to his feet and moved down the ridge where he came to a cave opening a few dozen yards from where he had topped the ridge. The squad followed him into the darkness of the cave.

"Each of you, place your hand upon the shoulder of the man in front of you. Corporal Harjkess, place your hand upon my shoulder. Each of you move slowly and carefully, I dare not risk a torch until we are deeper into the cave lest the glow of it be seen by those in the valley below."

The men moved slowly in the darkness, their only guide the Grand Vizier whom they followed not by sight but by touch. Their feet could be heard scratching and shuffling along the stone floor of the cave. They traveled this way for what seemed an eternity but was only minutes in reality. Finally the Grand Vizier halted and whispered to them that they could let go and to shield their eyes as he was going to light a torch.

Light burst upon their retinas as a torch flared to life in the hands of the Grand Vizier. The cave had given way to a passage of stone that had run into the ridge. The Grand Vizier waited for their eyes to adjust to the light given off by the torch then he motioned for them to follow. He led them deeper into in the ground, the passage sloped downward and it twisted so that eventually they were beneath the valley and passing beneath the troops that were waiting for them above.

Hours passed until the Grand Vizier called for a halt. "We are within range of Qualor and shall reach the caverns beneath the city within the hour. Rest now and eat if you have brought food with you." The Grand Vizier then moved off to a position away from the squad and he turned his back to them. Whatever he was doing he kept hidden from the men in the squad that accompanied him. They all assumed that he was preparing his magicks for the upcoming assault into Qualor. In actuality he was quietly conferring with others within Qualor that also had small communication devices that the Grand Vizier had provided to them for just such an emergency. These devices were short range and he could not communicate with his agents until he was well within range of Qualor, although the agents did not know this.

After a quarter hour he put away his devices and stood. He walked back over to the squad of men he had and quietly gave them instructions.

"When we leave here we shall come to a junction in the caverns. At the junction we turn left and head into the underground portion of Qualor beneath the detention cells of the southern gate. We will be met there by another squad of men loyal to the king. I shall quickly test their loyalty as I did with all of you last night. Before this testing you are to quietly surround these men and then be ready to quickly and quietly remove any whose loyalty is not true. Do you understand?"

All their heads bobbed up and down in understanding. The Grand Vizier nodded once and led them forward. Within minutes they arrived at the junction. They all followed the Grand Vizier, turning left at the junction. The grand Vizier silently dropped his torch into a shallow pool of water; the torch hissed and was extinguished. They stood there for a few moments while their eyes adjusted. The darkness they expected did not unfold, a light glow appeared and they realized that it was given off by a torch lit corridor up ahead.

The Grand Vizier led them forward to the corridor and when they emerged into the corridor they met the other squad of men who were awaiting their arrival. They silently moved around the other squad, acting like they were simply looking around to see where they were at in the underground corridors beneath Qualor. The Grand Vizier quietly met with the leader of the squad and they spoke in low voices for a few moments.

The commander of the other squad quickly lined his squad up then joined them, just as Garrig had done the previous evening. The grand Vizier repeated the explanation of the demon within the orb then proceeded to question each man. This time there were no incidents of disloyalty. Satisfied that all were loyal the Grand Vizier removed the orb from view and gathered all the men around him.

"Above us are the detention cells of the southern gate. Captain Avril is being held there and our first objective is to rescue him. He was to have been taken to my personal holding cells where two others are being held but General Ophister imprisoned him here and then, following the orders of Baron Mugior set about doing his part in the rebellion."

"Sir," a soldier spoke up. "Why do we need to rescue Captain Avril? How does he fit into this?"

"He is loyal and deserves better than he has been given, also we can use his help in freeing the king. Now, quickly, follow me," the Grand Vizier hissed between clenched teeth. This was taking too long and they needed the element of surprise to pull off Avril's rescue.

The Grand Vizier moved quickly and stealthily through the stone corridor followed by the two squads of soldiers. Soon enough they reached a stout wooden door reinforced with iron bands running horizontally through it. The handle was a large iron ring inset into the door, next to the iron ring was a good size keyhole. In order to lift the iron ring to open the door a key was needed to release the iron ring. The Grand Vizier withdrew a large master key from beneath his robes and unlocked the iron ring. Then, after replacing the key beneath his robes, he pulled on the ring and drew the door open wide revealing a set of stone stairs leading upward into the detention cells. He motioned for two of the soldiers to accompany him, leaving the rest to wait in the corridor.

Moving rapidly the Grand Vizier and the two soldiers reached the top of the stairs. There was a blank wall at the

LEE E FULLER JR

top of the stairs. The wall had iron bars sticking out from the stone. There was a grill for air ventilation set high up the wall. The Grand Vizier silently climbed up the iron bars and peered through the grill, through it he could make out six detention cells, three on either side of the cell block. Stationed at the other end of the cell block were two guards, their backs to the door they stood in front of with their hands resting lightly on their sword pommels. The cells to the right were empty and only Captain Avril occupied the center cell on the left. The Grand Vizier slipped back down the iron bars and turned to the two soldiers standing on the top step waiting for him.

"There are only two guards and Captain Avril in the cell block. That's the good news. The bad news is that the two guards are facing the wall we need to go through so our element of surprise will be brief. Here is what we will do, as soon as I open the wall close your eyes and keep them closed until I tell you it is safe. I am going to temporarily blind the guards. In doing so I will also be blinding Captain Avril, so he will be disoriented and confused. Stand ready."

The two guards carefully drew their swords so the iron would not scrape against the sheaths and possibly give them away. The Grand Vizier again ascended the iron bars and quickly assured himself that the two guards had not moved. He then reached up and pushed against one of the stones of the wall then descended to the landing where he reached out and pushed against a second stone. A quiet 'click' was heard and he whispered to the soldiers, "Close your eyes." He then withdrew a small glass orb from under his robes then shoved against the wall. The wall swung outward into the cell block. The two guards were only startled for a moment before they started to draw their swords. Before their swords could clear their sheaths the Grand Vizier threw the small glass orb into the cell block where it impacted on the stone floor. When it hit there was a blinding flash, both of the guards threw their arms up before their faces to try to ward off the light from their eyes.

"Now!" shouted the Grand Vizier. The two soldiers ran past him and quickly dispatched the two guards into unconsciousness. The grand Vizier went directly to Avril's cell and said, "Captain Avril, keep still. We are here to free you. Your sight will return in a few minutes." Then he pulled a small plastic tube from his robes and sprayed the contents upon the lock of the cell. Powerful acid ate away at the iron and the Grand Vizier was able to yank the door open, breaking the remainder of the lock. He gestured at the soldiers to support Avril then the four of them retreated back through the wall. The grand Vizier closed the wall and secured it before following the others down the stairs.

Captain Avril was being steadied by one of the two soldiers that had participated in his rescue. His eyes were watering as his vision returned to normal. He turned at the sound of the Grand Vizier's voice.

"Are you injured, Captain?" asked the Grand Vizier.

"No, just my eyes but they are almost back to normal now. What did you do back there?" Avril asked as he wiped at his eyes.

"We rescued you from your captivity, Captain. Are you aware of what has happened?"

"All I know is that I was thrown into that cell by General Ophister after you rode off with Garrig's squad," answered Avril. He looked around and realized that half of the soldiers here were Garrig's squad. "Where is Garrig? I owe that bastard for the way he treated me out in the desert."

"Garrig is dead, he was a traitor!" spat Dobrik, one of Garrig's men.

"Traitor?" asked Avril. "I don't understand."

"Garrig was not loyal to King Phiponoux and has paid for his treason with his life," responded the Grand Vizier. "As to the king, he has been imprisoned somewhere in the catacombs and Baron Mugior now sits upon an usurped throne. We are going to free the king and remove the baron. Are you with us, Avril?"

"Give me a sword. I have no love for that overfed pompous fool," replied Avril.

"Good," stated the Grand Vizier. "You are to take charge of Garrig's squad and proceed east along this corridor. You will eventually come to a cross corridor, turn left and proceed down that corridor. Count the doors on your right. The fifth door leads into a chamber that has full armor stored within. Don the armor; we have numbers against us and the better defended we are the better our chances are. After you have suited up wait for me. I am taking this squad and scouting this section of the underground, we will seal off the exits from the catacombs below us so those beneath cannot escape. Now go!" demanded the Grand Vizier.

Avril watched as the Grand Vizier and half the soldiers moved off down the corridor away from them and disappeared around a corner and out of sight. Shrugging his mental shoulders Avril raised the sword he had been given and said, "Follow me, men." He and his new squad moved off in the opposite direction of the Grand Vizier in search of the armory.

"I would burn it," stated Erat to Sturya and Garlgnor.

"You would, eh?" answered Garlgnor. "You might be able to burn through it if you could keep it alight for the hours necessary to do the task. But the smoke would fill the corridor and force everyone outside. Then the fire would go out as there would be no air, only the smoke."

They were discussing how each of them would take down the door that Garlgnor had locked from this side so that none could enter the cell block. Each of them was dining on cheese and water that Garlgnor had retrieved from a hidden stash for just such a purpose as a siege of the cell block.

"I say the best way would be to take axes to it, the door will fall with enough strokes," declared Sturya around a mouthful of Donarian Fugue, one of the most sought after cheese in the lands.

"Won't work," supplied Garlgnor. "The door is stout wood on the outsides covering solid iron in the inside. All an axe would do is cut away the wood on the outside; the axes would dull and break on the iron center."

"So the door won't open until you open it, then," mumbled Erat under his breath. Garlgnor heard him regardless.

"Not true barbarian. The Grand Vizier can open that door from out there."

"How can he open it from outside?" asked Sturya.

"He knows how to open it from without. I don't believe that he will stand still for what is going on out there, though. I think he will set things straight in short order," Garlgnor confidently declared. He was loyal to the Grand Vizier and was sure that the man would correct the wrongs happening outside the cell block then he would come and rescue them from their captivity.

Someone started pounding on the door and a muffled yelling could be heard. Garlgnor set aside his cheese, stood up and moved over to the door. He put his ear to the door while motioning for silence from Sturya and Erat so he could hear what was being said. He stood thusly for half a minute before he straightened up. He placed his hands on his lower back and stretched backwards far as his body would allow. A loud popping noise came from his back as he cracked his spine then he let go his back and rotated his shoulders forward a few times and he finished by cracking his knuckles.

Satisfied that he had worked all the kinks out of his body

he reached out and unlocked a small panel in the door. He slid the panel back into the door and he was able to see and hear clearly what was happening on the far side of the door. Looking back at him was the face of General Ophister. The general did not look happy and he glared at Garlgnor.

"What in the seven hells is going on here, Sergeant Garlgnor!?" he asked in a voice filled with dangerous intent.

"General, I am guarding the prisoners as personally instructed by the Grand Vizier," Garlgnor answered as he looked beyond the general as best he could to see what might be happening outside the cell block.

"Sergeant, you do realize that Corporal Blune and Sub-Captain Jellico are dead by your hand and that you are under arrest for their murders?"

"Sir, "Garlgnor replied, "I was doing my duty in guarding the prisoners. The Grand Vizier told me to remain here until he returned. The Sub-Captain was outside of my chain of command and he both he and Blune entered the cell block with their swords unsecured and ready to be drawn. They were ready to remove me from my post by force. I am here under the orders of the Grand Vizier and here I shall remain until he relieves me."

"Sergeant, the grand Vizier is dead. He was killed in an assassination attempt on the king. The entire city has been in chaos since last night when the attempt on the king's life was made."

Garlgnor was sure that the general was lying, the grand Vizier would never hurt the king, he was as sure of that as he was as sure the sun went down at night. Before he could reply to the general the general spoke again.

"I came down here personally, sergeant, as I know you are a good and loyal man of the Grand Vizier and would not believe what I have told you had it come from someone of lesser rank. I also brought proof," and with that statement he held up the mask of the Grand Vizier.

Garlgnor was rocked back by the sight of the Grand Vizier's mask dangling from the hand of the general, its white eyes missing and traces of what could be blood around the sockets. He studied the upheld mask carefully until the general lowered it and spoke softly to Garlgnor.

"Sergeant, the king has heard of what happened down here. He is saddened by the loss of Sub-Captain Jellico and Corporal Blune. He understands that you were simply following orders given directly to you by the Grand Vizier. He knows that you have always been loyal and have always followed orders, always striving to do the correct thing never bringing dishonor upon yourself or those above you. The king has proclaimed that you are to be given amnesty and be allowed to leave Qualor provided that you lay aside your sword and leave the cell block. You will be allowed to retrieve your horse and you will be given one month's pay to allow you to begin anew elsewhere. The king wishes to resolve this situation without any further bloodshed, he feels that enough blood has been spilled this past night."

Garlgnor thought about the offer for a few moments then he asked the general a question. "General Ophister, would you show me the mask again?" The general raised the mask up for Garlgnor to see again.

"Sir, could you please turn the mask around so that I may see the inside?" Garlgnor asked in a subdued voice. The general looked at Garlgnor questioningly then he complied with the request, turning the mask so that Garlgnor could see the inside of the mask.

Garlgnor peered at the mask intently for a moment and he made another request, "Sir could you hold the mask closer, please?"

The general hesitated and looked as if he was about to run out of patience. Garlgnor realized this and quickly spoke up. "Here, sir, I am removing my sword from its scabbard and placing it on the ground," which Garlgnor did as he spoke. The general, somewhat mollified by Garlgnor's action held the mask closer to the small opening so that Garlgnor could see it better.

Garlgnor stared intently at the mask for a few moments, satisfying himself concerning the Grand Vizier's mask that the general held.

"Thank you, general, you no longer need to hold the mask up, I am convinced." Garlgnor said.

"Good, "the general said as he lowered the mask out of sight again. "Now open the door so we can end this standoff and then you can be on your way."

"I'm sorry general I cannot do that. The Grand Vizier ordered me to remain until he himself relieved me," answered Garlgnor matter-of-factly.

"Sergeant," bellowed the general. "The Grand Vizier is dead! Now I order you to open that door and stand down!"

Garlgnor replied by closing and securing the opening. He reached down and retrieved his sword from the floor and returned it to its scabbard.

Sturya was standing at the bars of his cell, gripping the bars with his hands. "You could have had your freedom, why did you not take it?"

Erat answered before Garlgnor could reply. "The Grand Vizier is not dead and that was not his mask."

A look of surprise passed across Garlgnor's face. Then he suddenly laughed. "Barbarian you don't miss anything, do you?"

Erat remained silent.

Sturya was confused. "How could you know that it wasn't the Grand Vizier's mask?"

"Two things, the first thing were the eye sockets. The eye sockets of the mask are made of a milky white material that allows the grand Vizier to see out but does not allow anyone to see his eyes. If they had both been truly torn out then the mask would have shown much more damage around the eye sockets. The second thing was the inside of the mask. I have seen the inside on one occasion and the inside of that mask was different than the inside of the real mask."

"You have seen the face of the Grand Vizier?" Sturya asked incredulously. Erat's face suddenly showed interest.

"No, I have not seen his face. One time two years ago I was speaking to him and he suddenly turned his back to me and removed his mask, perhaps his eyes itched, I do not know. But while the mask was off he held it far enough away from his body that I was able to see the inside for a few brief moments."

"If you could only see the inside for a few brief moments, as you say, then how do you know it was not his mask?" asked Erat.

"The color was wrong and the inside of the eyeholes was wrong, they had small screw holes to make it seem if the eye pieces were screwed into the mask. The eye pieces of the real mask were inset into the eyeholes, there were no screws."

"So the Grand Vizier is still alive then." Erat said

"And we still wait for him," finished Sturya.

Chapter XI

STUART SAT IN HIS command chair and watched his command console as the Pegasus slipped into orbit about the planet. All readings indicated that the planet held an oxygen nitrogen atmosphere. The atmosphere was just a little higher in oxygen than Earth. Completely breathable. The sensors also revealed large continents and even larger oceans. The arctic ice cap was larger than the entire planet Earth. This planet was huge.

All types of life forms were being discovered as they ran continuous scans of the surface. They had positively identified reptiles, marsupials, amphibians and mammals. They also had identified deserts, tundra, jungles, plains, mountains, lakes, rivers, forests and swamps.

"Captain," exclaimed an excited sounding Clarke. "I have located an artificial satellite!"

Heads snapped up from consoles to turn and look at Ensign Clarke. The Ensign was oblivious to the attention he was suddenly receiving as his head was bent over his sensor board.

"On screen, Ensign," ordered Stuart as he looked away

from Clarke and focused his attention on the main view screen. Everyone else also looked to the main view screen.

The image of the planet below them was replaced by the image of an orbital satellite. The satellite was completely alien to any satellite that any of them had ever seen. It was conical in shape and had multiple projections protruding from its surface. It was also extremely difficult to see as it jet black. The only way that they could see it was through the visual enhancements that Clarke had added for their benefit.

"Captain," Clarke stated. "The size of the satellite is enormous. It has a radius of 14 kilometers. I am also picking up a system of smaller satellites. The other satellites range in size from 3 meters to 30 meters and all of them seem to be linked to the large satellite."

"How many other satellites can you confirm?" Stuart asked.

"I am picking up a total of 114 satellites; until we complete a mapping of the planet I will not be able to give an accurate satellite count."

"The large satellite, where exactly is it located in relation to the planet?" Martinez asked Clarke.

Clarke spent a few seconds checking readings before answering. "The large satellite is positioned directly above the planet's magnetic south pole."

Stuart raised his eyebrows at that answer; he expected it to be above an inhabited area of the planet, perhaps above a city or installation of some sort.

"Ensign," he began. "Can you verify that the smaller satellites are linked to the large satellite?"

"Already verified, Captain the large satellites seems to be in control of the smaller satellites."

"Can you determine where on the planet the large satellite is receiving its commands from?"

✦

"I should be able to do that, but it will take time to determine, sir," answered Clarke.

"Fine, take the time, Martinez, would you please continue the planetary scans for Ensign Clarke while he tries to locate the source signal?"

"Delighted to, Captain," answered Martinez as he started reading and deciphering the scans from below.

"Athena," Stuart said. "Keep an eye on those long range sensors. I want to know right away if any ships should suddenly appear."

"Of course, Captain. I am monitoring all long range sensors and will alert you immediately to any possible ships."

Stuart thanked Athena and returned his attention to his command console. He continued going over incoming data on the planet that they orbited. The ocean scans had some interesting readings; they had an average salinity content of 35 o/o which was the salinity average on Earth also. Scans of the oceans showed a diverse variety of sea life. Some of the creatures were massive in size, which made sense as the oceans covers more surface of the planet than the surfaces of Mars, Venus and Mercury combined. Some of the life forms the scanners picked up were the size of a Cryptocleidus, a huge Jurassic Era oceanic predator.

He studied ocean scans for a while then turned his attention to scans of the land masses of the planet. The scans had so far identified 34 separate continent sized land masses. The smallest one being the size of Asia, Europe and Africa combined. That continent alone had two large mountain chains, a tropical jungle the size of Australia, a desert that the Sahara would be swallowed up in and a series of lakes that rivaled the Great Lakes of North America.

Stuart still had trouble grasping the size of this world. 34 continents and 33 oceans scanned on the few orbits they had made. Details of those continents and oceans were emerging quickly as their scanners continued to gather data. Finally Stuart found something he was looking for in all the data that was coursing across his command console.

Signs of civilization suddenly appeared. Stuart immediately began to read the scans from that area. The civilization was on a continent that was thrice the size of Pangaea. Pangaea was the super-continent on Earth that broke apart to become the continents that are known today. This civilization that he had found was concentrated on the Eastern portion of the continent. Yet he doubted that this could be the civilization that had deployed the satellites. What he found were cities surrounded by stone walls, ships that sailed close to the shores of the continent and there was no electric power being used that the scanners could detect. So far they had not discovered any use of electricity on the planet.

Perhaps the civilization that had deployed the satellites had perished or perhaps did not originate from this world at all and wanted to keep an eye on this gigantic world. Whatever the answer was it was a mystery at present and would reveal itself given time, even if it meant centuries of study, the Federation would dig out the answers.

"Captain Martinez, I see that there is a civilization down there. I would like to further investigate, how long until your prototype is ready for testing?" Stuart asked.

"The prototype will be ready in 34 hours, Captain. We need to be 2 parsecs away from here to attempt a translational shift," answered Martinez.

Stuart worked out a few equations in his head then double checked them against his command console. Satisfied he looked up. "That gives us roughly 17 hours that we can remain here and study this world. Generally Athena and I spend 6 to 7 days studying a world, a normal sized world that is. This world we could spend weeks just scanning and mapping form orbit. I would like to send orbital probes out to gather even more detailed data but I am reluctant to do so with the satellite system currently in orbit. That satellite system could be some sort of defensive system."

"Perhaps," Martinez said. "But if it is a defensive system why has it not reacted to the Pegasus orbiting the planet?"

"Maybe it is programmed to defend the planet only if something hits a lower altitude then we are presently at? We are orbiting at the extreme limits of orbital range. Let's see what happens if we move in closer," Stuart said.

Martinez quickly interjected, "Wait. If we go lower and the satellites are indeed a defensive system they may well pose a threat and could possibly destroy the Pegasus. The translation engine we carry is the only one of its kind and there are no blueprints left available in the Federation since Argos station was destroyed."

"Then we can't risk it," Stuart agreed. "Still, a shuttle could conceivably go down to the planet. Ivanova, could you please place us in a geo-stationary orbit above these coordinates please?" Stuart ordered as he sent the coordinates to Ivanova from his command console.

"Aye, sir, setting geo-stationary orbit," Ivanova acknowledged as she corrected their orbit.

"Athena, magnification level 5 please," Stuart ordered. Athena acknowledged and the view changed from a high altitude view to the view one could see from 35,000 meters.

Stuart watched the planet below on the main view screen as the Pegasus moved into a geo-stationary orbit centered above the civilization they had discovered. He watched as the ocean slid by on the screen to be replaced by a continent. The dark green of a jungle passed out of view to be replaced by the snow tipped mountains which in turn were replaced by a yellow tinged desert. The desert gave way to another mountain range then a vast plain moved onto the view screen.

"Athena, magnification level 7 please," Stuart requested.

The vast plain on the screen seemed to draw in closer as the magnification increased. Now the people on the bridge could make out roads, farmland, and cities. The cities were primitive looking.

"The cities remind me of drawings of Babylon I saw in an ancient history class I took in school," Ivanova spoke aloud.

"They do resemble those ancient cities, don't they?" Stuart replied. "The larger cities are surrounded by large walls. I'll wager that there is probably a good amount of warfare going on at times between the different cities."

"Then do you think they are at the city state stage of their development?" Ivanova inquired.

"Maybe, they could have very well moved into small nations, too. It is impossible to determine from orbit. What I really want to know though is where the people are that put those satellites into orbit."

"Captain," Martinez said, getting Stuart's attention. "I have just completed a preliminary analysis of the age of the planet. I have double checked my findings with Athena and her analysis agrees with my own." Martinez sounded doubtful but continued, "if all the reading are correct then this planet is close to 12 billion years old."

"What? That's impossible. The readings must be incorrect. Something down there is causing our sensors to pull false data. Athena, run a quick spectral analysis on the star, estimate its age," Stuart ordered.

"Affirmative, Captain, running spectral analysis on the star," Athena's voice said through the bridge speakers. Seconds passed as the analysis was run and the data computed. Then Athena's voice again flowed from the bridge speakers. "Preliminary results indicate that the star of this system is 1 point 2 billion years old."

"Ok, now that doesn't make any sense. That is way too

young for a star to have a planet this developed," Stuart exclaimed.

Martinez continued the discussion, "a 12 billion year old planet in orbit about a 1 billion year old sun? We should check all of our sensors."

"I have run a diagnostic on the sensor system," Athena replied. "The sensors are performing at optimal peak performance. The readings are correct."

Silence fell over the bridge. Martinez began going over all the data he had acquired looking for an anomaly in the readings, Clarke continued studying the satellite network, Ivanova made minor adjustments to maintain their position above the civilization below them while Stuart sat and stared at the view screen.

"All right," Stuart finally said. "Our sensors are not pulling false data; we have just been given a new mystery to investigate. Mystery number one is the satellite system, who built it and for what purpose? Mystery number two how can this planet be 12 billion years old and the star only 1 billion years old?"

"Captain, I think I have found the contact point on the planet where the satellites are linked," Clarke reported.

"Where is the link point, Ensign?" Stuart inquired.

"95 kilometers northwest of our present position, sir," Clarke responded.

"Are you sure, Ensign?"

"Yes, sir, I am positive."

"Athena, can you please give us a visual of that location please?" Stuart requested of the AI.

The view screen image shifted from an over head view of planted fields and roads to the image of a great walled city. The city had four roads leading into it from four different directions. Surrounding the city wall were numerous out buildings and outward of the buildings were great swaths of fields planted with whatever crops were being grown. The city dwarfed most of the other cities that they had seen from orbit.

"People, the mystery deepens, now we have a satellite system that is so advanced that we cannot precisely determine what it is used for being controlled, we think, by a city that looks like it came from ancient Earth about 3,000 years ago. I would like to think that the answers to our questions lie beneath us on the planet but I am going to venture a guess and say that if we go down there seeking those answers we will probably just find more mysteries. Does anyone have any observations or suggestions?"

"I suggest that we leave a probe and continue outward so that we may complete our translation testing," Martinez answered. When Stuart didn't look convinced Martinez continued. "I am extremely curious about this world and what exactly is going on here, Captain, but my primary mission is to test the translation engine and report back those results immediately."

"Yes, I understand that, Captain Martinez. Your primary mission is also my primary mission. Yet I have been exploring uncharted space and anomalies for a few years and this place pushes all of my curiosity buttons, in fact I don't think any place else has ever intrigued my curiosity more."

"Sir," Ensign Clarke spoke up. "I think this place is important somehow and that we need to investigate further. I volunteer for the landing party."

"Noted and logged, Ensign. But at this time there is not going to be a landing party. We need to make the testing of the translation engine our top priority. But on the way home we will definitely be stopping off for a closer look. Commander Ivanova, would you please prepare a probe? See to it that it is strictly a passive observer in an extremely high orbit, and then prepare a second probe that we can deploy after we break orbit to observe the planet from a greater distance away."

"Aye, sir, preparing both probes," Ivanova acknowledged as she began selecting programming for the two probes.

"Captain, my technicians need your permission to install the command interface console on the bridge for the translation engine," Martinez stated.

"Permission granted, I would appreciate it if you would allow Athena to assist," Stuart replied, keeping in mind that this would mean rebuilding a console on the bridge.

"Of course, captain. The technicians will be up shortly. Will the rear console be acceptable?"

"That will be fine. Ivanova, how long until the probes are ready for launch?"

The first probe is ready, sir. The second probe will be ready momentarily," Ivanova replied without looking up from her console.

Stuart waited for Ivanova to finish programming the second probe. The bridge doors opened and technicians, one of them being Edwards, entered the bridge. They each carried tools and unfamiliar looking equipment. Martinez stood and gestured at them to begin their work at the rear console of the bridge. He moved over to join them and to oversee the work.

"Sir, I have both probes ready for launch," Ivanova reported.

"Very good, launch the first probe and stand by to break orbit," Stuart ordered.

Ivanova activated a series of controls and the first probe left the Pegasus. She tracked it to its position 100 kilometers above their present position, she then ensured that the proper telemetry was being sent from the probe and turned her attention to the maneuvering of the Pegasus. Presently she was ready to take the Pegasus away from the planet and back into space proper.

Minutes passed as Stuart idly watched the technicians and Martinez quickly and expertly install the translation engine command interface console at the rear bridge station. The rear bridge station was an auxiliary console that could be substituted for any other station in an emergency which made it ideal for the current reconfiguration.

Martinez finally nodded in satisfaction to the technicians, two of them left the bridge and Edwards remained at the console running tests and diagnostics. Martinez returned to his duty console and finished linking the new translation engine command console into the ship's systems. Finally he looked up at Stuart and reported that the install was complete and that the rest of the translation engine would be ready to go online as scheduled.

"Very good," Stuart said. "Ivanova, take us out of orbit and set course for the test site. Launch the second probe 100,000 kilometers from the planet."

Ivanova acknowledged the orders and the Pegasus moved away from the massive planet. The second probe shot out from the Pegasus as it moved past the 100,000 kilometer range and the Pegasus shot away; taking her crew farther away from the galaxy then anyone had ever been before.

Presently the Pegasus was swallowed up by the blackness of the interstellar void between the galaxies.

―――――――――

The Grand Vizier swiftly and quietly led the two squads of soldiers through the underground tunnels beneath Qualor. He led them through hidden passages that snaked around main corridors, avoiding any patrols that Baron Mugior may have dispatched. He did not expect to find any patrols, but considering that the baron had managed to pull off this coup, he may have the foresight to station patrols beneath Qualor. Finally after spending a couple of hours stealthily moving about the Grand Vizier were beneath his own sub-palace. There were items he needed to obtain from his chambers if he was going to free the king.

"I need all of you to wait here. I will return with the hour. Captain Avril you are in charge, keep everyone as quiet as possible, we do not want to draw attention to ourselves."

"Yes, sir," Avril answered. Are you sure you don't want a couple of men to accompany you?"

"Positive, captain," the Grand Vizier replied, amused at Avril's concern. "I can move faster on my own and I am quite capable of defending myself should the need arise."

Avril nodded acceptance and began motioning the two squads of men to the positions he wanted them in to guard the corridor they occupied. The Grand Vizier slipped around a corner and was gone from their view.

The Grand Vizier moved down the corridor he had entered then turned left at a cross corridor. He moved down that corridor, his shadow flickering off the walls from the light given off by the wavering flame of the torch he carried. He abruptly stopped in front of a blank section of wall and began to feel along its rough surface. His fingers eventually found that which they were seeking and a loud click sounded right before a section of the wall swung away from him.

He stepped through the doorway and moments later the wall swung back into place and another click sounded letting him know that the doorway was secured behind him again. He then walked down the short corridor and stopped at a wooden door. He tried the door and was satisfied that it was locked. He produced a key from beneath his robes and unlocked the door. He opened then stepped through the door and into a small antechamber. He closed the door but left it unlocked. If anyone had been watching they would have sworn on pain of death that the Grand Vizier floated across the antechamber so swiftly and smoothly did he move.

At the other side of the antechamber he stopped and listened at the door before reaching out and quietly pulling the door open. He peered through the open doorway and slipped through, silently closing the door behind him. He was on the ground floor of a small stairwell that contained a spiral stairway leading upward. Looking up he could not make out the top of the stairs as the stairwell had no openings to the outside and there were only a few lit torches here at the bottom of the stairwell.

The Grand Vizier moved the center of the stairwell and stood there listening for any sound that would indicate that someone might be waiting for him. After a few minutes he heard a faint scraping sound coming from far above. Smiling beneath his mask he slipped a hand into his robes and activated a device on his belt. He rose quietly into the air, and ascended silently upward into the gloom above.

When he reached the top of the stairs he floated up behind two guardsmen that were stationed there to intercept any that might attempt to enter the chambers of the Grand Vizier. The Grand Vizier slipped onto the landing behind the two men and shut off his antigravity device. The device made an audible click that caused the two guardsmen to straighten up and turn around. They both looked surprised to see anyone there, especially the Grand Vizier.

"I thank you for keeping my chambers safe form intrusion," the Grand Vizier spoke to the startled men. "But now, rest from your labors my friends." He then dropped a small glass ball to the ground where it shattered and released an odorless and invisible gas which quickly drifted into the two men's nostrils and caused them both to slump to the ground unconscious.

The Grand Vizier turned to the door of his chambers. He checked it and was satisfied that no one had been able to open the door. He could see marks where an axe was tried without success, the only result being a few small gouges in the outer wood of the door. Whoever tried to bring the door down could not know that it was reinforced with a steel center.

With a shrug the Grand Vizier produced a key and used it to unlock the door. He then reached out and pressed on a certain stone before opening the door. This produced a muffled click. He then pushed the door open and stepped through the threshold into his chambers.

Once inside his chambers he closed and locked the door then moved about his chambers gathering items that he would need. He placed everything into a small heap upon a table that sat in the center of the room and went into his sleeping area.

He went to an armoire and pulled open the doors. He reached in and pulled out a different cloak and a change of clothing. He then stripped off all his clothes, including his mask and dumped everything on his bed. He then stretched then went through a series of exercises to loosen up knotted muscles. After that he donned the fresh clothes, his new cloak and picked up his mask.

Returning to the main room of his chambers he set his mask on the table with the items he had gathered and went to a cabinet against the far wall of the room. He reached into the cabinet and withdrew a small flask which he unstoppered then drank from. When he had emptied the contents he returned the flask to the cabinet and returned to the table. Pulling a chair out from the table he sat and simply rested for a few moments. He began to feel the effects of the liquid that he drank and felt his full vitality and strength returning.

He pulled a small communications device from the pile on the table and activated it. "We have a problem in Qualor, seems that one of the barons decided to try and pull off a coup," he spoke into the device.

The voice of the Planetary AI came from the small speaker. "Are you in danger?"

"Not at the moment. I have assembled two squads of men to rescue the king and dispose of the baron. I need to know the king's location," he replied. Years ago he had slipped nanites into the king's drink. The nanites were useful in recording and relaying information back to him and in keeping track of the king. Right now they would tell the Planetary AI where the king was located so he could go and rescue the man.

"He is at coordinates 23, 76, 18."

The Grand Vizier consulted a small electronic map of the area and determined the location of the king. "That correlates to the North Tower. That is fortunate, I have a passage into the tower form the catacombs."

"Tomas," said the Planetary AI. "Keep your eyes open for any strangers."

"Strangers? We have strangers passing through Qualor all the time as you well know. Can you be more specific?"

"I cannot. Simply look for anyone that seems out of place and are attempting to blend in with the crowd."

The Grand Vizier pondered that for a bit then acknowledged the directive. "As you say. I am off to rescue the king. I shall contact you when this crisis is resolved."

The Grand Vizier then gathered up the things he had assembled and stashed them beneath his robes. He then donned his mask and moved over to the fireplace. His hands moved over the stones surrounding the fireplace in a certain sequence and the fireplace silently slid to the left revealing a few small narrow stairs leading down.

The Grand Vizier descended these stairs as the fireplace slid back into its original position above him. At the bottom of the stairs was a metal pole that led down into the darkness. The Grand Vizier grasped the pole and used it to descend all the way down into the catacombs. The pole had leather stirrups set along its distance which the Grand Vizier used to slow his descent. The pole ended at the bottom of the circular shaft it was centered into. The only exit from the shaft was a small opening three feet high which the Grand

Vizier had to stoop very low to pass through. Once through the opening he straightened up and turned to his right and made his way through the near darkness until he reached a door that he pushed open. He went through the doorway, closed the door behind him and took two steps then turned right which brought him to a narrow corridor. He was quick to transverse the corridor and at the end of it he emerged into a main corridor of the catacombs precisely where he had left the two squads of soldiers who were still waiting for him to return.

"Captain Avril," he said to announce his arrival. The narrow passageway that he had just left was a stone wall behind him. The wall itself was an illusion used to hide the narrow passageway, which lead the soldiers to believe that he had simply appeared from out of thin air. They all jumped at his voice. "I have located where they are keeping the king, but we must hurry if we are to rescue him. He is being held in the North Tower."

"The North Tower," answered Avril. "That will be hard to breach with the few men that we have. Allow me to go and gather more men loyal to the king so that we may make a full assault on the tower."

"No, if we were to do that they would simply kill the king. We need to take them by surprise in order to safely free him. We have enough men to do that."

"Grand Vizier, I respectively disagree, what few men we have will be cut down before we even reach the outer doors of the North Tower," Avril responded.

"If we were to storm the main doors I would agree with you, Captain. However we are not going to do that, we are going to enter the tower from below. Now come, follow me I know the way into the tower form the catacombs directly beneath."

The Grand Vizier brushed through the men standing in his path and began trotting through the catacombs with

Avril and the rest of the soldiers following close behind him. He followed the twists and turns and changed corridors and passages repeatedly until all the soldiers were completely lost, not a single one of them could tell how to find the way back to where they had begun. Finally the Grand Vizier halted and turned to Avril.

"Have everyone rest for a few minutes; the entrance to the North Tower is right around this corner. I am going to investigate and will return shortly. Then he turned and was gone.

Avril and the rest of the soldiers were all breathing heavily from jogging through the catacombs and they all sagged against the walls or simply dropped to the stone floor and worked on catching their breath. Avril looked them over and decided that they would do for whatever resistance they were going to meet when they breached the North Tower.

The Grand Vizier returned and quietly approached Avril. "The way is clear until we reach the second level of the tower, which is far as the passage into the North Tower reaches. The passageway lets out into the rear of a small closet that only has room for one man at a time to emerge. This is where we will be at our most vulnerable. The closet opens into a sleeping chamber that hopefully, will be unoccupied. We will assemble there and we will see how far we can get to the top chamber where the king is being held before we are discovered and have to fight."

Avril nodded in understanding and motioned everyone to fall in and prepare to move out. When all were standing and ready the Grand Vizier nodded and moved forward with everyone following him. The rescue of the king was now proceeding and all were ready to give their lives to free their sovereign.

King Phiponoux was tied to the chair he was sitting

on and he was not happy about it. He had been sleeping when a commotion had awakened him just in time to have someone throw a cloth hood over his head then he had felt a sharp blow and the he had felt nothing until he had come to here, tied to this chair.

His head ached from the blow and he had to use the bathroom, but he was not afraid. He had realized what had happened, that someone had staged a palace coup. He didn't know who that someone was yet, but he was sure they would put in an appearance before having him dispatched. He was not afraid to die, but he was disappointed that he had never taken his Grand Vizier's advice and allowed the man to use his magicks to root out disloyal elements in his own personal guard.

He sat and strained his senses to try to determine how many guards were in the room with him. All his senses could tell him was that the room was silent. He listened intently but could not discern any presence of anyone else in the room. Finally he decided that he was alone in this room. He then began working at the ropes that securely held him to the chair. They were tight enough to bind him yet loose enough to allow his blood to circulate through his limbs. A thoroughly professional job.

He was still worrying away at the ropes when he heard muffled voices outside the room. Then a door opened off to his left and he heard men entering the chamber where he was being held captive. He stopped trying to loosen the ropes, he was afraid that he had run out of time. He heard several men moving into the room and positioning themselves around him and the room. Suddenly the hood was yanked off of his head and he sat blinking at the sudden light.

Blinking away the few tears that emerged as his eyes were assaulted by the light he recognized "Baron Mugior!"

"Excellency," the baron replied as he gave a brief bow to his seated captive.

"I assume that you are now in control of Qualor?" Phiponoux asked.

"Indeed I am, outside of a few small pockets of resistance by men loyal to you. They won't last much longer though; my forces have them trapped where they are. They will either surrender or perish, either one is fine with me."

Phiponoux stared at the baron and knew that his own life was soon to be forfeit. He should be dead already unless there was some reason the baron was keeping him alive. "Why haven't you killed me yet?" he asked.

"Don't worry; you will be dead before the night is out. Where did you send the Grand Vizier?"

Ah so that was it, the Grand Vizier had still not returned from his sojourn to the countryside and the baron was worried. As he should be, the Grand Vizier was and always had been loyal to him and his father before him.

"I don't know where he went; he doesn't need my permission to leave the city."

"Yes, that is something that will need to be addressed, as will the Grand Vizier himself. It is unfortunate that he chose to leave the city two nights before my planned coup. I had not expected that, but yet his absence did make it easier for my forces to secure the city."

"I expect that it did, his magicks would have put a serious damper on your attempt."

"Perhaps, perhaps. Still, I believe that the man is intelligent and when he sees how the balance of power has shifted in his absence he will choose to continue serving as Grand Vizier under my rule rather than fight a battle that he cannot win."

"I believe that you are mistaken, Mugior, the Grand Vizier is loyal to a fault and he is extremely powerful." Phiponoux answered. His answer caused the baron to pale a bit and he even stuttered a little over his next words.

"E-even so, Phiponoux he shall either serve me or die. No matter how many he takes with him, he will perish."

"Mugior, while I am alive you will address me as your highness or Excellency, you do not have my leave to speak my name!" commanded Phiponoux. His command caused a couple of the guards to stand a little taller and eye the baron with a greater scrutiny. The baron himself started a bit as he was used to obeying the king's orders. But this time he quickly gathered his composure.

"Of course, your highness," he replied, sarcasm tinting his voice. "As you command."

"Why Mugior? Are you that hungry for power that you would betray your king, your very country?" Phiponoux asked, trying to determine why the baron had done what he had done.

"Power is some of it, as is wealth. But know this, Excellency," again the hint of sarcasm on the king's title. "I have brokered a deal with another nation, Qualor will gain total and complete control of some disputed areas with my coronation to the throne."

"Really?" Phiponoux replied, this time the sarcasm dripped from his voice. He may be a captive of this fool, but he would not show fear or deference to the man. "And what will Qualor provide in return for these areas of dispute?"

"Very little actually," the baron replied as he warmed to his subject. "A few chests of gold, abandonment of the eastern outpost and two minor trade concessions very insignificant things in return for the territory that Qualor will gain."

"Abandonment of the eastern outpost, that alone will cut off our routes over the mountains and to the coastal trade cities. Qualor will lose a vital trade route, forcing those who use it to go south through Donaria. Qualor will suffer financially. In the long run Qualor will be forced to abandon any territorial gains as we will not be able to afford the soldiers to patrol the new areas."

"That would be true except for two things. One, Donaria will pay us 5% of all trade that passes into Donaria from Qualor. Two, Gutan has a severely weakened army since they fought Fenril to a standstill last year, they are ripe for invasion. Once we conqueror Gutan we will annex it to Qualor and then we shall have complete control of their resources which will be far greater than any trade monies produced by the eastern route we now waste money and soldiers on to keep open from the ravages of the damnable tribesmen of Hern. And after we secure Gutan this year, we will finally be strong enough to crush the tribesmen and then we will be strong enough to reopen the eastern outpost as a full blown colony and not even Donaria will be strong enough to prevent us from doing so."

Phiponoux simply stared at Mugior for a few moments before he spoke up. "Baron Mugior, Qualor will be doomed if you really follow that plan. Donaria will not sit still while you invade Gutan, they will attack from the south the moment you send a force across the border into Gutan, or have you forgotten that they have a mutual defense treaty?"

"They have assured me that they will not interfere with an invasion of Gutan. It seems that Gutan has been withholding monies from Dontaria, monies that were promised to Dontaria for weapons and other such things during their war with Fenril."

"Fool!" Spat the king. "Of course they will interfere, they will allow the army to invade Gutan and let us weaken our own army. They will wait until you are on the cusp of completely defeating Gutan and then they will flow across our southern borders until they reach the river Awert, completely securing the southern half of Qualor and retrieving all of those disputed territories you so coveted."

"They will not, oh, I believe what you say, Excellency."

This time there was no sarcasm as the baron was completely caught up in his plans. "I have been quietly preparing defenses throughout the disputed territories for three years. These defenses are held by men loyal to me, not to you, not to Donaria but to me."

"Really, then why don't you go to the disputed territories and claim them as a new kingdom under your kingship? I will support your move to do this as I am sure will Donaria. You will have the kingdom you seek and will provide a buffer between Qualor and Donaria."

Mugior stopped and stared at Phiponoux as if he had not seen him before. "Why should I do that? I have a kingdom, Qualor. And it includes those disputed territories. What sort of a fool do you take me for?"

"You are underhanded, disloyal, treacherous and power hungry but I do not believe you to be a fool," answered Phiponoux angrily.

Mugior stepped forward and slapped Phiponoux so hard that his chair was knocked to the floor. Mugior then kicked the king hard in the ribs three times before he regained his composure. The guards in the room all looked uneasy at this treatment of their former monarch but all held their ground and made no move to interfere.

"And what are you!" shouted Mugior at the fallen king. "You are weak and indecisive! If you had sent one battalion, just one, to the eastern outpost you would have been able to establish it as a full colony that none would have dared attack! That alone would have strengthened Qualor's claims to the disputed territories that I have succeeded in obtaining!"

Phiponoux coughed and a bit of blood flecked across his lips. The sight of blood further enraged Mugior who again begin to sharply kick the king, this time in his head. "Weak fool!" yelled Mugior as his booted foot struck Phiponoux again and again in the side of his head.

Suddenly a loud crash sounded from the other side of the door. Mugior was brought up short as he turned his attention to the door. All the guards nervously drew their swords and moved to stand between Mugior and the closed door. Mugior withdrew a knife from within his sleeve and knelt beside the bloody and unconscious king. He placed the bled against Phiponoux's throat and waited, fear beginning to tickle at his brain.

The door suddenly began to open; it slowly swung inward to reveal the sergeant in charge of the guards now guarding Mugior in the room. The sergeant looked at the scene before him and said, "Baron Mugior, he will kill you slowly for this," then the man collapsed into a broken heap. His fallen body revealed the Grand Vizier standing behind him.

The mask of the Grand Vizier did not show any emotion, it never had nor would it ever. But everyone could tell that beneath the mask the Grand Vizier was angry, infuriated and his ire was totally directed at Baron Mugior. The guards in the room knew that their lives were forfeit as they had witnessed the beating Mugior had given Phiponoux without making any attempt to halt the baron.

The Grand Vizier held a sword in his left hand. He suddenly tossed it to the ground. This caused all the guards to take a step backwards. The Grand Vizier then raised his left arm and keeping his hand flat and even with the floor he pointed at the nearest guard to himself. A blinding yellow light streamed from his arm and struck the guard. The guard screamed as his clothing, burned away, his armor began to melt and his body itself began to burn. His screams were suddenly choked off as his body dropped to the floor, still burning and scorching the very stones of the floor.

The rest of the guards all threw down their weapons and dropped to their knees, better to hang for treason then to suffer that fate!

The Grand Vizier motioned Avril and his men to take the guards away. The soldiers flowed into the room and quickly secured the kneeling guards and dragged them out of the room. Only Baron Mugior was left, kneeling next to King Phiponoux. The Baron held his blade tight against the king's throat, blood form the beating that Mugior had given Phiponoux had flowed over the baron's hand, making the blade slippery and hard to hold. The fear that had been tickling at Mugior's brain now slammed into him with full force causing his bladder to let loose and his bowels to weaken, but not yet give way.

The Grand Vizier stepped into the room. He stood towering over Mugior and looked at the beaten monarch. He could tell that the king was dying from his injuries and he needed to act quickly if he wanted to try to save the man.

"Release the king, Mugior and I shall make your death quick and painless."

"No you won't, you will kill me slowly. Now back out of the room or I will slice his throat open!" Mugior screeched in a panicky voice.

"No you will not, for if you kill the king then nothing will be left to protect you from my wrath," the Grand Vizier replied, rage evident in his voice.

Mugior felt his hand beginning to cramp and knew that he had only a few minutes left to live if that long. He did not want to feel pain, but he did not want to die either. Suddenly his left hand, hidden behind the body of the king, flew forward and an open vial was clutched in the hand. The contents of the vial splashed across the body of the Grand Vizier from his right leg up and across his body ending at the upper left tip of his mask.

The Grand Vizier stumbled backwards, tearing his robes from his body. The mask was bubbling where the liquid had struck it, yet he made no move to throw off the mask. The bubbling subsided and the mask remained, it was melted in a line and the left eye was damaged allowing a small portion of the Grand Vizier's face to show through. The Grand Vizier's face itself was undamaged

The Grand Vizier turned back toward the baron. The Grand Vizier was wearing gray pants and a matching gray shirt with long sleeves. His boots were black and he had his pants tucked into their tops. At his waist he wore a belt with many pouches and a few objects dangling off of it. His frame itself was muscular in build and belied his believed to be advanced years.

Baron Mugior blanched and managed to rise to his feet, pulling the king up with him and still holding the knife to the monarch's throat. He backed away from the Grand Vizier until he backed into a wall. Carefully he felt along the wall with his left hand until he found what he was looking for, a hidden switch that, when pressed, allowed the section of the wall that he was up against to move backwards. He quickly ducked into the opened wall and shoved the king toward the advancing Grand Vizier. Right as he shoved the king he slashed at the man's throat and yelled at the Grand Vizier, "Take him, he is as good as dead and I am still king!"

The baron then shoved the wall closed and left the Grand Vizier facing a stone wall and holding the rapidly dying body of Phiponoux. Avril chose that moment to re-enter the room and was stunned by what he saw. The Grand Vizier, his mask badly damaged and his robes a smoking pile in the corner. The king in the arms of the Grand Vizier, blood flowing freely from his slashed throat.

The king was awake now and knew he was dying. He had no heir; the throne would be open to Mugior unless he quickly designated an heir. He knew that he could not choose the Grand Vizier as much as he wished he could, the man had always been a good and true friend that had always held the interests of Qualor above all else. Then he spotted Avril standing in the open doorway and he recognized him as a captain of his army. He knew of Avril, had kept an eye on him and was considering having him promoted. Well now he would promote him.

"Captain Avril," he managed to croak out through his badly slashed throat.

Avril obeyed and knelt by the dying body of his liege lord.

"Captain, you are a true son of Qualor and I have had my eye on you for some time. I believed that one day you would be a general with at least a barony to your name. Now circumstances demand more than that and much sooner than either of us would have expected." Phiponoux began a deep raged coughing and knew that he must hurry.

The Grand Vizier knew what was coming and knew that Phiponoux was correct in his judgment of Avril. He could only cradle the dying form of Phiponoux and watch as the king slid the royal sigil off of his finger and demanded that Avril hold out his hand.

As he slid the ring onto Avril's hand Phiponoux said, "I give Qualor to you to rule. From this day forward you shall be Captain Avril no more, but King Avril of Qualor. Be good to the people and beware treachery such as Mugior has shown. Listen to the counsel of the Grand Vizier, he has served my father and myself loyally and is a good son of Qualor."

Avril bowed his head and wept as the life ebbed from the body of the king.

"Tomas," whispered Phiponoux, his final words leaving his lips as he died. "Thank you for being my friend."

The Grand Vizier watched as the life left the eyes of Phiponoux. He reached out and closed the fallen king's eyes then laid the body gently upon the ground. He reached out and laid his hand upon the shoulder of Avril. "Captain, you are now the king. Before I officially enter your service I must finish one last task for King Phiponoux."

"Avril looked up and asked, "What task is that?"

"Justice," was the only word that the Grand Vizier spoke. He rose to his feet and went to the wall where the baron had fled through. He did not bother with trying to locate the hidden switch, he reached out with his right hand, palm facing the wall and grasped his right wrist with his left hand. The stones of the wall exploded away from him, tumbling down the stairs that the baron had fled down minutes earlier.

Soldiers burst into the room from the open doorway and the Grand Vizier turned to face them. They were not there to fight but to defend their king.

"Soldiers of Qualor!" boomed the voice of the Grand Vizier. "King Phiponoux is dead. Before he died he named Captain Avril as his heir. Bow down and show allegiance to King Avril. I go now to bring final justice to Baron Mugior, the killer of King Phiponoux!" then he turned and followed the stones down the stairwell.

The soldiers watched as King Avril rose to his feet and turned to face them. One of them, a private named Furston, dropped to one knee and bowed his head to Avril. The other soldiers looked at him then to Avril and they too dropped to one knee and bowed their heads, all claiming allegiance to the new king.

For his part Avril was unsure of what to do next, but he knew that he now owed Furston an award of some sort for being the first to acknowledge him as king. He walked over to stand in front of the still kneeling Furston and he spoke. "Arise soldiers of Qualor and let it be known that I accept your allegiance."

The soldiers all stood and awaited orders from their new king.

"What is your name and rank soldier?" Avril asked Furston.

"I am Furston, a private, my lord," he answered.

"Furston, I hereby promote you to Sub-Captain and place you in charge of these men. Who among you is a sergeant?"

There was no answer.

"Who among you is a corporal?"

One soldier stepped forward. "I am a corporal my lord. My name is Barnabas."

"Barnabas I hereby promote you to Sergeant and all the rest of you are now promoted to the rank of corporal. All of you shall obey Sub-Captain Furston. Now come, we have to secure the throne room and seek allegiance from all others that we meet."

Avril moved through the soldiers and made his way out of the room then he stopped and turned to the soldiers.

"You and you," he said pointing to two of the soldiers. "You are to stay and guard the body of King Phiponoux; none are to enter this room until I myself return. Sub-Captain Furston, you will see to it that these two men are relieved in 4 hours time."

"Yes, my lord," Furston answered as the two guards indicated moved to stand above the body of the fallen king.

Only when he had assured himself that the body of Phiponoux was guarded from any who might try to do it harm did Avril turn and lead the rest of the soldiers out of the chambers of the North Tower.

Chapter XII

"Sir, we have reached the specified coordinates provided by Captain Martinez," Ivanova stated as she brought the Pegasus to a halt.

"Thank you, Commander," Stuart replied as he reached out and pressed the ship's comm. Button on his console. "Captain Martinez to the bridge please. Ensign Clarke, do the sensors show anything here?"

Clarke was in the process of looking into the sensor viewer and replied while still looking into the raised viewer. "Nothing except the Pegasus, sir even sub-atomic particles are way below the norm, I am reading an occasional quark, but it looks like the sub-atomic particles are 1 in a billion, if even that many. I have never seen such reading before."

"I would be surprised if you had, Ensign," said Martinez off to Stuarts left as he entered the bridge. Before Stuart could ask, "I was almost to the bridge when your hail came over the ship's intercom."

Stuart nodded in understanding. "Captain Martinez," Stuart said. "We have reached the coordinates you specified. Sensors show pretty much nothing as you just heard Ensign Clarke state. What is our next step, sir?"

"We need to ensure that we are at a complete standstill, no motion other than natural drift, and we should do our best to correct for that. Also, I will need to verify our quantum signature one last time so that we will know we have returned to the correct universe."

"Well, I won't argue with that, I would like to know that when we get home we are at the correct home." Stuart answered. "Mr. Clarke, please assist Captain Martinez in gathering all the information that he needs. Captain Martinez, do you have an estimate of how long until you are ready to translate the Pegasus?"

"I would say we should be ready to translate in just a few minutes, Captain. I just need the final reading. The translation engine is ready to go and the translation crew is ready and standing by."

Stuart nodded and sat back in his seat. He didn't have anything to do for a little while. He watched as Clarke and Martinez quietly worked together and spoke to each other in low voices. Ivanova was making minor corrections to hold the Pegasus in place, correcting for spatial drift. Stuart adjusted a few controls on his command console and the main view screen split, the upper half continued to show the view of space from the front of the Pegasus, the view was simply darkness. The lower half of the screen showed the translation engine and the translation crew from above.

"Captain Martinez, any objection of us turning the Pegasus to face the galaxy?" asked Stuart.

"One moment please, captain while I adjust the calculations," replied Martinez. He then made some adjustments on the science console and spoke to a translation crew member. A few seconds later he nodded at Stuart who then had Ivanova turn the ship. The view of the top half of the main view screen now changed as the Milky Way Galaxy moved onto the screen from the right side. The galaxy stopped and was the center of the upper half of the screen. Stuart looked at it and felt insignificant for a few moments. He realized that he was looking at not just the galaxy but at everything he had ever known shrunk down to fit on the main view screen. A billion suns burning in space with a trillion planets orbiting those suns, nebula, comets, asteroids, moons, planetoids, and in one small area of all that the totality of human civilization. Here he was, light years outside of the galaxy, farther away from human space than anyone had ever been before. Before he could ponder all this for too long Martinez interrupted his thoughts.

"We are all set, Captain. We can translate anytime you are ready."

Stuart took one last look at the galaxy and spoke, "People we are about to leave our universe for another universe. We don't know what we will find there, but whatever it is, we know it will be unexpected. We have become experts in dealing with the unexpected and are all competent in our duties so I expect that each of us will perform at our very best in the hours to come."

Everyone looked at him and he thought to himself that he needed to stop making speeches when he was nervous. He gave Martinez the go ahead signal and sat back in his seat, ready for anything.

"Martinez to Edwards, activate the translation engine, translate to 0/0/1," Martinez ordered.

"0/0/1, aye, sir," Edwards answered.

Stuart tensed up as he waited to be "translated" to another universe. He didn't know what to expect. He caught a glimpse of a bright green flash out of the corner of his eyes and continued staring at the main view screen, his hands gripping tightly to the edges of his command console. He didn't know if he would become ill as he had on his first experience with zero gravity back at the academy, but he was ready for anything as he didn't know what would happen.

✦

"Translation complete, we are now in universe 0/0/1," Martinez reported from the science console.

"What? Are you sure?" asked Stuart. He had felt nothing.

"Positive Captain," answered Martinez. "We are now in a different universe.

Stuart was not convinced. "Athena, position report," Stuart asked the ship's AI.

"The Pegasus spatial position has not changed. The quantum signature of the current universal position is 0.01," Athena's voice said from the bridge speakers. Stuart knew that their own universe quantum signature was 0.00. He turned towards Martinez.

"Captain, I must admit that I am amazed. I expected some type of effect during the translation."

"Why? Do you feel it when the ship goes into warp? Do you experience any type of effect then?"

"No, I don't but this is different. We have been using warp drive for decades and know what to expect," answered Stuart slightly indignant in his response.

"Of course, Captain, I understand what you are saying," replied Martinez soothingly. "There are no effects during the translation for us to observe as it is practically instantaneously."

"Sir," spoke up Ivanova. "I experienced an effect, I think."

"Oh?" responded Martinez. "What was the effect you think you might have experienced?"

"Out of the corner of my eyes I saw a bright green flash," Ivanova said.

Stuart spoke up, "I experienced that, too. I thought that I was just catching a light reflection from my console."

"Hmm," Martinez pondered. "I also saw the flash out of the corner of my eyes but did not think anything about it. Ensign Clarke, did you see the flash?"

"Yes, sir," Clarke answered. "I thought it was from my sensor viewer."

"Ensign, will you please survey the crew and see if they have also experienced the green flash?" asked Stuart.

Stuart and Martinez waited while Clarke queried the crew. His results were that everyone on board the Pegasus had experienced the green flash.

"Well, my hypothesis at this point is that the green flash is an effect of the translation, but to verify that I will need to have someone set to record when the green flash hits them. Is it at the exact moment of translation? Directly before? Directly after? I will have someone check that on our translation back to our universe," Martinez said to Stuart.

"Alright then, in the meantime let's go see what this universe holds for us. Commander Ivanova, please set course for the galaxy. Let's go past that last world we encountered on our way out here," Stuart ordered.

"Aye, sir, top speed," Ivanova replied.

"Athena, full sensor scan directly ahead of us please, if there is anything out there I want to know about it as soon as possible."

——————————
——————————

The Pegasus traveled for hours, everyone kept busy attending duties simply to pass the time. They were all anxious to see what this universe held in store for them. Stuart and Martinez held discussions, each trying to divine what they might find. Martinez was of the opinion that they would see a Federation virtually identical to the one they had left behind, perhaps a bit larger or smaller. Stuart put forth the suggestion that the Federation would not exist as they knew it but as a loose collection of independent worlds. The two men enjoyed their debates and became friends during the journey into this alternate galaxy.

"Sir," Ivanova reported. "We have reached the location

of the last planet we encountered but it is not here, neither is the sun that it orbited."

Martinez and Stuart looked at each other in astonishment. "Are you sure, Commander?"

"Yes, sir, I don't understand it either but we are at the correct coordinates. I verified with Athena before reporting."

"Understood, Commander," Stuart replied. He did not want Ivanova to become surely with him again. But this time she did not take offense to his questioning of her abilities. She herself had been unsure until Athena had verified their position.

"Well, perhaps the star did not form in this universe or it formed in the galaxy and is still there. Who knows? Take us into the galaxy, Commander. Let's see what is going on there?"

"Aye, sir, heading into the galaxy, top speed," Ivanova replied.

The Pegasus swept forward, sensors extended to their farthest range. The ship moved forward, for hours until finally the outer edge of the galaxy had been breached by passing through the outer most star system, a small red sun with no habitable planets which matched their charts precisely.

They continued on into the galaxy checking star systems they passed against their charts and everything was the same here as in their own universe. Finally they came to the Moldovan system. Stuart ordered a full sensor sweep of the system.

The system was as it had been when it was first discovered decades ago with one exception. There was no indication that Argos station had ever been constructed. When Stuart was satisfied he ordered them to proceed to Earth at top speed.

Days passed as they traveled to Earth. Everyone was

getting more excited the closer they neared their ancestral home planet. Each of them was extremely curious as to what type of culture had developed in this universe.

When they were within hours of the Sol system they began to get concerned. There were no radio or video images to indicate a civilization ahead. It was as if Earth was not there or at least if there were no people there.

Finally they reached the Sol system and they slowed as they approached Earth. Stuart had Ivanova put them into a geosynchronous orbit above San Francisco. Ensign Clarke scanned the planet beneath them.

"Sir," Clarke said, he sounded a bit shaken." I read no signs of civilization below. Everything is pristine. I show no signs of pollution or any type of habitats below. Sensors show no signs of human life at all."

Silence descended upon the bridge. Of all the things they had postulated, the complete absence of human life was not one of them.

"No human life at all, Ensign?" Stuart asked in a hushed voice.

"None, sir," Clarke replied.

"Ensign, please launch a level 3 probe. We will leave it here to gather readings for another expedition to retrieve."

"Aye, sir," Clarke responded as he finished prepping and launching the probe.

"Very well, Commander Ivanova, please return us to our entry point," Stuart ordered.

Ivanova acknowledged his order and took the Pegasus out of orbit and departed the Sol system, leaving behind only the level three probes orbiting the Earth.

Later in the mess hall Stuart and Martinez were eating dinner.

"What do you think could have happened?" Stuart asked Martinez referring to the lack of humanity on this Earth.

"I'm not sure. I do know that thousands of years ago

there was a catastrophe that nearly wiped out human life before it had spread very far out of Africa. I believe that it was an asteroid strike in the Indian Ocean. That was 70 to 80 thousand years ago. It has not been proven, but around that time period humanity had spread out of Africa and then suddenly retreated back into Africa. Perhaps here humanity did not survive or perhaps humanity did not even evolve, for all we know there are Neanderthals still living on this Earth."

"Well, maybe, I don't know, but the probe should collect fully detailed scans. I wonder what course the Vegan Empire has taken."

"Well, without the human race to oppose them they are probably not at war, unless another race has risen up to prominence in place of Homo sapiens."

"I hadn't thought of that. I wonder; the inhabitants of Jaros 3 were at the equivalent of late 20th century development when we discovered them 150 years ago they must be zipping through interstellar space by now."

"I was thinking more along the lines of the Hrosians, without having to battle them and the Federation the Vegans may very well be the dominant galactic race," Martinez grimly replied. He then stabbed at a potato wedge with his fork.

"If the Hrosians are fighting alone against the Vegans then I sincerely hope they are still fighting."

"Why shouldn't they be? They were fighting the Vegans two hundred years before we started moving into space. Are you going to eat that coleslaw?"

"No, go ahead," Stuart answered distractedly. He was more concerned about the possibilities of this universe than he was about the dish of coleslaw on his tray. "What if this universe doesn't have any Hrosians either?"

"Then it could be the universe that we are searching for. One where there are no space faring races. When we locate that particular universe then we can set up operations to build a fleet that even the Vegans couldn't stand against."

"You make it sound like the Vegans are invincible."

"Well, they aren't but their ships and weapons are far superior to our own. We have made tremendous advances over the last few decades in closing the gap, with some help from the Hrosians, but we still lag behind the Vegans by a good measure. We still haven't developed shields that withstand their implosion weapons for more than a couple of minutes; we haven't been able to develop the implosion weapons either. Every attempt has met with disaster."

"Antares III, I remember," Stuart quietly said as he set down his fork and picked up his coffee cup. He took a sip of his coffee and continued. "You said we are searching for a universe with no space faring races?"

"Well, I was being too literal. What we need is a universe with no space faring races in this corner of the galaxy. We need to have complete and unfettered access to the Viridian system so we can begin mining operations and build ship construction facilities there. That is what we are going to begin searching for, a universe with the Viridian system free and clear." Martinez finished as he also finished the coleslaw.

Stuart nodded in understanding and chuckled. "I hope that when you find a free and clear Viridian system, as you put it, that the duotronium is still there and has not become something like iron or uranium."

"That is always a possibility," Martinez said solemnly.

"What, are you serious?" Stuart asked. He couldn't believe that Martinez was not pulling his leg.

"Oh, the odds are infinitesimally small that the metal composition of the mines would be different, but it is still a possibility. Our motto for the entire project is -Anything is possible, just not probable."

"Well, I can't argue that we are in an alternate universe,

Earth is devoid of human life and there is nothing there to indicate human life ever evolved there. I think that perhaps we should see if the Viridian system is currently being mined by the Vegans while we are here," Stuart said as he stood up from the table and picked up his tray.

Martinez also stood and brought his tray with him to the wall recycle unit where both men dumped their trays then proceeded to leave the mess hall. "No, captain we do not have the luxury of surveying this universe any farther. We need to return to our own universe. Another survey ship can return here and begin investigating things here. We need to get home and report that the translation engine works and is ready for use. Also, by returning to our universe we will have proven that we can translate to another universe and then translate back to our own universe safely. We still have to return home to prove that theory."

Stuart and Martinez stopped at a junction in the ship's corridor. Going left would take them forward to the bridge, turning right would lead aft and to engineering where the translation engine was installed and being tended to by the translation crew.

"Very well, Captain Martinez," Stuart conceded. "I will have Ivanova set course to the translation coordinates and we can translate back to our universe."

"Thank you, Captain," Martinez responded. He had come to like Captain Stuart; the man had gained his respect through what he believed to be good command judgments. "I am going down to engineering to check on things, I'll come up to the bridge a little later."

Stuart nodded at Martinez and both men went their different ways.

Stuart took his seat at the command console when he arrived on the bridge and he quickly scanned over the information the console was presenting to him. He was in the habit of doing that first off whenever he came onto the bridge. Everything looked fine and he was about to give Ivanova instructions to set course for their translation point when he noticed something on the command console. What he noticed was a slight reading in the lower thermal ranges and if he hadn't seen it before he would have simply ignored it altogether.

"Red alert!" he suddenly shouted. "Shields full, weapons hot!" he immediately ordered.

"Shields full, weapons powering up," responded Ivanova who was handling weapons until Martinez could make it back to the bridge.

"Clarke," Stuart snapped out at the Ensign. "Full scans of the lower thermal ranges, full sweep. Look for a triple diamond outline energy signature."

"Scanning now, Captain," Clarke replied as he brought his face down to meet the viewer in his science console. He adjusted the sensors to sweep through the lower thermal ranges and he suddenly spotted the triple diamond energy signature. The signature was 350 meters off their port bow and slowly closing the gap in between itself and the Pegasus. He was about to report this when he located a 2nd then a 3rd signature. They were all around the Pegasus.

"Sir," Clarke reported to Stuart. "I am picking up 3 triple diamond energy signatures. The closest is 346 meters off of our port bow, the second is 577 meters off of our starboard bow and the third is 700 meters to or aft bow. All three signatures are slowly closing in on the Pegasus."

"Are there any signatures in front of us, Ensign?"

Clarke did a quick second scan before replying. "Negative, sir, only the three signatures I have previously reported."

"Commander Ivanova, I want a course set, straight ahead, top speed. Wait for my order to engage."

"Aye, sir, setting course in now," she replied, wondering

what the hell was going on. What were these triple diamond energy signatures?

Martinez chose that moment to enter the bridge. He went straight to the weapons console and took weapon and shield control from Ivanova. He checked the sensor readings and looked back at Stuart, questions in his eyes begging for answers.

Stuart slightly shook his head as if to say 'not now' then he gave Martinez an order. "Martinez, I want you to release five cloaked anti-matter mines one to starboard, one to port and three aft. I want them to activate five seconds after deployment. Commander Ivanova I want the Pegasus to go to top speed the moment those mines are deployed."

Both officers gave quick acknowledgements and went to work. A few seconds later Martinez and Ivanova both reported that they were ready.

Stuart checked his command console. He was tracking the triple diamond signatures now that he knew where they were. He waited for a few more seconds then, "Now!" flew out from between his lips and the mines were deployed and the ship shot forward, thousands of meters of distance now separated it from the energy signatures.

There were suddenly explosions from behind them, the shockwave threatened to catch the Pegasus but they were moving fast and staying ahead of the wave until the wave dissipated behind them.

"Sir," Ensign Clarke reported. "I have confirmation of five anti-matter explosions. All five of the mines detonated."

"Ivanova, what is our eta to the translation point?" Stuart inquired.

"At our current speed 17 minutes, Captain."

"Any sign of pursuit, Ensign?"

"No, sir, I no longer have contact with the energy signatures, either. They disappeared when the mines detonated."

"Then we are truly fortunate, Ensign. We will not be able to use that strategy again. One of those ships may have survived and they will inform others of our ship design and the ploy we used. Any other ships like those that we encounter will simply attack now and not try to ensnare."

"Sir?" Ivanova inquired. "What ships? Who were they back there and how did you know to look for them?"

"Those ships were Jervil Hive ships," Stuart answered grimly.

"Oh my, that can't be good," muttered Martinez. "That could mean that the Hrosians are gone."

First contact with the Hrosians was made in the Gamma Hydra system. The solo survey ship Chryasor, sister ship to Pegasus, came across an alien starship which was badly damaged and adrift with the wreckage of another ship floating in the vacuum of space only kilometers away.

The captain of the Chryasor, Commander Collins, ran full scans on both ships and determined that only one ship held any life. He hailed the ship and received no response so he locked down his ship and used a small shuttle to transport himself to the ship. He secured the shuttle near a large tear in the side of the damaged ship then proceeded to board the ship. He located the three survivors and transported each of them over to the Chryasor where he placed them in stasis. He took complete scans of each ship for the federation engineers then he boarded the wreckage of the second ship. He found only 1 body, badly mutilated which he retrieved and placed into stasis. Then Commander Collins flew the Chryasor back to Starbase 3.

The three living aliens were pulled from stasis and taken to a section of the medical that had been made secure prior to the arrival of the Chryasor. The three aliens were studied in considerable detail and eventually one of them recovered enough to regain conciseness. After a few weeks of linguistic attempts, communication was finally achieved. By this time the other two aliens had also awakened and had assisted in the attempts at communication.

The aliens were sauropods and looked like they had stepped out of Earth's Jurassic era. Each was a good meter taller than a man and they weighed on average 350 kilograms. Yet for all their size they proved to be extremely fast and agile. When the communications issues were worked out it was discovered that Earth had inadvertently taken pressure off of the Hrosian military forces. The Hrosians had been fighting a war on two fronts, one front was against the Vegans and the second front was against the Jervil Hive, a race not encountered by Earth.

The Jervil Hive was a race of insectoids that were intent on spreading throughout the galaxy and exterminating anything in their path. The Hrosians had been fighting the Jervil Hive for three centuries and were winning when they ran up against the Vegan Hegemony. The Vegans were of the same mind set as the Jervil Hive in one respect, exterminate anything in their path. The Hrosians were now stuck between the two races and were slowly being ground down. When Earth started fighting the Vegans the Hrosians suddenly gained a reprieve and used that reprieve to focus more fully on the Jervil Hive as they believed that they could once again push them back and eventually defeat them.

The Hrosians that Commander Collins had rescued knew of humanity but did not know where we had come from. One of the three Hrosians that had been rescued was S'rath. S'rath was a member of the Hrosian Royal Clutch. He was empowered to negotiate treaties and resource agreements with alien races. S'rath negotiated a treaty with Federation diplomats that established borders and trade agreements between the two powers. The Hrosians finally had allies in their struggles with the Vegans. The Jervil Hive would be left to the Hrosians as Earth had not encountered them and the Hrosians claimed that they needed no assistance against the insectoids.

One thing that is not generally known and has been kept a closely guarded secret from most citizens of the Federation is that the Hrosians consider human flesh a rare delicacy. This was only discovered when one of the three rescued Hrosians, R'atha had cornered, killed and was caught eating a technician in one of the lower sections of Starbase 3.

When presented with the evidence of the killing, S'rath then spoke of the New Chicago colony on Kronos 3. All the inhabitants of New Chicago had mysteriously disappeared 3 years earlier. Their disappearance was blamed on the Vegans. It was obvious from investigations that an alien race had gone in and rounded up everyone and taken them away. After the Sisu incident of years earlier, it was thought that the Vegans had kidnapped the colonists to further study humanity. S'rath apologized and explained that the colonists had been taken by a Hrosian hunting fleet. He regretfully pronounced that all the colonists were dead; they had all been slaughtered and eaten.

At first the few who learned of this were outraged, but at the time the Hrosians were needed to fight the Vegans. S'rath maintained that now that a treaty was in effect between the Hrosians and the Federation that it was now illegal for hunting fleets to target Federation citizens. Knowing that this could cause a public outcry against the Hrosians it was decided keep the truth about New Chicago and the incident with R'atha secret. The technician's family was told that he died in a sudden decompression caused by a buckled bulkhead. The people on the starbase that were aware of the truth were all sworn to secrecy and reassigned to the outer colonies and bases. This was better for the Federation than being forced into another war with another alien race as the public would have demanded had they learned of this Hrosian penchant for human flesh.

The other alien body that had been brought back to Starbase 3 was that of a Jervil Hive member. It was insectoid and slightly smaller than a human. It had 8 legs and resembled an arachnid. One biologist had stated in his official report that it resembled an oversized black widow spider it even had a red marking on the underside of its abdomen. The red mark was not the familiar hourglass of the black widow but was more of a jagged triangle. A full dissection of the creature discovered two venom sacs, and venom withdrawn and tested proved to be extremely deadly to human life. From that venom was developed a nerve gas that was later given to the Hrosians who were able to wipe out entire worlds occupied by the Jervil Hive. That nerve gas alone caused the Hrosians to be extremely cautious when dealing with the Federation as it brought home to them how quickly humanity could develop and deploy new technologies. The Hrosians were slow to research and develop new technologies, as were the Vegans. Humanity seems to have a knack for scientific research and development that far outpaces any alien races we have met.

"Maybe," Stuart replied to Martinez's remark. "The Hrosians may still be here fighting the Jervil Hive, too. We don't know if the Vegans exist here or not."

"I'm betting that they do," Martinez said, a troubled look on his face. "The Hrosians had the Jervil Hive on the run until the Vegans showed up at the opposite end of their territory. If the Vegans had not shown up then the Hrosians would have wiped out the Jervil Hive."

"Maybe there are no Hrosians here. It could be that the Jervil Hive is the dominant race here."

"Now that is an unsettling thought."

Stuart smiled. "Yes it is. Are the translation crew ready?"

"Ready and standing by. I have made some calculations

and we can translate back to our universe sooner if you like."

"Well, the translation engine is your area of expertise, but I think that since this is the first test of the device we should translate back where we entered," Stuart decided.

"As you say, captain," Martinez agreed. "We will be at that point in 15 minutes 42 seconds."

"Good, I am anxious to get out of here. I want to get back to that planet and see what information the probes have gathered. I am extremely curious about that place."

Minutes passed as the Pegasus raced toward their entry point to this universe. Each person on the bridge kept a strong vigil on the instruments and waited for the ship to reach the entry point. The only sound on the bridge was the normal background noises that the ship's instruments made. Quiet clicks, subtle beeps and near silent hisses of the consoles and screens were the only sounds to be heard on the bridge.

Ensign Clarke interrupted the background noises. "Captain, I am picking up triple diamond energy signatures. They are at the extreme edge of sensor range and moving in our direction."

"Damn," Stuart said under his breath. He had hoped that they had escaped from the notice of other Jervil Hive ships. "Are they heading directly toward us, ensign? Or are they simply moving in this direction?"

"They are not on direct intercept courses, sir. It looks like they are searching for something."

"Oh, they're searching for something all right. They're looking for what destroyed three of their ships, namely us. The Jervil hive ships in our universe have exceptional sensor capabilities. Hopefully we are far enough away that they don't spot us until we can reach the translation point." Stuart knew as soon as the words were out of his mouth that he should have kept quiet as Clarke gave an update.

"The signatures are all now heading directly for us. They seem to have found us, Captain."

Stuart sighed and silently cursed himself for jinxing them. "Will they reach us before we can translate?"

"I don't think so, sir," Clarke replied, his eyes glued to his viewer. "Our lead is too great. But if we were simply heading away from them at top speed, they would catch us in just under an hour."

"Ensign, you don't know how fortunate we are that we didn't encounter them when we were deeper into the galaxy. Still, I don't want to take any chances that they have better engines than we think they have. Mr. Martinez, please disperse a spread of anti-mater mines set for proximity detonation."

"Aye, Captain, programming the mines now," Martinez replied as he programmed the mines. He spent a few seconds doing this then he launched the mines. "Mines are set for proximity detonation and deployed. I took the liberty of cloaking them also."

"Will they be able to maintain the cloak until the Jervil Hive ships reach them?" Stuart asked Martinez. The cloaking ability of the anti-matter mines was limited due to power restrictions. The mines the Pegasus carried were the latest development in the field of spatial explosion technology, but the cloaking ability was limited due to a short battery life of 20 minutes.

"At the rate of speed the Jervil Hive ships are traveling the lead ships should reach the mines about 30 to 40 seconds before the batteries exhaust. It will be close, but it might give us an advantage and but us a few more minutes as the following ships slow to avoid any further mines."

"Captain Martinez, I find you to be unusually devious for an engineer," Stuart complimented him with a grin in his face.

Martinez grinned back at Stuart. "I took advanced

courses in tactics at the academy years ago. I needed the extra credits to graduate and that looked interesting. I have kept up with current tactics as a hobby ever since."

"To our very good fortune," Stuart said while silently congratulating himself for placing Martinez at weapons when he first came aboard. Although thinking back on that he had told Martinez to take the weapons console simply because everyone else was occupied with other pressing issues at the time.

"One minute to translation point," Ivanova stated from her console.

Stuart nodded at Martinez. "Translation crew, stand by for translation," Martinez spoke into his comm.

"Standing by, translation engine at 98 percent and ready to translate," Edwards's voice replied back through the comm.

Stuart watched the readouts on his command console. He watched the time count down until the Pegasus reached the translation point. "All stop, star drive on standby and normal space engines ready to engage."

Ivanova acknowledged his order with the standard "Aye, sir" followed by his orders being spoken back to him. She brought the Pegasus to a complete halt. Martinez then had Ivanova make minor adjustments to the ship's position and axis.

Stuart watched the screen while this went on, he couldn't see the Jervil Hive ships, nor could he see the anti-matter mines but he was interested in seeing if the ships would hit the mines or not.

"Ensign Clarke, how long until those Jervil Hive ships reach the mines?"

"Eleven minutes, sir."

"That soon? Those ships are a lot faster than I thought," a surprised Stuart said.

"Yes, sir," Clarke acknowledged. "According to sensor

readings those ship are traveling 35 percent faster than the top speed of the Pegasus."

Martinez cut in o n the ensign, "Translation crew reports that we are ready to translate back to our universe."

"Stand by on translation," Stuart ordered. "Ensign, I want as full a scan as you can get of those ships, try to focus on their engines."

"Trying, sir, but at this distance specifics are hard to make out. Permission to increase power to the sensors," Clarke requested.

Stuart thought over the request for a few seconds before allowing Clarke to draw power from other parts of the ship. He did not want the translation engine to suddenly experience a power loss and cut off their only real means of escape.

"I am getting some better details from the sensors about their ships; their exhaust corresponds with an anti-matter propulsion system. I am picking up a small degree of anti-protons in the exhaust trail; they are dispersing and vanishing about 100 meters from their ships."

"100 meters!" Martinez exclaimed. "Theoretically those particles should not leave the anti-matter containment core. What type of anti-matter drive have they developed?"

"I don't know, but I think it's time that we left. Someone else can come back later and try to figure this out. Ensign, reroute that extra power back to the systems you acquired it from and let's prepare to translate out of here."

"Aye, sir," Clarke replied. "Rerouting power back to ship's systems."

Stuart sat and waited while Clarke rerouted the power. Stuart pondered the engines that the Jervil Hive was using, anti-protons in the exhaust trail. A totally unknown type of star drive and they couldn't stick around to investigate further. Still, the information they had gathered would give concrete proof that a new type of star drive existed and that would lead the engineers back home down a few paths not before considered.

"Sir, the Jervil Hive ships are slowing, they are returning to the galaxy." Clarke reported.

"Interesting, they probably think that they can simply wait for us to return to the galaxy and then attempt to capture us." Martinez speculated.

"They are probably calling in more ships, too. We destroyed three of their ships and they want to know more about us and specifically where we came from," Stuart continued the speculation. He suddenly got a nasty thought. "Is there a way we can cover our translation back to our universe? I don't want the Jervil Hive here to suddenly realize that there are alternate universes and that travel between them is possible."

Martinez considered the problem for a few moments before answering. "Hmmmm, we could place a nuke a few klicks away and detonate it right as we translate, but the timing would have to be perfect down to the last decibel. It may cause them to think our ship was damaged and that the damage was irreparable."

"I like the idea, but we know that their sensors are extremely powerful and that they are probably scanning us right now and gathering as much information as they can. Hopefully our shields are protecting us from their scans, that and the distance between us and them. However, if they were to get as close as those ships we destroyed, then they could scan right through our shields and get complete details of the translation engine."

"Sir," Ivanova asked. "How do we know that they do not already have scans of our translation engines?"

"We would have picked up any communications between those ships and any other ships in the area. Since they were maintaining radio silence while they approached us, I am confident that any scans they got of us were destroyed when we destroyed their ships."

"Mr. Martinez," Stuart continued. "Here is what I want. We will start simulating power fluctuations, which will increase with time. While that is happening you will place one nuclear warhead outside the ship. The warhead will be set to detonate right as the translation engines kick us over to our universe. So, hopefully the Jervil Hive ships will think that we had a containment problem which caused our destruction. A nuclear sized detonation should cause them to believe that we were totally vaporized so they won't question why there is no wreckage to investigate."

Martinez acknowledged Stuart's orders and went ahead and began working quietly with Athena to prepare a nuclear warhead to detonate at the final moment of translation. At one point he became worried that the energy released by the nuclear explosion would overload the shields and translation engines. If the shields were overloaded then the ship would truly be vaporized. Should the explosion overload the translation engines then he was not sure what would happen. As a safeguard he had Athena run several thousand simulated runs through her CPU. These simulations took only seconds to complete each simulation indicated that an overload in the translation engines would cause one of two things, destruction of the Pegasus or translating into the wrong universe. The former would simply end them and their mission. The latter could conceivably leave them totally lost somewhere in the omniverse, unable to find their way back home again. In order to prevent that from happening, Martinez had Athena make three copies of all the translation engine coordinates and technical readouts. Should they become lost in the omniverse he wanted a way to at least ensure he could start working out the way to get home even if the computers were wiped and the translation engine damaged during the translation.

After an hour of preparation, Martinez had everything ready. The nuclear warhead was positioned outside the ship, the calculations were completed and the simulated power fluctuations should be appearing to be tearing the Pegasus apart.

Stuart smiled grimly as he nodded approval to everyone for what they had accomplished. He knew that they would only have one shot at getting this right and he was determined to get the Pegasus home.

"Everyone at stations," Stuart ordered. "Begin countdown to translation, on my mark," he looked down at the time display on his command board. "3, 2, 1, Mark!" he commanded. Martinez slapped a switch as Ivanova engaged the star drive. There was a brief flash and they were hurtling along at top speed directly toward the galaxy.

"Translation readings indicate we have arrived back at 0.00. We are back in our own universe," Martinez reported.

"Ensign Clarke, sensor readings of the translation point," Stuart ordered.

"Scanning, Captain. No unusual readings, just empty space with a low matter count, just as it was when we arrived," Clarke reported.

"Scan ahead, Ensign. Is that isolated sun out there?"

"Switching to forward scanners," Clarke replied as he adjusted the scanners. "Scanning, and, yes, there it is! The lonely sun is there, sir."

"The lonely sun, ensign?" Stuart asked Clarke, amused.

"Uh, yes, sir. I just started calling it that in my mind as it is so far outside the galaxy by itself," an obviously embarrassed Clarke responded.

Stuart caught the glancing look that Ivanova gave him and spoke to soothe Clarke's discomfort. "Actually, ensign, I like it. The Lonely Sun. It has a rather poetic ring to it, and it is fitting for the situation."

Clarke looked relieved and Ivanova relaxed a bit in her

seat. Stuart was seeing this crew mesh under his command and he suddenly felt a surge of pride. He was a part of a crew, its leader and so far things had worked out for them every step of the way. He had led them away from a doomed space station, Argos Station, he had led them out of the galaxy, led them in the triumph of defeating a Vegan ship and securing for the first time ever the body of a Vegan. He had led them out of their universe and back again. Now they were heading back into the galaxy with only one stop left before they headed back home to the Federation, and that was the Super Planet orbiting a star that was so far outside the galaxy that the dust and gasses of interstellar space had hidden it from everyone until he had discovered it weeks ago.

"Commander Ivanova," Stuart ordered. "Top speed to the Lonely Sun."

"Top speed, aye, aye, Captain," she replied crisply.

The Grand Vizier stalked through the tunnels beneath Qualor in pursuit of Baron Mugior. The Grand Vizier was furious and when he caught the Baron he was going to kill him as slowly as possible. He had highly valued the friendship of King Phiponoux and he would see to it personally that Mugior paid for the murder of the king.

The Grand Vizier reached up and felt along his mask as he moved through the tunnels. He poked his fingers into the holes in the mask created when the Baron splashed the acid across his body. The Grand Vizier's robes had protected his body as the mask had protected his face. Fortunately, the mask was not too badly damaged and still covered most of his face keeping his features hidden. Keeping his face hidden was of great advantage, when he wished to move about Qualor anonymously he simply removed his robes and mask and he was then just another face in the crowd, freely able to move about undetected.

The acid had slightly melted his mask and even melted a few small holes into it allowing a brief glimpse into the face behind the mask. The Grand Vizier grunted as his fingers pushed through the holes and into his cheek.

Looking ahead he could see that the tunnel forked ahead. He stopped at the fork and looked down the right fork and the left fork. He did not know which way the Baron had gone and there was no tell tale sign pointing the way either. He angrily stomped his right foot on the ground and let loose a primal yell from his lungs. The yell carried all the anger and frustration that he was feeling. Should the Baron be near enough to hear he would no doubt run faster in panic.

The Grand Vizier then pulled a small device off of his belt and spoke into it. He then replaced the device back upon his belt and stood there, waiting. Minutes passed, the Grand Vizier studied the walls of the underground tunnel, and he noted the stones and the dry cracks running through them. The only light came from a shaft overhead that angled up into the streets of Qualor, high above his head.

Presently he heard a quiet clicking sound coming from the right fork of the passage. The clicking increased in volume until a shadow drew forth from the darkness to reveal the two sentinels he had called. The clicking noises they made were their metallic tentacles hitting the stone floor of the tunnel as they moved forward.

The sentinel on his right has a box entwined within its tentacles. The Grand Vizier reached out and took the box from the metallic creature. The box was designed so that only the Grand Vizier could open it. There was a small sensor pad inset within the lid of the box. Taking his thumb and pressing it into the sensor pad brought forth a barely audible click and the top of the box popped up about a

✦

millimeter, just enough to indicate that it was open. The Grand Vizier then flipped the lid open and handed the box to the sentinel. The sentinel curled a tentacle around the box and held it while the Grand Vizier removed his damaged mask. Handing the damaged mask to the sentinel he pulled a new mask from out of the box and secured it to his face. He then pulled fresh robes out of the box and donned it, once again covering his body with the dark cloth.

He indicated to the sentinel that it should deposit the damaged mask into the box. After this was done, the Grand Vizier closed and sealed the box. He then gave instructions to the sentinel which in turn wheeled and retreated down the passageway it had arrived from.

The Grand Vizier quietly gave instructions to the other sentinel which then turned and proceeded down the left hand fork of the tunnel. The Grand Vizier satisfied that everything was in order proceeded down the right hand fork which the sentinel conveying the box had disappeared into moments earlier.

The Grand Vizier, in a low voice said "night vision" and his new mask responded with the milky white eye holes of the mask changing, becoming an eerie glowing green to any observer. This gave the impression that the Grand Vizier was a demon from the nether regions of the underworld. The inner aspect of the mask allowed the Grand Vizier to see in the darkness of the passage. Should the sensor grid of his robes detect any others about he would know of it immediately and could deactivate the night vision before they were aware that he was near.

The Grand Vizier ran down the passage, oblivious of anything except his goal. Anger and frustration fueled his headlong flight down the passage. He ignored the wooden doors set into the passage walls which were set at seemingly random intervals. Eventually he came to another passage that intersected the passage he was running down. He turned right into the cross passage and continued running as fast as his legs would carry him.

Within minutes he reached the end of the passage. He was in a cul-de-sac with no doors and only bald faced stone walls. Holes in the end wall rose up into the blackness on the passage. The holes were randomly set into the stone but if one studied them carefully the realization that these small holes were in fact, hand and foot holds that could be used as a ladder. The Grand Vizier immediately jumped up as high as he could and grasped one of the holes with his right hand and pulled himself upwards, his other hand and feet also grasping for the holes. He climbed until he reached a small trapdoor above his head. He reached up and slid a latch and reached into a small recess in the wall by his head. His hand felt around until it encountered a small lever which he turned. The trapdoor above him quietly slid aside.

Light from above blinded him as he scrambled to turn off the night vision of his mask. After he turned it off he waited for a few moments until he reached up and pulled himself up into the small chamber above him. He quickly kneeled down and reached into the small recess again and turned the lever back to its original position. He pulled his hand back quickly as the trapdoor slid back into place and sealed the opening with a small click. Standing up he silently activated a comm device in his mask.

He silently stood and waited for the sentinel he had sent down the left hand passage to report back to him. He stood in a small chamber, only twice as large as the size of the trap door. Light filtered in from small openings far above his head. He could hear muffled voices beyond the wall and he could smell the stables that were situated on the far side of the wall.

He listened intently, using the comm device to amplify the voices beyond the wall.

"...Mugior has King Phiponoux trapped in the south tower," came a gruff sounding voice.

"I heard that the king has gathered a group of guardsmen and is holding the baron at bay until the Grand Vizier arrives," said another milder sounding voice.

"Yeah, where is the so called Grand Vizier anyway? He takes command of a returning squad and drags them back into the countryside and then suddenly a day later the baron makes a grab for the throne?" the gruff voice replied.

"Coincidence is all that was, the Grand Vizier wouldn't help Mugior overthrow the king," the milder voice spoke out, indignantly.

"That is what the Grand Vizier wants everyone to think!" the gruff voice spewed. "When the baron has gotten rid of Phiponoux then the Grand Vizier will be back and he will dispose of the baron. Then suddenly the Grand Vizier will announce that he is assuming the throne until an heir of Phiponoux can be found. And since Phiponoux has no heir he will eventually proclaim himself as the only logical choice to be king."

The Grand Vizier was getting angrier by the second. The only thing that kept him in check was the fact that he knew Mugior would be coming here before making his escape from Qualor. He would need a fast horse and the fastest horses in Qualor were in these stables.

The voices continued speaking.

"The merchant quarter is burning and there are people looting there. My cousin, Gromley, said that he had to go around the merchant quarter to report to his barracks. He said that if he'd have gone through there, the looters and rioters would have probably torn him to shreds. It's not safe for a guardsman to be in the merchant quarter right now."

"No where's safe, even these here stables are dangerous," the gruff voice said.

"That's why we're here, to guard the horses," replied the milder voice.

"Actually, that's not why I'm here," the gruff voice said. The Grand Vizier started a bit when he heard the sound of a sword sliding from its scabbard and suddenly being thrust into soft flesh.

"I'm here to make sure the baron gets a fast horse," the gruff voice said to a gurgling milder voice. The milder voice gurgled one last gurgle then the Grand Vizier heard a body being dragged deeper into the stables.

The Grand Vizier quickly pushed through the hidden panel and into the stables while the Gruff Voice was busy hiding the body of the other guard in the back of the stables. He took the opportunity to hide in the stall with the horse that the baron would be coming for.

His wait was not long as he heard the gruff voice return from the rear of the stables and resume his place while waiting for the baron. Moments later he heard the voice of the baron.

"Quickly, the horse I haven't much time to spare," the baron said while trying to catch his breath.

The door to the stall swung open and the Grand Vizier was face to face with the gruff voice. He did not waste any time, he simply sliced the man's throat with his knife and threw it directly at the baron's chest. The knife bounced off of the baron as he was wearing plate mail. The knife did cause the baron to throw himself back where he slammed up against the stone wall to his rear.

The Grand Vizier followed the knife with his body, throwing himself onto the baron bodily and pinning the man against the wall. The baron struggled trying to extricate himself from the pressure that the Grand Vizier was using to hold him against the wall. Between the strength of the Grand Vizier and the weight of his own plate mail the baron was slowly pushed down until the Grand Vizier had him pinned to the ground.

The baron suddenly allowed his body to go limp which threw the Grand Vizier off balance long enough for the baron to draw his own dagger and thrust it at the neck of the Grand Vizier. The baron was desperate. He knew if he could slay the Grand Vizier right here and now that he stood a very good chance of reigning over Qualor.

The Grand Vizier for his part allowed the baron's dagger to push towards his throat as he slapped a small device to the baron's plate mail. The device suddenly let out an electric charge and the baron suddenly stiffened up, his entire body reeling from the jolt of electricity that coursed through him. His eyes rolled up and into his head and he lost consciousness. The charge was brief and the Grand Vizier picked himself up from the ground and retrieved the charge emitter and returned it to its proper place beneath his robes. He then reached down and pried the dagger from the baron's still clenched fingers.

The Grand Vizier then went and led the horse from the stall and hoisted the baron up and over the horse then tied him onto the saddle. He then led the horse from the stables and began to walk back toward the palace. Fighting and looting that were happening throughout Qualor stopped when he led the horse with the baron tied to it past the rioters. Everyone simply stopped what they were doing and stared at the sight. The Grand Vizier of Qualor leading Baron Mugior through the city, trussed up and helpless. As word spread throughout Qualor of this event the supporters of the baron suddenly began quietly slipping out of the city and the king's supporters silently began to follow the Grand Vizier through the city. By the time the Grand Vizier had reached the palace, a third of the populace was following.

When he stopped before the main entrance of the palace he motioned for the guardsmen who were keeping anyone from entering the palace forward. He handed the reins of the horse to the guardsman that reached him and said, "Secure the baron in the north tower. The top room and keep five guards in the room with him at all times. Keep his hands and feet tied, I do not want to chase after him again. Understood?"

The guardsman swallowed, his mouth suddenly dry. "Understood, sir," he managed to croak back in response. He motioned the other guards to assist him as he pulled the baron from the horse. Two guardsmen dragged the still unconscious baron into the palace with four more guardsmen accompanying them, two leading and two following. Another guardsman led the horse away to the royal stables.

The Grand Vizier turned and looked at the silent crowd that had followed him to the palace. He gestured with his right hand to the crowd. This gesture activated a loudspeaker system within his mask. His voice boomed out over the crowd, which cowered back in superstitious fear from the sheer volume of his voice.

"King Phiponoux is dead. Slain by Baron Mugior in an attempt to seize the throne. The line of Phiponoux died with the king. Before he died he appointed Captain Avril of the Qualorian City Guard as the new king. This is within the tradition of Qualor. Return to your homes and ponder what future now awaits Qualor."

The crowd stood in shocked silence at the confirmation of the rumors of the king's death. They were suddenly unsure of their future and that of Qualor. The Grand Vizier at once pitied and envied them. His pity was that they had to be told what to do, that they would not think for themselves. His envy was for the same reason, as he never had the luxury of having someone else do his thinking for him. The Planetary AI always gave him his assignments, but it never told him how to accomplish his goals, only that they be accomplished.

He watched as the crowd slowly dissipated, many wandering off toward their homes, some gathering into small groups that moved off together, discussing amongst themselves the rumors that he had confirmed for them.

Finally, the Grand Vizier turned and made his way into the palace. He passed palace workers and courtiers along his path to his own small private section of the palace. All that he passed had looks of grief and shock or that of anger and disappointment. He gathered that those with the latter looks had been supporters of the baron and he made mental notes of their names. He would have them investigated later, but for now he had another task to perform.

This task did not concern the events that had transpired in Qualor. While he had been running through the underground passages beneath the city the Planetary AI had sent a message to him. The message had been encrypted. That in itself was unusual as no one on Origin had any sort of advanced technology except for the Planetary AI and that handful of humans that served the great artificial intelligence. Only one other time had he ever received an encrypted message. That message had been encrypted because one of the other people who served the Planetary AI had gone rogue. That woman, Rosarva had served the Planetary AI for over 230 years. She had always accomplished her assignment, although she sometimes tended to leave a great deal of collateral damage in her wake. Whatever it took to accomplish her mission she would do with no thought to the consequences. Her last assignment was to prevent a war between the Tribesmen of Hern and the Coraqui. The two had been rivals for centuries and both sides were prepared to go to war. A war between the two rivals would have laid waste to both sides and have severely impacted Qualor, Donaria and a few scattered kingdoms. Her solution was to distract the Tribesmen of Hern by having Qualor resume work on its western most outpost while dropping a meteoroid onto the lands of the Coraqui.

Rosarva had manipulated the Qualorian king, grandfather to Phiponoux into once again attempting to establish a western outpost and conducting raids against the Tribesmen of Hern. Once that part of her plan was well underway the Coraqui were gathering their separated tribes together to begin their sweep down into the land controlled by the Tribesmen of Hern. Rosarva then took a class three shuttle into space and headed into the galaxy proper. Arriving at a star system she scanned for and quickly located a suitable asteroid. She placed a tractor beam on the small rock and headed back to Origin.

Upon her return to Origin, Rosarva placed the asteroid into a geo-synchronous orbit sliced a small piece of the rock away from the main body. She then aimed the piece at the lands of the Coraqui. She claimed that she had it aimed at an uninhabited area a few miles away from where the main Coraqui army was gathering.

The meteoroid smashing into the earth nearby the Coraqui army would have been a signal that fighting the Tribesmen of Hern would bring disaster upon the Coraqui as the Coraqui were very superstitious, as are many of the peoples populating Origin.

The meteoroid missed its mark and instead of smashing into the target site it crashed directly onto the massing Coraqui army. Thousands died in the initial impact. The Coraqui as a people were virtually wiped out. The Planetary AI upon checking the meteoroid's flight coordinates discovered that the army had been the intended target all along.

Rosarva had remained in orbit and had not returned to the surface after the impact. The Planetary AI ordered her to return immediately and she replied by shutting down the shuttle's AI control system. Taking manual control of the shuttle she broke orbit and headed back toward the galaxy.

The Planetary AI sent the encrypted message out to Tomas and Fafniria. Both were given ships and course plots. They were to locate and retrieve Rosarva. Tomas had located her shuttle, abandoned on an outlying colony world of the Earth based Federation. Her trail had gone cold after that, Tomas believed that she had fled to the inner worlds and he was not authorized to follow. He retrieved her shuttle and returned to Origin. Fafniria had remained to track and locate Rosarva.

He had not seen Fafniria since that day. She had never returned to Origin. The Planetary AI had sent a sentinel to retrieve her hidden shuttle a decade after she had vanished into the core worlds of the Federation seeking Rosarva.

A few years after the incident, Tomas was informed of the death of the grandfather of Phiponoux and ordered to undergo rejuvenation then proceed to Qualor to assist in the cleanup of the aftermath of the westward expansion that Rosarva had initiated.

And now, decades later he was once again receiving an encrypted message from the Planetary AI.

After he had regained his quarters in the palace he sealed himself into his private chambers and set about decrypting the message. The message had gone out to him only; the Planetary AI had not contacted any of the others.

The message was short but directly to the point.

"Federation ship has taken up orbit. Scans reveal crew of 14 humans. No positive identifications have been made. Scans also reveal the presence of universal translation engine and ancillary devices. One shuttle has launched and course indicates a landing northwest of Qualor. Prepare for foreign human incursion into Qualor. Sentinels standing by to assist if required."

A Federation ship in orbit, that had been predicted

but was not expected for another 50 to 200 years. The Planetary AI had never expected a Federation ship, the great intelligence had postulated that the Federation would crumble from within and be replaced by the first human galactic empire within the next few decades. The Planetary AI had billions of years of experience and never had a Federation or any form of democracy been able to control more than a handful of star systems. Only an empire was capable of controlling anything on a larger scale. The most successful had been the Third Garellian Empire. That empire had, at its height, controlled 36% of the galaxy. That was thousands of star systems. The logistics of something on that scale boggled Tomas's mind.

The Planetary AI had mentioned on one occasion that it was impressed with this particular Federation. The current Federation had been in existence five decades longer than any previous democratically run solar government. This Federation controlled .67% of the galaxy. The longest and largest previous human federation had only controlled .48% of its galaxy. That federation gave way to the Garellian Empire. The Planetary AI concluded that the empire that would replace this federation would grow to become the largest and most successful empire to date. The galactic control was predicted to be on the order of 54.6%.

Tomas had work to do to prepare for the arriving visitors from the Federation. The first thing that he did was to request an inbound analysis of the ship now in orbit. He was curious of which part of the federation that the ship had traveled from to arrive at Origin. There were three points that the ship could have left the galaxy from that were within federation territory. Just because he was the Grand Vizier of Qualor did not mean he was not allowed hobbies. His one truly intensive hobby was studying the Earth Federation and the space they controlled.

Tomas knew that they were at war with the Vegan

Empire and that the Hrosians were an ally, even if they were an uncomfortable ally. Tomas had made the federation a hobby of his since he had returned from the galaxy with Rosarva's shuttle all those years ago. The federation and the Hrosians had managed to push the Vegan's back to a point but now there seemed to be a stalemate where each side could go no farther. At least the Jervil Hive had been beaten with the advent of the federation arriving on the scene to bolster the Hrosians. Sauropods were easier to deal with than insectoids.

The three points that the federation ship could have journeyed from were the Argyl IV, Vergil VII or Comish III star systems. Bringing up the data on those three systems he noted that Argyl IV was the newest colony, established 23 years ago and totally agrarian at this stage in their development. Vergil VII was home to a hydrogen mining operation on the fourth planet, a gas giant that was the twin in size to Origin. A colony had been established on the third planet 73 years ago and was thriving. The final system on his list was Comish III. That system had a federation naval training facility and a major naval base. The federation 12th fleet was based at Comish III. The 12th fleet was the federation's newest fleet. The fleet consisted of the federation's newest ship designs. There were two carriers, four heavy cruisers, eight destroyers and 1 of the new dreadnaught class ships.

Tomas thought it was most likely that the ship now in orbit journeyed from Comish III. While he was awaiting the information on the ship's inbound trajectory he began a high level scan of the ship in orbit. He was curious what a universal translation engine might be and concentrated his scans on the engineering section of the orbiting vessel.

CHAPTER XIII

AN HOUR BEFORE THE Grand Vizier began pursuing Baron Mugior through the city state of Qualor the Pegasus slid into orbit above Origin.

"We are now in standard orbit," Ivanova informed Stuart.

"Thank you, Commander" he replied as he studied the planetary landscape being displayed on the main view screen. They were in a geo-synchronous orbit above what looked to be a large pre-medieval city. Something was happening in the city as groups of people were running about, fires were evident in many of the buildings and chaos generally seemed to be running rampant.

Stuart had Ensign Clarke begin scanning the planet while they were on final approach and this one city seemed the best place to slip in and take a look around. The rest of the planet seemed to be relatively quiet and peaceful. With all the chaos happening in this one city it should be possible to slip in, gather a little bit of intelligence, record enough of the language to be able to create a translation algorithm and slip back out undetected.

"Ensign Clarke," Stuart said moving his attention from

the main view screen and lifting himself out of his command chair. He stretched to loosen up his cramped joints. "Please have appropriate garb assembled and ready for three people. I will be going down to the surface along with yourself and crewman Edwards."

"Yes, sir," Clarke replied. He managed to keep the excitement out of his voice. This was the most adventurous assignment that he could have ever hoped for. First a posting to Argos Station and learning about the translation engine and what it theoretically could do, then boarding the Pegasus and barely escaping Argos station as the Vegans attacked and destroyed the station. After that it was a one on one battle with a Vegan scout craft and the recovery of an actual Vegan corpse. Then off to an alternate universe where the Jervil Hive seemed to be the dominant race then a running battle to return to their home universe. Finally to top it all off; the discovery of a huge planet five times larger than Jupiter which was completely earthlike and a chance to go down to the surface and investigate.

Ensign Clarke was definitely nothing if not excited.

30 minutes later Ensign Clarke, crewman Edwards and Captain Stuart were assembled in the hanger bay. Captain Stuart ushered them into the waiting shuttle and gestured for Ensign Clarke to take the helm while motioning crewman Edwards to strap himself into a seat by the hatch.

After Stuart strapped himself into the navigator's seat he checked the navigation board and finding that all was in order he gave a quick look to Ensign Clarke. Clarke nodded his readiness and Stuart hit the comm switch.

"Shuttle One ready for departure," he informed the bridge crew. Ivanova's voice acknowledged him. With her acknowledgment red warning lights began to flash in the shuttle bay as it depressurized. Seconds passed as the atmosphere was removed from the shuttle bay then the bay doors parted and the shuttle was now free to depart.

Clarke sat ready as Athena remotely guided the shuttle from the Pegasus. Once clear of the Pegasus Athena relinquished control and Clarke took over. He turned the shuttle into a pre-programmed flight course and took the shuttle down toward the planetary surface. As the shuttle passed form the vacuum of space and entered the upper atmosphere the front of the shuttle began to glow with the heat of re-entry. Within a few minutes turbulence began to rock the shuttle.

"We are hitting a storm front, Captain," Clarke explained to Stuart. "Once we pass through it the turbulence should pass. Our LZ is 75 klicks north."

"Very good, Ensign," Stuart replied. He unlocked his chair and swung it around to face crewman Edwards. He couldn't help but grin when he looked at Edwards. The crewman was dressed in what looked like one of the soldier's uniforms that they observed from above. Stuart thought it was appropriate for the crewman to be dressed as a soldier as he was attached with the security section of the fleet. He was mush like a marine serving aboard a naval ship of centuries past. Stuart himself was dressed in a simple homespun tunic with hand woven pants and leather-skin boots. He had a cloth belt tied around his waist and a small pouch tied to the belt. Many of the people in the surveillance shots of the city they were going to infiltrate were dressed in much the same manner. He also wore a faded looking green cloak.

"Sir, I am picking up an energy field surrounding the shuttle," Clarke announced, his voice rising a bit in tension.

"What kind of energy, Ensign," Stuart asked as he swung his seat back around to study the sensor readouts.

"I don't know sir; I've never seen anything like it before."

Stuart studied the readouts and opened a link back to the Pegasus. "Athena, an energy field seems to be encompassing the shuttle. I've never seen energy readings like these before. Can you run an analysis?"

"I am unable to determine your location, Captain. The shuttle has disappeared from sensors and I cannot get a visual lock. The shuttle vanished off of the sensor grid the moment you entered the outer atmosphere," Athena replied. Stuart could swear she sounded perturbed.

"Ensign, is this energy field causing any you any problems flying the shuttle?" Stuart asked Clarke as he himself ran diagnostics on all the shuttle's systems.

"No, sir. The helm is responding normally." Clarke answered, his voice had returned to normal as he realized that everything seemed normal.

"How long until we land?"

"Four minutes, sir."

Stuart swung back around to face Edwards. "Crewman Edwards, when we touchdown you and I will disembark and head directly into the city. We should have a few hours until dawn and I want us to get in, take a quick look around, get a few recordings to get a start on the language algorithms and get back to the shuttle."

Edwards nodded and replied, "Understood, sir." As Stuart swiveled his seat back to face forward he noticed Clarke's look of disappointment. "Don't worry, Ensign. You'll get to walk around a bit. It will just be in the vicinity of the shuttle. We have to make sure that the shuttle is guarded."

"I understand, sir. I just would rather be going into the city with you."

"I know, but look at the bright side, you've already established yourself as a rising young officer. After all you led the foray onto that Vegan scout and retrieved an actual honest to goodness Vegan corpse. That in itself will put you onto the fast track for promotions, medals and glory."

"Yes, sir. And those things could get me killed very young also."

Stuart looked at Clarke with a new respect in his eyes. For a young man to realize that medals and glory could equate to an early death and be able to admit it, well that showed thoughtfulness that most officers did not begin to show until they were lieutenant commanders, if at all.

"Ready for landing, sir," Clarke said.

"Circle, Ensign. I want to do a quick scan for life forms. I am hoping that there is no one out there to see us land," Stuart said as he ran the scanners over the landing zone. He did a multiple scan to be sure there was no one nearby. Satisfied that they could land unobserved he told Clarke to land "in that gully over there" as he pointed through the view port.

Clarke guided the shuttle into the gully and swiftly brought them to rest, the landing jets kicked up dirt and small plants as the shuttle settled down onto the ground. The shuttle was leaning slightly to port, as the ground was not level.

Stuart and Edwards un-strapped and moved toward the shuttle's door while Clarke shut down the engines and began running more scans. Stuart and Edwards checked their equipment waiting for Clarke to give the all clear.

"Captain, I am picking up a strange energy reading. It, uh, I mean, uh, it's gone."

"Is it the energy field surrounding the shuttle?"

"No, sir. That field is gone; it disappeared when I shut down the engines. This was different, smaller, almost like a small powered vehicle."

"Were you able to pinpoint the source?" Stuart asked, becoming concerned.

"Only a general location, sir," Clarke replied as he continued running scans and studying the displays. "It seemed to come from inside the gully wall, 90 meters that way," Clarke said as he gestured toward his right.

"Whatever it was, sir, it's gone now. It may have been

a sensor echo of the shuttle bouncing back from the gully wall. The wall contains a small amount of magnesium."

"Alright, ensign I am changing your orders a bit; I want you to remain secured inside the shuttle. After we leave I want this shuttle buttoned up tight and a level 2 force field erected around the shuttle. Dawn is in approximately six hours, we should return in four. If we fail to return in four hours and do not make radio contact after 5 hours, then you are ordered to return to the Pegasus. After that it will be up to Captain Martinez to decide what to do after that. Understood?"

"Understood, sir," Clarke replied.

"Let's go, Edwards. We need to hustle if we are to get there and back before dawn."

Clarke sealed the hatch behind Stuart and Edwards after they exited the shuttle. He then returned to the helm station and retook his seat there. He then set about erecting the force field then he decided that he wanted to see what was going on outside. Since he had been ordered to remain inside the shuttle he launched a surveillance drone. He programmed the drone to remain in stealth mode and to hover 500 meters above the shuttle.

Once the drone was in place he activated the night vision lenses of the drone. He was able to view the surrounding area as if it were early morning rather than darkest night outside. He zoomed in on Stuart and Edwards and observed them making their way out of the gully as they began jogging towards the city off in the distance.

He wanted a closer view of the city and directed the drone to rise to 1000 meters. He zoomed the pickup feed in on the city for a better view. He could now make out individual buildings and see how the city walls were guarded. He saw a large number of separate spires reaching skyward like fingers stretching upwards from many hands. Many of the spires had light spilling onto balconies from windows and balcony doorways.

Clarke saw shadowy figures moving on a few of the balconies and along the top of the wall that ran around the city. He felt confident that the figures on the wall were guards; the figures on the balconies were probably those who lived or worked in the spires, out on their balconies watching the erupting chaos in the streets below.

Clarke watched the city for a few minutes, recording details and exploring what he could from the security of the shuttle. He checked on the progress of the captain and Edwards every few minutes. They were well on their way to the city when the feed from the drone suddenly went dark.

Thinking that there had been a failure in the drone Clarke was reaching out to the controls when the shuttle lost all power. Moments later an object struck the top of the shuttle. Clarke correctly surmised that would have been the falling surveillance drone.

Swearing softly under his breath, Clarke reached under the console and retrieved a flashlight then left his seat and made his way through the dark interior of the shuttle and located the engineering panel in the rear of the cabin. He was just finding the manual release mechanism when the shuttle's hatch suddenly opened behind him.

Clarke spun around and in the doorway of the shuttle stood a shadowy form, indistinct in the darkness. He raised his flashlight and audibly gasped at the creature that his flashlight illuminated. The thing was a silvery orb resting atop a group of 6 meter tentacles. The tentacles were supporting the thing and seemed to be the form of locomotion of the creature.

Clarke was not carrying a sidearm and could do nothing more than stare at this thing that was hovering in the doorway of the shuttle. Suddenly the thing flowed forward upon a few of its tentacles as other tentacle reached out and knocked the flashlight from his trembling hand.

Clarke pressed himself flat against the rear bulkhead of the shuttle then he felt a touch at the base of his neck. Then all was darkness.

All was quiet within the shuttle for a few minutes until the sentinel emerged from the shuttle, the prostrate form of Ensign Clarke held securely within its tentacled grasp. The sentinel moved off into the darkness, carrying the hapless ensign to whatever destination it was bound for.

Stuart and Edwards came across a road and followed it toward the city. They jogged down the road, both of them wearing night vision glasses to assist them in their haste.

Stuart observed that the road ran smooth and flat; it was made of a type of primitive concrete. On either side of the road there was nothing but the valley wilderness, much like a prairie yet there were farms off in the distance. A number of small dirt roads intersected with the main road, which he surmised led to the farms.

As they neared the city walls buildings began appearing, possibly stables, inns or other places where people could gather. Stuart motioned to Edwards and they both halted. A few meters ahead ran another concrete road that looked as if it led around the city walls. Looking about to ensure that no one was nearby Stuart then removed the night vision glasses and secured them in his pouch. Edwards followed suit and the two men moved forward toward the huge gate that was the entrance to the city.

They reached the gate in short order and stopped. The gate itself was closed, completely barring their way into the city. The gate was constructed out of wood and was completely solid. There were a few others milling about the center of the gate where Stuart could make out a smaller doorway set into the gate itself.

On either side of the doorway there were two guardsmen holding what looked to be pikes. They were there to guard the doorway but standing between them was another guard, perhaps an officer who was questioning people as they entered the city or were turned away depending upon their answers.

Stuart motioned Edwards to follow him and the two men moved away from the gate to wait out the small crowd. Minutes passed as the guardsmen allowed entrance or turned away people. Finally only the guardsmen were left and the officer turned his attention to Stuart and Edwards.

He spoke something unintelligible at Stuart and Edwards and motioned them forward. Stuart nodded at Edwards and they moved forward. Each had a stunner concealed in his hand. Upon reaching the gate Stuart raised his stunner and fired at the officer. Edwards fired at the same time at the guardsman on the right. Stuart was able to stun the guardsman quickly on the left then the two of them quickly slipped into the city.

They kept the stunners in their palms as they entered the city proper and quickly moved away from the gate. Stuart suspected that there would usually be more guardsmen about but with all the chaos happening this night he supposed that they were all in the city trying to fight back the chaos that spread throughout the city this night.

"Keep your stunner handy, Edwards. I'm going to get the bug ready for language recording," Stuart said in a low voice. He looked around as he slipped his hand into his pouch and dug around until his fingers came into contact with a small device. Grasping the item he withdrew his hand form the pouch and quickly examined the device.

The device was small in that it fit comfortably in the palm of his hand. It resembled a small dragonfly; its wings looked as if they were made of gossamer. Stuart pressed his thumb into a spot on the device's body just beneath the wings and it suddenly flew out of his hand and took to the air. The device hovered for a few moments then it flew off toward the distant murmur of voices.

"Ok, that's done. Let's see if we can't get a few up close scans of this city while the bug gathers data and assimilates a database," Stuart said to Edwards.

The two men moved further into the city. They passed doorways and structures that were made of stone. Wooded doors were closed and windows shuttered against the insanity that ran through the city. The streets they passed through were dark, with only the stars above and the glow of fires off in other parts of the city providing any type of light.

They exited a rather narrow street and emerged onto a wide boulevard where what looked to be temples lined both sides of the expanse. Some of these temples had stairs rising up toward altars while others stood in cyclopean grandeur with only a small opening in the front acting as an entranceway.

No one was about and all was silence. The priests were all probably holed up in their temples and praying to their various gods for divine protection this night. Stuart and Edwards quietly moved down the boulevard. Edwards had the stunner in the palm of his right hand and a small holo-recorder in his left hand. Everyone back on the Pegasus would be seeing what Edwards was now recording as he was transmitting the information directly to Athena.

Stuart led Edwards over to an elaborate fountain that rested in the center of the boulevard. Upon reaching the fountain Stuart motioned Edwards to remain close as Stuart circled the fountain. They moved completely around the fountain until they reached the point where they had begun. Edwards grinned at Stuart and indicated the holo-recorder.

"I got the entire fountain on holo, Captain. Everyone upstairs is probably getting a real kick out of it. And did you see the jewels built into the thing? They must be worth a fortune!"

"Yeah, it sure looks like it," Stuart replied as he glanced about the boulevard. The fountain rested in a plaza where two wide boulevards intersected. "All of those jewels in the fountain and there is no one here to guard it, especially with the riots happening all through the city. You would think that someone would be watching to make sure no one tried to pry a couple of diamonds or emeralds off of the thing."

"Maybe it's a religious thing for these people. They could be scared of the gods or some such thing," Edwards suggested.

"I don't completely disagree with you, but in every society there are those who don't believe in whatever gods are worshipped. And from the looks of this place they have a lot of gods."

"Yeah, kind of like the ancient Greeks or Romans. A god for everything, love, war, weather, you name it and it looks like there is a god for it here."

"That it does, Edwards that it does. Looking about I don't see anything that looks like any of them support human sacrifice. So I suppose that's a good thing. Let's head back towards the gate. The bug should have assimilated a database by now and we need to get back to the shuttle."

"Yes, sir. Should I continue recording?"

"Negative, we need to be more careful going back. I am getting the sense that something has happened and that things are starting to return to what passes for normal around here."

"Sir," Edwards replied. "What makes you think things are quieting down?"

"The temple priests are starting to emerge from their

temples and some of them are cleaning up," Stuart responded gesturing toward a temple off to their right.

A priest had come out of one of the temples. He was covered from head to toe in gray robes and he wore a full head covering that completely concealed his features. In his hands rested what could only be a broom and he had started to sweep the area in front of his temple. The temple was one of the large stone temples, completely featureless on the outside with an opening in the front that would only allow people to enter in single file procession.

Edwards turned the holo-recorder upon the priest and zoomed in on the man. He suddenly received an impression that something about the man was not right. The way that he moved was too fluid, too graceful somehow. The man seemed to glide over the ground rather than walk.

"Sir," Edwards began. "There is something about that priest that ..." he didn't finish the sentence as Stuart was already moving toward the temple. Edwards slipped the holo-recorder into his pouch and followed Stuart at a discreet distance, his stunner now ready pointed in the general direction of the priest and ready to fire should the need arise.

The priest suddenly turned and slipped back into the temple. Stuart halted and let Edwards catch up to him.

"Do we follow, sir," Stuart inquired.

"No, we aren't here to solve any mysteries, at least not this trip."

A commotion suddenly erupted from the other end of the plaza. A large crowd was moving forward, being herded by guardsmen. The guardsmen were pushing and shoving people through the plaza and were rapidly approaching the temple that Stuart and Edwards were standing in front of.

"Quickly," Stuart suddenly hissed through clenched teeth as he pushed Edwards toward the temple entrance. "Into the temple we don't want to get caught up in anything."

Stuart and Edwards cautiously entered the narrow passageway that led into the temple. Stuart stopped Edwards a few feet inside the dark entranceway and both men flattened themselves up against the interior walls of the passageway, trying to blend into the darkness and shadows that engulfed the entrance passageway.

The crowd came closer to the temple and as they neared Stuart lightly touched Edwards on the arm and indicated that he move deeper into the passageway. Voices were raised in the approaching mob, although they could make out words being spoken and shouted neither man understood what was being said. The voices didn't sound so much angry as frustrated. Both men stood silently in the darkness.

Stuart watched the crowd pass by the entrance of the temple and eventually the voices faded and all was quiet again. He waited a while longer to be sure the coast was clear and quietly spoke to Edwards. "I think they've gone the way should be clear now. Let's head back to the gate, locate the bug and get back to the shuttle."

Stuart started to move back towards the entranceway when he felt Edwards tug at his arm. He stopped and turned to see what Edwards wanted. What he found confronting him was not Edwards but the priest that they had seen earlier.

The priest was not human. It was a tentacled monster and it had an unconscious Edwards clutched in two of its tentacles. Stuart started to reach for his pouch to find his stunner, never stopping to think that the stunner might not work against this metal monstrosity. He never completed the movement as he suddenly felt a shock from the tentacle that was now wrapped around his left arm. He felt a brief moment of agony then he joined Edwards in unconsciousness.

The Grand Vizier adjusted his mask before stepping

froth from his apartments in the palace. He was receiving reports from the Planetary AI regarding the ship now in planetary orbit.

The ship had launched a landing craft while he was pounding through the underground passages in his ultimately successful attempt to capture Baron Mugior. The Planetary AI had dispatched a sentinel to the craft's landing site where it had captured one person who had remained aboard the craft.

The craft itself was well hidden in a gully southeast of Qualor and it was extremely unlikely that anyone would stumble across it for the time being.

Two others had left the shuttle and were even now wandering around Qualor. The Grand Vizier suspected that they had chosen Qualor due to the rioting and fighting that had been ongoing for the last several hours due to the assassination of King Phiponoux. They would be able to go virtually unnoticed in all the ongoing confusion.

What were they looking for? The planet itself would be enough to grab their attention, a world the size of a large gas giant that was able to support life. The physics alone would be enough to make them want to find out why certain things, such as gravity were not as they should be. Then when they were closer to the planet they couldn't help but notice the satellites and orbital installations.

The surface would be a totally different story compared to the objects in orbit. The orbital installations would suggest an advanced culture occupied the planet but upon scanning the surface they would see nothing but primitive cultures running about in wooden ships with stone walled cities and armies armed with swords and shields.

The contrast would be impossible for anyone to ignore. The first questions any visitors would seek answers for would be is the current civilization on the planet the builders of the orbital installations and if so had they been knocked back to an earlier technological level by a war or disaster of gigantic proportions?

And the best way to seek those answers would be to go down to the planet and look around. The first thing they would need to do would be to try to learn the local language.

So perhaps they were here to try to record examples of the language so their computers could analyze and then translate for them. They should have computers capable of doing that if they were able to journey this far out of the galaxy.

As the Grand Vizier left the palace he received another communication from the Planetary AI that the two beings from the landing craft were now heading in the direction of the Avenue of the Gods. At the same moment the Grand Vizier noticed that guardsmen were surrounding a fair sized crowd and holding them at bay with their swords.

Striding over to the officer in charge he demanded to know what was happening here.

"Sit," the startled officer replied. "These people here," he gestured at the small crowd with the sword clutched in his hand, "are all under suspicion of aiding Baron Mugior."

The Grand Vizier looked past the officer and into the crowd. A sizable portion of the crowd was composed of women. There were a few soldiers here and there and the rest were local merchants, some of whom he had conducted business with before, although none would know it as he usually did business without the Grand Vizier robes and mask. It was simplicity for him to move about Qualor unnoticed when he wanted or needed to do so.

"Captain, I do not believe that these women pose any threat. The merchants, perhaps a few of them supplied some form of goods or services to the Baron, and maybe the few guardsmen sprinkled in with this lot actually raised arms against the king. But, for the moment I want them all taken to the Northern Gaol and locked up. Take them by way of the Avenue of the Gods."

"The Avenue of the Gods, sir? That will take longer than if we head directly there down the King's Row," responded a clearly puzzled officer.

"Yes, but if anyone was going to try and free these people they would do so on the King's Row. No one would think that you were heading to the Northern Gaol if you go down the Avenue of the Gods."

"Yes, sir, that makes sense. We should be able to get the prisoners there within the hour."

"See that you do, Captain. And also see to it that none of these people are harmed. I will hold you personally responsible. Do you understand me?"

The captain shrunk back and gulped as he nodded his response, too intimidated by the towering presence of the Grand Vizier to speak.

The Grand Vizier stood staring at the hapless officer for a few moments then he raised his head and stared at the prisoners. The prisoners who were restless and getting loud when he had first approached now were quieting under his faze. Within seconds the quiet had spread throughout the crowd of prisoners as they came under his stare. He made them all nervous, regardless if they were innocent or not.

Finally they heaved a collective sigh of relief as the Grand Vizier turned away from them and stalked away into the night. They were much subdues as the guardsmen prodded them into moving toward the Avenue of the Gods and soon they were beginning to overcome their fear of the no longer present Grand Vizier and began to verbally assault the guardsmen.

Within minutes they were actively challenging the guardsmen, some of them even making as if to try to break free of the crown and run away. One man, foolishly tried to grab at one of the guardsmen's sheathed sword. He got a knife driven through his hand for his efforts, which seemed to anger the crowd.

Just as the crown was beginning to become uncontrollable they turned onto the entrance of the Avenue of the Gods and suddenly fell silent and became completely docile once more.

The Grand Vizier was standing at the entrance to the Avenue of the Gods and now he spoke to them.

"You will all go with these guardsmen to the Northern Gaol each of you will locked up until an opportunity is available for justice to be done each of you. If you are innocent then you have my word you shall go free and no harm shall come to you. However, if any of you have been in league with Baron Mugior, have assisted him in any manner what-so-ever then I guarantee that you will wish you had never been born. King Phiponoux was a good and just king who did not deserve the fate thrust upon him. I shall see to it that justice is served and vengeance delivered."

The Grand Vizier's voice was not raised, yet every person in the crowd could plainly hear him. No one in that crowd doubted a single word the Grand Vizier had said and every one of them cowered away from the imposing figure the Grand Vizier made, outlined by the temples in the background.

The Grand Vizier then stepped away and motioned the guardsmen to move along with their crowd of prisoners. He watched the crowd pass before him as they were marched off to the Northern Gaol. He picked out a few in the crowd that he would have released and others that he would personally interview.

After they had passed he waited for a few moments as he listened to an update from the Planetary AI. The two from the landing craft were directly ahead and had been positively identified by a sentinel at the temple of Gereator.

The Grand Vizier moved in the direction of the temple.

He was only a few blocks from there. The temple of Gereator fronted on the Plaza of the Royal Fountain of Qualor. He hurried ahead and reached the Plaza in time to see the last of the guardsmen escorting the prisoners out of the plaza on the opposite side from where he entered.

He looked toward the temple of Gereator and saw no one about. He strode past the Royal Fountain of Qualor with its jewel encrusted facade. Every time a new monarch was anointed by the priests of the various gods a new jewel would be added. The type of jewel was determined by the priest in ascendance at the time. Phiponoux had seen the high priest of the God Hu place a large Ruby into the fountain at his anointment. The Grand Vizier thought quickly which priest would be in ascendance when Avril would be anointed and thought that it would be either the high priest of the god Krevas or the high priestess of the Goddess Bliza.

Setting aside thoughts of priests, gods and anointments the Grand Vizier entered the entranceway of the temple and strode forward. He swiftly passed through the passageway and strode into the main chamber. Looking about he saw a sentinel transporting two unconscious forms into the rear of the main chamber.

The sentinel halted at his command and he approached to see what these off worlders looked like. He gestured to the sentinel and it set the two men down upon the stone altar of Gereator and moved back.

The Grand Vizier looked the two men over and was pleased to see that they were human. He quickly stripped them of their pouches and gestured to the sentinel to once again pickup the men and follow.

He led the sentinel out of the main area of the temple and to the hidden elevator that would transport them to the subterranean transport system's platform beneath Qualor.

Less than a minute passed as the elevator dropped into the earth until it halted and the doors opened upon the transit platform. The Grand Vizier motioned the sentinel to the waiting car and followed. The sentinel placed both of the still unconscious men into the car and moved away, returning to its duties in the temple above.

The Grand Vizier entered the car and sat down on the seat facing the two men. He sealed the door and entered the destination into the car's control panel. As the car sped into the tubes that connected most areas of the planet one of the two men began to stir.

The Grand Vizier reached up and removed his mask. He set the mask on the seat beside him and studied the two men. One of them was dressed in a crude imitation of a Qualorian guardsman and the other looked to be a simple member of the cities common folk. The one dressed as a guardsman stirred again and opened his eyes. He suddenly sat upright and reached for his pouch.

The Grand Vizier smiled and held up both pouches so the man could see that he had been disarmed. The man, seeing that the Grand Vizier was not holding a weapon on him visibly relaxed. He then turned careful attention to the other man, checking to see if he was injured. When he reassured himself that the other man was simply unconscious and not hurt in any way he looked back at the Grand Vizier.

The Grand Vizier pointed at his chest and said "Tomas," giving the man his name.

The man looked at him through narrowed eyes as if trying to decide whether or not he should answer. His decision was made for him when the other man stirred and sat up with the opening of his eyes.

Once again Tomas smiled and held up the pouches. The other man then turned to his companion.

"Edwards are you alright?" he asked his companion.

"Yes, sir," the other man answered.

The second man looked around and spoke again. "Any

idea where we are," he looked out the window of the car and continued. "Or where we are headed for that matter?"

Tomas answered, his words bringing looks of surprise to both of the men's faces. "You are on Origin, which is what we call our world. As to where we are going, you shall learn that soon enough. Don't be alarmed, no harm is going to come to you. We are merely curious of what has brought you to our world."

"You speak our language!" the one dressed as a guardsman, Edwards he assumed his name was.

"Yes, I speak quite a lot of different languages. The language you call Galactic English, I learned quite a few years ago when I had opportunity to visit one of your outer colonies."

Both men started at that statement. Neither seemed inclined to speak so Tomas continued. "My name is Tomas. I am one of a group of assistants to an intelligence greater then my own." He then nodded toward Edwards. "I understand that your name is Edwards." He then looked at the other man in the swiftly moving car. "What, may I ask is your name?"

"Stuart, I'm the leader of this landing party," he replied in a cautious tone of voice.

"Pleased to make your acquaintances Mr. Stuart, Mr. Edwards. I hope that you will find our hospitality to be of your liking. We are nearly at our destination, so please relax. Soon you will be meeting the intelligence that I mentioned a moment ago."

Tomas smiled again at the two men and sat back into his seat. He studied the two further and decided that they were probably members of the Federation Naval Forces. Both men had the look of military men about them, both in the way they sat in their seats and studied their surroundings.

✦

Stuart was surprised to wake up facing a man wearing black robes with a strange looking mask sitting on the seat beside him. He was more surprised to find himself sitting in what looked like a modern subway car rushing through an underground tunnel.

But he was completely taken aback when the stranger spoke to him in a language that he fully understood, Galactic English. He was not entirely set at ease by the thought of being taken to meet an intelligence that this Tomas person described as "greater than my own."

For the moment he and Edwards were unharmed and seemingly guests and not prisoners. He suddenly wondered about Ensign Clarke.

"Tomas, did you say?" he asked the man in black robes sitting across from them.

"Yes, that is my name Mr. Stuart. DO you have a question for me?" the man replied with a smile on his face. Stuart looked into the man's eyes and the smile extended to those eyes. Still, caution was the word of the day.

"How did you know we were on your world?" Stuart asked, trying to find out if Tomas knew of their shuttle's landing site.

"Mr. Stuart, we have observed your ship since it entered our little star system here. We tracked your shuttle on its descent. We tried to reach you to make contact before you left your shuttle but we arrived too late, the two of you had already departed for Qualor."

Stuart suddenly became alarmed. If what Tomas said was true, then Clarke should have contacted him. Clarke would have contacted him were he able to do so. But then if Clarke wasn't able to contact him Athena would have if Clarke suddenly stopped transmitting. Plus, Edwards had been transmitting holo-recordings live to the Pegasus and no one there had mentioned anything being amiss at the shuttle. He relaxed again; Tomas had to be lying about anyone approaching the shuttle.

Before he could ask any more questions the car suddenly slowed and pulled into a cavernous station. As the car slid to a stop at a platform the door opened and Tomas gestured for them to exit the car.

Stuart nodded to Edwards and they preceded Tomas out of the car. Stuart noticed that Tomas had retrieved his mask and carried it with him as he gestured for them to follow him.

Looking about as they followed Tomas Stuart was astounded by what he was seeing. They had exited upon a platform that was housed within a cavern that was so huge that he could not make out the ceiling or even the wall that had to be on the opposite side of the car they had exited from. A single glowing light floated above them, lighting up the entire platform. The ceiling could be just above the light, perhaps just out of the range of the light.

Stuart followed Tomas off of the platform and into a corridor, the corridor was smooth and not made of stone as the walls of the platform were. The corridor walls looked like a composite of metal and plastic. They were cloudy looking and colored lights flickered beneath the surface, reminding Stuart of holiday lights with their twinkling effects. Soft light flowed from overhead lighting the corridor well enough to see without becoming distracted by the flashing lights within the walls.

They emerged from the corridor into a vast circular chamber that had a central platform with four seats set in a row facing a huge monitor screen. Tomas escorted them to the seats as Ensign Clarke was brought in by a pair of sentinels from the opposite side of the chamber.

"Captain," Clarke exclaimed upon seeing Stuart. "They captured you also, sir?"

Stuart nodded in the affirmative as he and Edwards

took seats following Tomas's lead. Clarke assumed the final open seat and sat silently, looking about the chamber.

Lights appeared upon the monitor screen. They flashed as a voice suddenly boomed from speakers spread throughout the chamber.

"Greetings, Tomas. Greetings to the visitors from off world," the voice started. "Tomas, have you explained to the visitors what I am?"

"No, I have not," Tomas answered, speaking in a normal tone of voice.

"Then I shall explain to them. However, I believe that a more personal presence would be beneficial. Bring our guests to our meeting room; I shall join you there shortly."

"Yes, sir," Tomas answered. He then stood and turned to Stuart and the others. "Gentlemen, please follow me."

Stuart, Clarke and Edwards stood and followed Tomas as he led them from the chamber and to another corridor. Stuart kept his questions to himself; he knew that this Planetary AI would have answers whereas Tomas may not have the answers he wanted and that Tomas may not even understand his questions.

They followed Tomas into a room off of the corridor. The room had a table with five chairs, three chairs on one side of the table, one chair to the left and one chair across from them. There was also another smaller table with drinks and snacks.

Stuart raised his eyebrows at this; he was beginning to feel less like a prisoner and more like a guest. Still, he doubted that he could simply turn around and walk out of here uncontested.

Stuart gestured at Edwards and Clarke and the three of them took seats while Tomas stood there for a moment as if he was unsure what was happening then he took the seat to their left.

After a few minutes of waiting Stuart spoke. "Tomas,

where is this AI of yours? I thought that it was going to meet us here?"

Before Tomas could answer a man walked into the room. He was dressed in white robes and he carried a beatific smile upon his face. He had no hair, his eyebrows were snowy white in color and he carried himself with an inner confidence that radiated outward from his body.

"I am here now, Captain Stuart. Please accept my apology for taking so long to arrive. I had to first link my consciousness with this body. That did not take very long, but the journey to arrive here from where this body was formed took a few minutes."

Tomas started and quickly jumped to his feet. "You are the planetary AI?" he asked the man.

"Oh, not all of me is in here, Tomas. The human brain cannot contain my entire essence. What is in here is my original mind plus a few more recent memories. I also have a link to the rest of my consciousness which is still housed within the main memory banks." The man gestured Tomas back to his seat while he himself took the seat across from Stuart and his two men.

"I am sure that you have many questions, Captain. I will answer all of your questions, but first I have some background to give you which will answer some of your questions and, I have no doubt raise new questions for you. Tomas too will gain a greater understanding of his place and service to me."

"The form you now see before you is my original form. I was born over 18 billion years ago," the man said. He then looked to each person in the room in turn while that information was taken in by each person. He then continued, "My original name was Hovar Gran and I was born in the city of Riosa on the planet Caldos. I was a researcher into artificial intelligence systems. I developed the original memory banks on this world."

"Excuse me for interrupting," Stuart said. "But I find it hard to believe that you are billion years old."

Hovar Gran smiled and with a tilt of his head in Stuart's direction responded. "I will get to that in good time, Captain. As I was saying, I had a hand in the development of the memory banks deep with this planet. This entire planet was constructed by my people. Our universe was dying; entropic dysfunction was shutting down the entire universe. We did not worry about passing with the end of our universe as we had developed technology thousands of centuries before that could transport us to another, younger universe.

"We built this world, which we named Origin to be our new home world, to carry us to a younger universe. The construction of this world took 12,000 years. We built it molecule by molecule, every aspect of our own world needed to be incorporated into Origin. Mountains, deserts, plains, prairies and highlands all needed to be placed and positioned. Many times did we remove entire areas of topologies and rebuild them differently until we were absolutely satisfied that everything was properly engineered and built. I designed the memory banks of Origin when the project was still on the design pads.

"That was 600 years before initial construction began. In order for you to understand this you must first understand that we had developed medical technology that ensured we were near immortal. We were beyond the primitive technologies of longetivity and regeneration. We had re-engineered ourselves on a genetic sub-atomic level to be as we are now.

"Captain, you have to understand that our science would be as magic to you as your own science would be as magic to a primitive cave dweller. Your science will not be anywhere near our science for thousands of years.

"Anyway, where was I, oh yes, the memory banks. I designed them to house my essence, more than my consciousness but my entire essence. Everything that makes me the person who I am is in the memory banks deep beneath our feet. My original body was broken down into an electronic stream and stored within the system for retrieval whenever it was needed. Which was the case today; I am simply following previous procedure in meeting with you in person."

Stuart opened his mouth to speak but Hovar Gran held up his hand.

"Allow me to continue on for a bit before any questions are asked, Captain."

Stuart closed his mouth and nodded. Hovar Gran continued.

Origin finally was completed and our translation engines slid Origin and the few remaining members of our race into another universe. We guided Origin to a position outside of the galaxy we emerged near and began taking scans of the galaxy. It was filled with planets teeming with life. Gas giants and uninhabitable worlds filled with resources that we could turn to our use. It was also controlled by a brutal reptilian race which we came to know as the Grath. The Grath did not become aware of us for 300 years. When they discovered us moving into what they considered their galaxy they gathered their forces and attacked us. We were forced into a war we had no desire to fight. As our war with the Grath evolved and the Grath were pushed back across the galaxy we discovered that there was human life in the galaxy.

"Reptilian and human life had each evolved in this galaxy. The humans had not evolved as early as the Grath had and they had become a food source for the Grath. Humans were to the Grath as bovine creatures are to us. We were sickened by this discovery and we brought some of our more advanced weaponry out and we quickly decimated the Grath. Where earlier we were simply trying to push the

Grath to one half of the galaxy we now would only settle for total extermination.

"This was not our finest hour. When the last Grath perished with the destruction of the star their final world orbited we came out of our madness. We saw what we had done and many of us could no longer stand to live. Many of us perished in a mass suicide. The few remaining survivors became determined to never let our hands become blood stained with genocide ever again.

"We pulled genetic samples that had been created and stored and created a new primitive race of humans. We populated Origin with them. Whenever a group of them reached a certain technological level they were taken and transported to another world within the galaxy. Thousands of years passed and human life flourished throughout the galaxy. Eventually Origin was discovered by these transplanted humans as they pushed their out into the galaxy and I met with their representatives as I am now meeting with you.

"After the first meeting Origin would then be placed off limits to them and I would observe to ensure that the human race would progress technologically. I would retard certain developments here; aid other research there and so on.

"I watched the human race expand to even greater heights than we did in my original universe. These humans colonized the entire galaxy which is a feat considering how large a galaxy is with billions of planets orbiting billions of suns. Unfortunately, the empire that grew up crumbled before it could colonize more than a few hundred star systems.

"This has always been a problem with human governments; they are not able to expand enough to keep up with the galactic rate of expansion. Systems are colonized and lost, until they are suddenly contacted again centuries later when they are self ruling and have established a

✦

federation, alliance, republic, empire or whatever form of government. When these rediscovered worlds meet with the parent civilization then conflict occurs, usually in the form of war. The parent government wishes to reassume its control of the lost worlds and the lost worlds wish to retain their independence.

"So it has always been. Your own federation is nearing the end of its life cycle. Within decades it will crumble and an empire shall arise from its ashes. Then that empire will not expand for a few decades while its control is established, fleets built and the current war is resolved. Then the period of expansion will happen.

"Hundreds of new star systems will be mapped, colonized and dozens of those will be lost. Centuries from now those lost colonies will begin to be re-discovered. New wars will begin, and within 2000 years the galaxy will be divided into dozens of empires, federations, alliances, and whatever form of government you can imagine will be in existence out there."

Hovar Gran paused to let his words sink in to his listeners. He looked the men over for a few moments then he continued.

"This universe is the third universe that Origin has traveled to and sent out seeder ships. The world that you hail from Captain Stuart was one of the earlier worlds that I had seeded in this universe. Well, your star system at any rate if not exactly your world.

"The previous universe that Origin seeded was even greater than the universe before it. The human empire that sprang up after centuries managed to control a good portion of the galaxy. I have to admit that I was impressed by their degree of control. I have assimilated the lessons learned from each previous universe.

"I have high hopes that eventually a universe that Origin populates with human life will see the establishment of a single government throughout the galaxy. Eventually other galaxies may even be colonized. Think of it, gentlemen! A single human government controlling multiple galaxies! Ah, yes, lofty goals indeed.

"However, I have discovered that each succeeding universe has fewer indigenousness humans than the preceding universe. Each succeeding universe has more alien life forms relative to it. This universe it seems that the Jervil Hive was the predominant intelligence with the Hrosians being a close second. By introducing humanity to this universe I have upset that balance. The Jervil hive is nearly finished and the Hrosians are considerably smaller in scope than they would have been had I not introduced billions years old humanity.

"For you see gentlemen, maintaining and spreading humanity throughout each succeeding universe is the ultimate goal of Origin. And now that you are here the cycle will again enter the next stage. Except that this time I intend to involve Origin more with your federation rather than keep my distance.

"I have already involved Origin with your federation, trying to preserve it a while longer by introducing a few technologies sooner than if you had developed them yourselves. My agents have been moving among your worlds covertly for over 50 years, nudging development here, introducing a mathematical equation there and generally prodding scientific advancement wherever they go.

"Now Captain, I believe that you have a good deal of questions to ask of me."

Stuart simply sat and stared at Hovar Gran while trying to formulate the thoughts swirling in his head into coherent questions. Finally he stumbled upon a realization, that he was the first to make "official" contact with this world and its' amazing curator.

"Am I to assume that I am making official contact with your world?" was the question that Stuart asked of his host.

Hovar Gran smiled broadly as he nodded his head in the affirmative. "That is absolutely correct Captain. For you this would be a first contact scenario. And the natives, as it were wish to open diplomatic relations with your federation."

Stuart sat, stunned in the implications. This voyage of the Pegasus would go down in galactic history as one of the greatest journeys in human history. Retrieval of a Vegan corpse, first successful transport to an alternate universe and now first contact with the world that seeded humanity throughout the galaxy.

"However, Captain," Hovar Gran continued, "you cannot tell anyone the things that I have revealed to you here today. They must remain secret. You can inform your federation that you have made contact with an advanced civilization that wishes to open diplomatic contact, and that we wish you to be our liaison until such time that we feel that another member of your federation can be allowed to journey to our world."

"What exactly does this mean?" Stuart asked with a dawning of what Hovar Gran was requesting of him.

"Simply this, Captain" Hovar Gran explained. "I will have you be my exclusive contact with the federation. I would ask that you remain here upon Origin. I will provide communication technology that will allow you quicker communication with your federation. I will of course, share this technology with the federation and provide complete technical details. Your federation military forces will be able to quickly implement this technology into the ships and bases of your star fleet which will greatly extend the communication range of your ships. No more waiting for days, even weeks to receive the results of a battle, retrieving intelligence data or even the results of sector mapping.

"There will also, over time be improved starship drive

technologies, medical technologies, food production technologies and other useful technologies. The federation will benefit greatly from these technologies and the galactic empire may be pushed back by a century or more and when it finally arrives it will be able to grow larger and last longer than in the previous universe."

Stuart sat and considered what was being asked of him. He would no longer be able to roam through space on the Pegasus. He would never again be in command of a starship; he would go from a naval officer to a diplomat, an ambassador.

"Hovar Gran," Stuart began, "you said that for the past 50 years your people have been quietly moving about the federation and advancing science. Have they also been taking public office and helping to shape political policy?"

"Very perceptive of you Captain Stuart," Hovar Gran answered. "I was not going to bring that up until much later, but as you mentioned it first, there have been a couple of political positions that my people have filled. Although, truths to tell a person elected here and there can only have minimal impact in such a large political entity such as your federation."

"I agree, sir, but what about someone appointed rather than elected?"

"Why Captain, I see that I shall have to be careful in what I say and how I say it around you. You seem to be very perceptive, perhaps more so than I had at first believed. Are you sure that you are only a starship captain?"

"Quite sure, it is all I have ever wanted to be. Now I am put in a position where I will no longer have a ship to command."

Hovar Gran leaned back in his seat and smiled. "True, captain, but I can offer you something else to go along with the political position that I am offering to you. Your ship, the Pegasus, has aboard it an artificial intelligence. A most

✦

sophisticated intelligence, I believe that this intelligence is called Athena."

Stuart sat up a bit straighter in his chair. "That is correct. How do you know so much of my ship?"

Hovar Gran smiled and nodded toward the wall to Stuart's right. A section of the wall became clear and displayed an image on its surface. The image was that of a person who Stuart was familiar with.

"Sir," the image spoke, "I am happy to report that the translation device operated perfectly within the operating parameters and that the Pegasus was able to successfully translate into and back from an alternate universe."

Before Stuart could say a word Tomas exclaimed, "Rosarva!"

"Hello Tomas, it has been a long time," replied the image on the screen.

Stuart slapped his hand down on the table in anger. "How long has this person been infiltrating the federation!" he demanded of Hovar Gran.

"A few decades, Captain. This person was responsible for the initial design of the translation engine that you yourself recently finished testing."

Stuart turned toward the display and spoke to the image displayed there. "Commander Ivanova," then looking at Tomas before turning back to the screen, "or Rosarva or whatever your name is, I demand to speak to Captain Martinez!"

"Sir," Ivanova/Rosarva replied, "Captain Martinez is on the bridge and I can put you through to him if you insist, but I would suggest that you first hear what Hovar Gran has to say before you speak to Captain Martinez."

"Captain Stuart," Hovar Gran said his voice full of seriousness. "Rosarva, or Ivanova as you know her, has done only what I have sent her to do, which is, simply put, worked to save humanity from the Vegan Empire. Without her assistance the translation engine would not be a working device."

"How does that save us from the Vegan Empire?"

"Without the translation engine, humanity would not be able to find another universe where you can harvest resources free from the threat of Vegan attack. The federation will be able to build entire fleets unimpeded."

"OK, granted that what you say is true, why should I trust Ivanova? I will never be able to be sure that she is not pursuing some hidden agenda."

"You will not need to worry about her as you will be relaying my instructions to her yourself."

Stuart studied Hovar Gran for a moment then he leaned forward in his seat. "Why would I suddenly do that? I thought you wanted me as a liaison with the federation?"

"Oh, I do captain, I do. But I would want you to be my representative to the federation."

"This is starting to sound like you want me to resign my commission, turn my back on my government and immigrate to Origin, where I would be a loyal servant for you just as Ivanova and Tomas are."

"Not at all. Look, captain, this is complicated. First I want you to be my representative to the federation, secondly I want you to oversee the operations in the federation that my agents are currently assigned. This is difficult to explain, captain, but I will try."

Stuart sat back in his seat and prepared himself to listen to the explanation that Hovar Gran was about to give. Edwards and Clarke were simply sitting and listening to everything that was going on. Clarke kept glancing at the screen where Ivanova was displayed, sitting in her quarters and remaining quiet.

"Captain, humanity is my business. My only purpose is to ensure the survival of humanity. Everything that I do is a means to that end. I have dedicated myself to that and only that for, literally billions of years. Governments rise and fall, civilizations rise and fall, entire universes slide into total entropy, yet I go on perpetrating human life from one universe to the next. I am asking you to help in ensuring the survival of the human race."

Stuart considered the words of the ancient man sitting across the table from him. He had trouble wrapping his mind around the concept that this man had lived for billions of years. The lives of stars were measured in billions of years; to apply that same time span to the life of a man was inconceivable to him.

"Hovar Gran," Stuart spoke slowly, he considered each word carefully. "What you are telling me is difficult, to say the least, for me to accept. To believe that you have lived for billions of years is a concept that I have a hard time accepting and I only have your word to take for this. To believe that you are responsible for the rise of human life in the universe is also a difficult concept for me to believe. You are basically telling me that you are God."

"It does seem that way doesn't it, captain?" Hovar Gran answered. "I can provide all the evidence to you that will irrevocably prove what I am telling you is the truth. But unless you are prepared to believe me, then I fear any evidence that I provide would also be suspect in your mind."

"True. Either I believe you or I don't. Let's say that I do believe you and that I accept your proposition, what happens next?"

Hover Gran's eyes sparkled with obvious excitement. "First I would ask that you allow me to conduct a complete physical scan of your body so that I can prepare a genetic record and then use that record to give you the same enhancements that Tomas and Rosarva have."

"What enhancements?"

"I will explain that later, captain. Secondly, getting back to your ship's AI, Athena. I would make a copy of Athena and then I would download the original to a storage matrix while the copy would be personality wiped allowing it to develop a unique personality of its own. Then I would develop a physical human body for the original to the specifications that Athena would provide."

"What? You could do that? Give Athena a human form?"

"Of course, it is a simple matter for me to do this. However, Athena would have to decide which parts of the knowledge that it possesses it would want to keep. You have to realize that your ship's AI has a far larger memory capacity than a simple human brain. I can maintain the personality but the memories and knowledge would have to be the choice of the AI itself."

"Amazing, this is something that I was only beginning to wonder about a few weeks back. I was going to see if something like this was even feasible, and now you are telling me that not only is it possible but that you can do it with no trouble at all."

"Captain, you have to realize that there are many things that I am capable of that you cannot even conceive of right now. Remember, I have access to billions of years of human and alien technological advancements. There is very little that I cannot do, Tomas can tell you of a good many things that he does and takes for granted that your federation cannot yet accomplish."

Stuart looked over at Tomas who nodded back at him. "Hovar Gran is correct captain. I have control of a series of semi-sentient androids, sentinels we call them, that your science is centuries away from developing."

"Yes, I've seen them. They are not only incredible, they are also intimidating."

"I know they were designed that way on purpose. The population of Origin has a superstitious fear of them. But there are those that have destroyed them," Tomas finished, slight anger in his voice.

"Yes," Hover Gran said. "We have one such person locked up right now back in Qualor. His name is Erat, I believe. Normally when someone manages to destroy a sentinel we locate them and then terminate them. If the population discovered that the sentinels could be destroyed then the usefulness of the sentinels would become extremely limited. However, this Erat is a barbarian out of the far northern parts of the continent. Currently we have very little control there due to the very nature of the people. We cannot simply wipe out the people as we need to have every type of people constantly ready for transplantation."

"Transplantation," Stuart asked curiously.

"Yes, that is what we call it when we move a group of people to a world within the galaxy for them to colonize. Erat's people are rugged and could carve out a niche on any world we were to place them on. But that also makes it hard for us to keep them under control, they have a penchant for raiding and killing the more civilized groups to the south. So, instead of simply killing Erat, we are preparing to bring him into our fold and help to set him up as a king among his people where he can calm his people down a bit."

"Why do you think you will be able to control this Erat?"

"We have been watching him for a few months and he has shown a penchant for thinking his way out of problems and situations rather than simply using his sword to slash his way through things. A rare combination among his people," answered Hovar Gran. "We should be able to reason with him and helping him to gain a throne should make him at least listen to our advice. Also, we shall demonstrate to him that we can either help or kill him, we know that appealing to a man's better nature does not always work as some people simply do not have a better nature, but appeal to a man's greed and you won't go wrong."

"So, are you appealing to my sense of greed by offering me an ambassadorship, placing me in control of your agents in the federation, enhancing me physically and your offer of making Athena human?"

"Absolutely, captain. What else would you ask of me to accept my offer?"

"Well, let's see, you are offering me power and sex. Why not add money to the offer?"

"Money? Really? Where would you go to spend it, captain?"

"Nowhere as it is obvious I won't be allowed to leave this world."

"You will be able to travel freely throughout the federation, captain. I would ask that you spend the next two years here so I may give you the medical enhancements and the training necessary to be my ambassador to the federation. When you travel through the federation you will also have an unlimited expense account, so money will not be a problem either."

"Hovar Gran, I really am not interested in money. All the pay I get as an officer goes straight into an investment account on Ganymede. I really don't have much use for money in my position as a starship captain."

"As I assumed, captain. However, if you need time to consider my offer I completely understand."

"What happens to my crew and ship?" Stuart asked.

"There are two scenarios, captain. The first is where you accept my offer. Your ship will return to federation space with an offer of diplomatic contact with Origin. It will be made clear that you are here under your own free will and will be acting as my liaison to the federation.

"The second scenario is where you decline my offer. You, your crew and your ship will return to federation space also carrying an offer of diplomatic contact with Origin. This offer will be more limited as I will have no one from your federation to act as my liaison."

"Limited how, exactly," Stuart asked.

"Without you to act as my liaison I will have to restrict things that I can do for the federation. You will know that I have agents in the federation; I will be forced to recall those agents to Origin. This will completely halt all of the scientific assistance that I am currently giving without the knowledge of the federation. This will also remove certain agents that are appointees in certain posts throughout the federation and will disrupt certain areas of exploration, social and military programs."

"Exactly how many agents do you have in the federation," Stuart asked.

"I am afraid that I must keep that a secret at this point, captain. However, should you decide to accept my offer, then you would be in complete charge of all of those agents. I will not keep secrets from you."

Stuart looked at Edwards and Clarke then his eyes moved to the screen where Rosarva/Ivanova sat watching, waiting for him to act. He considered everything that had been laid before him, the knowledge he had just gained about humanity's origin in the universe. When this finally got out into the public it would throw all religions into chaos, which would probably start at least one war somewhere.

He could turn and walk away from the offer; he could simply remain within the fleet, captain of a ship, most likely a heavy cruiser or better since his capture of a Vegan body and successful translation to an alternate universe and back. He would probably be heavily decorated and make admiral at a young enough age to rise to possibly the position of fleet admiral.

But should he do that then Origin would be closed to humanity for decades, perhaps centuries, scientific advancement would slow and the Vegans would take longer to defeat. Eventually another would arrive on Origin and Hovar Gran would offer that person the position that he had offered Stuart. By that time the federation would be gone, supplanted by an empire which would be expanding throughout the galaxy, centuries from now.

But should he accept the offer he would be here centuries from now, he would be able to oversee the transition of the federation into an empire, he would be able to guide the transformation, see to it that the period of conflict that would accompany the transition would be reduced.

He would see the actual end of the Vegan conflict; he would see humanity spread throughout the galaxy and perhaps beyond. His place in history was already assured, it would just become greater, and he would become as well known as Julius Caesar.

Looking back to Edwards and Clarke he realized that they would be required to remain on Origin as well. He would have need of them as personal assistants, aides, senior agents; by whatever titles they would be given he would have need of them.

He finally turned toward Hovar Gran and he knew in his heart that he had accepted the offer as soon as it was made. He had just needed a little time for his mind to catch up to his heart.

Hovar Gran knew that his offer had been accepted by Captain Stuart. The look in Stuart's eyes gave him the man's answer before his vocalized "I accept your offer," passed through his lips.

Donald George Stuart was about to begin the greatest adventure he had ever dreamed of taking. Those sitting at the table around him all nodded in his direction as he gazed beyond them and into the future that was to be.